A UNICORN

For Jacqui
Best wishes
Paul S. Firth

A UNICORN DIES

A Novel of Mystery and Ideas

Paul S. Fiddes

Firedint Publishing Oxford

Acknowledgements & Permissions

I am grateful to a number of people who have allowed me to draw on their expertise in writing this novel. My wife Marion has given me a wealth of general details about the John Radcliffe Hospital, and Jenn Sula Minns has given me specialist information about the system of signs in use there. Alexander Vinter has put his vast experience of portering in the same hospital at my disposal. Fleur Talbot has helped with medical knowledge, and Kathryn White has checked and corrected my account of police procedure. Students from Georgetown College, Kentucky, have enlightened me about the customs of American college fraternities. The lecture on 'The Unicorn and the Platypus' described in chapter 22 is closely based on a lecture given by Professor Martin Kemp, Emeritus Professor of the History of Art in the University of Oxford, entitled 'Unicorns: Can We Believe Our Eyes?', on May 5, 2015 at St Barnabas Church, Oxford; reference is made to the lecture with the kind permission of Professor Kemp. The manuscript has been read by my colleague Bethany Sollereder, and I am grateful for suggestions she has made. John May provided scrupulous proof-reading of an early published text. Richard and Rosemary Kidd accompanied Marion and myself on a unicorn hunt to Stirling Castle, and the account in chapters 23-24 has benefited from their interest and enthusiasm. Despite all this assistance, any errors remain my own.

I should make clear that all the characters, the plot, the colleges of the University of Oxford referred to, Horne Grant College, the house at 81 Observatory Street and the 'Alternative World' website are imaginary. Other places, all the works of art and the unicorn lore are real, or at least as real as I can make them.

Contents

Acknowledgements and Permissions   5

1. Hannah   9
2. Tutorial   16
3. Scapegoats   23
4. About Benedict   30
5. Death   38
6. Postcards   51

Illustrations : the six postcards   61

7. Memorial   68
8. Suspended   79
9. Horn of Ulf   91
10. Montmartre   103
11. The Lady   112
12. Oxford   123
13. Afternoon in Rome   137
14. Maiden   148
15. Alternative World   158
16. In class   171
17. Alpha Mu Omega   183
18. The Cloisters   192
19. Another death   205
20. Colmar   216
21. Another hospital   229
22. Oxford again   240
23. Stirling Castle   252

Illustration : the seventh tapestry   265

24. The upper path   266

25. The river   273

1

Hannah

On a May morning Giles Questing was walking through the University Parks in Oxford, thinking about the approved method for catching a unicorn. He had no expectations of finding any examples of the beast in the immediate vicinity, but the means to entrap it was –he presumed – somewhere on view around him, and he had an active imagination. He also had the advantage of having just read John of Trevisa on the subject in the English Faculty Library, and so he knew that the essential point was this: first find a virgin. The next step was to sit her under a tree.

He sat down on the bench dedicated to the memory of J. R. R. Tolkien, stared at the pleasing mixture of grass, birches, willows and water, and gave himself up to dreaming. Which of the many girls in his field of sight would be the most suitable to use for luring a unicorn to its fate? And which tree should he select for her? He could feel the gnarled wood pressing into her back and hear the swish of hooves through the grass as the creature approached, dipping its head in acknowledgement of her beauty, shyly laying its single horn in her lap, and glancing up at her with its milky-blue eyes. It could then be relied upon to go to sleep and give the hunters their chance, hidden so unsportingly in the bushes.

Her lap, he thought. Yes, her lap. If this were a medieval scene then the lap would be mysterious in its many folds of silk, an open apron, spreading wide and covering the ground. The heavy head would sink into the space so generously provided, between limbs delicately outlined in the cloth. If the unicorn were to appear here and now in the haze of the afternoon, then there would no doubt be other kinds of lap offered. Giles thought of the wonderful triangle made by a short dress and two long legs. The head would be held more tautly on such material, and the smooth white jaws of the animal would brush against bare skin.

Two girls padded by, on their jogger's circuit through the Parks, lycra-clad. Glancing at them covertly, Giles found neither mystery nor wonder there. Though there was flesh to be seen it was exposed in too practical a way, as well as covered in a light film of sweat. A whiff of something rancid in the air as they passed made him recall that, according to ancient authorities, the unicorn was remarkably sensitive to odour, and could sniff out a suitable maiden at a distance. How, after all, could a virgin be identified on such brief inspection? Giles had done a little reading around his subject in the library, and some medieval writers had been both enthusiastic and respectful about what they called 'the odour of chastity', which the unicorn would detect as he stepped along the forest path. Other writers depended on the holding power of the eye for recognition; there was something in the look, as they gazed at each other, beast and maiden, that gave the clue. The indomitable Abbess Hildegard of Bingen was particularly emphatic about this, and had even suggested that increasing the number of maidens would intensify the charge of the eyes. In defiance of the male point of view, she had advocated replacing the lone virgin under the tree with a bevy of girls wandering round the woods collecting wild flowers. Giles had a definite preference, however, for the more established version.

Giles, it must be said, was a dreamer. Oxford conspired to keep him in a state of perpetual somnambulism. It was not the dreaming spires of the advertising copy for Oxford that had this effect on him; indeed, looking around him now, he could see fewer spires than cranes, building one more addition to the science blocks on the southern side of the Parks. He was permanently sleepy during the hectic eight weeks of each term for a combination of reasons. The Oxford tutorial system encouraged him to spend long hours in the libraries which were heavy with the book-dust of the ages, inducing the resting of head on hands for a snatched sleep; knocking off at lunchtime for a pint in one of Oxford's pubs hardly helped attention during the afternoon. Then essays were invariably written during the night before the tutorial; keeping vigilant in the tutorial itself, sufficiently to engage in a cut and thrust of argument with the tutor, was certainly possible, but it exacted a heavy toll in the following two days. At least once a week he spent until the early hours of the morning in one of the night-clubs where the young of Oxford danced, and began the next day with a deficit of alertness.

He shook himself awake, continued down Oak Walk alongside the river, past the duck pond where children were torturing young frogs with sticks as they tried to clamber out of their birthing pool, and paused by the bench simply marked 'Cholmondeley'. He was still a little early for his appointment at Observatory Street, and so he sat down again. He knew, as he would not have known a year ago, how to pronounce the name carved into this seat as a dignified, yet supremely self-confident, memorial. No more than the single word was needed to evoke generations who had been Lord Great Chamberlains of England. According to the special spelling rules of the upper classes, the name was to be spoken as 'Chum-ley', and uttering it as written when greeting someone bearing it would evoke the same kind of sideways smile as referring to Magdalen College as anything other than 'Maudlin'. To meet a Cholmondeley at Magdalen and get both wrong at once would be a social nightmare.

Giles was sensitive about names, as he had suffered a great deal from his own at the West London Comprehensive school where he had completed his earlier education, and where his mother had worked as the school secretary. When younger he had not greatly minded being dubbed 'Giles Questioning' by teachers who made this response to his constant curiosity, and who without fail thought they were the first to make the joke. His fellow-students in adolescent years were less gentle, and came up with such variations as 'Giles Queering' and 'Girls Chesting'. He had vowed to get even with them all by escaping from the featureless suburbs of London to Oxford, though he had suffered something of a setback at his interview when, on offering the name of the London Borough of Ealing where his school was situated, he had been greeted by the response, 'Isn't that where the train stops on the way to

Paddington?' Recently, having found the genre of medieval romances, he had become reconciled to the name 'Questing', and liked to think that it expressed some special sense of searching or yearning that he felt within him, and which he did not yet realize was common to most young people of his age.

He looked in a sleepy way at the scene in front of him. The grass of Picked Mead was strewn with clumps of trees, and some were gathered together into a small-scale grove, yew, cypress, ash and hawthorn giving it a mysterious and sacral air. A little distance away a girl was sitting under one of the trees, with the remains of a picnic spread out around her. She was wearing a summer dress and had a lap, certainly. He could also just discern a mass of long curls surrounding her face. The term 'Pre-Raphaelite' crossed his mind, but was quickly identified and dismissed as a cliché. She seemed, one might say, a suitable candidate for catching unicorns. He was just imagining the fabulous animal moving gently towards her from among the trees when a young child, five or six years old, suddenly shot out from behind a bush and advanced upon him, waving a stick in a menacing manner. Giles had learned from any number of tabloid newspaper stories that he should not attempt bodily contact in any circumstances, and so he made haste to get himself out of harm's way. He stood behind the bench, out of range, and smiled what he hoped was a friendly and placating smile. The boy at once flung down his stick, burst into tears and ran towards the girl, shouting for help. As he buried his head in her lap she comforted him, and looked suspiciously at Giles. He thought the best thing was to make his way out of the Parks, hoping that she would not pick up a mobile phone and contact the police.

As he walked briskly away, despite his anxiety he could not help reflecting that the girl was probably not the best candidate after all, as she was most likely the boy's mother and so evidently not a virgin. Passing the cricket pitches, where a player was brandishing his bat in a threatening way, he recalled that some medieval authors reported that a unicorn, having divined that the maiden set before him was not virginal, would grow angry and run her through with his horn. Reaching the gate opposite the multi-coloured brickwork of Keble College, thrown up by the High Church movement of the nineteenth century, he added a mental qualification. He had read that some texts of the Syriac Church were less concerned about the strict virginity of the woman set to trap the unicorn, and portrayed her as positively seductive. Experienced, at any rate.

By now Giles had reached the road, and looked about nervously for signs of a police car. None appeared, and Giles made his way from the park gates to Observatory Street, free from pursuit from the police cars, but not from harassment by cyclists who clearly believed that they were exempt, by some law made for the benefit of users of two wheels alone, from the restrictions of traffic lights. He turned in from the main road to the quiet side street, looking for number 81, which turned out to be near the end. He knew that, like much else in Oxford, the appearance of things belied their reality. He saw a road flanked by a row of small, narrow houses, few more than one window and one door in width. They had been made for the labouring classes a century before, in the expansion of the city northwards when dons had finally been loosed from the confines of the colleges, permitted to marry, have families and commute into their colleges to teach and enjoy the cordon bleu cookery of the high table. By night they returned to their villas of sandstone in the new wide streets and were served by those who crouched, in their humility, in the cramped dwellings of such roads as Observatory Street.

But now the face of things was deceptive. Just as the blank walls of the colleges in the centre of the city concealed roomy quadrangles and expansive gardens, glimpses of which could be caught through the small wooden doors that guarded the entrances; just as the ragged and dirty student uniform of jeans and sweatshirts concealed bodies nourished in the best private schools; so the façade of Observatory Street hid architectural extravaganzas which burst out into the gardens beyond the rear walls. Behind the mean frontage were extensions which stretched like the interiors in Dutch paintings, or like a tunnel of images made by facing mirrors, providing their academic and professional inhabitants with music rooms, farmhouse-style kitchens, sun-lounges and exercise areas. Giles was not surprised that the apparently limited area of number 81 was able to accommodate not only the owner of the house but also three lodgers.

13

He was surprised, however, by his potential landlady. The door was opened by a girl whom he at first presumed was one of the students living in the house. On asking for Ms Hannah Grace, and giving his name, she disconcerted him by exclaiming, 'Oh dear! I am so sorry. But it's the bathroom, of course.' Hastily he disclaimed any pretence to being a plumber, and explained that he had come about the room that he hoped was still spare for next year.

'I know', she said with an unsettling calm. 'Your friend Emily telephoned me and apologized for not taking the room after all. It seems she's got an offer to live with a group of friends. She said she was sending a friend who was interested in renting, but she didn't say what sex. I assumed she meant a girl.'

She had coloured at the word 'sex', flushing just noticeably beneath a slightly dark skin. Giles took in an appearance which was a little Persian, an oval face with high cheek bones and wide-set dark brown eyes, framed by a neat curtain of dark hair falling to the bottom of her neck. Her mouth was fairly wide for her narrow face, and throughout their conversation was mostly set in a serious line, but at the moments when she smiled her whole face opened up in welcome. Her eyes regarded him solemnly, though something humorous flickered there. He felt both attracted and uncomfortable.

'What I mean', she continued, 'is that I've let rooms in the past to male students and I'd rather hoped to keep to women from now onwards. It's a question of the bathroom, you know. I've had too much experience of the women having to clean and clear up after the men have used it. I'm sorry, but I don't think I can help.'

Over her shoulder he could see the ground floor of the house, with the garden beyond, and could see that it was only slightly extended – probably to provide the bathroom mentioned, and making a larger kitchen underneath. It looked welcoming, plain but bright, with white walls and sunlight coming in from the garden.

'I suppose it wouldn't make any difference if I said that I was quite good at clearing up, and that I dislike dirty bathrooms extremely?' he queried. She looked at him quite directly, and again he felt disturbed, but not unpleasantly. She laughed and hesitated, before shaking her head regretfully again.

Giles was disappointed, and realized that he was probably facing a long search, having left things far too late in the year for much of a choice of lodgings. As he said goodbye and turned away from the door he found himself remarking, 'Well, I must get back to my essay on unicorns.' Thinking about it later, he was at a loss to account for why he had blurted this out. Perhaps it was just for something to say to cover an awkward moment, or perhaps he sensed that she was someone it was easy to go on talking to. Whatever the reason, her reaction was unexpected.

'Wait a moment, then', she said, and he turned back to face her. She was looking at him carefully once more, although he felt that he had already had her full attention from the beginning of the conversation. He was surprised to see that she was apparently reconsidering her decision. 'Perhaps we can work out the room situation, and you must have a talk with Benedict.'

Later she telephoned to offer him the room, and when he returned to look at it she told him that she had been half-inclined to agree anyway, and his mention of unicorns just tipped the balance. But at the time it seemed to him as if he had uttered a secret password which had given him entrance to a desired but forbidden realm. The apparently magical effect of the mention of unicorns may well have contributed to his obsession with the subject and led to all the consequences that were to follow. The promised conversation with Benedict, Hannah's fiancé and a theological research student at Helwys College, had to wait until after the summer vacation.

2
Tutorial

Giles settled back, rather uncomfortably, into an armchair that was showing more evidence of springs than horsehair, and began to read his essay.

'The medieval Bestiary', he began, 'is a rag-bag of information and misinformation about animals. It has no single author, but grew through additions made by many hands over the years. It began from a Greek book called the *Physiologus*, written in fourth-century Christian Alexandria, which collected animal lore and drew morals from it, in the manner of Aesop's fables. As it was translated into many languages, more animals were added, from first-hand observation and from the authority of ancient literature. In the virtual zoo it presents us with, the most interesting animal is the unicorn.'

He paused, suddenly aware that his tutorial partner, Emily, was shifting in her seat and leaning forward about to interrupt. He deduced that it was his essay and not the chair that was causing her discomfort, and was immediately proved right.

'Wait a moment', she protested, 'I've read the only medieval English version of the Bestiary there is, in the Exeter Book, and there's no unicorn in it. I even went to the trouble of reading the whole bloody thing, not just the selections in the reader we were given. I found it in the notes at the back and looked it up in the library – it's a manuscript in the British Museum and there's absolutely no unicorn in it. No way. There's ...', she consulted her own essay, 'a lion, an eagle, a serpent, an ant, a hart, a fox, a spider, a whale, an elephant, two kinds of doves, a panther and a seductive-looking mermaid, but that's all. I was rather fond of the elephant, myself.'

She leaned back, and looked for approval at the tutor, but he said nothing, beyond murmuring 'That's traditional for mermaids, but one has to beware of drowning, of course.'

Giles found to his surprise that Emily was more interesting than he had thought, and he tried not to look at her plunging neckline, barely covering an expanse of rounded, freckled skin, which was rising and falling more quickly with the effort she was making to get her point across. Her head with its reddish hair was tilted up aggressively as if welcoming a fight. She had, he observed, some kind of top tucked into a denim skirt reduced in length for summer and getting shorter still with every agitated move. She wasn't wearing tights and a sandal dangled precariously from her foot as she hitched one leg over the other. But he checked himself and returned to the argument.

'The English Bestiary's only a selection from a Latin version', he pointed out. 'There are about one hundred and fifty animals in the twelfth century Latin text, and the unicorn's definitely there.'

'I thought that we were reading English', she retorted. 'It's a bit unfair, bringing in the Latin. This is a *Medieval English tutorial*, you know.'

'John of Trevisa, 1397', he murmured.

'What did you say?' she said, startled.

'In 1397 Trevisa translated a Latin commentary on the Bestiary written by someone called Bartholomew Glanville in the thirteenth century, who himself was following an older writer called Isidore. It's not got the whole works in it, but it's got much more than the English poem we were talking about. It's a kind of second-hand bestiary. Trevisa wrote in English, and the unicorn's there, really there. I read the notes at the back of the reader as well, and found the Oxford edition of Trevisa on the shelves in the college library. I was just skimming through it to see what animals it had, and I found a unicorn, though he starts off by calling it a rhinoceros.'

And, he thought, I haven't been able to get it out of my mind since then.

The tutor agreed that Trevisa could indeed be counted as medieval English prose. He indicated, delicately, that Giles had shown promising initiative in the matter of footnotes and that this augured well for the future. Emily was silenced for the moment, yet not unwillingly as she was becoming intrigued by what looked like the most passionate engagement with literature that she had yet seen from Giles.

'So what did you learn from John of Trevisa about unicorns?' enquired the tutor, scanning his bookshelves intently as if he expected to see the ancient author emerging from their dark recesses.

Giles continued to read his essay. 'Trevisa reports that the Unicorn is an extremely strong beast, with one horn in the middle of his forehead which is very sharp and at least four feet long. No hunter can catch him, but he can be caught by a stratagem. A virgin girl is led to where he lurks around, and there she sits down. She opens her lap, and the unicorn comes and lays his head in it, losing all his fierceness. Drawings in various manuscripts show her sitting under a tree and holding him affectionately by the horn. The hunters, hiding near by, can easily catch him or spear him to death. The image which Trevisa offers us is a symbol of love that has endured through the ages. In the thirteenth century, the "Bestiary of Love" by Richard de Fournival portrays love as the skilful huntsman, and the lover as "dying the death" to which he was doomed as he sleeps in a maiden's lap. The story has gone on inspiring poets and painters such the Pre-Raphaelite Dante Gabriel Rossetti, presenting us as it does with a lover who is willing even to die for the sake of the one he loves.'

'Hold on there', interrupted Emily tersely. 'Hold on. Don't you see that it's the old story, all over again? It's the woman's fault. She's the deceiver, the betrayer. She not only deceived Adam but now this darling little unicorn as well. And it's all to do with sex, in fact *her* sexuality. He lays the horn in her lap – there's a phallic symbol for you – she even holds his horn in her hand, good God, I shouldn't wonder if she doesn't lick it with her tongue, and then he gets himself killed. He suffers death because of the sin of the woman and the sin of her fascinating lap.'

Giles sat, appalled. He saw the picture he had been carrying in his head for a week get blurred around the edges and then slowly dissolve into a dirty smear. This was a perspective on the myth that he hadn't seen before. He'd realized about the horn – you could hardly miss it – but betrayal? Sin? He fought back.

'This is typical feminist revision of literature' he said. Women critics are always wanting to find their own meaning in literature, spoiling it for others'. He was quite upset.

'Not really fair', said the tutor quietly. 'The more vivid details of Emily's imagination are not in the sources, either in the text or...', he paused, 'the pictures, but the theme of deception is quite strong, and it's a bit puzzling that the woman is both the lover and the betrayer, life and death to the unicorn. Scholars of the myth find all kinds of ingenious ways to reconcile them: for instance, if the girl sitting out alone in the wood is the earth goddess, or Mother Nature, and if the unicorn represents the moon – its single horn looking like the crescent moon, don't you see – then it's a cycle of nature for the moon to die at dawn, and then be reborn at sunset. There are of course other explanations...', his voice trailed away, 'but I fear that none of them really excuse a patriarchal society.'

He looked quite gloomy, and glanced again at his shelves as if seeking comfort in the women authors arranged there.

Encouraged by this support, Emily looked again at her own essay.

'If you really want to catch a unicorn', she said, ' why not use the strategy provided for elephants? The medieval English *poem* we were *asked* to read has a good device for catching elephants, which were rather too large for the average hunter in those days before guns and darts tipped with anaesthetic and so on. The hunter takes advantage of the well-known fact that elephants like to rest against trees, and gets ahead of the beast by sawing right through the trunk at the bottom but leaving it standing where it is. The unsuspecting animal leans against it, the tree falls over and so does the elephant. Before it can get up, which naturally takes a fair time, the hunter is on top of it. This could', she concluded with a glint in her eye, 'no doubt be adapted for unicorns. It would certainly let the woman out of the whole messy business.'

Giles smiled. 'Wouldn't the smaller size of the unicorn stop this working?'

Emily became more inventive. 'Well, say that the hunter stands in front of the tree, hiding it, and when the unicorn charges at him with its horn lowered to gore him horribly, he just skips out of the way and wham! four feet of sharp and glittering horn gets buried in the tree. The poor unicorn's stuck, and the hunter's got him at his mercy.'

It was the tutor's turn to smile. 'Brilliant', he said. 'You've just discovered the alternative method of catching a unicorn as found in some of the best sources. Do you know the line from Shakespeare's *Julius Caesar*, "He loves to hear that unicorns may be betrayed by trees, and bears with glasses?" But, leaving the bears out of it for a moment, can either of you see the link between the two methods?'

Giles and Emily looked at each other, and there was a prolonged pause. Then they both replied at once, 'The tree'.

'Yes', said their tutor, 'the suitable virgin who is to seduce the unicorn sits under a tree. I wonder why?'

Giles realized that neither 'to rest her back' or 'to keep out of the sun' would really do.

Emily forged on. 'It's back to the Garden of Eden, isn't it? Adam was led into sin by Eve, because she was attracted by the apples on the tree. It was the tree that really mucked things up, by having such luscious fruit. They were both tempted by the tree. In my essay I say that the Bestiary extracts this moral from the story of the elephant, but of course it could apply to the unicorn as well. The tree betrays them both.'

'Right' said the tutor approvingly. 'Some of the pictures showing the capture of the unicorn have the hapless girl sitting under an apple tree.' Then he frowned. 'But it wasn't an apple, you know. People are always getting that wrong. The book of Genesis says 'the fruit of the tree of good and evil', and the Latin word for wrong – *malus* – got confused with the word for an apple – *malum*. It hasn't done the reputation of a perfectly respectable fruit any good at all.'

He seemed distressed by the thought.

Giles was getting restive. 'I'm not so happy about all this religious symbolism', he ventured. 'I know that the Bestiary attaches what it thinks is natural history to spiritual meanings, and this is the point of the rest of my

20

essay. I go on to say that the religious application spoils the effect of the symbol. Trevisa misses these bits out, and that's just as well in my view. I imagine that the Bestiary must also moralize about the unicorn.'

The tutor, it seemed, wanted to be helpful. 'You imagine rightly', he said. 'If you read the Bestiary in Latin, you'll find that the writer in fact compares the unicorn with Christ; they're both captured and killed, and the writer says that they're both a kind of scapegoat.'

'There you are', said Giles. 'I suppose that they both die of love, but a religious application like that seems to narrow the meaning too much, and we lose what I thought was an image of human passionate love. The symbol's got lost in the allegory.'

The tutor made sympathetic noises, but he also appeared to be dissenting. 'It may be that bringing together the tale of the unicorn and the story of Christ opens up all kinds of new meanings that expand and can't be controlled. Perhaps there's a metaphor here that goes beyond a merely mechanical allegory. And there's quite a bit more about the analogy I haven't mentioned that's really interesting.'

Giles and Emily looked expectantly at the tutor, but he only scanned his shelves once more, as if looking for a long-lost friend sandwiched between the books, and said, 'Why don't you read a poem in celebration of the Virgin Mary attributed to a Kentish vicar, William of Shoreham, in the early fourteenth century?'

Tutors, they thought, did annoying things like this. You wanted them to give you information, and they sent you off to find things out for yourself. Back to the library on a summer's afternoon for what seemed like a good deal of hard work.

Meanwhile, the tutorial turned to other, more linguistic matters as the tutor made sure that they could translate the passages from the reader, and understood the difference between participles and adjectives. He collected Emily's essay to read later, and they left the room as the hour struck.

'What about a drink in the college bar?' said Giles. I owe you one for putting me onto the house in Observatory Street. I was surprised at how young the landlady was, by the way. Is she a student herself?'

'I had quite a long conversation with her when I was planning to take the room', replied Emily, 'and found out that she finished her degree only last year. She's got a job as a graduate management trainee at the John Radcliffe Hospital, something to do with arranging accommodation. It seems that a favourite aunt who used to live in the house died, and left it to her. Oh, and she's got a partner, and is actually engaged to him.'

'I just about discovered that,' said Giles. 'Let's go the bar. We could discuss a further claim by John Trevisa – that the unicorn often fights with elephants and conquers them by wounding them in the belly – though actually he says "in the womb."'

Emily punched his arm in a friendly way. 'I'm not sure whether that's a dirty joke or not,' she said.

Giles blushed, as this hadn't actually crossed his mind.

'Anyway, you can buy me a drink', she agreed.

Later, Giles came to regret that he had not followed his tutor's advice to extend his reading about the unicorn. Perhaps it was that, in the confidence of youth, he thought he had understood what he had read well enough. Perhaps he wanted to keep the image of the unicorn and the virgin just as it was, bright and fresh, in his mind. Perhaps it was the fact that exams were looming and there were other subjects to revise. Anyway, it was not until nine months later that he heard a verse from the poem about Mary his tutor had mentioned, and a great deal had happened in between.

3
Scapegoats

A few days before the Michaelmas Term began, in the period that Oxford, with its imperial annexation of the calendar, calls '0' week, Giles was moving into his new lodgings. His mother had driven him and his belongings to Oxford, and at his insistence had left him and his piles of books, clothes and electrical goods on the pavement outside number 81. He knew that he was not behaving well, and that his mother was hurt by not being asked to come into the house, or to have lunch with him somewhere in the city, but he felt a strong urge to make a division between the parts of his life in his West London suburb and in Oxford. He relished returning to Oxford and the separate life he was making there, and though he knew that his parents cared for him, he was also at the age when he was embarrassed by them. Like all the students he knew, parents were a kind of guilty secret; source of financial support, even – at times of crisis and the major festivals of the year – a source of love, they were best kept invisible to friends, tutors and sexual partners.

It had not been a particularly good vacation. His father, though pleased to see him, after a few perfunctory enquiries had soon reverted to his usual rhythms of work and pottering around in the garden. His mother had been delighted to have him home, but had exasperated him by supposing a knowledge of his life which was almost totally misinformed by her experience as a school secretary. She had picked up the patter of student life which applied to almost every university except Oxford and Cambridge, and so would enquire how the 'semester' had been at 'uni', whether 'hall' had been comfortable and whether he was tired by going to all the lectures. Giles had found it impossible to communicate the particular nature of existence at Oxford, suspended as it was between the dizzy freedom in which undergraduates made virtually their own timetable, and the intense pressure of producing written work each week, sometimes twice a week, of a standard to satisfy tutors who would prefer to be reading papers written by their colleagues in research.

Despairing of giving his mother entrance into his world, he took a brief satisfaction in hearing that he had passed his first public examination with respectable marks, spent a few weeks stacking shelves in the local supermarket, declined ungraciously to go on the family holiday, and read nineteenth-century novels voraciously in preparation for the coming academic year. His spare hours were also filled with some confusing images, partly of Emily and partly of Hannah. Dwelling upon them with the help of furtive fumblings beneath his duvet at night, they sometimes seemed totally different women, and sometimes merged into the same mysterious figure, sitting under a tree on a May morning.

Set down now on the pavement in the street in front of his lodgings, he was already proving a hazard to pedestrians walking their dogs, or taking a short cut between the two larger thoroughfares that were joined by Observatory Street. One woman picked her way between his boxes, giving his computer and stereo system a kick that could charitably be regarded as an accident as she passed, and another walker was forced out, muttering, into the road. Hastily Giles turned his key in the door and began to pile boxes and loose clothes into the narrow passage beyond. As he did so a young man, slightly older than him, came out from the bright rectangle of light beyond the hall.

'So, you're the man who's come to keep the bathroom clean, are you?' he greeted him.

Giles remembered the first time he had knocked at this door, and guessed that the mocking tone belonged to Hannah's fiancé, Benedict. He found himself facing a slight, medium-height figure with close-cropped hair, a bony skull with skin stretched over sharp angles, dark eyes, one ear-ring, and a challenging stare. Though he was at least six inches taller, Giles felt threatened, and drew back instinctively. He wondered with alarm whether he was about to be thumped in the chest. Then Benedict laughed suddenly and held out his hand, and Giles felt that, on closer acquaintance, he might be able to like him.

'Let me give you a hand', offered Benedict, 'or we'll offend the neighbours for ever. The time's long gone when an undergraduate came to Oxford with one trunk and had it carried from the station in a push-cart.'

Together they carried Giles' goods upstairs to his room, all the paraphernalia now needed for modern living during eight weeks of term, and deposited them in a heap on the floor and against the walls. Giles said thanks, and then, on an impulse, decided to return Benedict's opening greeting with a thrust of his own.

'I believe you're the man to talk to about unicorns,' he said.

Benedict looked hard at him, and Giles felt some of the initial belligerence returning. Again, however, he relaxed and smiled.

'Before the unicorns', he replied, ' we need to talk about the goats.'

'Right', responded Giles, 'you mean the scapegoats'.

'I can see that you've done some thinking and reading about this', said Benedict approvingly, and Giles felt he had passed a kind of initial test. Benedict slumped onto the only chair on the room, and Giles perched on the bed, feet on a box of books.

'It was the idea of the scapegoat that interested me at first. I'm writing a thesis in theology, and I've long been intrigued by the theories of a scholar called René Girard. Have you heard of him, a French Professor who went on to teach at a University in the United States? He writes in your area, you know, literature.'

Giles noticed that Benedict had been told by Hannah what subject he was reading, and had remembered it. He admitted that the name of this particular scholar had escaped him so far.

'Girard points out that the fundamental drive in human affairs is desire. We all desire to possess what seems attractive and valuable, but only because we imitate each other in what we want. We desire what others desire.'

A UNICORN DIES

Benedict looked straight at Giles at this point, and Giles said faintly, 'I see that this can be true, but it seems to me that sometimes we desire someone, even before we know that someone else desires her.' He swallowed hard and hoped that Benedict would not draw any conclusions about Hannah.

'But in general', Benedict continued impatiently, 'We learn from each other what *sorts* of things to desire, and this leads to conflict in society, because there are never enough desirable objects – or people – to go round. Society will break up in mutual violence unless this conflict can be removed and harmony re-established, and that's where the scapegoat comes in. Some individual or group of people are singled out as being at fault for whatever's going wrong in the world – usually immigrants or outsiders who don't really belong – and everyone projects their sense of guilt onto these victims. These are the impure ones, dangerous, poisoning the water or the banking system or the minds of the young. They are the cause of the plague. Finally the scapegoat is killed by an act of collective murder, and this releases tensions in the community and restores harmony for a period. But conflict will re-assert itself and the need for the killing of a scapegoat re-emerges.'

Giles rocked to and fro on the bed, appalled by a kaleidoscope of images that suddenly overwhelmed him. He smelt the roasting flesh as flames seared the feet and legs of witches bound to the stake, some mercifully choked into unconsciousness by the smoke first. He felt the heat of another fire lit in modern times, unquenched for five years, as Jewish children were parted from their parents on the selection ramp, and all went, neatly sorted by age and gender, to the double embrace of gas in cyanide chambers and the crematorium. He saw Roma caravans overturned and their inhabitants stoned as they crawled out from the wreckage in Eastern Europe. He heard the thud of boots of the police kicking street children to death in a South American state, and the repetitive liturgy of the machine gun in Hindu temples or Christian churches in India, turning prayers of praise into bitter lament, communion wine into blood on the pews. He was, for a moment, breathless, suffocated under the bodies of the victims of the ages, but as if from a distance heard Benedict continuing with his explanation.

'Girard shows the place of religion in all this. The killing of the human scapegoat is echoed by the ritual making of a sacrifice. This has been human sacrifice in the past, such as among the Incas, but more usually an animal has been substituted. So the sacrificial system in religions promises to make society secure and healthy through violence, and the gods are dragged in to support the whole institution; they have the power to restore well-being and prosperity, and they approve of the sacrifice. It's the gods in the end who are using violence to redeem.'

'I think I see where you're going', said Giles. 'Isn't this where the unicorn comes in? It's hunted and killed like a sacrifice. But isn't there a problem here? It's not real – it's a figment of the imagination. Nobody actually has a religion in which unicorns are killed.'

'Hold on,' protested Benedict. 'You're going much too fast. It's going to take some time to get from the scapegoat to the unicorn. In the case of collective murders of actual people in our society, it's essential for the persecutors to maintain that the scapegoat was guilty all along. If violence is going to redeem, then people have to believe that the victim really was unclean and dangerous. This is the lie that society perpetuates, the lie of the powerful. Myths are created to justify the violence. The human scapegoats are depicted as unnatural and sub-human monsters. So stories about them are claiming that the scapegoats are guilty of all kinds of crimes.'

A memory of past reading of Greek myths tugged at Benedict's mind. 'Wasn't the Minotaur a monster like that, living in a maze in the royal palace in Crete?'

'Exactly', responded Benedict with approval. 'The Minotaur was half-bull and half-man. Dragons, who get a generally bad press, are part-snake, part-lizard, part-bird with definite human characteristics, like hoarding gold.'

'Wait a moment', cried Giles in excitement. 'We've got to the unicorn now, haven't we? The unicorn is a sort of monster, a mixture made of bits of animals that do exist. The unicorn is part-goat, part-horse, and part-rhinoceros. It may look elegant, but it's still unnatural, and all the books say it's very fierce. It's definitely an outsider, because it lives on its own away from human habitations and from other animals. And…', here Giles' excitement grew, 'its attachment to virgins has the feeling of something human about it, and – though I hate to say this about a noble animal –

something forbidden and bestial as well. I bet your French Professor, Girard, sees the unicorn as a typical scapegoat myth.'

'Actually', said Benedict with a grin, 'he doesn't say a word about unicorns. That's me – that's what I'm doing in the thesis. And we still haven't got there yet, though I must say I'm impressed by your hasty deductions. You've forgotten about...', he paused as the door-bell suddenly rang loudly and persistently, '...Jesus Christ!' For a moment Giles was disturbed by his strong reaction to this interruption. It seemed to be a return to his earlier aggressive manner. Then he realized that he was completing his sentence as well as registering his surprise. It seemed a characteristically complex move.

Reluctantly, since there was no one else in the house, Giles got up and went downstairs. On the doorstep, he found Emily, who had, she said, come to help him move in. Since he had stepped in to take up her contract, it was the least she could do. Normally, he would have been pleased to see her, but he was disappointed that the thread of the argument had been broken. Benedict was coming down the stairs, the mood of the moment dissipated.

'Please', said Giles, 'I do want you to finish what you were saying. We still haven't really got to the unicorn bit properly. Please do explain your thesis subject. And I'm sure Emily would be interested too. Last term we did a tutorial together on the unicorn in the Middle Ages.'

Benedict seemed to look cross, or perhaps he was just absorbed in his own thoughts. 'All right', he responded, 'but I really ought to be in the library now. Why don't we all meet for a drink tonight? Say nine-o'clock.'

'What about the Bird and Baby?' Giles had named a local pub, more formally though infrequently called the Eagle and Child. Benedict frowned angrily.

'No. Not there. The landlord's banned me – unfair, but there's nothing to be done about it. Let's meet opposite at the Lamb and Flag.'

They agreed, Giles resisting the temptation to ask what Benedict had done to get himself barred from the premises of one of Oxford's most popular student meeting-places. He guessed that the enquiry would not be welcome, and might lead to losing the chance of having the rest of the discussion. Benedict went out in the direction of the Faculty Library, and Giles took Emily up to his room.

The next hour was spent in unpacking and getting the room into some sort of order. Emily reminded him that, despite what he'd said to Benedict, their last tutorial together wasn't meant to be about unicorns. He'd highjacked it in that direction, and she still hadn't entirely forgiven him. Still, she was interested to hear his account of what Benedict had said about the scapegoat. Telling her, while sorting his books out, Giles was shaken by some unexpected emotions. He skipped over the images of human brutality that had seemed so vivid to him earlier – this was not time to revisit them – but he found himself stirred by the association of the unicorn with sex and death. Who was it, he tried to remember, who had said that the orgasm was a 'little death'? Medieval and Renaissance poems were full of the lover's yearning to die in his beloved's lap, or on her breasts, wounded by Cupid's arrows. Death to one's self, no doubt, in being open and vulnerable to the one who is the object of intense desire, death to worries about reputation and – for one brief moment – a falling into delicious lack of conscious control over the body, abandonment to a sheer current of pleasure running strong and deep. What did D. H. Lawrence call it? 'Lapsing out', that was it. 'When the sweet tickling joys have come to the highest' was a phrase he also suddenly remembered from his reading of scurrilous poems attributed to John Wilmot, court-rake and death-bed penitent. He could not help the references floating into his well-stocked mind, and they increased his arousal rather than damping it down.

It was not surprising that when Emily sat down on the newly-made bed, flushed and with her hair and blouse in disarray from her exertions on his behalf, he felt he should thank her with nothing less than a kiss, and that this somehow became prolonged when he felt her willing response. She was wearing rather more, in early October, than in the May tutorial, but she helped him with various buttons and hooks, easing his clumsy haste and slowing him down a little. In someone so forward and confident, someone of whom he had been a little afraid at times, he had not expected to find such softness. Afterwards they had to re-make the bed, and Giles made sure that the bathroom was clean after their showers.

4
About Benedict

By nine that evening, Giles and Emily, feeling for the first time a little strange and awkward with each other, had found their way to the Lamb and Flag. Benedict was waiting for them at the bar and, after Giles had bought a round of drinks, he led them up a couple of steps into the snug. It was smoky, but empty. They looked at each other over their glasses of local ale, and it seemed difficult to know where to pick up the subject. Then Benedict said, slowly and deliberately, 'Jesus Christ.' As earlier in the afternoon, Benedict had the odd sensation that this was partly an oath and partly a hint that he was going to say something about the person named. There was a flicker of anger there, suppressed but not entirely hidden.

'How to break free from the circle of violence, victimization and scapegoating, that's the question', said Benedict, 'that's what Professor Girard was asking, after all his researches into literature, sociology and the rituals of far-flung tribes. He'd written several books about violence and collective murder as the foundation of society, and wasn't particularly happy about human prospects. Then he made a discovery, or it came to him with the force of something new. The story of the crucifixion of Jesus Christ in the Gospels isn't the usual justification of the powerful. It carries all the marks of the killing of a scapegoat, and one of the Gospels even puts the dramatic line into the mouth of a high-priest that "it's necessary for one man to die for the people." But this story is different. It's written from the point of view of the victim. Unlike the great myths, it asserts the innocence of the scapegoat.'

Giles fiddled with his glass, uncomfortable with this sudden turn towards what seemed a positive view of religion. He had been happier in the last conversation when religion was being condemned as blood-thirsty, demanding human sacrifices.

'So what does it do, this story, for the victims, the scapegoats? Surely it's just a story.'

Benedict leaned forward and spoke more strongly: 'The story of Jesus exposes the lie of the powerful in society. Girard suggests that it's when we read the story, when we see ourselves as one of the persecutors, that we are liberated from the myth of sacred violence. From the perspective of the cross of Jesus we can understand all victims of collective murder as innocent. Human life can be transformed by the revealing of the truth.'

Giles still was unhappy about emphasis on religion. 'That's a lot of weight to put on a story', he complained, 'especially one in the Bible.'

'Don't forget I'm a theologian', said Benedict. 'It's my story, after all. And there's a community that lives by the story, making a counter-culture to oppose the culture of violence, imitating the way of Jesus rather than the way of desire for possessions which results in conflict. The trouble is that the followers of Jesus soon swallow the lie again and lapse back into thinking about a vengeful God who demands to be appeased by sacrifice. And so, perhaps, we come at last to the unicorn.' Benedict hesitated, then asked, 'What do you know about hunting the unicorn?'

Giles and Emily looked at each other, and then Emily replied, 'We've come across two kinds of hunt in the literature we've read. There's the love-allegory, and there's the Christian allegory. In the first, the unicorn's like a lover, laying his head in the woman's lap and being overcome by her beauty; so he's hunted and slain by love. In the second, the unicorn's like Christ, hunted to death for the sake of divine love.'

'Actually,' said Benedict quietly, there's a third kind of hunt, but I think I'll leave that on one side for the moment.'

Giles had the odd sensation that he'd heard something like that opinion before, and after an effort to remember he thought that his Medieval English

31

tutor had said something similar. But for the moment he only said, 'When I first came across these themes, I thought the religious application rather spoilt the whole story. I've gone on holding that view, but I have to say I'm not quite so sure now I've listened to you.'

'It's hard to separate the two hunts', said Benedict. 'In the past it seems that people were quite content to see the unicorn as a sign of divine and human love, and to live with both. You might have pictures of both kinds of hunt hanging on your walls, for example, if you were wealthy enough. One of the lucky ones was the family that owned a chateau in Verteuil, France. They had seven marvellous unicorn tapestries, made at the end of the fifteenth century. One of them portrays the unicorn in captivity, chained to a pomegranate tree, bleeding from the wounds of love. Fastening the beast to a tree was a symbol that the beloved had subdued her wild lover and got him committed to marriage with her.'

Emily snorted audibly at this point, and Giles guessed she was on the verge of saying something about the way commitment should be understood today, in the light of the liberation of women. But he avoided catching her eye, and diverted the subject into asking whether Benedict had seen the tapestries himself.

'Yes, but not in France. The chateau was looted at the time of the French Revolution, and all seven tapestries ended up being used by the peasants to cover their fruit trees and potatoes from the frost. They were briefly restored to the chateau, and were then bought by John Rockefeller and given to the Metropolitan Museum of Art in New York. I've seen them there, in an outlying gallery called The Cloisters.'

'Did you say that they weren't all about human love?' asked Giles, who was getting interested in the religious theme, despite himself.

'Yes, I was going to mention the second kind of hunt', replied Benedict. 'Four of the tapestries, a different set from the one that has the 'Unicorn in Captivity', show the unicorn being hunted to death in an allegory of the passion of Christ. In one image of this series, the unicorn is at bay, fighting the dogs and facing the spears of the hunters. It's clear that the unicorn represents Christ because one of the hunters, blowing his horn, has a caption on his scabbard reading – in Latin – 'Hail, Queen of Heaven'. This hunter is

32

probably the angel Gabriel in disguise; we can tell this because his motto recalls his words 'Hail, Mary' at the annunciation of the birth of Jesus. So nobody, you see, thought it was peculiar to hang these two kinds of hunt together. The unicorn is a lover *and* is Christ; the unicorn is wounded for the sake of the beloved *and* dies to redeem the world.'

'So that's what your thesis is about, is it?' enquired Giles. 'I can see how the two kinds of story about the unicorn weave together , but I'm still not sure how all that you've told us about the scapegoat fits into the unicorn. Perhaps I'm just a bit slow.'

Benedict was about to reply, when the snug was invaded by a group of noisy drinkers, laughing and joking among themselves. They sat down at a nearby table, and the three attended to their drinks in a sudden silence among themselves. Giles recognized a final-year student from his own college in the group and nodded slightly to him. Another of those who had come in, who was clearly at the lively centre of the conversation, glanced across at them, noticed Benedict and stiffened suddenly. He seemed about to ignore him, but then couldn't restrain his fury.

'Bloody hell!', he exclaimed, 'This isn't a way to spend a pleasant evening. I can't say that I fancy the company.' He looked again at Benedict, with contempt, and added 'It's just my humble opinion, I know, but I reckon that Oxford would be a more civilized place without your bloody presence. Come on', he said to his companions, 'let's get out of here and breath some fresh air.' He slammed down his half-empty glass and walked out of the pub. After some hesitation, and a quick finishing-up of drinks, the others followed him.

Giles and Emily hardly dared to look at Benedict. When the man had started haranguing him, he had risen quickly to his feet as if to start a fight, but had then clenched his fists and sat down again. He was staring intently at the table and tracing a pattern in his spilled beer, trembling slightly. For a few minutes he said nothing, and seemed in a state of shock. Then he shook himself, recovered his poise somewhat and looked Emily and Giles in the eye. 'I'm sorry you had to hear that', he said, 'Nick Stoney and I go back a long way, and I may have made a bad decision a few years ago. He doesn't usually lay into me that much, but perhaps he'd had too much to drink tonight.'

While naturally curious to know how justified this assault on Benedict had been, they thought that being supportive was the best immediate course.

'Your thesis sounds like a marvellous subject', said Giles, who seemed now to have forgotten his earlier aversion to the religious angle.

'I wish my supervisor shared your enthusiasm', replied Benedict, his face taking on its customary, slightly hostile look. 'He thinks I've bitten off more than I can chew, what with tapestries and old French romances alongside the theology. He thinks I shouldn't worry too much about the unicorn as a lover, and should focus on the Christ-allegory. He says that investigating both kinds of hunt thoroughly may be too ambitious – though mind you,' he added, 'he knows a fair bit about the first hunt himself. Perhaps too much for his own good.'

The expression on their faces made clear that this last revelation was even more fascinating than the academic discussion, and he seemed to realize he had gone too far.

'We'd better stop there for now', he said quickly. 'I realize I haven't yet answered your question properly about the way that the scapegoat and the unicorn fit together. Actually, that's the whole point of my thesis, but we'd better leave it for another day.'

Several days later, Benedict was having a session with his supervisor, Mark Goodall, chaplain of St Paul's College. Mark handed back the re-drafted version of one chapter of Benedict's thesis, commenting that he thought Benedict was making real progress with the subject, and that he had himself learnt a great deal from it. He also grumbled that computers made a supervisor's life even more difficult than need be. A student used to make revisions in ink on the typescript so that it was immediately obvious where changes had been made, but now, using a word-processor a student could hand in a completely clean version in a couple of days – sometimes several in one week – and the hapless supervisor had to start reading all over again. Students seemed incapable of using the tool called 'track changes', or else they were such perfectionists that they refused to leave any traces of their mistakes and changes of mind.

Benedict had heard this complaint before, but waited until it was over before saying, 'I've got an apology to make to you, Mark. I was talking to a couple of undergraduates the other evening about my thesis, and I'm afraid I got rather carried away. Anyway, I was talking about the love interest in the unicorn story, and just happened to let slip that you'd had some problems in that area. I suppose it might get back to you.'

Mark sat as though stunned. 'How the hell could that just *happen* to come up?' he demanded. 'I'm really disappointed. Do you make a habit of talking about my personal affairs?'

'I don't really understand how it happened myself', Benedict said unhappily. 'It just seemed to come out of the conversation. I'd had a fair amount to drink in hall and then in the pub, and I'd also had a bit of a shock about something. I know that this isn't an excuse, and I'm really sorry. I didn't go into details, and I hope I haven't done any damage.'

Mark continued to look upset, but then sighed and said, 'Well, it can't be helped, I suppose. Apology accepted.' As a sign of forgiveness he offered Benedict a glass of his cut-price sherry, and Benedict swallowed it as a penance. But, for the next couple of weeks, relations between them were not as easy as they had been.

Somehow, time could not be found in the following weeks for Benedict to take up the subject again with Giles and Emily, and to fulfill his promise of explaining more clearly what the image of the unicorn had to contribute to the theme of the scapegoat. One mystery was, however, cleared up. One day Giles and Emily were ordering lunch at the bar of the 'Bird and Baby' and Emily, in her direct way, asked the barman taking their order why Benedict Green was barred from the premises of the pub. The man hesitated, looked annoyed at the question and then laughed shortly.

'I don't mind telling you,' he said. 'In my view he's an officious bloody prig. My son, you see, he's an undergraduate at this guy's college and he's studying theology – though I don't know why.'

'Reading theology, we say in Oxford', corrected Giles mentally, but was careful not to say it out loud as he wanted his lunch.

'Well, the other day here in the pub this bloody pompous Green accused my son of being one of a crowd of drunken undergraduates who'd broken into a car outside here on St Giles one night, hot-wired it and driven it away for a laugh. He said he'd recognized him easily from tutorials with him. He had the nerve to say that he was in two minds about whether to go to the police about it.'

The barman gestured indignantly towards the corner of the bar adorned by an ancient fire grate where a notice hang proudly proclaiming that C. S. Lewis and J. R. R. Tolkien had once sat there with their friends and read their book manuscripts to each other. This was where, for example, *The Lord of the Rings* and the *Chronicles of Narnia* had first been heard. 'Would real scholars and gentlemen like that have grassed on their own students?' he asked indignantly – ' if they'd done anything, of course,' he added hastily.

Giles could have replied that the barman was assuming a lot about the ethics of people he'd never met, and that the disciplinary code of the university, which college Fellows were obliged to uphold, was more stringent than in the 1940s. If found guilty, the barman's son would have faced likely expulsion. Though strictly irrelevant, he could also not help recalling that Lewis and his friends had moved to the Eagle and Child across the road when the landlord of that time decided to modernize the pub and took the wall of their snug away. But he suppressed all these responses and only asked, 'Did the landlord really have authority to bar him on those grounds?'

'Not exactly', admitted the man. 'But of course my son denied the accusation and told him to take it back, with a few frank words. Green reacted strongly and a bit of a fracas followed. I just told the landlord that he made a habit of brawling with other customers, and got him banned for that', he explained with some satisfaction. 'He needs to watch out, does Green, that he doesn't take to walking in the dark in the back alleys of Oxford. I don't know how he's got the nerve to go on teaching Tom after what he did.'

All this left a nasty taste in Giles' and Emily's mouths which made lunch less enjoyable than it would have been before the disclosure. It also confirmed their impression that Benedict had a hasty temper, did not tolerate fools easily, and was prone to make enemies. It did not, however, stop them from admiring him in many ways.

5
Death

During the following weeks of the Michaelmas Term, Giles plunged into nineteenth-century English literature. His general tendency to dreaminess was enhanced by reading the romantic poets, especially Shelley, but received a strong antidote from the socially-realistic novels of Dickens. A brisk walk in from his lodgings to college also helped to wake him up in the morning, whereas before he had moved only a few paces from his bed to the college library. He found plenty of evidence of an interest in things medieval among the Victorian novelists and poets, and he spent a whole day in the company of Tennyson's knights and ladies, but for the most part the unicorn was an unknown wonder to them, and his conversation with Benedict drifted out of the forefront of his mind.

He got to know his fellow-lodger in Hannah's house – Jacqui Watt, a mathematician, who seemed rather more playful and jokey in manner than he would have expected from those of her craft. She was snub-nosed, with cropped blond hair and vivid blue eyes, and he found her friendly and open to late-night conversations about the nature of time and space. Indeed, reflection on quantum theory, as Jacqui explained it to him, had an even more powerful effect on his detachment from the visible world around than the romantics did. He wondered whether Jonathan Swift, had he known about modern physics, would have added a fourth volume to his Gulliver's Travels, and made his hero visit the miniscule world of the quanta where atoms could apparently spin in opposite directions at the same time, or perhaps at two different times simultaneously.

On one occasion Jacqui also had some unexpected comments to make about Benedict.

'I used to talk a lot to Benedict. We agreed that you probably need as much imagination in thinking about the quantum world as you would about unicorns. But we haven't spoken for a while.'

'I'm sorry to hear that,' responded Giles. 'What's the reason?'

Jacqui looked embarrassed and flushed slightly. 'I don't want to go into that, but I'd have thought it was obvious. Hannah, you know.'

Giles wasn't sure he understood properly, but Jacqui was so obviously uncomfortable about saying more that he thought he should not push the matter.

He went on seeing Emily, though they were no longer sharing tutorials. They developed a pattern of spending the late evening, one or perhaps two days a week, dancing with friends at some nightclub, and then returning to Giles' room for the rest of the night hours. Giles had no idea whether Hannah was aware of this part of his life, or whether it might infringe on the conditions of his tenancy. He was reluctant to mention it to her, for some reasons that were obvious and for others that he was prone to push to the back of his mind, but of which he remained dimly aware. Hannah appeared now and again in his fantasy life, but for the most part he was faithful in his thoughts and dreams to Emily.

The two of them were beginning to drop into a steady relationship, but neither wanted to talk of the future – which, in the roller-coaster pace of Oxford existence, meant beyond the end of the Michaelmas Term. Hilary Term seemed a distant mirage, hovering beyond the desert wastes of the six-week Christmas vacation. Both had had short-term relationships before, but this one seemed at least to have the potential for some extension. Emily made Giles laugh, and kept him mentally alert with her sharp, often piercing, insights, but he sometimes found her exhausting. She, for her part, found him an intelligent and considerate partner, but astonishingly ignorant of life beyond either Oxford or the London suburb just fifty miles down the motorway. Hers had been a family in the diplomatic service, and she had grown up in various places where her father had been posted, most recently in Nairobi. She was making plans to travel together to East Africa with a group of friends in the summer, and she hoped that Giles would be with them.

Part of their habit for their nights together was to wait to appear the next morning in the kitchen downstairs until Hannah had left for work at the hospital. This was an unspoken arrangement, which suited them both. Sometimes Jacqui would join them for breakfast. One particular Monday morning, in the sixth week of term, Giles and Emily came unsteadily down the stairs at half-past nine, scarcely half-clothed, to put on the kettle, and found Hannah sitting at the kitchen table. Their first reaction was to retreat back upstairs, but then Giles saw that Hannah was staring blankly ahead of her, with a look of misery on her face. She was compulsively twisting her engagement ring round and round her finger, but otherwise seemed frozen, too numb to cry. Absurdly, the thought popped into Giles' mind, 'It's as if the air's too cold for it to snow'. He went to her and put his hand gently on her sleeve, noticing that she had rubbed her finger raw with the thin band of gold.

'It's Benedict', she whispered. 'The police phoned about half an hour ago, and told me that something terrible had happened to him. I think he must be dead, but they wouldn't tell me that over the phone. Someone's coming straight round.' She added, as if the information mattered, 'He always carried my name with him, you know, as the first person to be contacted, just in case.' Emily ran forward and held Hannah in her arms.

A mile away, in the set of rooms occupied by the chaplain at St Paul's College, Detective Inspector Matthew Longley was gloomily surveying the scene in the bathroom. In the centre of the floor was a large Victorian bath. It was free-standing, with feet like eagles' claws in burnished brass, and with a wide lip running all around it. With ornate handles on each end of its casting it had the appearance of a huge, ceremonial urn, funereal black outside and clinical white within. It was full of a crimson liquid, some of it trickling over the edge and running down the sides. Floating in this container was the body of Benedict Green, wrists cut open, but no longer pumping out the blood that had mingled with the water to produce this scene of pompous death. Rigor mortis was over, and the limbs of the body moved gently on the red viscous surface, as a breeze blew in from the open door and the room beyond. Benedict's clothes, from which his wallet had been carefully extracted for identification, were piled neatly on a wicker-cane chair nearby, and a fluffy brown towel stood ready on a stand. It had not been needed.

D.I. Longley shivered. As if to underline the finality of death it was cold, icy cold, as all the heating was shut off. The police doctor, who had had no difficulty in certifying death, had found it more difficult to make a suggestion about the exact time of death, as the cooling of the water – presumably at least warm at the critical moment – had slowed the process of decomposition down, but he had estimated some time between 6.00 pm on Friday night and 6.00 am on Saturday morning. The pathologist would perhaps be able to be more precise. Without disturbing the body, the doctor had also found a sharp ornamental paperknife at the bottom of the bath.

The D.I.'s sergeant had reported what he had learnt from the chaplain who had himself found the body and called the police. Dr Goodall had apparently been away the whole weekend, from Friday afternoon, helping to install the new rector at a church in Birmingham of which the college had patronage. He had returned by an early train that morning, in time to take tutorials before lunch, and had stumbled on the tragedy when he opened up his rooms. Benedict Green, it appeared, was one of his research students, and he had recognized him instantly, despite what he had called 'the unusual circumstances'. He was still deeply shocked, and was now praying in the college chapel.

The policeman thought that the chaplain could be left to his orisons for the time being. He would interview him later in the morning when the body had been removed to the mortuary, and the plug removed from the bath. Meanwhile, there was a job for the Scene of Crime Officers to do, and he stood aside to let them enter the room. It looked, he reflected, like suicide, but he wasn't jumping to conclusions.

'I can't believe he's dead', Hannah was saying in a choking voice to her parish priest. The young policewoman who had called to give Hannah the news of Benedict's death, had summoned him at her request. He was, wisely, sitting with her in silence rather than trying to offer hollow words of consolation or explanation.

'I know he was angry', said Hannah. 'He was angry at himself, though people usually didn't understand that, and he was angry with God. He often shut himself up in his emotions, as if he were alone in the world because of something bad that had happened to him in the past. I used to tell him that other people had the right to be angry as well, but I don't know whether he understood what I was saying. Was he angry enough to do this?'

The priest was silent. He felt that the question wasn't actually directed at him. He was a good theologian, and had read all the right books in the reading list headed 'The Problem of Suffering'. But he said nothing.

D.I. Longley, accompanied by his sergeant, was interviewing Mark Goodall in his study. The body of Benedict had been taken to the mortuary at the John Radcliffe Hospital, to await autopsy. The SOCOs had finished what they wanted to do for the moment, and how much more would need to be done would depend on the decision of higher authorities about how to treat the incident. The cast-iron bath, stained red, was still looking like an altar of human sacrifice. Mark had decided that as soon as he had permission from the police he was going to have it removed, and replaced by a modern one made of fibreglass.

'What I don't understand, Sir, is how Mr Green could have got into your bathroom', began the policeman.

'There wasn't time earlier to explain the whole position to your sergeant', replied Mark. 'As a doctoral student, he was assigned some undergraduates to teach, and when I was going to be away I used to lend him a key to my rooms so that he could use my study to take tutorials. Otherwise he had to use a seminar room in his college, which wasn't quite the right atmosphere. Since he only had a shower in his graduate flat at Helwys College, I also said he was welcome to use my bath.'

'Very generous, Sir, I'm sure', said the policeman, making it sound like an accusation. 'So that's what happened on this occasion, was it?'

'It certainly was, Inspector. Benedict came by after lunch on Friday, and I gave him the key. He told me that he was taking tutorials at 4 and 5, but I had left by 3 o'clock, on the train to Birmingham. As you know, I didn't get back until 8 this morning, and found him here.' His voice, firm until now, began to waver.

'You went rather early, didn't you? I thought installations usually happened on a Sunday, when the congregation was due to gather.'

'In this case', replied the chaplain, 'it happened on the Saturday afternoon, so there could be a parish meal in the evening. It was also the only time the Bishop had available for the licensing. I wanted to be there on the Friday, to prepare my address in my hotel away from the distractions of college. I then stayed on to preach for the new rector at Sunday evensong. All this meant I had to leave at an appallingly early hour on Monday morning to get back in time for morning tutorials.'

'Did you leave the hotel on the Friday evening?' asked the inspector.

'No, I didn't', replied Mark quickly.

'Not even to get a meal?' enquired the inspector, with a note of surprise in his voice.

'I bought sandwiches at the station and took them in with me', explained Mark, 'so that I could get on with the address while I ate. There was tea and coffee in the room.'

'Can anyone verify that?' persisted the inspector. 'Did you call anyone from your room during the evening?'

'Well, no. I was totally occupied with working out what I was going to say. I wanted to amuse and inspire, you know, and that's not easy.'

The inspector reflected that this wasn't a combination he usually aimed at in his reports to his chief superintendent.

Mark thought for a moment. 'I suppose you can ask at the reception desk. I'm sure they'll say they didn't see me until the next morning.'

The inspector paused and then took a new direction. 'Why was it so cold when we arrived earlier on?' he asked.

'Well, I asked Benedict to turn the boiler off when he'd finished, to save gas, and I suppose he must have done this before getting into the bath.'

The inspector had left one significant question to the end, to see if it caught the chaplain off-balance when he imagined the interview was over. It was a technique he had been perfecting over a number of enquiries. 'One more thing, Sir, if you don't mind. Is this your paperknife?' He held up the exhibit in a sealed plastic bag. Even through its cloudy surface the small wicked blade was clear, ending in an ornamental handle surmounted by a pearl.

The chaplain's startled face was gratifying, even if not actually incriminating.

'It's mine!' he admitted, 'a gift from a grateful Arab student. I keep it in its stand on the table in the living room.' He shivered. 'Is that what Benedict used in the bath? You might as well keep it. I don't want it back.'

D.I. Longley's next stop was with Hannah. She got the impression of a thin, rather severe-looking middle-aged man who was trying to be kind in a clumsy way. He saw an attractive young woman who was obviously upset but trying to be composed.

The inspector introduced himself and his sergeant.

'I'm sorry to disturb you further at this distressing time, Miss', he went on somewhat formally, 'but I'm afraid I've got to ask you a few questions. When did you last see your fiancé?'

Hannah thought about the Thursday night they had spent together, and scenes flitted through her mind. The thought suddenly hit her that this was not only their most recent night but their last. Yet she only said, 'Early on Friday morning'.

'Weren't you surprised that you didn't hear from him again over the weekend?' asked the inspector.

Even at this painful moment Hannah could not help reflecting that the question showed what different worlds policemen and scholars lived in. 'He was writing his thesis', she explained patiently, 'and sometimes he got so absorbed he lost track of time altogether and couldn't think of anything else.'

Even me, she added silently, while knowing in her mind that any lingering resentment was completely out of place.

'I see,' said the inspector doubtfully. 'And had you noticed anything different about him in the last few weeks?'

'Do you mean, did he seem so depressed that he'd kill himself?' burst out Hannah. 'I just don't know. He'd been worried about something for a long while, and he wouldn't tell me about it. It put him on edge, and spoilt things now and then, but I'm not sure it was getting any worse.'

'You really have no idea what the problem was?' pressed the sergeant.

'Don't you think I'd tell you if I knew?', cried Hannah. 'I want to know what happened as much as you do.'

Shortly after the two policemen took their leave, saying apologetically that they might need to come back if they found they needed more information. On the way out they ran into a young man who had come quickly down the stairs as if he had heard them going.

'Are you the police?' he asked. I want to say that I'm not sure that Benedict killed himself.'

'Oh really,' replied the inspector, 'Have you got any information that would be useful to the police, or is this just a hunch?'

'Not exactly information', said Giles, but I find that chaplain at St Paul's suspicious. I hope you're checking him out.'

'That's a serious accusation', said the sergeant. 'You can trust us to do our business, and I hope you'll keep to yours.'

Shutting the door behind them, the inspector said, 'Good put-down, but you should check out the parson's story with the hotel in Birmingham anyway.'

Late in the afternoon, Benedict Green's mother, a thin, pinched woman, visited the mortuary. She had taken the first available train from her home in Manchester, but could not contact Benedict's father, having lost contact with him five years ago. She had wanted to see Benedict before the necessary invasion of his body by the autopsy, and she made the formal identification, despite not having seen him for over a year.

She sat with him for ten minutes in the small, cheerful viewing room (almost like a hotel-room, she thought, not at all like the stainless steel caverns that you see on television), and lost herself in memories. On the way out she failed to recognize Hannah coming in, having never met her, or even known of her existence.

Tucked away on one corner of the hospital site as the mortuary was, Hannah had never visited it before. As she had parked her car, the thought had come into her mind that she had never found a parking-space at the hospital so easily before, and that perhaps some of this space could be made available for those visiting the still-alive in the buildings over the way. Sitting beside Benedict, she traced her fingers over a face that seemed less angry, more relaxed, and said out loud, 'All passion spent.' It was then that she cried for the first time.

In a busy day D.I. Longley was now interviewing the porter, in his glass case in the lodge of the college. It was constructed, by some quirky academic planning decision, side-on to the entrance passage, so that the porter could see who was coming in if he looked out to his right, but when attending to an enquirer at the front hatch his attention would be neatly diverted from passing traffic. This would not matter so much if the CCTV camera were in operation, but on this occasion there had been no tape in the recorder, the porter evidently feeling that the mere presence of the camera was sufficient deterrent to potential wrong-doers. He confirmed that two undergraduates had indeed come for tutorials at 4 and 5 on the previous Friday, since they had asked to be directed to the chaplain's rooms. He also remembered seeing Benedict Green go out of the front door at 6.15 pm with the second student. He could not recall seeing him come back in again later, but this did not mean – the porter said, stating the obvious – that he hadn't.

In his last task for the day, D.I. Longley tracked down the 5.00 pm student through phoning the director of studies for theology at St Paul's college. The undergraduate, Tom Naylor, confirmed that after the tutorial he had walked out of the front gate with Benedict Green, and that they had parted immediately afterwards. He reported that his tutor had not seemed unduly disturbed, though he was a bit distant and detached as he had been throughout what had been an uncomfortable tutorial hour. The inspector got the impression that student and tutor did not get on well, but he had known many other situations like that when interviewing students. Relations could vary from clubbable sessions at the pub which stretched over a couple of hours to frigid conversations, based on too-little reading done, in which the ending of the hour could not come too soon for both participants.

That night, Giles and Emily were talking together, in subdued tones, about the events of the day.

'I suppose he must have killed himself', said Giles. 'Anything else seems unthinkable, but I'm beginning to wonder about other possibilities.'

'He appeared very clever when I met him, but a bit weird as well. Perhaps he was depressed', mused Emily. 'He did say some bloody odd things that evening we spent in the Lamb and Flag along with all the fascinating stuff about scapegoats and unicorns. What was it he said about his supervisor, that he knew too much about the love-hunt for his own good?'

'I've mentioned the chaplain to the police', said Giles, 'but I don't think they took it very seriously.'

'And that Nick person clearly had it in for him, as well as the undergraduate he had a fight with', recalled Emily. 'He must have been under a lot of pressure.'

Two days later, D.I. Longley had the autopsy report in front of him. Death, as he had expected, was due to blood loss resulting from deep cuts to the radial veins at the wrists. Unexpected was the finding of substantial amounts of LSD, mixed with PCP, in Benedict's urine, blood and liver. There were also small traces in his hair. The dose he had apparently taken was not enough to be fatal, but it would have produced severe hallucinations and could well have rendered him unconscious, depending on the state of his metabolism. The pathologist had done no better than the police doctor in fixing the exact time of death.

They went back to Hannah, as they must, to ask about the drugs. She had heard of LSD, but Phencyclidine, popularly known as 'Angel Dust', had to be explained to her. She seemed shocked, and protested that she knew nothing about Benedict's use of them.

'I'm inclined to believe her', remarked the inspector to his sergeant. 'She seems a truthful person, though she's also perceptive and it seems odd that she never suspected anything.' He was not usually an imaginative person, but a line from a Shakespeare play he had recently seen performed by the local amateur dramatic society passed through his mind unexpectedly. 'Love sees not with the eyes, but with the mind.' He shook himself from his momentary reverie and said to his sergeant, 'How did you get on in Birmingham?'

'Nothing conclusive one way or the other', he replied. 'The staff at reception confirm that Dr Goodall arrived there at 5.00 pm, and they don't recall seeing him going out afterwards, but it was a busy night. People were arriving for business conventions until late on from several countries, and they were occupied until after midnight coping with the rush. They could easily have missed him slipping out and in. Unfortunately there was no CCTV. Apparently the guests don't like it.'

'The timing's a bit tight', commented the inspector, but he could have returned to Oxford, drugged and killed his student, and got back by the last train.'

'But how could he have been sure that Benedict would have been there in his lodgings?' objected the sergeant. 'And we've found no motive for wanting him dead.'

'So we've got two possibilities', said the inspector. 'The most straightforward one is that this young man took the drugs himself, got into the bath and cut his wrists before he passed out. The other, much less likely, possibility is that someone gave him the dose, in a drink or something God knows when or where, and when he was unconscious put him in the bath and cut his wrists for him.'

'Using the chaplain's deadly paperknife', added the sergeant. 'Can't we get forensic evidence from that?'

'All the finger-prints have been dissolved by the water', replied the inspector. 'I suppose we could try for DNA, but it's only worth doing if we think there's something suspicious about the death. That's the first thing we have to decide.'

The sergeant tried again to be helpful. 'I'm a bit puzzled about the fact that the heating was turned off. How do you read that?'

'It could point in various directions', replied the inspector. 'If he killed himself then – as Dr Goodall suggested – he must have turned it off before taking the bath, perhaps even before taking the drugs. I must say that it seems a bit over-conscientious to want to save the chaplain money when he's about to lose the fees from a research student, but he was probably in a confused state of mind. If there's a murderer, then this unknown person turned the heating off, possibly to confuse us about the time of death.'

'Or perhaps', added his sergeant, 'the murderer turned it off to *make it seem* that his victim had planned to die.'

'That's a bit too complicated', retorted the inspector, reflecting that his sergeant might be over-reaching himself in a desire to impress.

'I don't like the fact that there's no suicide note', went on the inspector, 'especially since he was engaged and you'd expect him to write something to his fiancée. On the other hand, she tells us that he was worried about something he was keeping from her.'

'I wonder whether the relationship was as good as she makes out,' remarked the sergeant, seeking to redeem himself. 'She seemed quite cool and collected to me during the interviews.'

'Be that as it may,' replied the inspector, who had actually been impressed by Hannah, 'there's a piece of evidence that tips the balance for me. The traces of LSD found in Benedict's hair would have had to build up over three to six months, and they show that he was a habitual user. That makes it likely that he drugged himself that night, and so in the absence of any suspicious signs I'm going for the obvious conclusion, that this was suicide.'

The inspector reported his findings to his chief superintendent, who took a few days to mull over the facts while further forensic investigations were done at the melancholy site, but finally he agreed with his subordinate officer. The inspector relayed the decision with some satisfaction to his sergeant.

'I'm closing the case. The chaplain can have his bath back. It'll need cleaning.'

The inspector lifted the restrictions on entering the bathroom that he had kept in place in case the room was determined to be a crime scene. Benedict had earlier on made a 'living will', requesting that in the case of accidental death his body should be donated for medical experiment. Ahead of an inquest fixed for two weeks' time, the coroner released the body for this purpose. The inspector reflected that this probably meant that its destination was to lie under the hesitant scalpels of first-year medical students in the dissection lab, though it was just possible that Benedict might contribute more to the sum of human knowledge through research after his death than he had achieved in his life.

6
Postcards

A memorial service was planned for Benedict, to take place shortly after the inquest. This would take place after term, in the Christmas vacation, but this scarcely mattered as far as university people who knew Benedict were concerned. Apart from Giles, Jacqui and Emily these were mostly postgraduate students for whom the boundary lines of term and vacation meant far less than for undergraduates. For supervisors, any difference had long ago disappeared under the demands of their students to read multiple drafts of chapters from their theses just as soon as they had finished revising them for the third or fourth time. Aware that they were now the subject of assessments by their students on the on-line electronic reporting system, to be reviewed by the directors of graduate studies in their faculties, supervisors hastened to oblige. The balance of power in Oxford had shifted. Long gone were the days when a supervisor would advise a graduate student, 'Come and see me when you've written something', confidently expecting this offer to be taken up in a year's time. Now the supervisor was faced by the forbidding question on the on-line system, 'How many times have you seen this student since your last report?' To tick the box labelled 'none' seemed to invite retribution.

In the intervening couple of weeks before the service, Hannah was clearing Benedict's room at St Paul's College, assisted by Giles. In exchange for this help she had allowed Giles to stay on in his room in her house into the vacation without charge. The bursar of the college had been anxious to have the room vacant for a new letting in Hilary Term, and a pleading letter to Benedict's mother to empty it had gone unanswered. He therefore judged the fiancée to have authority in the matter of clearance, and asked her to act promptly. They found, of course, drafts of the thesis and notes for it, and Giles noticed that much of it was familiar from the conversations he had had with Benedict. But it was while sorting through Benedict's miscellaneous papers that they made two unexpected discoveries.

The first find was half a dozen small pieces of paper, about 2 centimetres square, printed with the head of a unicorn. These were puzzling, but they passed over them quite quickly, their attention being caught by something else. There was a series of six postcards bearing different pictures of unicorns, bundled together with a rubber band. They were all postmarked Oxford, and all addressed to Benedict in the same way – a laser-printed label. They had been numbered in sequence in a hand that Hannah recognized as Benedict's, but otherwise – apart from one – they were completely blank.

The unicorn images came from various art galleries and museums. The card numbered 1 was a photograph of a medieval artefact from the treasury of York Minster, an ivory drinking-horn named the 'Horn of Ulph', which the short description on the postcard dated from the early eleventh century. The pictorial engraving on the horn was confined to a narrow band around the mouthpiece, and so the detail was not clear on the card, but it appeared to include a unicorn and a lion on either side of a tree. The card numbered 2 was more colourful, and again showed a unicorn and a lion, this time with an ornately-dressed woman standing between them and touching the unicorn's horn. The legend on the card identified the image as one of a set of six similar tapestries called 'The Lady and the Unicorn', woven in Flanders about 1500, and kept in the Musée de Cluny in Paris. The third postcard reproduced a painting by Raphael, from about the same period, depicting a young woman with yellow, braided hair and looking apparently just over the shoulder of the viewer. She was sitting and holding a baby unicorn in her hands. The printed description on the postcard recorded that the painting was probably influenced by Leonardo da Vinci's Mona Lisa, and that it was kept in the Galleria Borghese in Rome.

The fourth postcard was vaguely familiar to Giles from his conversation in the Lamb and Flag with Benedict some weeks earlier, though it was new to Hannah. It showed a tapestry from the series held in The Cloisters, the medieval collection of the Metropolitan Museum in New York. As Benedict had described it, the scene was of the unicorn lying contentedly in a garden full of thousands of small flowers, enclosed by a fence, and tethered to a tree in which ripe pomegranates were visible. The description on the card informed the reader that this was one of a series of seven tapestries woven in the South Netherlands at the same period as the last two images, and that it was usually called 'The Unicorn in Captivity'.

The fifth postcard inserted a religious theme into the series. It reproduced a painting which depicted the Virgin Mary sitting in a walled garden with a unicorn apparently about to jump onto her lap. She was touching its horn and holding its front hooves in her hands, and over her head hovered God the Father sitting majestically in a cloud. The printed description on the card identified it as from the circle of Martin Schongauer, painted again at the beginning of the sixteenth century as part of a Dominican altar-piece, and kept in the Unter den Linden Museum in Colmar.

The final postcard introduced a jarring note, and carried the only written message of the sequence. It showed a tapestry in which the unicorn was depicted at bay, about to be killed. It was being harassed and bitten by dogs, blood was streaming down a wound in its flank and four spears were poised to strike it. Again, Giles hazily remembered it from Benedict's earlier description as another one of the tapestries hanging in The Cloisters in New York. But surprisingly it had not been issued by the Metropolitan Museum of Art there. The printed note on the card identified the tapestry as one of a series woven recently to be hung in Stirling Castle, under a commission from Historic Scotland, copying and recreating the set of tapestries in The Cloisters. On the card was stuck a computer-printed label like the address labels, carrying the message: 'Think you're an archangel? You bastard.' It crossed Giles' mind that modern printing methods had completely removed the possibility of solving a crime, as in old detective novels, by examining the peculiarities of type-writer keys – a chipped corner of a letter, for instance.

Hannah and Giles looked at these images a long time, pondering their significance.

'They were obviously background for his thesis', observed Hannah. 'Some friend must have sent them to him, thinking they'd be useful.'

'He did tell me and Emily about two of them', confirmed Giles. 'But the postmarks show they were sent over a period of nine months. That's a bit odd, isn't it? And the sixth one isn't at all friendly. Quite threatening in fact. I can't help wondering if they've got something to do with Benedict's death.'

'That's a bit speculative, some leap', retorted Hannah. 'Don't you think you're letting your own interest in unicorns run away with you?'

'Well, perhaps', replied Giles reluctantly. 'But let's try and work out how they fit together. The first two images and the fourth seem to belong to the theme of the 'love hunt', where the unicorn is caught and held by his lover. Probably the third fits here as well. The last one, according to what Benedict told us, belongs to the theme of the passion and death of the unicorn as an allegory for the death of Christ. That's what interested him so much. I admit I'm having difficulty fitting the fifth one in. I suppose it could belong to either of the two stories, but because it's religious I'm inclined to think it relates more to the second.'

'You're the expert – or at least you know more about unicorns than me', conceded Hannah. 'But what do you mean about being connected with Benedict's death?'

'I think I mean,' said Giles slowly, 'that there are two possibilities. One is that receiving the postcards somehow increased his despair and pushed him into taking his own life. The other is that they were sent by the person who murdered him.'

'But only the sixth card could be understood as a threat,' countered Hannah, and we don't even know what the message on it means.'

'It's certainly hostile,' pointed out Giles. 'The person who sent it was angry, that's for sure. It must have something to do with what happened, either way. I think we should let the police know about the postcards before the inquest, in case they want to make any further investigations.'

'It's rather too late for that,' said Hannah sombrely. '"Boys and chimney-sweepers come to dust" and so on. Or,' she added with a half-sob, 'or at least they come to the dissection table. I can't stop you, but I'm not happy. I can tell you that the police won't be interested. Surely you don't want to take the little squares with the unicorn on them as well?'

'Oh, I don't think so', said Giles, a little upset at the turn the conversation had taken, and at even the hint of a disagreement with Hannah. If he could limit the damage to their pleasing amity he would. He wondered why it seemed so important to find the truth about Benedict's death. It was partly because he thought it might help Hannah cope with the terrible event, but help in finding the truth would now, it seemed, have to be offered to Hannah against her inclinations and with considerable tact. There was another reason, too, of which Giles was only half-aware. The whole theme of the unicorn seemed to be tied up with his own sense of what made life worthwhile. He was finding himself, he dimly perceived, in finding the cause of Benedict's death. And ultimately, he was finding the unicorn.

The next day he telephoned the police station in St Aldate's, Oxford, and asked to speak to D.I. Longley. When the inspector came on the phone Giles reminded him that they had run into one another when he was leaving Hannah's house after interviewing her about the death of Benedict Green, and he explained that he had some new information to offer about the death. Though the inspector made what Giles felt to be a grudging response, he did invite Giles to come in and talk with him later in the day.

The police station had the usual aroma of a public building, a mixture of smells of paint, cheap floor covering and bodily sweat. The desk-sergeant let the inspector know that Giles had arrived, and they met in a dingy interviewing room.

'Well, what have you got for me?' asked the inspector. 'You know that the case is closed, I expect. It will have to be something good to open it up again.'

'It's this,' said Giles, spreading out the postcards in front of the inspector. 'We found these bundled up when we were going through Benedict's papers. You know Benedict was writing a thesis about unicorns.' He nearly added 'and scapegoats', but he had some sense of self-preservation in how much it might be wise to say. 'The message on this one, marked number 6, makes me think they've got something to do with his death. I thought you should know about them before the inquest.'

The inspector glanced at the postcards, and spent a little more time reading the message. He closed his eyes, though whether this was to continue thinking or to express frustration Giles was not sure. He did not have to wait long to discover which it was.

'Unicorns!' said the inspector, making it sound like a swear word. 'Have you any idea about the thorough, scientific way we investigate deaths that might be suspicious? Then you arrive wittering about unicorns. The message is obviously a joke of some kind, the sort of thing that students send each other when they haven't got anything better to do. Or do you want to add angels to unicorns? I suppose you can't fill me in on how these pictures explain the death of Mr Green? Are you suggesting that a unicorn appeared in the bathroom and killed him with a paperknife? Or an angel? I suppose they do teach you at your college that unicorns don't exist?' He passed no judgement on angels.

Giles flushed with embarrassment. 'I can't exactly see how the postcards connect up with Benedict's death. I just know that he was interested academically in the subject, and I think there's something sinister about getting this series of postcards over a long period. At least the last one looks to me like a threat.'

'Well, thank you for your public-spirited action', responded the inspector, injecting a heavy dose of sarcasm into his remark. 'But I suggest you follow the excellent advice given to you by my sergeant when we bumped into you at Miss Grace's house. Let us get on with our business and we'll let you know when we need any help.'

Dispirited, Giles gathered up his cards and made his way out past the unsympathetic gaze of the desk-sergeant, relieved to be back in the open air.

'I did warn you', said Hannah seriously when they met again in the house that evening, though it was typical of her that she didn't seem to imply a triumphalist 'I was right and you were wrong.' 'But I've been reading the thesis', she went on, 'and I thought you might be interested in the following passage.'

They sat around the kitchen table and Giles realized with mounting excitement that he might at last learn what Benedict thought was the point of bringing together the images of scapegoat and unicorn. Benedict had promised to tell him and Emily, but had never had the opportunity. Now Giles heard, through her voice, the tones of Benedict, slightly sardonic but intensely interested in his subject.

> 'The question is this: what is the myth of the unicorn doing? What's the impact of it when it's told, or painted, or woven into a tapestry? Professor Girard suggests that the history of Christ debunks the myths of the powerful, by insisting on the innocence of the victim. He does not consider the unicorn, but we must ask: does the Christian use of the unicorn story redeem this myth as well? If it becomes obvious that the unicorn is innocent through identifying it with Christ, then the myth cannot work in the usual way that myths do, to defend collective murder by society. It is not only the Gospel story of Christ that exposes the lie of violence and sacrifice, and stops people scapegoating others. Whenever the unicorn myth is told or portrayed it can have the same effect as well. It can turn people towards the life-giving power of the story of love that the unicorn also embodies.'

'Yes, that must be it!' interrupted Giles. 'Isn't it clear to everyone that the unicorn is innocent? Everyone loves a unicorn.' He paused. 'But wait a moment. Benedict was telling us that the unicorn might be seen as a kind of monster, a sort of more user-friendly version of the Minotaur. I'm not sure how that fits in.'

'Just listen,' commanded Hannah. Benedict goes on to deal with that.' She continued reading, unconsciously imitating the rise and fall of Benedict's voice.

> 'But the myth of the unicorn has many sides to it. It might not be redeemed by the story of Christ. If the unicorn is seen as guilty in some way, or even has a whiff of the dangerous about it, then the myth might actually be used to justify the

violence of the majority against the outsiders. "Killing the unicorn" could become a cipher for persecuting the Jews or burning witches. And the unicorn *is* an ambiguous symbol. It's very fierce, and is sometimes portrayed as preying on other animals. What's more, the Syriac version of the *Physiologus* underlines the irregular relations between the unicorn and the girl in the story. The virgin grasps the unicorn's horn with her hand and offers her breasts to him; the unicorn sucks them and generally makes himself familiar with her. The Waldensian version from Provence actually identifies the unicorn with the devil, who can only be overcome by the virtue of the virgin, though it must be said that this is unusual. Later on, when the unicorn is running rampant over the heraldic shields of Europe as a symbol of knightly chastity, Leonardo da Vinci regards it as an image of intemperance, a lack of sexual control.

So the question for my thesis is this: is the unicorn an innocent victim, or one that gets what it deserves? Does the myth undermine the scapegoat syndrome, or strengthen it? What does this tell us about those who appeal to the story?'

Giles was frowning. 'I can see that this is an open image, with lots of possibilities. Benedict convinces me that the unicorn story *could* encourage people to make minorities in society into scapegoats. But surely he wants to say that making Christ the unicorn has the power to overturn all that. As soon as you say, unicorn equals Christ, then surely it ceases to be sinister and monstrous. Why doesn't that always work?'

'You're really getting the point of this', exclaimed Hannah with a note of admiration in her voice. 'I wish Benedict had been able to discuss this with you. I don't think he had a sympathetic listener like you and that's why he got so frustrated. You're exactly anticipating what he goes on to write. Listen.'

'However much the story of Christ redeems the myth of the unicorn, there is always the other image of the unicorn lurking in the shadows. There is always another kind of picture hanging on the walls. And there is another factor to be considered. If Christians relapse back into the idea of a God who demands blood sacrifices to pay for sin, who actually hunts Christ to the cross with help of his angels, then this God might approve of other sacrifices for the good of the church and Christendom. Purging Europe of the Jews, or ridding the church of heretics, could be a logical extension of the crucifixion.

In this thesis I shall be taking a selection of instances of the unicorn story, in poems, art and devotional books, and I shall be seeing how it actually works in each case. I shall also be exploring the society and church of the time, to see what was troubling people, and then try and put two and two together. The canvas is a vast one, and in this thesis I only expect to make a beginning.'

Hannah stopped reading, her voice faltering. So much promise, she was thinking, wiped out. 'So you see,' she concluded, 'he was obviously collecting the postcards, with someone's help, to illustrate the examples he was going to study in the thesis. They're just traces of his research. Nothing to do with his death at all.'

Giles wasn't going to give up so easily. 'We've still got the time-frame to consider. Since the postcards were sent over a nine-month period and are numbered one to six they look as though they're telling a story. And I can't get away from the threatening tone of the sixth.'

'Doesn't the passage I've read from the thesis change your mind at all?' asked Hannah.

'If anything it tends to confirm my impressions', replied Giles, as gently as possible. 'In my view it's a great thesis. At last I can see what Benedict was doing, even though I'm a mere undergraduate. It could revolutionize all the scholarly studies of unicorns that I read when I was writing my essay on unicorns. But it also tells me that the image of the unicorn can be a dangerous as well as a happy one. There is a dark side to the unicorn. It could be used to threaten someone with death as much as to celebrate love.'

'We're just going to have to disagree', said Hannah unhappily.

Giles found he took a kind of comfort from the fact that Hannah was upset by the slight breach between them. What this meant for his relationship with Emily would have to be worked out later, he decided. When the inquest took place, and Hannah was called to give evidence, he was not surprised that she said nothing about the discoveries they had made of the postcards and the mysterious unicorn squares. The verdict, as expected, was suicide while the balance of Benedict's mind was disturbed, due to drugs. All was clear for the next stage of the memorial service.

Illustrations:
The six postcards

The images that follow are those on the postcards, in the order in which they were received and numbered by Benedict. Identification and copyright details are to be found on the 'Acknowledgements and Permissions' pages.

Postcard 1

Postcard 2

Postcard 3

Postcard 4

Postcard 5

Postcard 6

7
Memorial

The day of the memorial service was suitably overcast, but a watery sun emerged just before the Evensong which was to be the occasion for remembering Benedict in his own college. The light was just enough to kindle the late-afternoon glow from the yellow stone which is Oxford's best magical trick that it produces consistently for residents and visitors alike. Only Oxford can do this, due to its centuries-long project of making a faithful commitment to sandstone. Cambridge, for all the vertical glory of King's College Chapel, cannot achieve the same effect since it has had divided loyalties to granite, red brick and whitewash.

Some perpetual denizens of Oxford go on appreciating the miracle of the stone although they have seen it for decades, while for others habit has staled the wonder they once felt. Although he had lived for more than a year in Oxford, Giles greeted the transformation with an ever-grateful heart. As the light washed over the roof of the chapel, the collection of hobgoblins, fiends and bishops that made up the wild company of the gargoyles stood out in sharp outline. Among them, for the first time, he noticed a unicorn head. It seemed an omen of the event to come.

A mixed group was moving towards the chapel door at the torpid pace that the expectation of an hour's prayer, hymn-singing and sermon usually engendered. Nobody was hastening with a purposeful step. There were a few undergraduates who had known Benedict, mainly through tutorials, fellow-graduate students and a handful of college Fellows garbed in surplice and hood. It seemed that the largest part of the congregation would be the choir. Giles was accompanied by Emily, Hannah and Jacqui, but he broke away from them when he spotted a figure he'd seen a few weeks ago in the Lamb and Flag. To his astonishment, Nick Stoney was coming to the service.

Giles approached Nick and said, 'I didn't expect to see you here after what you said the other day about Benedict.'

'I don't think I know you', replied Nick, startled and in a brusque, unfriendly manner. 'What do you mean?'

'I was in the Lamb and Flag with Benedict when you expressed your feelings in no uncertain manner.'

'Oh, right. Perhaps I've just come to make sure the bastard's really gone after all. Perhaps it's a sense of unfinished business. Benedict and I go way back. Perhaps I just don't know why I've come.' He hesitated, and then added, 'I owe you an explanation if you were a friend of Benedict's, and anyway you ought to know what he was like.'

They paused on the path to the door and moved to one side for a moment to let others go past. Giles asked his friends to keep him a seat in the pew, and turned to listen to Nick.

'We were at school together, in the sixth form', he explained. 'I was using amphetamines and ecstasy, and when I had a few left over I passed them around my friends, for whatever they could afford. Benedict got to know about this and shopped me to the headmaster. I was expelled for drug-dealing, and it took a load of private tutors and a lot of hard work for me to get back on track to Oxford and end up where I am now. What really sticks in my gullet is that when I asked Benedict last year whether he'd ever taken drugs he admitted that he'd starting experimenting with LSD. Trust Benedict always to tell the truth, whatever the consequences – to others or himself. But in my book that made him a bloody hypocrite.'

'Isn't there a difference between consuming drugs and dealing in them?' asked Benedict.

'I knew you'd take his side', retorted Nick angrily. 'Tell you what, I don't need any of this damn hassle after all.' He swung round and marched off in the opposite direction.

A UNICORN DIES

Giles sighed, and reflected that Benedict had been a complex character. Brilliant in mind, awkward in manner, oddly compelling when he was enthusing about his academic passions, lovable to some – certainly to Hannah – and with a compulsion to tell the truth that frequently got him into trouble. He was interested to hear what the chaplain would say about him in his eulogy. He entered the chapel and found his way to the front pew where Hannah had a reserved seat for herself and her friends. In the front pew opposite he observed a woman whom he guessed must Benedict's mother, sitting miserable and crumpled up. He did not have the social skills to say anything, and he noticed that she spoke to no one either before or after the service.

He allowed the choir to carry him across the regular contours of Evensong. Beginning with remembering his faults and failings – never difficult for him to do – he then listened to the choir singing a passionate, ancient Hebrew song filled with the emotions of love, hatred, despair and hope in the unemotional tones cultivated in Anglican cathedrals and copied in lesser places. A witness to faith in God handed down in Scripture from both Jewish and Christian communities of the past was followed respectively by songs from long ago attributed to a young woman and a man near the end of life, expressing determination to wait for deliverance in time of trial. The order of service called them the Magnificat and the Nunc Dimittis. The choir continued to lead the congregation in opening its lips in praise, pleading with God for help against its enemies (whoever they might be) and asking God to save the Queen. The choir then showed off its skill by singing a complicated anthem, more prayers followed, and finally – attached, it seemed to Giles, as an afterthought – there came the address by the chaplain.

Giles had been a passive participant in the service, wandering through it in a kind of daze. But his attention had been caught at a couple of points. In the lesson from the Old Testament the writer was enquiring sarcastically, 'Will the unicorn be willing to serve thee? Canst thou bind the unicorn? Wilt thou trust in him because his strength is great?' In the psalm, the choir intoned in its urbane way, 'Mine horn shall be exalted like the horn of an unicorn: for I am anointed with fresh oil.' At each point when the word 'unicorn' appeared, Giles caught sight across the chapel of a young man and woman sitting together who looked significantly at each other, and nodded as if they had recognized something.

The address of Dr Mark Goodall was, in Giles' estimate, a disappointment. He paid tribute to Benedict's academic ability and the considerable potential he had as a scholar, regretting a sad loss to the college as well as to Benedict's family and friends. He mentioned his effectiveness as a tutorial teacher, and his capacity to inspire young minds; perhaps as an attempt at humour he added that not everyone appreciated his approach. There was a little nervous laughter, quickly suppressed, from the congregation. There was also one odd moment when the chaplain mentioned Benedict's 'originality of thought' and seemed to stumble, as if he were suddenly embarrassed. However, he recovered his confidence and ended on a high note by speaking about Benedict not only as a student but 'as a friend'. Giles was sorry to find no references to unicorns, even though it was obviously the chaplain who had chosen the scripture reading and the psalm in which they had made their unexpected entrance. In all, the address did nothing to dispel Giles' suspicions about him.

On the way out, Giles had to pass the chaplain who was hovering around diffidently at the door, uncertain as to whether members of the congregation wanted to shake hands with him or not. Giles did proffer his hand, thanked him for the address, and then added on the spur of the moment, 'but I felt there was something important on your mind about Benedict that you didn't mention. To do with unicorns and love. Am I right?'

The chaplain started violently and dropped Giles' hand, and a look which Giles was sure was guilt spread over his face, with hints of fear. He stuttered and began to say something, but other members of the congregation were pressing on them, anxious to leave, and Giles was swept onwards. He remembered the look, however, and often thought about it later.

Outside in the gathering gloom of the early evening he passed the young man and woman whom he had noticed in the service. He thought he caught the word 'unicorn' and could not help interrupting them.

'Excuse me, but did I hear you mentioning unicorns?' he broke in. 'They appeared in the words of the service, you know.'

'Yes, we did notice,' said the man in a friendly voice. 'We thought it was appropriate because of Benedict's interest in the subject.'

'How do you know about that, if you don't mind me asking?' enquired Giles, encouraged by the response. 'Were you fellow-theologians with Benedict?'

'We're graduate students, getting on a bit now, but not in theology,' replied the man readily. 'My name's Justin Webber and I'm the President of the Unicorn Society here in Oxford. This is Rosie Jones, the Secretary. Benedict was a much-valued member of our little society.'

Giles expressed his astonishment. 'I didn't know there was such a society', he exclaimed. 'I might have wanted to join since with Benedict's help I've been doing quite a close study of unicorns – I mean their history, habitat and associations with other fabulous animals' – like scapegoats he added in his mind. 'But I've never seen the society advertised.'

'Well, we don't put ourselves on display at the Freshers' Fair,' replied Rosie, 'and you have to be nominated by other members of the society to join.'

'What about coming round for coffee with me next term,' continued Justin, 'and we'll talk about unicorns?'

It was clear that Giles was not going to be invited to join this exclusive society spontaneously. There was evidently some kind of test he would need to pass, even if it was just a scrutiny of his opinions and sociability.

'I'd like that,' he replied, and agreed to email Justin at his university address when he was back in Oxford for Hilary Term.

Due to Hannah's generosity over his lodgings, Giles did not need to deliver post over Christmas to make ends meet, and only spent one week at home. Even this felt something of an ordeal, and he was glad to hasten back to Oxford. Hilary Term was designated for study of Shakespeare, and he spent the week before term reading as many of the playwright's comedies as he could ahead of tutorials.

Though he had already seen several of the comedies performed, his conversations with Benedict about unicorns and scapegoats gave him a different perspective on what he had previously thought to be unclouded happy endings, marked only by feasts and dances. It now struck him that the cost of a reconciliation between lovers or friends was being paid by someone who was being excluded as an outsider, or was excluding himself from the charmed circle. There was Malvolio, vowing 'I'll be revenged on the whole pack of you', Jacques absenting himself with the remark, 'to see no past-time I', Don John for whom the happy couples would 'invent strange punishments'. The *Merchant of Venice* which he had previously viewed as the triumph of mercy appeared to him now to end with two outsiders – obviously Shylock, but also Antonio whom he now saw to remain as sad at the end as at the beginning, with no partner for his loneliness and consumed with a scarcely-acknowledged passion for Bassanio. In short, the comedies were inhabited by scapegoats.

Prompted by Benedict's thesis, Giles set himself to work out in what sense the scapegoats might also be unicorns. This question could have resulted in some brilliant tutorial essays during the term which would have pleased his tutor, but unfortunately Giles was so preoccupied by his quest for unicorns that the thought of having to read critical commentaries, actually to write the essays and then present them to a tutor was burdensome. From the beginning of term he began to skimp the time he was spending on preparation for tutorials, and his essays became increasingly brief. Emily was no longer his tutorial partner, or she might have noticed what was going on and had success in getting him to do some conventional work as required by the Oxford system. This situation was hardly helped by a conversation he had with the President of the Unicorn Society in the third week of term, which set his thoughts off in many other directions.

After an email exchange the President, Justin Webber, invited him to his room in the university graduate accommodation in Wellington Square. The square was reached through a street filled with stately Georgian houses in yellow Bath stone, recently cleaned of a century's grime, which gave way to attractive red-brick Victorian town-houses on the largest part of three sides of the square itself. At the centre of the square was one of Oxford's secret patches of green – a circular, sunken garden complete with shrubs and trees and surrounded by wrought-iron palings. All this charm was somewhat undermined by the concrete blocks of the modern graduate building on the fourth side of the square, and even more by the last section of the third side which was filled by the concrete layers of the university administrative building. Bare, concrete platforms and ramps which carried futile notices forbidding skate-boarding led up to the glass doors. Giles had seen Japanese tourists taking selfies in front of the sign which proclaimed 'University of Oxford', under the apprehension that this was indeed the university campus.

On entering the President's room, which boasted a view over the secret garden, Giles was startled to find himself facing a large tapestry, covering most of one wall, reproducing a scene that was familiar to him from the second of Benedict's postcards. It was not exactly the same tapestry, but remarkably similar, showing the same unicorn, lion and lady. He admired it, and Justin responded.

'It's from a series of tapestries you may know about. I picked up this reproduction when I was in the Cluny Museum in Paris.'

He did not appear to want to say any more about it, and so Giles reminded him of the scripture readings at Benedict's funeral. 'Despite reading a lot about unicorns, I hadn't come across these references before.'

'There are others too', replied Justin. The first one you heard was from the Book of Job when God is reminding the miserable Job that he knows a great deal more about the mysteries of creation than Job does, and so Job shouldn't try to work out the reason for his suffering. There are more fabulous beasts there, such as Leviathan and Behemoth wallowing about in the water – probably based on a crocodile and a hippopotamus. The second was from Psalm 92. Apart from Psalm 29 when the unicorn is skipping about like the high hills, references are mostly to the strength of the animal. The chaplain could have chosen six other texts from the Old Testament, but only of course if he was using the old King James Version of the Bible. ' Justin's voice, normally soft and lilting, had taken on a lecturing tone.

'Didn't the writers in the Bible know that unicorns don't exist?' asked Giles.

'Actually, the original Hebrew text doesn't have the word "unicorn" at all', answered Justin. 'Modern translations of the Bible usually translate the Hebrew word *re'em* as a "wild ox". But it seems that the translators into Greek didn't know what the Hebrew word meant, and so used the word *monoceros* – a one-horned animal. Then Jerome, saint though he might have been, didn't know any better either and translated the Greek word into *unicornis* in the Latin Vulgate. Finally, from the Geneva Bible in 1560 onwards, English translators followed suit. So the unicorn made its entrance onto the stage of holy writ, and that had huge results.'

'What do you mean?' asked Giles. 'All this Hebrew, Greek and Latin seems a bit obscure to me. What did it really matter whether translators got it right?'

'Well', answered Justin, 'the fact that the word "unicorn" appeared in the Latin Bible, which was used all over Europe, convinced people that unicorns must exist. After all, the Bible couldn't deceive. That was one of the two big things that made unicorns credible. There they were in infallible scripture. The other thing was that people had the horns, between four and nine feet long, striated just as you see them in the old prints.'

'What?' exclaimed Giles. 'They had the horns? But they couldn't have'.

'They did,' replied Justin teasingly. 'They cost a king's ransom. You can still see one today in Chester Cathedral. The Cathedral of St Mark in Venice has three of them, but then the Venetians always had the money and the contacts for vulgar excess.'

'You must be making fun of me' accused Giles, not sure whether his world had just been turned upside down, and now half-believing in unicorns himself.

Justin relented and explained. 'Of course the horns came from the narwhal, a whale sometimes called "the unicorn of the seas", and the horn isn't really a horn but an ivory tooth extending from the narwhal's mouth, not its forehead. But where the horns came from was a tremendous secret. The arctic fishermen of Canada, Greenland and Russia made a very good living out of exporting the tusks, and managed to conceal the truth for hundreds of years. When their trade-secret finally came out, it didn't put an end to the unicorn story but supported it. The natural philosophy of the period held that there were parallels between land and sea animals, and so if there were a unicorn of the water there had to be one of the land as well. People could still believe *their* horn, on which they'd spent a fortune, was from a land-unicorn. They went on believing this until the eighteenth

75

century. Until then theologians, philosophers and naturalists had heated disputes about whether unicorns existed. The renowned and ultra-sensible Sir Thomas Browne writes about five kinds of unicorn in 1646 and a Danish scholar illustrates his 'encyclopaedia of unicorns' with pictures of twelve different types as late as 1672.'

'But I still don't understand why owning a horn was so important', complained Giles. There must have been a good reason for spending all that money.'

'There was', replied Justin. 'Poison. Poisoning was the deadliest weapon of the time. Kings and popes as well as anyone with a reasonable amount of goods to hand on, or with a young enough wife to have a lover, feared it. Poison could be smuggled into a meal with little fuss and so it was a favourite weapon of women. The great thing about an alicorn, or unicorn's horn, was that when it was placed on the dining table it would show the presence of poison by breaking out into a sweat. Or, when it was ground up into fine powder and swallowed in a drink it would act as an antidote to poison. It was best to drink from a cup actually made of alicorn, if you could afford it. The monarch's food would be touched by a piece of unicorn horn just to make sure, and poorer people would purchase a few grains as a prophylactic against "poisonous diseases" such as the plague.'

'Did it work?' asked Giles curiously.

'What do you think?' replied Justin. 'People believed it did, and belief can have wonderful powers.'

'But wait a moment,' objected Giles. 'I've been learning about two unicorn themes – the love-hunt and the passion story. Where does all this business about poisoning fit in?' Giles was anxious not to be diverted from what seemed to be the heart of his quest, and especially from learning more about the tapestry from the Cluny Museum. As Justin piled on more and more arcane detail about owning an alicorn, it seemed to Giles that he was wandering away from the kind of interest that Benedict had in unicorns.

'Perhaps there's no connection', admitted Justin. 'But the supposed virtue of the horn probably links to the story that unicorns dipped their horns into a pool of water to cleanse it of noxious substances so that other animals could drink from it safely. In 1389 John, ruler of Hesse, was travelling in

76

Palestine and claimed to have seen a unicorn purifying the water like this in the very place, called Marah, where the Bible says that Moses made bitter water sweet with his staff. What John actually saw, if anything, God only knows but his report certainly helped to substantiate the fable. This generous act by the unicorn was sometimes associated with the theme of Christ the unicorn, redeeming the world. Sometimes it was just mentioned as another well-known fact about the unicorn.'

Giles was going to press Justin further about this, but then remembered something else he wanted to ask. 'There were half a dozen small pieces of paper among Benedict's belongings, stamped with the picture of a unicorn's head. Are they something to do with the society, like a membership card or entrance tickets to meetings?'

Justin seemed interested in this piece of information. 'Did Benedict ever show you them while he was alive?' he asked.

'No, I just found them among his papers after his death', replied Giles.

'Well, I don't expect they mean much', Justin went on. 'They're certainly nothing to do with us. You might as well throw them away.'

Just at that moment there was the sound of a key in the door, it was flung open and a young, fair-haired man burst in and greeted Justin affectionately. From the way Justin responded, Giles suddenly realized that he was gay.

'Well, then,' Justin said. 'Peter and I are just going out for lunch together and I'm afraid we'll have to stop there. I hope I've been some help. You really ought to talk to our secretary, Rosie Jones, who's probably got a different angle on unicorns. If you drop her an email I'm sure she'd be glad to meet you. Look her up on the university directory.'

As Giles made his thanks and took his way out of the building he had the odd feeling that he'd just failed whatever test he'd been set. The President hadn't, at any rate, invited him to join the society.

The next day he reported most of this conversation to Emily at one of their regular meetings. They occasionally still spent a night together, but over the last couple of weeks meetings usually meant coffee in the covered market. To his surprise she manifested considerable impatience.

A UNICORN DIES

'I'm getting a bit fed up with all this unicorn business', she snapped. 'It was all right when we were studying it for an essay in the medieval course, but aren't you getting a bit obsessed by it? Can't you move on? And when you're not talking about unicorns you're always going on about Benedict's death. I suppose Hannah's encouraging you.'

'Actually she's not,' replied Giles, thinking 'I wish she were.'

'Well, I'd like you to bloody talk a bit more about *us*', Emily complained. 'Have you decided yet about coming to Kenya in the summer?'

Giles was uneasy about the turn the conversation had taken. 'It's rather expensive, and anyway I think my time's going to be taken up with research.'

'You mean more unicorns', retorted Emily. 'Giles, it's been fun to have this time together, but I think our relationship may have come to an end. Don't think I haven't noticed that you find Hannah attractive. And I have to tell you that my tutorial partner, Jake, wants to go to Kenya with me even if you don't.'

Emily had become rather breathless getting all this out, in her usual direct way, and Giles got the impression she had been wanting to say it for a while. Pausing for a moment, he stared past her at the way the iron supports of the market roof curled up into the glass canopy, the work of an unknown artist. The moment seemed suspended as he noticed a spider weaving its web around a lower decorative arch of the support, launching itself out with abandon on its thread into empty space. Examining his feelings, he found that he had been expecting something like this, and that he did not mind so very much after all. He swallowed hard and threw himself into the void with the spider.

'Emily, I'm really sorry it's come to this', he said in an unsteady voice. 'I'm terrifically grateful for all we've had together, but I think you're right. I'm going to miss you dreadfully, but I hope we can still be friends.'

'I don't see why not', replied Emily, with a bright but peremptory smile. 'You might even tell me about unicorns – but please, not just yet.'

78

8
Suspended

It was shortly after the meeting with Emily that Giles made contact with Rosie Jones, the secretary of the Unicorn Society. She invited him to her graduate accommodation, which lay over Magdalen bridge, at the point when the urbane curve of the High Street gives way to the huddle of shops and houses that fill the 'Plain', and Oxford begins its metamorphosis from stately sandstone into the colourful patchwork and international vitality of the Cowley Road. She appeared to be a confident woman with a brisk manner and an intensity that reminded him of Benedict, but he detected reservoirs of warmth lying beneath the surface. She greeted him with the same restrained friendliness as the President had done, but what she had to say took a very different direction.

'Did you learn anything about unicorns from our Justin?' she asked as soon as he was seated and they had mugs of coffee in front of them.

'He told me about translations of Hebrew and Greek, and about medieval customs of poisoning,' replied Giles.

'Well, he's a historian, interested in manuscripts and old paintings,' she pointed out. 'I expect you saw the tapestry on his wall that he picked up from a museum in Paris. I'm an anthropologist myself, and I'm not really interested in ancient objects or classical fables. It's human behaviour today that fascinates me.'

'There doesn't seem to be much of an opportunity for unicorns there', observed Giles.

'You couldn't be more wrong', retorted Rosie. 'You've obviously never put the word "unicorn" into Google or other search engines on the internet. Cyberspace is chock full of people claiming to be unicorns, or calling other people unicorns, or trying to retail things by branding them with unicorns. This is a unicorn-obsessed age, especially among the young.'

Giles was startled. 'What do you mean, claiming to be unicorns?' he demanded. 'That doesn't make a lot of sense to me.'

'I don't mean literally', she said with a slight smile, 'but claiming the image to say something about themselves or others. There are dozens of blogs announcing "I am a unicorn" to the world. There was a very influential episode of an American sitcom where the teenage hero came out as gay in an election to be class president and asserted his identity and values by calling himself a unicorn. I know at least three pop songs called "I am a unicorn" or – more stridently – "I am *the* unicorn". The singers, two of them women, are wanting to say, "I'm unique, I don't have to conform to your view of me, I've got my own future, I can stand up against the general direction society takes."' She closed her eyes and began to quote in a sing-song tone:

'I can't show my face or I could be found,
No one else like me is ever around...
I could never be anything you tell me to
Nothing's true, I'm not you, let me through.
I'm flying and you'll never stop me.
I am the unicorn. You'll never stop me.'

Giles got the distinct impression that this might be Rosie's creed as well. But he objected, 'If that song's by a woman then that makes the unicorn female, while we know from all the myths and allegories that the unicorn's actually a male.'

Rosie laughed. 'People adopting the unicorn identity usually don't know much about the scholarly history. Popular culture gives the unicorn wings and has it flying over rainbows, even farting rainbows. The sex doesn't matter. The point is the brand, the claim to uniqueness, being special and –

above all – authentic. On the web you can find men and women claiming to be all kinds of unicorns, or asking their readers "Are you a unicorn?" There are spiritual unicorns, who believe they have an extraordinary sensitivity to truth and beauty, who claim an instant empathy with others whom they feel to be unicorns too and who say things like "I don't really belong to this world". There are healing unicorns, who invoke the energy of the unicorn "for faith, healing and power" and exhort you to "take a deep breath and let the spirit of the unicorn fill you." There are wicca unicorns, promising to teach you "elemental magic" and witchcraft. There are lesbian unicorns, using the unicorn as an emoji in their emails, gay unicorns and political unicorns.'

Giles could not help interrupting. 'Political unicorns?' he exclaimed. 'Whatever can that mean?'

'Well, it's when someone supports a political candidate or party you wouldn't expect them to. Like a gay endorsing a very conservative candidate. Or a liberal voter switching to a nationalistic party. They're showing they can't be catalogued or typecast. There are articles in the serious press after every election analysing the "political unicorn". These unicorns can cause quite an upheaval. They're unicorns to be feared.'

Giles thought briefly of Benedict's thesis about the dark side of the unicorn. 'Did Benedict ever talk to you about these modern unicorns?' he enquired.

Rosie laughed again. 'I was always trying to get him to pay more attention to them,' she responded. 'He kept getting stuck in historical examples and I would tell him that he was neglecting real life all around him.'

'So how do you explain this fascination with unicorns?' asked Giles. 'You're an anthropologist – you must have thought about it.'

'Oh, I have,' replied Rosie. 'Partly it's commercialism and the global market. Half of the unicorn sites on the web are about selling goods with the unicorn brand or the unicorn image – prints of unicorns by thousands of artists throughout the world, sports' clothes, mugs, and video-games. There are hundreds of T-shirts for sale with slogans like "Time to be a unicorn" and "Keep calm. I'm a unicorn." Partly, though, it's about looking for one's own identity in a world where the traditional identity-giving structures like churches have broken down. It's a feature of postmodernity that people get suspicious about the "big stories" they're being given by religion, or politics, or the state and so they want to make their own stories instead. Stories about being a unicorn. Sometimes you can't tell whether the internet site you're looking at it is selling something or offering an identity. Sometimes it's both at once – buy this expensive clothing or this piece of wall decoration and you'll be making a statement about yourself.'

Rosie's voice had taken on the tones of a tutorial teacher, just as Justin's had done, but in her case Giles found himself being distinctly charmed. He caught himself reflecting that he wouldn't have minded being taught by her. Perhaps it was just that her interest in unicorns was refreshingly different from the world of art galleries and medieval manuscripts he'd been immersing himself in.

'I'm amazed', he said. 'This is a whole new world. I'll certainly do a bit of browsing on the internet myself. Thanks so much for telling me about it.'

'There's a lot more I haven't mentioned,' added Rosie. 'Be ready for a few shocks. I haven't said much about the sexual uses of the term. One of the more harmless romantic ones is where a man is looking for his ideal woman, someone perfect in every way, beautiful, intelligent and sympathetic, who will just adore him. She's a unicorn because she's rare, and probably doesn't exist. She's the invisible pink unicorn.'

A slight note of bitterness seemed to have appeared in her voice, but Rosie seemed disinclined to talk about other sexual meanings, and Giles respected her reticence while inwardly determining to make his own explorations online. Before he left, he rather hoped that she would say something about joining the Society, but she did not raise the possibility. He suspected that she and Justin had discussed it earlier.

Giles was not a newcomer to the internet. As a student of his generation, reared with a smartphone as a natural extension of his hand, he could hardly be a digital novice. There always seemed to be time in the day to consult the social network of Facebook, and most days he posted on-line a few nuggets of news about what he was doing, regardless of whether anyone was likely to read it or not. A few years previously, having established a couple of on-line 'friends', he was surprised to find how many people the obliging software suggested he might want to ask to be his friends. It seemed that the user was immersed into circles of other people's friends, and they multiplied alarmingly. As time went by he became more selective about requesting and accepting friends, though he had been gratified recently to find that Justin's face had appeared as someone's friend of a friend, and Justin had accepted Giles' invitation, perhaps (thought Giles) by a reflex jerk of the finger. But Giles' on-line life had been largely confined to email and Facebook. Over the next week in the Bodleian Library he was to expand it considerably. While he was supposed to be reading for an essay on Shakespeare's tragedies, he plugged his laptop into the sockets so conveniently provided, and spent most of time investigating sites he reached by putting 'unicorn' into his browser.

He saw immediately what Rosie meant about the plenitude of unicorn blogs, and recognized most of what she had been telling him about. He made a few errors identifying the sites. 'The Unicorn Preservation Society' looked promisingly eccentric, until he discovered that it was devoted to maintaining H.M. Frigate Unicorn, a 46-gun frigate in the Royal Navy built in 1824 and located in Dundee. Another confusion was over 'The Fat Unicorn'. It took him a while until he worked out that there were in fact two different sites naming themselves like this, one the home of 'unique and creative digital marketing', and another a society established to recognize, support and aid over-weight people who designated themselves as unicorns. The experience drove home Rosie's point that there were two main motives for the modern proliferation of unicorns all over the net – the urge to sell and the search for identity.

He also found that unicorns of the fluffy, pink kind populated many children's cartoons and TV programmes, and that they had even taken over from fairies in the solemn pronouncement, 'Every time you refuse to believe in unicorns a unicorn dies.' One campaign for making awards to advertising agencies in South Africa had capitalized on this phrase with its strap-line, 'Every time you make a bad ad a unicorn dies'.

But Giles' most startling discovery in his travels through cyberspace was of a different kind. In street-language, it seemed that 'unicorn' could be a term for a bisexual person, usually but not always a woman, who was willing to make a third in a sexual partnership with an existing heterosexual couple. Looking for such an obliging person, he learned, is often called 'hunting the unicorn'. But the term was, it seemed, used in a highly complex way, with layers of meaning. It could relate ironically to the assumption of the couple that the 'unicorn' would do nothing to disrupt or threaten their own relationship, but could be used simply to complete their own pleasure, and perhaps also help with the rent and the housekeeping, without making further demands on them. The word 'unicorn', he gathered, flags up their unrealistic expectations, and warns that they are exploiting a third person as a mere figure of fantasy.

Armed with this knowledge, some of the blogs that had puzzled him before began to make more sense. He began to follow links, and by a winding trail ended up on sites that frankly astounded him. He learned more about what people claiming to be unicorns did, about the way that a unicorn horn could be used, and about the positions in which it could be employed – not to say inserted – than had ever occurred to him before. Some of the sites offered pictures as well as words, enticing the user to send a credit card number and pay for even more explicit photographs and even live performances. Giles never paid any money, and passed over the images offered as quickly as possible, though he was undeniably fascinated by the sites. He told himself that he was getting a further glimpse of Benedict's 'dark side of the unicorn'. Darkness of quite another kind was offered by many photographs of horses and goats 'adapted' by having single horns strapped on them, and seeing these shabby and unhappy specimens made him nostalgic for the graceful and bewitching animals of paintings and manuscripts.

Towards the end of his week of discoveries, he had only the bare bones of an essay on *King Lear* to show for his habitation in the Bodleian Library. He was forced to make an all-night effort to scrape an essay together for his tutorial, though the result was – predictably – that he exhausted himself by reading it out to his tutor and was too tired to hold a proper conversation with him and his tutorial partner for the rest of the hour. He had just started reading for the next essay, without much enthusiasm, when he received an official-looking letter from his college Dean, summoning him to a meeting in two days' time. Although he had previously had little contact with him, he knew that the Dean was the disciplinary officer of the college, and he felt alarm.

With some trepidation, Giles arrived at the door of the Dean's office on the appointed day. A frayed, hand-written paper label identified the occupant, and Giles felt a pang of sympathy. The college could surely have given the Dean a piece of inscribed brass or even embossed plastic. But this was not the issue that most concerned him. He knew that the summons meant he was in deep trouble, and he had failed to identify what it might be. He thought that if his work was the problem, his tutor would have warned him.

'Good morning, Giles', said the Dean with a serious look on his face. 'Thank you for coming to see me. I'm sorry that this such a formal affair, but we need to arrange a hearing with the college disciplinary committee, and it's my task to explain to you, with regret, what the college charge against you will be. I'll then confirm this in writing to you, and you'll have an opportunity at the hearing to present your case. You can have a friend with you when the committee meets, or a legal advisor, like a solicitor, if you wish. This is a serious matter, and you could be rusticated for a year from the college, or even be expelled from the university. The process is all written up in the college disciplinary code, and since I expect you've lost your copy since you came up to college, I'm going to give you another one now. Does that all seem quite fair?'

'I suppose so,' said Giles, panic beginning to seize hold of him. He wasn't sure what 'rustication' meant, but he was even less sure what the whole fuss was about. He wondered whether he was the victim of a terrible mistake, or even some kind of cruel practical joke. But he'd always respected and even liked the Dean whom he knew to be doing his best. He stared at the bookcase behind the Dean's shoulder, noticed the entirely irrelevant fact that the books seemed to be arranged exactly by size, and swallowed hard. His mouth seemed to have suddenly gone dry, and he almost croaked rather than spoke.

'I just don't know why this is happening. What am I supposed to have done?'

'I have to say that I'm surprised we're in this situation as well', replied the Dean, attempting a friendly smile, which appeared on his face more like a grimace. 'The point is that the college has had a complaint from the University Computing Services. They've tracked your use of pornographic websites. Accessing them is against the policy of the university, and opens you to disciplinary action which a college is obliged to take. It's a very serious abuse of university facilities. Do you admit that you've been visiting these sites? I have to say that unless someone else has been using your computer and password the evidence is very strong – in fact, in my view, incontestable.'

'Oh!' exclaimed Giles. 'That's right, but it's been quite harmless. I didn't intend to access them. It just happened when I was looking at other sites. I didn't enjoy them. It's really not a habit.'

'It looks quite habitual', remarked the Dean, 'and it seems to have "just happened" quite frequently.' Consulting his own computer screen, he went on, 'I've got a list of at least twenty occasions here.'

'It's like this', said Giles desperately. 'I've got interested in the way that people today are fascinated by unicorns, and want to become unicorns themselves. I've been visiting unicorn sites, and some of them lead on to pornography. Not all of them do, of course, but with some you've made a link with something pornographic before you know it. After it happened a couple of times, I got interested in discovering how many of the sites were like this.' An idea occurred to him on the spur of the moment, which sounded fairly convincing: 'I suppose you might call it research.'

'You mean you're writing an undergraduate dissertation on the subject?' asked the Dean helpfully. 'You could have cleared this with the university ethics committee. It mightn't be too late, though I can't promise anything.'

'Not exactly', admitted Giles. He looked at the corner of the Dean's mahogany-coloured desk and despite the acute situation he was in, he was interested to see that the veneer facing was peeling back, exposing chipboard underneath. The Dean had seated himself, in a pastoral way, in front of his desk rather than behind it, and as he shifted his body uneasily while talking, he kept catching his jacket in the rough edge. The thought flitted across Giles's mind that the college must be saving money on its supply of furniture to college officers, as well as on door signs, not to speak of the drop in both quality and quantity he had observed in student meals recently. He went on quickly, 'I'm interested in unicorns because I think they might help me solve the mystery of someone's death.'

The Dean's expression moved from an attempted warm expression to a more severe one, modulating back to friendly anxiety. 'This someone wouldn't be Benedict Green at Helwys College would it?'

Giles was surprised. He indicated that it was, and wondered how the Dean had guessed.

'I have to tell you', said the Dean, 'that we've heard from Inspector Longley of the Oxford City police. He was worried that you might be developing an unhealthy obsession with Mr Green's death, and thought that the college welfare staff should know about it and keep an eye on you. We've been worried too, especially as your tutor reports that your work hasn't been up to your usual standard recently. You've missed writing a couple of essays, and you've failed to turn up to a tutorial. You're in danger of being summoned by the academic standards committee. Don't you think you might be taking all this a bit too far? If you're feeling depressed you should really get a doctor's certificate. I must say that you don't sound to me quite in a normal state of mind.' The Dean hesitated. The last part had not come out exactly as intended, and he suspected that his pastoral skills were being over-stretched by this conversation. He corrected himself: 'I mean, you sound a bit stressed.'

'What do you mean?' asked Giles, even more alarmed than before.

'Well, this thing about people wanting to "become a unicorn", and thinking that unicorns could you help solve a mysterious death – not that', he added hastily, 'there's anything mysterious about Mr Green's death at all, or for that matter, that unicorns exist. You must admit that it sounds a bit odd.'

Giles looked again at the bookcase. He now saw that the arrangement of books by size had nothing to do with their subject at all. It was neatness without purpose, and seemed somehow symbolic of the moment. Further explanations seemed too complicated, and a sudden weariness overtook him. Perhaps he did need to consult a doctor. He said nothing.

The Dean was relieved that this uncomfortable interview seemed to be drawing to an end, and that he hadn't had to cope with any emotional outbursts.

'I'll write to you formally, as I've said, and you must choose how you're going to respond. I should also remind you that if the decision goes against you, you can appeal to the Master of the College, and if you're not satisfied with his decision, you can appeal further to a committee in the university. It's all in the code.' Handing over the document he was confident that he'd laid out the position quite clearly, but remembering the advice he'd been given on pastoral care when he'd agreed to be Dean, he added, 'Is there anything you'd like to ask me?'

'I don't think I'll bother', said Giles in a resigned tone.

The Dean was startled by what seemed an aggressive tone. 'It's really no trouble to answer any questions you have', he assured Giles.

'Oh no, you've been very helpful' said Giles politely. 'I mean, I won't bother to appeal.'

And he did not. On the day when the disciplinary committee met, he took neither friend nor legal advocate with him, admitted everything, and took his sentence of one year's rustication with equanimity. He was tired of trying to keep his essay work up to date as well as working on the unicorn problem, and he would welcome a break. The college advised him to get some medical advice as soon as possible from the college doctor, and required him, before being re-admitted at the beginning of the Trinity term in a year's time to get a doctor's letter verifying that he was in a state of mind where he could take advantage of study. Meanwhile, Giles had discovered from the helpful if officious college code what rustication meant. Deriving from Latin, like most of the Oxford academic jargon, it could be literally translated as 'moving to the country' – or leaving the town of Oxford for a temporary period of suspension from the college and the university. During this period he couldn't use university facilities or receive any teaching.

Giles did not, in fact, intend to leave Oxford for the country. He was going to stay and solve the mystery of Benedict's death without help from the police. He wanted Oxford to be his base, while he had in mind to do a good deal of travelling. He explained this to Hannah when they met that evening over a meal.

'Now I've been forced to take a year out, I want to do something to really make it worthwhile. Investigating Benedict's death in a low-key way has got me into trouble, so now I want to take it more seriously. My idea is to follow up the trail marked by the postcards, to visit the places where they came from in the order they're numbered, to look at the artworks they portray and see what they might tell me. You've already said that you're not keen on the idea of spending more time on the cards, so I don't expect you to approve of the plan. I'm ready to move out of the house, and I'll do casual work to pay for a room somewhere else.'

'Got to keep an eye on you', pronounced Hannah solemnly. 'It's silly, but I feel a bit responsible for what's happened to you. I don't know what you thought you were doing, playing around with the internet like that in the Bodleian, but I sort of encouraged you by asking you to help clear out Benedict's room. If you've absolutely made up your mind to travel around like this, I'll help you as much as I can.'

'That's terrific', enthused Giles, who had been secretly hoping for this response. 'I'd really like to talk over the results of my visits with someone, and you're the ideal person.'

'Well, that's settled,' said Hannah. 'You need looking after, as this whole disaster makes clear. I'll lower the rent on the room since you're not on a student loan any longer. But just remember – we don't know Benedict was murdered at all, and even if he was, we don't know the postcards have got anything to do with it. I want to know the truth, but don't rush to conclusions – that's all I ask.'

Giles readily agreed with her, and thanked her again profusely. He promised to let her know where he was going and where he would be staying, and to email or text her when he arrived each time, as she asked. He hoped this showed the beginnings of affection as well as solicitous concern. In any case, he intended to post a general account of his adventures on his

Facebook page, without giving too many details away, especially about the unicorn quest. Over the years he had got into the habit of blogging about his activities, before, during and after they happened, and there seemed no reason to stop now. He liked to share his sense of anticipation when he was travelling somewhere, so that he could compare his feelings about a place before he had seen it with his reactions in the light of reality. He had found that his readers – few though they were – enjoyed these stories of discovery.

In light of Hannah's generous offer about the room he decided now only to go home for a week at Easter. It was going to be difficult enough to explain to his parents that he was about to take a year out from Oxford. He had decided to present it as his own decision, pleading the need to cope with exhaustion, and he did not want too many questions asked. He could hardly wait until after Easter, when he had planned to visit the Horn of Ulf in York. He had saved enough from his student loan from the previous term to afford a train fare to York, on a student railcard. On his return to Oxford, telling Hannah where he was going as he had agreed, he set out.

9
Horn of Ulf

For his trip to York Giles was staying with an old friend from school who was studying philosophy at the University of York. He was grateful to sleep on the floor in his friend's room in a student residence block, which had been designated a 'college' in the manner of Oxbridge by those who had founded the university in the early 1960s, academic venturers riding a new wave towards ever-wider shores of higher education. If he were inclined to compare the blank concrete panels of these buildings and the concrete cube of the clock-tower with the neo-Gothic stonework of his own college, to York's disadvantage, he had to admit that the students he saw around him, jostling the paths round the central lake and carefully avoiding the plentiful duck excrement that smeared them, seemed to have just the same questing intelligence as his contemporaries in Oxford. In fact he had to admit that they seemed more eager to frequent the lecture rooms and libraries than his fellow-students, and that more lively conversation seemed to go on in the restaurants and coffee-shops than in his own ancient dining hall.

The day after he arrived he made his way in early morning to the bus stop, taking the postcard of the Horn of Ulf with him. To get there he crossed a bridge across the ornamental lake, first passing a small pool surrounding massive heating equipment and boasting the trickle of a fountain, the water making a desultory attempt to spurt out from the depths. Once again he could not stop himself from comparing the view of the pool, lake and guano-spattered grass with the grander vistas of the University Parks in Oxford with its winding river and charming tributaries. This did not look like a propitious place for hunting a unicorn, even though in the warm days of early Autumn there were plenty of examples of laps to be seen on which a unicorn's head might lie. He soon stopped his comparisons, however, when he recollected that no Oxford undergraduates actually lived in the Parks – unless they were exceptionally unfortunate with their lodgings. It took him fifteen minutes to reach the Parks from his own college, while students here could stagger from bed in the morning and be immediately invigorated by the sight of a sheet of placid water, reflecting the light and fringed by weeping willow trees.

He took the bus to the city centre, passing through a maze of red-brick houses in the back-streets, to be rewarded by the sight of the medieval city walls, sections of which could be glimpsed along the way or at the end of nearly every narrow side-street. Just before entering the walled city Clifford's Tower reared up on a grassy mound, a reminder that society – as Benedict had pointed out in his thesis – always demanded a scapegoat. From his medieval studies Giles knew about the massacre of the Jews of York in 1190. Anger had spread from an outrageous rumour that the Jews had sacrificed a Christian boy, a myth created largely by Christians who owed money to Jewish lenders. Crowded for safety into a keep of the castle on the spot now occupied by Clifford's Tower, and threatened by a murderous crowd outside, the whole Jewish community of one hundred and fifty people perished. Many men died by suicide, having first killed their wives and children, others were murdered by the mob, and all were burned when the wooden tower was set on fire. The ringleaders went straight to the Minster to start another fire, burning the record of their debts that had been held there. Giles reflected that the terrible event showed how society rejected the strangers in its midst, and targeted them as a substitute for its own anxiety and fear. Behind the jagged tooth of broken stone, protruding from a green skull, Giles felt he could see the shadow of a unicorn's horn.

Sobered by these thoughts, Giles left the bus and made his way through the medieval streets to the area of the Minster. Threading his way through crowds, outdoor café tables and markets he felt he was truly on a unicorn hunt. By way of High Petergate he arrived at the Minster entrance, avoiding the throng of Chinese tourists taking selfies in front of the ancient wooden doors. Here he met his first blockage, unexpectedly being confronted by a substantial reception desk, complete with tills, demanding an entrance fee. Even for a student it was £5, and he only had £3.20 change in his pocket for the bus and no credit card with him.

He could linger in the short distance between the door and the desk, getting a glimpse of the nave and lighting a candle in memory of the dead. He thought of Benedict, and nearly left things at that, but he was only too aware of the postcard in his pocket and his need to get to the undercroft where the horn was apparently housed. There must have been something desperate in his eyes, as he approached the custodian at the desk.

'I don't have £5', he confessed, 'but I really want to get in'.

'Well, how much do you have?' came the query.

'£3.20', he replied hopefully.

'Have you come to pray?' the custodian unexpectedly enquired. 'We don't charge for prayer.'

Giles searched his conscience, thought again about Benedict but then, admitting to himself that the main purpose of his visit was to visit a museum, answered, 'Sort of'.

'Well, then, we can "sort of" charge', replied the custodian with the hint of a smile. 'How about £3.00? I think the Minster might just be able to bear the loss this time, but don't tell everyone or we won't be able to repair the roof.' He informed Giles that the ticket was valid for repeated visits over 12 months. Giles would have to walk back the two miles to the university, but he thought he could cope with that.

On enquiry he was told that the undercroft housing the Minster's museum was to be entered through the transept, and he wandered forward through the stone forest of the nave, as planned by its thirteenth-century builder. Pillars thrust upwards, and arches leapt with them, bursting from foliations which budded from the pillars, and branching into a cluster of smaller arches which reached up into the light of the clerestory windows. Finally the trunks stretched themselves far into the roof, forming a new tracery of stone foliage studded with golden bosses like constellations of stars in the firmament. Slightly dazed, Giles reached the crossing where light poured in from the great tower above, turned north and found himself, not in the undercroft but in the chapter house.

He stood in the octagonal space, looking with amazement at the zoo of medieval heads, animals, demons and fabulous beasts that peered out at him from the elaborately carved stone arches above the seats of the now absent monks. Some faces were smiling and laughing with holy joy, others grimacing in fear and hatred; animals or demons were squatting on top of some heads or in the process of devouring them. One unfortunate victim looked suspiciously like a bishop and Giles could only think that the panorama was fixed before the monks' eyes as a warning as they came to vote on the life of the community, Turning round 360 degrees, searching without success for a unicorn in this company his head began to spin. Dizzy through walking through the streets after breakfast consisting only of coffee and powdered milk, amazed by the proportions of the Minster, and preoccupied with his quest, his mind was full of turmoil about Benedict's death and his own confused feelings about love. He thought he was going to fall right in the centre of the red-tiled floor. He staggered out of the chapter house and found himself in the choir facing an embroidered panel depicting a unicorn.

The panel was the work of the Minster's embroidery group and a notice informed him that it copied a carved unicorn's head that was part of a heraldic device on an oak panel in the south aisle of the choir, dating from 1580. Giles was not at all sure where this might be located, and was disinclined to search further, but he took the image as a hint that he should make his way immediately to the undercroft to find the Horn of Ulf. This time he turned south in the transept and found another large wooden reception desk next to an aluminium stairway leading downwards. A young woman with a more severe expression than the custodian at the entrance sat at the desk and looked at him suspiciously. He took out his postcard and showed her the picture of the horn.

'Is the undercroft the place where this is kept?' he asked.

'Well it is', she replied grudgingly, 'but can't you see that the undercroft's closed?'

She pointed to the ornamental rope which was hooked to brass fixings across the stairway and which he'd missed on first glance.

'The undercroft is closed until further notice for re-arranging the exhibitions', the young woman went on. 'You might try coming back next month.'

'But I won't be here next month', said Giles with exasperation.

'I can't do anything about that', the woman said remorselessly. 'Regulations are regulations, and the undercroft's shut.'

Giles walked away slowly with a sinking heart and a deep sense of anti-climax. His plan to crack the code of the postcards seemed to have failed at the first step. Close by the desk was a side-chapel with yet one more invitation to light a candle and pray for someone, and this time he did take a candle from the dozen or so provided and light it in memory of Benedict. Though he was only able to put 20 pence into the box provided for offerings he thought that neither Minster nor God would mind in the circumstances. Leaving the Minster through the shop his dizziness returned for a brief moment as passed a cluster of carved heads and animals reproduced from the chapter house, together with stuffed toys made in the form of demons, their legs hanging in a sinister way over the edge of the shelves.

He sat in the square outside the Minster for a quarter of an hour, refreshing himself from a street water-fountain which had probably been there for centuries for the sake of travellers and pilgrims. He enjoyed the weak Autumn sunshine, sitting at the intersection of six narrow medieval roads, and watching the busy mass of shoppers. Feeling distinctly better, he remembered he still had a valid entrance ticket in his pocket along with the now useless postcard, and thought he might as well use it in looking for the oak panel with the carved unicorn. He'd like a picture of it on his smartphone to send to Hannah.

'Back again so soon?' asked the friendly custodian.

'Well, I left because I found the undercroft closed', explained Giles.

'Of course it's closed until 10.00 am each day', replied the custodian. You came a bit early, but it should be open now. Turn south in the transept.'

'But I was told that it was closed for a month', exclaimed Giles in surprise.

95

'Someone's been pulling your leg', said the custodian. 'You'll find I'm right.'

Giles hurried to the stairway and found that the rope had indeed been removed, and visitors were already moving underground. He turned to the desk to make a righteous protest, but found the forbidding woman gone and another person there who knew nothing about the message given to Giles earlier. Giles was puzzled, and disturbed. He couldn't help wondering whether someone wanted to stop him seeing the horn, or discourage him at an early point from carrying through his whole plan. Perhaps showing the postcard had identified him and triggered a plot against him. He also thought he might be becoming paranoid, and that he might just have been the victim of a mistake. He was far too anxious to see the horn than to worry further about this, however, and so made his way down the stairs.

Walking briskly through an exhibition about the history of the Minster and the discoveries made in excavating under it, he arrived at a brightly lit exhibit in a central area. The horn had pride of place in a separate glass case, and was so well displayed and illuminated that the carving on its ivory surface stood out much more sharply than in the images reproduced either on the postcard or the museum website. Giles was excited to see how clearly the unicorn was standing with its horn stuck in the trunk of the tree, just as he himself had described one version of the myth in his tutorial with Emily. The tree itself was budding with branches and leaves, and on the other side of it crouched a lion with a deer in its paws. A notice informed Giles that the horn was made of a single elephant tusk, and had been presented to the Minster in 1180 by a Viking nobleman named Ulf as a symbol of a gift of land to the Minster. Tradition records that he filled it with wine and placed it on the altar as a sign of his dedication of the land to God. The horn was probably made in Southern Italy, the notice further stated, and the motifs on it came from Syrian and Babylonian art. Quickly Giles took photographs on his smartphone to send to Hannah.

Close by the horn Giles was interested to see another exhibit featuring a tree, this time more obviously Christian. There was a fragment of stone from a tall cross made in the ninth century, showing a tree of life in the form of a vine scroll, recalling Jesus' words from St John's Gospel that 'I am the true vine'. Animals too were associated with the tree, sheltering in its branches. He failed to spot any obvious unicorns, but the association between Christ and the unicorn tugged at the edge of Giles' mind. He couldn't see how, but he had the impression that at some point the connection would become a key part of his quest. He mentally filed the thought away and turned back to the horn.

Next to the glass case was a plaster cast of the horn, which visitors were invited to lift, feeling its weight. Giles ran his hands over the reproduction of the carving, following the line of stress from the horn into the tree, and sensing the way that the tree held together in tension the unicorn on one side and the lion on the other. He looked at the finely carved lion on the cup and felt its outline through his finger-tips on the reproduction. The lion was holding the deer in its paws, one could almost say in its hands, in a curiously gentle way, with a benevolent, even beatific look on its face which was not one of ferocious hunger but could only be called love. Perhaps the carver intended the scene to reflect the biblical text that the lion shall lie down with the lamb. As he held it and handled it he became more certain about the message of the postcard. It was as if the lion was saying, softly, 'I'm holding one fleet beast already in my paws, but you are next. You will be a captive of love.' It was a warning and also a promise.

Giles searched his memory for what his tutor had said in the tutorial, which now seemed a long time ago. In some works of art the unicorn, he recalled, might represent the moon with its crescent horn, and the enticing woman might recall mother earth. Here was no woman with her waiting lap, but a lion. The notice in front of him told him no more than that there might well be a Babylonian or Syrian origin for the symbolism, but the explanatory piece on the horn of Ulf he had downloaded more recently had suggested that while the unicorn represented the moon, the lion stood for the sun. The unicorn was often associated with the holly tree, and the lion with the oak, and it was a tree with oak leaves in which the unicorn was firmly caught. Perhaps the scene depicted on the horn was a mythological expression of the overcoming, or even the devouring, of the moon as mistress of the night by the blazing light of the morning sun. Possibly the tree represented the 'tree of the world' which sprang up from the dark underworld and held all earth and the heavenly bodies in its branches. He now had a view on all this mythology that he did not have that day two terms' ago in his tutor's room. Whatever might have been, he thought, the origin of the symbolism he was looking at in this little scene – he'd leave that to the cultural historians and the anthropologists – what he knew through his eyes and fingers was more to do with human passions, and he thought he had heard the voice of the lion confirming this.

Giles made his way out of the underground museum, passing the Anglo-Saxon York Gospel sitting in its own glass case on the way. It was too much to expect that there would be a picture of a unicorn in the margin, as in several manuscripts of the time, and indeed there was not. A unicorn head did appear, as promised, on the wooden panel for which Giles duly went to hunt on his way out. The panel turned out to celebrate Sir George Gale who died in 1556, having been Lord Mayor and Treasurer of the King's Mint, and the memorial carried his coat of arms, complete with a unicorn surmounting the helmet. Giles reflected that the image had been frozen and diminished into a motif for a wealthy man's commemoration. Below ground there was a scene on the horn which expressed life, personal challenge and danger. It was the very stuff for a postcard sent, it seems, with the aim of starting a love-affair. It was, in every sense, earthy. Above ground was an image which asserted a man's position in society, portrayed proudly on his memorial in a medallion like a Roman emperor. There was a remnant of life in the perky, assertive pose of the unicorn placed on the heraldic device, but it had been suppressed into a status symbol. He did not bother to take a photo. No lover would send it to another. Giles suspected that the new obsession with unicorns, spread across the world-wide web, was an emerging of the subterranean unicorn into the political and economic world above the ground. He wasn't sure this was altogether a good thing, but perhaps this was because he had a head-ache.

Making his way through the obligatory shop, Giles thought he caught a glimpse of the disobliging woman from the desk on the pavement outside, but by the time he reached the door she had vanished. Giles walked back to the university in a state of mounting excitement, despite the throbbing in his head. It seemed quite a short walk as now and then he glanced at the pictures he had taken on his mobile phone, thought about them more and sent a few of the unicorn ones to Hannah. On his Facebook 'wall' he posted photos of the Chapter House he had managed to take before dizziness had overcome him, and in the evening in his friend's room he added to them his impressions of that extraordinary place. He felt he was well launched on his quest.

Back in Oxford the next day Giles was discussing his experiences with Hannah over a cup of coffee in her kitchen.

'Let's get this straight', said Hannah. 'You're proposing that the first postcard is a coded message from a woman who's already had one lover, who now believes that Benedict's attracted to her and she wants him to know that she quite likes the idea.'

'Obviously', added Giles hastily, 'this was all before he met you. But it seems to fit.'

'Not entirely', responded Hannah. 'I can see from your photo that this lion's got a mane, and so must be male. If Benedict's the unicorn, then your reading of the message of the picture really calls for a lioness.'

'Not necessarily', said Giles. I was talking about the beginning of a love affair. I didn't say anything about a woman.'

'I would've thought that I'd have bloody well known if Benedict had been gay,' she retorted impatiently. But she thought for a moment, absorbing the suggestion. 'I suppose it's not impossible he was bisexual, but you've shocked me. I'll have to live with this for a bit to make sense of it.'

'Let's not be too literal', Giles replied. 'We could be looking for either a man or a woman. This mysterious person's got to do the best with what's available, and all the myths portray lions, not lionesses, in association with unicorns. Surely what matters is the attraction and the passion.'

It was clear that Hannah was not at all happy with the turn the conversation had taken. Giles saw how disturbed she was, yet it seemed to him that in her fair-minded way she was not immediately dismissing the possibility. Still, she had another protest to make as well.

'It seems a bit unlikely that a previous lover murdered Benedict just because he'd moved on to someone else, if she – or he – really loved him.'

A UNICORN DIES

'I'm not saying that this person must have been the killer,' replied Giles
quickly. 'There are other people in the frame with other motives – you know
how suspicious I am of Dr Mark Goodall for example, despite his alibi, or it
might have been someone we haven't come across yet at all. I think we
should just follow this trail up to see where it leads. I can't help thinking that
unicorns have got something to do with it, and it's really all we've got at the
moment.'

Over the next six weeks Giles aimed to get enough money together to
make a trip to the next place marked out by the postcards. The easiest way to
collect money was to work stacking supermarket shelves with stock. He was
on the minimum wage, but Hannah was providing his room free of charge
and he often shared an evening meal with her. He worked by day, and in the
evenings worked on researching the unicorn quest. Some of the time he spent
on exploring the internet, now with his own private broadband account and
released from worries about infringing university rules. He frequently talked
over the results of his researches with Hannah, following up the thoughts that
had come to him looking at the memorial of Sir George Gale in York
Minster.

One evening he had been enthusing as usual about unicorns ancient and
modern, when Hannah suddenly observed, in her straightforward manner,
'Of course, there's Benedict's mother to be thought about as well.'

'Why, you don't imagine she had anything to do with it, do you?' he
asked, surprised. Hannah sighed gently, and Giles suddenly saw himself as if
through her eyes, while not able to stop himself thinking at the same time
what wonderful brown eyes she actually had. 'I guess I'm on the wrong track
– please put me right', he said humbly.

'I only meant,' she replied, her neat curtain of hair swaying around her
serious face, as she made her points, 'that we mustn't forget about her loss in
making a kind of game of discovery out of Benedict's death. I was worried
about her failure to reply to the bursar at Helwys College, and so I got her
address from him and I've been writing to her every couple of weeks. It was
typical of Benedict that he never took me to see her, and I've discovered that
she knew nothing about me, or any of Benedict's previous girl-friends, but
she's been interested in my memories of Benedict, and I think that's helped

her a bit. She's been divorced since Benedict was ten and he was her only child, so she's been hit really hard by the tragedy.'

Giles was upset by the word 'game', but he had to admit to himself that Mrs. Green had never once crossed his mind since he had spied her, hunched up miserably, in the front pew at the Memorial Service, and failed to say a word. The revelation of Hannah's insight where his had utterly failed, deepened his growing love for her. The term 'sweetness of mind' floated up from his stock of literary phrases, though he immediately balanced it in his thoughts with 'sharpness of mind'. And he was entranced by the way her hair brushed across her high cheek bones as she moved her head.

'I've visited Margaret once in Manchester, but it's difficult to find the time with so much to worry me going on at work,' added Hannah.

Giles reproached himself for being so wrapped up in his own quest that he had failed to ask about Hannah's own day-to-day concerns. 'Tell me about it,' he urged.

'Well, I'm having some problems about finding accommodation for doctors and pharmacists who are on call during the night. Each department has at least one room set aside for them, but there's such a pressure on space that they're using the rooms for other things – offices, storerooms, consulting areas, even teaching. I haven't got control over the rooms myself but I'm always blamed when on-call doctors have to bed down on sofas in lounges. I sometimes dread going in to the office in the morning in case I find one of them waiting for me to complain and demand what I'm going to do about it. I'm sometimes late leaving work because these kind of clashes happen right at the end of the working day before the night shift starts.' After a moment's thought she added, ' I suppose it's no big deal compared with what my parents are coping with in Uganda, but I'm finding it taxing.'

Giles felt this was just the opportunity to show he was not totally obsessed by his own concerns, and pressed her to explain this unusual reference to her parents, about whom he knew nothing.

'I'm rather proud of them', she said. 'After years as a country G.P. near Wadebridge in Cornwall, where I grew up, he's volunteered to do community health work in a rural part of Uganda. My mother, who's a nurse, is helping him with health education for local women. I talk with them by Skype once a month or so.'

Giles thought he had an inkling now about why Hannah had chosen to work in the health sector herself. He guessed that she had not wanted to bother her parents with her troubles, and she seemed relieved to have been able to use him as a sounding board instead. He resolved to be more interested in her job in the future, but he had done little to fulfill his resolution by late November when he was ready to travel again.

10

Montmartre

S itting on the bus from Oxford to Heathrow at 5.00 am, Giles
calculated that this 70 mile trip down assorted motorways of the
southeast was costing him almost as much as his budget airline flight
to Paris. As the bus slowly ground its way through a series of stops on the
way out of the city, before freely and joyously taking flight down the open
road towards London, Giles took the second postcard out of his pocket and
examined it for the hundredth time. The lady was standing proudly tall with
one hand holding a spear from which fluttered a banner, and with the other
hand holding, even caressing, the horn of a unicorn. The unicorn was looking
distinctly pleased, and as on the Horn of Ulph was accompanied by a lion,
who – unlike the Ulph lion – bore a look on his face that could only be called
aggrieved, disgruntled and even incredulous. An oak tree was visible among
three other species of trees, but in this picture it was the Lady and not the tree
that stood between the two beasts and made the drama. Scattered about the
tapestry was a whole menagerie of animals enlivening the stage, and Giles
just managed to pick out two rabbits, two monkeys, two wild animals with
spotted fur, a falcon, heron, partridge and a pheasant occupying a red ground
strewn with myriad flowering plants.

Giles knew from the entry on 'The Lady and the Unicorn' in Wikipedia
that this was one of five tapestries that appeared to depict the five senses, this
one obviously representing 'touch' since the Lady was grasping the unicorn's

rampant horn. His guidebook confidently asserted that the sixth one, showing the Lady standing in front of a regal tent and flanked by the lion and the unicorn, was the climax to the series, representing the abandonment of the sensual life depicted in the other five tapestries. The Lady was portrayed wearing a glittering necklace in the series on the senses, while in the final tapestry she appeared to have taken it off, and the moment was being captured – according to the guide – when she was laying it aside into a casket, renouncing vanities. What was the message of the 'Touch' image? wondered Giles. How might it continue the message of the Horn of Ulph?

It had been an early start, Hannah waking him at 4 am with a welcome mug of tea, and as the bus moved on he slipped into an uneasy half-sleep. Through his drowsiness he heard the driver instructing him to fasten his seatbelt, and in the shifting, phantasmagorical images of his waking dream, he was riding the unicorn, lifting up from the ground, feeling the wind from the beating of great wings above him. Even in his dream he protested that this was all wrong, that the winged unicorn was an invention of the modern, romantic imagination and that the unicorn he knew, the unicorn of the Lady and the Horn of Ulph, had no such aerial paraphernalia. It must have been his anticipation of the flight to Paris in the mechanical Pegasus provided by Air France that kept the image in his mind so that it could not be shifted by the odd logic of the half-waking state. At least no rainbow appeared.

The feeling of his swift carriage through the air lingered with him as he took the distinctly prosaic 490 bus towards Richmond which stopped on its way at airport terminal 4, surrounded by early morning workers who disembarked at the Cargo building and the catering preparation area. As the plane lifted off the ground Giles dropped into a broken slumber once more, scarcely hearing the useful admonition from the safety announcement that no oxygen masks were provided in the toilets. He found himself again on the unicorn's back, but this time the flight was not a smooth one. The beast seemed to be swooping, veering and bucking, and Giles felt himself violently shaken from side to side. He could not stop himself slipping off, and to his horror fell towards the water of the English Channel beneath. It appeared at first icy blue, and he could scarcely distinguish it from the clouds through which he was passing, but then a small patch of red appeared on the surface, and as he fell towards it, it spread wider and wider until the whole expanse of water was crimson. As he watched, with increasing dread, the blood-red waves breaking on the troubled surface, the Channel shrank inwards towards itself, until a white rim formed around the edges and Giles saw with horror that he was plunging into a bath of majestic proportions.

With a start he woke, in sweat and panic, and discovered that the plane was passing through unusual turbulence in its descent towards Charles de Gaulle Airport. He had been told that Benedict cut his wrists in the bath, and though he had not seen the place of death for himself, it seemed that his imagination could readily supply what he could not have witnessed with his eyes.

In a sombre mood Giles took the RER train to the Gare du Nord of Paris, and kept himself awake for the remainder of the journey. From there he took the metro two stops to Château Rouge and arrived in the district of Montmartre where he had booked a bed in a dormitory of a backpacker's hostel. He was not at all sure why he had chosen Montmartre as the place of his one night's lodging, but several cheap hostels in that area had come up at the top of the Google list when he had gone online, and the name 'Montmartre' had stuck a chord in his memory about artists in Paris at the turn of the twentieth century. Names like Toulouse-Lautrec, Renoir, Van Gogh and Picasso had swum through his mind. He had the half-remembered impression that they had all lived there and had appreciated the scantily-dressed chorus line of the Moulin Rouge. The online description of the environment of the hostel had promised him a village atmosphere with winding cobbled streets, whitewashed cottages, old-fashioned street lamps and charming little squares; so it was with a deep sense of disappointment that he emerged into the daylight from the Metro station underground. He was confronted by a busy main road, choked with traffic trying desperately to navigate the road works that blocked the centre of a large junction, flanked by the same collection of shops, their walls smeared by graffiti, that could be found in any inner-city scene. If Montmartre was really as the website described it, then he must be in the wrong part of it.

Despite his first reaction, Giles used his smartphone map to find the hostel he had booked for one night, not far from the Metro. He was sharing a dormitory with five others in bunks, and the bathroom and toilet were also shared, all for the price of 15 euros a night. But the staff were welcoming and the place seemed clean enough. Time was passing by now, especially as he had lost an hour in leaving British Summer Time behind. There would hardly be opportunity to get to the museum where the Lady and the Unicorn Tapestries were housed and hung and spend a reasonable amount of time there before it shut, and so he resolved to visit the next morning before his afternoon return flight. He would spend what remained of the afternoon exploring Montmartre to ascertain whether he had indeed turned up in an untypical area on the fringes of the old village.

It was then that he noticed a number of posters pinned up around the hostel, advertising a *Danse pour l'égalité des sexes* in the open-air venue of the Place du Tertre that very afternoon and evening. The French he had learned at school was sufficient for him to translate 'Dance for Gender Equality', and he was intrigued by the prospect. The online information had also mentioned festivals and carnivals as characteristic of the area, and so he was inclined to experience some of the colour that had been denied him so far in the dismal hinterland of the station. His decision to go was clinched when he found an advertising bill for the event on his bunk which he must have missed when he arrived, with the handwritten scrawl, 'please come!'.

Consulting his smartphone once again, he found that the square named for the event lay on the other side of the Basilica of Sacré-Coeur, so he made for this well-known landmark of Montmartre. His electronic direction-finder had failed to inform him that some of the streets on the map were in fact steep pedestrian alleys consisting of hundreds of stairs uphill, and he ruefully recalled that the 'Mont' in Montmartre meant a hill. Clambering up them he began to appreciate the description that had been cruelly contradicted by his first impressions. The Montmartre beloved by its famous artists began to reveal itself, as he finally arrived at the Basilica with its breath-taking view of Paris spread out below. The church itself was a confection of white domes, turrets and towers and seemed more oriental than a Western Catholic cathedral. Having panted his way to the top of the hill, he decided to go inside the building that surmounted it in such a grand way.

Entering a somewhat gloomy interior, he was confronted immediately by a reminder of Benedict's death. On each side of the entrance was the expected holy-water stoop in which worshippers could dip their fingers, but these were less the size of cups and more like miniature baths. Images of the bath in his dream flitted across his mind. Boxes of candles were stacked high on each side of the side aisles for visitors to purchase (2 euros for a small one, 10 euros for a large), place in the adjacent racks and light in memory of the saints or their own loved ones who had died. Giles reflected that the cathedral here was taking the whole business more seriously than York Minster, and had almost made an industry of remembrance. A heavy silence reigned, broken only as the severe-faced attendants 'shushed' any visitors who dared to raise their voices above a whisper.

The gloom was dispersed only in one place: a fresco of the resurrected Christ filled the apse with hands outstretched, and powerful spotlights lit up the gold of his halo and the bright red mosaic of a beating heart exposed in his chest. Below the figure, mirroring the heart, a golden tabernacle for the host shared in the illumination. There was little doubt that this was a cathedral dedicated to 'the sacred heart of Jesus'. Giles lingered in the nave, thinking about Benedict. Only those who were intending to pray were permitted into the centre of the nave, but Giles supposed that his thoughts might well count as prayer, as in York. He wondered anyway how the attendants could ensure that visitors were fulfilling the requirement.

After a while he made his way out into the sunlight of the late afternoon, still bright and hot on the head and shoulders. A couple of hundred yards away there was the Place du Tertre, from which the white dome of the Cathedral, ethereal in the light, could be seen floating over the top of the buildings that flanked one side. It was a small square, lined on each of its four sides with restaurants, bars and coffee shops, many of them showing the patina of age from the time when Montmartre was a vine-growing village quite separate from Paris. One of the restaurants promised, in fact, to provide its clients with wine from the sole remaining vineyard in Montmartre.

Most of the square was taken up by a large, slightly raised central platform which was crammed with more restaurant tables, souvenir shops, and stalls where artists were selling local views and executing lightning-quick portraits of tourists. This left a kind of narrow channel between the platform and the surrounding buildings of the square, and this was crammed with colourfully-dressed dancers, circulating with a whole mixture of steps, swaying, jigging, twisting and jerking to the heavy beat that was issuing at a nearly deafening volume from loudspeakers. Tourists and onlookers swelled the crowd, but there was so little room that it was difficult to tell the dancers from the observers, and in fact the aim seemed to be to draw everyone into the flow of music and movement. From time to time, dancers would break off, refresh themselves at the restaurant tables or in the cafés bordering the square, and would then re-join the seething, gyrating mass.

Making the theme clear, a number of placards were held up by groups of dancers. Giles could distinguish: '*égalité pour les gais*', '*égalité pour les lesbiennes*', '*égalité pour les transexuels*', '*égalité pour les bisexuels*', and even '*égalité pour les hétérosexuels*'. It all seemed very French, but he did not need a dictionary to translate the messages, whose language was international. Nor did he have any trouble reading one placard which, unlike the others, was in English, and which read: 'We are the unicorns'. The group of about six people around it was, if possible, more wild and extrovert in its twirling movements than the others, and they stood out in virtue of wearing unicorn heads made of papier mâché, with flowing white manes and complete with horns. Their antics frequently drew applause from the onlookers, and Giles moved closer to get a better view of the heads.

Suddenly he found himself surrounded by the dancers and one of them shouted, 'What's your name? Tell us so we can dance the unicorn dance for you.'

Startled, he replied 'Giles', and the dancers took up the name and repeated it several times, weaving it into the rhythm and the music as they moved to the beat, tossing their heads and waving their horns in the air.

Giles felt the pressure of bodies against his own, and had the impression that one who came particularly close was a woman. He found himself being jammed against the central plinth, and couldn't escape. Half-stifled, he felt his jacket being pulled above his head by the joyous and yet strangely threatening Bacchanalian throng, and blinded, fell against the stone side of the low platform. His head was whirling with lack of sleep, the hot sun, the merry-go round of dancers and the insistent throb of the music. Images coursed through his mind. The water in the basins of Sacré-Coeur had turned as crimson as the water in Benedict's bath of death must have been, and over them hovered like an eagle the red, pulsating heart of Jesus. He felt himself again falling from a great height towards the surface of the water, and knew with the certainty of a dream that if he plunged into the depths he would never be able to rise from them. Panic gripped him, but then he felt himself arrested in his fall, gently held and placed on the back of a great beast which had swooped gracefully into the square from the direction of the dome. He was no longer trapped in the jostling, suffocating crowd but being carried up and away into a country where he could breathe freely once more.

'Are you feeling all right? That was some fall.'

The anxious enquiry came in an American accent, and Giles recovered his consciousness to discover that he was being helped up from the ground by one of the diners at the tables placed towards the edge of the central platform. He collapsed onto a chair to recover. His rescuer helped him to pull his jacket down, and once again Giles could see the whole scene bathed in bright late-afternoon light before him. Of the unicorn dancers, however, there was no sign. It was then Giles noticed with alarm that his passport was no longer in the top inside pocket of his jacket where he had stowed it for security. He looked anxiously around him on the ground, but it was nowhere there. With a hollow feeling in the pit of his stomach he realized that the dancers must have trapped him and stolen it.

Walking back slowly to his lodgings, still feeling dazed, Giles counted his luck that he had a second passport with him, which he had earlier deposited in the security box provided in the hostel. At the age of sixteen he had reluctantly accompanied his parents on the last of their family holidays to a cheap hotel near the beach at Tel Aviv in Israel. It had been a dismal week for him, as the last thing he had wanted to do to celebrate the end of his GCSEs was to sit on the beach, and his parents had ruled out any enjoyment of the lively nightlife of the city on the grounds of his age. Then, just the previous year, he had wanted to accept an invitation from a Lebanese friend in his college to spend a week with him in Beirut, and had discovered that his passport with an Israeli stamp in it was not acceptable at the border. He had acquired a second one, leaving him with his original which still had a number of years left to run. He had discovered during the week that he and Costa had much less in common than he had supposed, and they had drifted apart since the new academic year had begun in the way that college friendships quickly change, but he had been left with two passports. For some reason Giles had packed both for this short trip to Paris, and in his anxiety in being in a strange place had kept them separate.

He reflected that if he had not been so well provided, his visit to the Musée de Cluny would have ended right then. He would have had to have spent all of the next day until his flight at the British Embassy getting emergency travel documents. As it was, he found after going online from his phone and looking up 'lost or stolen passport' on Google that he would have to report the theft at a gendarmerie and get a police record of his visit. He would use his second passport to get back and the rest of the tedious business with the passport office could wait until he was back in the UK.

The interview with the French policeman at the gendarmerie he located in the 18th Arrondissement did not go well. He only had rudimentary French and the gendarme only had broken English. Giles knew the French word for unicorn, since he had read on his postcard that the tapestries in the museum were called *La Dame à la Licorne*, but it turned out that using the word 'Licorne' in a situation where communication was difficult was a bad mistake. The gendarme obviously thought that Giles was trying to report that his passport had been stolen by a unicorn, and his reaction was not unlike that of D.I. Longley in the English police-station when Giles had shown him the postcards of the fabulous beasts. The gendarme's first response was to suspect Giles of being a practical-joker who wanted to waste his time, and the second was to doubt his mental stability. 'Il n'y a pas de licornes' he kept repeating, his voice increasing in volume each time to drive the point home.

Finally Giles decided to drop any mention of unicorns and just report that his passport had been stolen during the outdoor dance in the Place du Tertre, which the gendarme knew about since he had given permission for it in the first place. Giles gathered that the gendarme, in vociferous French, was stressing the danger of pickpockets, drawn by the hundreds of tourists in the summer months to that square in particular. Once unicorns were off the agenda, the gendarme seemed not at all surprised by Giles' loss, and Giles got the impression that he had written a similar report for foreign visitors dozens of times already that year. The episode did supply Giles with what he thought was amusing material for an anecdote he posted on his Facebook page, to accompany photos of the more picturesque parts of Montmartre.

Later that night, kept awake by the snores and other nocturnal noises of his fellow-sleepers in the dormitory, Giles suddenly made a connection with the confusion he had encountered at York Minster about opening times for the museum. It struck him that someone might be trying to prevent him seeing the tapestries and breaking the code, someone who had a lot to lose because they were implicated in Benedict's death. It seemed incredible, and yet it was possible. To be sure, an enemy could not have counted on the fact that Giles would go to the dance, or that he would be carrying his passport. But someone, he reflected, could have taken the opportunity when it presented itself, and might otherwise have attacked him in some other way, perhaps with greater violence than he had actually suffered. It was a deeply unpleasant thought, and he tried to push it to the back of mind as he drifted off to sleep with the sight of the Lady in the tapestry in his mind's eye.

11

The Lady

The next morning Giles' fears of the previous night had faded in the light of day and in face of his anticipation of seeing the unicorn tapestries. Perhaps, he thought, the Lady had been his guardian angel keeping his nightmares at bay. He decided to see Montmartre one more time, and to walk to another Metro station, at the Place des Abbesses, from where he planned to take the train to Cluny-La Sorbonne in the Latin Quarter, close by the Cluny Museum. Though laden this time with the extra weight of his rucksack, he re-traced the hundreds of steps up the hill to Sacré-Coeur, quickly admired the panorama of Paris spread out below him beneath the fringe of trees on the upper slopes, and pressed on to the square where he had suffered such an unpleasant experience the afternoon before.

He steeled himself to pause and order a cappuccino and croissant for breakfast in one of the cafés that bordered the square. The scene looked harmless enough in the early morning, positively tranquil before the wave of tourists arrived. The only evidence of the turbulent scenes the afternoon before was the rubbish littering the square and overflowing bins that had not yet been emptied. He wandered around the empty tables on the central plinth, hoping that he might find his passport kicked under one of them, but he was unsurprised to see no trace of it.

He followed the map on his phone down the further side of the hill, descending the steps of several narrow alleys. The whitewashed walls of the small houses that bounded the paths were certainly there, in fulfilment of the online promise of picturesque scenes, but they had become the canvases for graffiti artists whose initials and tags in glaring colour lined the way. Giles noticed one message that appeared stencilled several times in inelegant capitals, accompanied by a roughly-drawn unicorn head: 'Put up a fight for what you love.' The instruction rang in his ears as he made his way to the Place des Abbesses where, his guidebook informed him, the Abbess of the women's abbey of Montmartre had once been seduced by Prince Henry of Navarre. His lieutenants and the other nuns had followed the example of their leaders, but the hapless Abbess was shortly afterwards deserted by her royal lover. She had, it seemed, failed to put up enough fight to keep him as he ran off with her cousin. Sitting in the Metro on the way to the museum, Giles reflected that the unicorn myth was capacious enough to contain the truth of every tragic relationship in history.

In the medieval grandeur of the Musée de Cluny, Giles paid his entrance fee and followed the signs for 'La Dame à la Licorne'. The designers of the museum had ensured that visitors, in making a rush to find the Lady, would not overlook the other riches of antiquity they guarded, and so had placed the tapestries in the twelfth room. On his way, Giles found several reminders of the fatal event that continued to lurk at the back of his mind, ready to push its way forward at every excuse. There was a Roman bath, a wide excavated enclave in the ground where the remains of Roman and Medieval architecture merged into a pillared room of vast proportions. Another room contained stained glass from the thirteenth century, one piece showing Christ being baptized by St John, not in the river Jordan but standing in a bath-sized font. On the way to the stairs leading to the rotunda in which the tapestries were hung, Giles passed a massive stone container, reminiscent of the shapes of both a font and a bath which a notice informed him was the basin of a fountain from a twelfth-century monastery in Languedoc.

All dark thoughts receded, however, when he entered the tapestry room. He was immediately overwhelmed by the riotous profusion of flowers, animals and trees on a rich red ground that surrounded him from four walls, providing the background for the key actors of the Lady, the lion, the unicorn and – playing a subsidiary role – the Lady's maidservant. Later he discovered that there were some forty different varieties of flower. There were wild flowers of the fields and woods, as well as cultivated flowers from the garden, and they brought a breath of Spring into the room with its subdued lighting. The hangings were all, like his 'Touch' picture, dotted with animals and birds, and he was fascinated to spot a young unicorn among them in one of the tapestries, image of the adult unicorn that took such a prominent place. Then there were four kinds of tree, two on each side of each hanging, whose positions shifted around in the series. The effect that six tapestries made all together was, he thought, nothing less than sublime – and as a student of literature he had some idea of what 'sublime' meant, beyond its popular over-use. As the poets experienced it, the sublime swamped the senses and overturned mere reason. He was having that experience now.

There to the right of the door, first in line in the series, was the large-scale original of his now familiar postcard – 'Touch'. He stood, moved to admiration, gazing at it for a couple of minutes, and then picked up the viewer's guide to the tapestries, in English, conveniently provided at the doorway. This essentially substantiated the brief account in his guidebook, but filled it out with much more background material from the culture of the period. While there was no evidence as to the order in which the tapestries were originally placed, the guide proposed that they should be ordered according to the hierarchy of the senses which was widespread in the philosophy of the Middle Ages. Arranged according to their supposed proximity to the soul, the tapestries should be placed in the order: touch, taste, smell, hearing and sight.

Arranged accordingly, the first five hung on three walls of the room where he stood. For touch, the Lady held the horn of the unicorn, as he already knew. For taste, the Lady was feeding a parrot with titbits from a basket held by her maid, and a monkey sat eating at her feet. For smell, the Lady was plaiting a crown of carnations, taking them from a basket again held by her maid, and for hearing she was playing a portable organ while her maid pumped the bellows. For sight, she was holding up a mirror for the unicorn to view himself as he placed his forelegs familiarly in her lap, her arm encircling his neck. Each time the Lady was flanked by the lion on the left and unicorn on the right. In three cases the two beasts both held spears from which floated banners or pennants depicting the armorial bearings of the Le Viste family, which had evidently commissioned the tapestries. In 'Sight' however, the unicorn had abandoned his spear in order to rest on the Lady's lap, and in 'Touch' neither beast had spears, while a single spear and banner was held by the Lady. In 'Sight' and 'Touch' the unicorn had a more intimate posture with the Lady – lying in her lap or having his horn held – while the lion enjoyed no physical contact with her throughout.

Occupying the fourth wall was the sixth tapestry, larger than the others, and apparently the key to their meaning. The Lady was standing in front of a royally appointed tent, whose flaps were being held open by the lion and the unicorn in their accustomed positions, while they were also managing with great skill to hold their spears and banners at the same time. The Lady's maidservant was holding a small chest, evidently crammed with attractive jewels, and the Lady was holding a necklace over its open lid. The accompanying guide-sheet, like Giles' guidebook, proposed that she was returning the necklace she had been wearing to the chest, symbolic of renouncing the life of the senses for something higher. The inscription over the open entrance of the tent read, 'To My Sole Desire' (*a mon seul desir*), and the guide noted that – while there was an air of mystery about this – it probably referred to the faculty of the will or the 'heart'. The guide even proposed that this could be read as the 'sixth sense' to which some poets and philosophers of the Middle Ages appealed, a mental or spiritual dimension of life which transcended the merely bodily senses. This, proclaimed the tapestry, was what the Lady really desired. As the final piece in the series it carried the message that the viewer, typified by the Lady, should be cultivating the soul. The guide did admit, however, that the word 'desir' had an ambiguity about it, since the 'heart' was also seen as the seat of love and amorous desires. Despite this, it was content to hold to its interpretation, and claimed a good deal of scholarly support for its conclusions.

As Giles was absorbing all this information, he was wondering how it might relate to the choice of 'Touch' by the unknown sender of the postcards, and becoming puzzled. Why hadn't the unknown person sent a picture of this key tapestry? He was also aware of being somehow dissatisfied with the explanation given. It didn't seem to address the rivalry between the lion and the unicorn which spoke loudly to him from every scene, as the beasts did not just stand there but leapt about the scenes. The explanation was reducing the beasts to mere banner-holders. Just as he was thinking this, he heard the voice of a living guide who had ushered in a party of visitors.

'Don't tell the curators of the museum this', she was saying, 'or I'll lose my job, but in my view they've got the order of these tapestries all wrong. I think that the large '*A Mon Seul Desir*' tapestry is the beginning of the series, and 'Touch' is the last and the climax of them all.'

One or two of the group looked vaguely interested in this opinion, but for the most part the members were content to wonder at the tapestries and to take photos of them with their mobile phones. In particular they were anxious to take photos of each other in front of the tapestries or take selfies. Some of them even had extension sticks for their phones to get as much of the tapestry in as possible with themselves in the foreground. The unicorn room was apparently the end of the tour, as the guide shortly dismissed the group and they made effusive, if insincere, thanks.

Giles caught up with her as she was leaving the room, and said, rather embarrassed, 'I hope you don't mind, but I couldn't help hearing what you were saying about the order of the tapestries. I'd be very grateful if you'd explain what you meant.' To make his request more convincing, he added, 'You see, I've got a particular interest in the 'Touch' tapestry.'

'Have you?' asked the young woman pleasantly, speaking English with a French accent in a slightly husky voice. 'I'm very glad to hear that, because it's often overlooked. It's the one where the unicorn wins, you know, and so it has to come last. Not first, as they've put it here.'

'But I thought that medieval philosophy settled the matter about the order', responded Giles, with a surge of hope that he was going to learn why this particular postcard had been selected.

'Oh, philosophy', replied the woman contemptuously. 'Artists couldn't be ruled by philosophy. The point is that these tapestries show a war going on – a gentle war, but still a war, or at least a contest. Haven't you noticed that the spears that hold the banners and pennants are uncapped, with sharp ends? That should give you the clue.'

116

'I didn't notice', said Giles humbly. 'But I did get a sense of conflict. You can't help that, just looking at the tapestries. So you think the large tapestry comes first? Why's that, please?'

'Well, it sets up the whole scene', replied the woman. 'That's the kind of tent that you put up on a battle-field. The Lady's come out of her tent to start off the action between the lion and the unicorn. You know the text from the Gospels, "Where your treasure is, there will your heart be also"? The Lady isn't putting the necklace back but taking it out of the treasure chest, ready to put it on for the rest of the series. The question is this: where is her treasure, signified by the necklace she wears? What is her desire? Is it for the lion or the unicorn, for power or for love? It's all going to be about the heart – the printed guide's right about that. But where's her heart? She's going to discover that through her five senses, not despite them. The soul can only operate through the body, not without it. You mentioned philosophy. The best philosophers knew that.'

The woman was becoming so excited as she warmed to her theme, that her voice was rising in volume and she was positively declaiming, if not – Giles thought – preaching. His attention was caught by the custodians at the doors who were shifting uncomfortably in their chairs, and he believed that, if they had not known the woman, they would have intervened to hush her. Giles was anxious to hear the rest of what she had to say, and so motioned her into the corridor outside the room where they had a bit more privacy.

'This is beginning to make a huge amount of sense,' he said. 'I'm so grateful. But what did you mean about the unicorn winning?'

'Just look at "Touch" replied the woman. 'It's clear that the Lady's chosen love.' She paused and then added with a slightly flushed face, 'She's holding his horn, dammit, and I'm sure you know what that means. Not just his neck, his horn. She's making a statement about her choice by holding the spear and banner herself rather than leaving it to the beasts. Look how the upright spear echoes the upright horn. And the lion's outraged. She's taken his spear away to signify the contest is finished, and he doesn't like it one bit. All the commentators notice his bulging eyes and say how different his look is from the other times he's pictured. They don't appear to recognize why. Then there's the trees.'

Giles' interest was further quickened. He'd run up against trees several times in his quest of the unicorn already. 'I know that the oak tree's associated with the lion', he said. But what about the other trees?'

'As well as the oak, there's a holly, a pine and an orange tree' replied the woman, 'but the other significant one's the holly, which traditionally belongs to the unicorn. You can see the progress of the contest by the position of the trees, left and right. You must have noticed that they move around from tapestry to tapestry.'

'I've read that the unicorn can represent the moon and the lion the sun, with the conflict as their rising and setting each day', remarked Giles in an attempt to show he was not completely ignorant.

'That's as may be', said the woman shortly, 'but I think there's a much more straightforward drama going on here. What's going to get the Lady's heart? Is it power, dignity and influence, or is it love? You can tell how the struggle's going by the trees. They're a kind of medieval score board that anyone can read. In the opening scene the lion and the unicorn start off each with their own tree on their own side, the lion with the oak and the unicorn with the holly. With 'Taste' they've got one blow in each – the oak's now on the unicorn's side and the holly on the lion's. With 'Hearing' the lion's beginning to get the upper hand – both the oak and the holly are on his side and he's looking pleased. Probably it's because the organ is associated with ceremonial and noble music; if it had been love music the lady would have been playing a lute. With 'Smell' they're back to being equally balanced, each having their own tree. With 'Sight' one still can't get the upper hand over the other – each is still keeping their own tree. There's more than a hint, however, that the unicorn's about to play a master stroke as he kneels and lays his forelegs in the Lady's lap, and the victory is confirmed by 'Touch', when the unicorn has finally bagged both the trees.'

'Well, that's fascinating', said Giles, 'though I can't help thinking it's a bit of a neat scheme.'

The woman looked slightly crestfallen at this note of doubt from someone she had obviously come to feel was her disciple.

'I admit that I may not have got the sequence exactly right, but I'm definite about the last stage and fairly sure about the two before that, for another reason.'

Giles wanted to make amends for having disappointed her with his criticism, and anyway the corridor was becoming increasingly public. 'Why don't we go and get a cup of coffee?' he suggested. I spotted a Starbucks across the road if you'd like.' She made a Gallic shrug, not unlike one he'd seen from the gendarme the previous evening, but in the end conceded that the coffee shop selected had become sufficiently converted to French culture to be tolerated.

Over cappuccinos, Giles proffered his name, and she admitted to Françoise. She had, he thought, a striking appearance, with long black hair down to the level of her chest, framing a heart-shaped face. Her eyes were a very dark brown which were almost black, and her mouth, painted a vivid red colour, moved in a quick smile which came and went as rapidly as her manner of speech, and was accompanied by a passing glint in her eyes. As she spoke she pushed her long hair back behind her ears, but it kept falling over them again as she warmed enthusiastically to her subject. She was fairly tall and slim, a good four inches taller than Hannah, Giles estimated, and carried herself elegantly. The reason for her husky voice became apparent as she took out a packet of *Gauloises* and played with it as they spoke, taking cigarettes out and pushing them back in, though there was no chance of smoking in the coffee shop.

Giles prompted her to continue about the 'other reason' she had mentioned for thinking she had the last three stages in the conflict between the lion and the unicorn in the right order.

'I should warn you that it's a bit erotic', she replied. 'But you may notice that in what I'm proposing to be the last three senses the Lady is becoming increasingly intimate with the unicorn. In 'Smell' the Lady has pinned up her outer skirt to display her underskirt, and so has her maid, arranging their clothes in the way medieval women would do to appear attractive. In 'Sight' she's actually allowing the unicorn to rumple up her outer dress. The mirror in which the unicorn is looking at himself is the same shape as her face, and so recalls the courtly love tradition that the lover sees himself and his desires

119

reflected in the face of his beloved. I've already mentioned what the Lady's doing in "Touch". These scenes recall the old legend of the catching of a unicorn by a maiden, and so the Lady isn't just choosing the unicorn over the lion but positively seducing him. All this ought to give us the clue that the conflict is moving towards an end.'

'Thanks so much', enthused Giles. 'You've really shown me why "Touch" makes the impact on me that it does when I stand in front of it. There's a stillness about it, unlike the other pieces, which gives out the message that everything's been resolved.' He did not explain about the postcards, but he was now confident about what the second was signifying, and he could hardly wait to discuss it with Hannah.

Françoise seemed mollified by his response, and even pleased. She offered her card to him, and he saw that she was a research assistant in the history of art at the Sorbonne. He reflected that she would have enjoyed meeting Benedict, and felt flattered that she was willing to keep contact with someone who was obviously still an undergraduate. He resolved to invite her to become a friend on Facebook. He had, in fact, had the curious feeling throughout their conversation that she already knew something about him, but it was – he reflected – probably the intimacy of her manner that gave this impression. It did cross his mind that he might be fated to be lectured by women cleverer than he was, but the sting in the thought was soothed by the fact that he found her undeniably attractive.

Wanting to express his appreciation of her, as well as her opinions, he ventured a hesitant, 'Might I say that your English is superb?'

'Well, I thank you,' she replied, accepting the compliment gracefully. 'As a matter of fact I spent a year as an assistant at the Ashmolean Museum in Oxford while I was finishing my thesis. Do you know that there's a pen and ink sketch there by Leonardo da Vinci called 'A Maiden with a Unicorn'? Could you get there and look at it some time?'

'Actually I'm an undergraduate at Oxford', replied Giles. 'I'll certainly look it up. Did you ever happen to run across a research student in theology called Benedict Green while you were there? His thesis was about unicorns.'

Françoise thought for a moment, and replied that she could not remember anyone like that. She then hesitated again, took a final sip of her coffee, and went on slowly, 'I do find a problem with my reading of the tapestries. Not so much as an academic, but as a feminist. If these tapestries were made for a marriage, let's say of Claude the daughter of Jean Le Viste, then they could be read as urging the bride to be willing to give up the power and authority she has as a single woman in favour of submitting to her husband. The lion may recall Lyon, home-city of the Le Viste family. Claude would have had status in the city when she was unmarried, but medieval women lost their independence as well as all their property when they married. The lion must give way to love. That presents me with real issues as a woman.'

And so it would Hannah, thought Giles. So it would Hannah.

Françoise brightened a little. 'Still', she added, 'you can always read the pieces more allegorically, as being the story of Everyman – or,' she corrected herself, 'Every Person.' After all, the soul is usually portrayed as feminine, *anima*. If the pictures are an appeal to every viewer, man or woman, to put love above power and reputation then I suppose it's all right to apply it to Claude.'

The intonation of her voice had risen again into the sermonic, but again Giles did not mind. He did think secretly that – while she was without doubt right about 'Touch' being the climax of the five portrayals of the senses – it might still be possible to read *A Mon Seul Desir* as the ending rather than the beginning. Perhaps the whole point of the sequence was that the largest piece could be read either way.

'So, let's get to the point' remarked Hannah the next day when Giles had returned to Oxford, bursting with ideas, and they were once again sitting round the kitchen table. 'While the Ulph postcard marks the beginning of attraction, the Cluny postcard marks the beginning of sex.'

'Absolutely', agreed Giles. 'In the Ulph card, the unknown sender is saying 'I think something is happening between us', while in the Cluny card he or she is saying 'All my senses are inflamed by you and I'm glad we've got as far as we have.'

'He or she?' echoed Hannah with a query in her voice. 'Surely the Cluny pieces confirm that it must be a woman. It is 'The *Lady* and the Unicorn' we're talking about after all.'

'Not necessarily', replied Giles. 'I think we now have to identify the unicorn as Benedict, but remember Françoise's point that the Lady might be Everyman ...' hastily adding 'Every Person.' 'Or the person might not want to be pinned down to a particular gender identity', he went on, remembering the Gender Equality Dance in Montmartre. 'More than that,' he concluded, 'in the internet age people like to take on different personas. Many men have internet identities as women. They're experimenting with what it feels like to be the opposite sex. A man could be saying "Let's play at unicorns and maidens. You be the unicorn and I'll be the lady." For the moment we should keep our options open.'

'And don't forget', interrupted Hannah, 'that we're also keeping an open mind about the cause of Benedict's death. The postcard sender isn't necessarily a killer, and Benedict might not have been killed at all.'

'I'm getting more sure there is a connection between the cards and Benedict's death,' responded Giles, and proceeded to tell Hannah about the incidents in York and in Paris that had very nearly prevented his seeing the tapestries. He had gradually been coming to the conclusion, he explained, that someone was trying to stop him seeing the images of the unicorn and solving the mystery of the cards.

Hannah was not impressed. 'Those events are quite different', she exclaimed, 'and I don't see why you should lump them together. No one tried to prevent you getting a ticket at the Cluny Museum, did they? It's just coincidence. And you *are* always getting into trouble.'

Giles did not bother to point out that if anyone *had* been working against him with malicious intent they could hardly have known about his second passport, and might have thought they had succeeded. He could see that Hannah was getting irritated, though he was not sure why, and he did not press the matter. Anyway, his suspicions seemed even to him to be far-fetched now that he was back in the familiar setting of Oxford. He did decide, however, to change the settings for his postings on his Facebook 'wall'. He had been leaving these as 'public', open for anyone to see. As a precaution, from now on he would tag his Facebook posts from his journeys to be viewed only by his friends. He had nothing to fear, he was sure, from any of them.

12
Oxford

Giles had returned to the occupation of stacking supermarket shelves on a zero-hours contract when, about a week after his return from France, he had a day when he was not required to be in. Coming down to breakfast about mid-morning, he was surprised to find Rosie Jones sitting at the kitchen table having an obviously cordial cup of coffee with Hannah. He had one of those moments when someone familiar is met in an unexpected place, and for a moment the everyday world seems to have been turned upside down. When he thought of her, he had always mentally pictured her in her apartment just beyond Magdalen Bridge, and had unwittingly confined her there like the maiden in the tower in fairy tales.

'What on earth are you doing here?' he stuttered, realizing immediately just how rude this sounded.

'I suppose I'm allowed to be', responded Rosie somewhat tartly, but with a hint of amusement. 'As you can see, I'm enjoying a cup of coffee with a friend.'

'It was Benedict,' said Hannah in her usually abrupt way, but looking away out of the window. 'He introduced me to Rosie at a party, and ever since we've met up now and then. It's good to talk with someone Benedict knew. '

Obviously, thought Giles, it's not enough to talk with me, and then was immediately ashamed of the thought. He had liked Rosie, and was quite pleased to see her again, even though it was the leads she had given him that – indirectly at least – had resulted in his rustication.

'Actually, Rosie's just going,' went on Hannah. 'But could you hang on? There's something I want to tell you.'

Giles was certainly going to 'hang on', as he had not yet had breakfast, and when he was amply supplied with toast and Hannah had seen Rosie out, he waited to hear what Hannah had to say.

'It's Jacqui,' she began slowly. 'I wanted to tell you that she moved out of her room today. She's gone to share a flat with a friend.'

'I'm sorry to hear that,' replied Giles. 'I've had some interesting conversations with her'.

'Well, I'm not sorry,' responded Hannah. 'To tell you the truth I've felt uncomfortable with her for some while, and I've been wondering what to do about it. Now she's solved the problem herself.'

Giles felt that he had been unobservant and insensitive. Hannah had evidently been troubled and he had been too preoccupied to notice it. 'Would you like to tell me about it?' he asked tentatively.

'I'm probably being silly,' she replied, 'but while Benedict was alive I felt that Jacqui was attracted to him. Just one or two things she said.' She hesitated, and then went on, 'And this is probably even more absurd, but I got the sense that she wouldn't have minded a relationship with both of us. I thought this was too ridiculous to be true and so I pushed it to the back of my mind.' As if emphasizing this, she pushed back her hair which had fallen forward over her face, in a gesture that aroused some intense, if exquisite, feelings in Giles as he listened. 'But it all came back when you were telling me about the way that some people call themselves unicorns nowadays.' A slight flush crept up her face as she said the word 'unicorn'.

Giles instantly regretted having disturbed her with his speculations, and began to get some inkling as to why she might have been impatient with some of his ideas. 'Thanks for telling me', he said sincerely, 'but please don't think about it any longer. If there was anything in it, Jacqui's not around any longer to worry you.'

'Don't infantilize me', said Hannah sharply. 'I'll deal with it in my own way. For the moment I don't think I'll let the room to anyone. I can get by, and I don't want to get caught up in anyone else's life just for the moment.'

Giles reflected that he hadn't handled things well, but he was, he had to confess to himself, intrigued by the scenario she'd painted. He decided to have a talk with Jacqui, to probe her as gently as he could and to test things out, so he phoned her on her mobile to say he was sorry they would not now see each other as frequently as before. They arranged to meet for a drink in The King's Arms on Friday evening of that week.

Pushing his way through the usual crowd of drinkers and eaters, some out for the evening and some refreshing themselves after a hard day's reading in the Bodleian Library opposite, Giles found his way to the bar. All around him the conversation rose like incense to the heaven of the ancient beams, and he heard snatches about the progress of theses, the success of the university cricket team and the latest gossip about being invited – or not – to a college ball. In the scrum around the till he found Jacqui and was relieved to find that she had already bought her own pint. Stacking shelves was not that well paid, and he had a number of journeys to provide for. Finding a corner in the snug behind the bar, he asked whether Jacqui was well settled in her new flat.

'I'm actually with my partner, Alexia,' replied Jacqui with a satisfied look. 'We're going to see how it works out'.

Giles mumbled his congratulations, and thought secretly that this might be relevant to the questions he had in his mind, but did not intend to voice.

'Actually, there's a bit of a story behind this,' went on Jacqui, 'involving Benedict. It's amusing, I think.'

Giles encouraged her to tell the story, and Jacqui did not seem reluctant to do so.

'Well, you know that Benedict and I used to talk about his thesis. As a mere scientist I found the theology really quite interesting. Benedict told me all about unicorns, and it all seemed a bit theoretical to me. So I suggested that he should try being a unicorn, in Alternative World.'

'What do you mean?' replied Giles, astonished. 'How could he get into an alternative world?'

'Not *an* alternative world', said Jacqui. '"Alternative World" – you know, the online world you can visit and inhabit.'

'Oh, a computer game,' responded Giles. 'Benedict didn't seem to me to be the type to play cyber-games.'

'No, not a game', said Jacqui impatiently, 'That's not the point of it at all. It's an environment where you can live another life, or even three or four. You can travel to countries, buy land, build a house and – in particular – meet other people. Business companies hold online conferences, there are all kinds of societies, and churches even set up their own places for religious worship. You pick an avatar, or an identity to represent you in the world. You can go as yourself if you want, or you can be a different gender, or you can be an animal or some fantastic beast. For a while the Anglican Cathedral had a flock of dragons in the congregation but I think they've flown off now.'

'Do you enter the Alternative World often?' asked Giles curiously, wondering when Jacqui found time to write her thesis.

'Not very often now, since I met Alexia there. After getting to know each other online we agreed to continue the relationship in the "real" world, though the world "real" is only relative, I think. In fact we met "outside" for the first time in this pub.' Jacqui reflected on a pleasant experience. 'Anyway, getting back to the story about Benedict. I persuaded him to join Alternative World as a unicorn – I mean choosing a unicorn for his avatar – just to see what might happen. I'm a scientist, and I'm all for experiments and empirical evidence.'

'What happened, then?' asked Giles, really intrigued by now.

'Well, I have to confess that I partly suggested it so that I could get a bit closer to Benedict. I'd got a hint that he might be open to something more physical than we'd had together so far, and I was really very fond of him.'

Giles thought that he was getting a bit nearer to what he wanted to know, but he could not help objecting. 'Physical? Isn't that just what a cyber-world isn't? Isn't cyberspace outside the body, just in the mind?'

'Clearly, you haven't tried it', riposted Jacqui. 'It can get very physical. Virtual sex isn't just in the mind. And you should know as a literature-buff that you can't separate the mind from the body anyway. I'll be one of your friends on Facebook, if you like, and give you a few ideas. But to get back to the story, we entered the Alternative World together, sitting side by side with our own laptops, with Benedict as a unicorn and me as Jack.

'Jack?' interrupted Giles, startled. 'Did you say Jack or Jacqui?'

'Jack, of course,' replied Jacqui. 'This is an alternative world, you know. Being Jack enabled me to work a few issues of identity out that I needn't go into. I gave myself a really super muscular body. I thought we put a lovely shape together for Benedict, really entrancing with a flowing white mane, delicate hooves and a sharp horn, just designed for penetration. The obvious place to go was the medieval world scene, and so we transported there immediately. That's where things began to go wrong.'

'I suppose you went there because of the medieval myth of the unicorn and the virgin', suggested Giles. 'Did you find any virgins?' he added, remembering his own thoughts in the University Parks what seemed like an aeon ago.

'Hold on a moment', interrupted Jacqui. 'We hadn't got into the Middle Ages before we had a row. You see, you can't enter the medieval environment without wearing the proper clothes, and you have to buy those at a special store. I'd already had to spend quite a lot of money kitting out Benedict as a unicorn. He didn't need anything medieval as unicorns obviously don't wear anything except their virtue, but I had to dress up as a knight. That cost quite a lot more, in AWDs.'

'AWDs?' queried Giles.

'Alternative World Dollars' explained Jacqui. 'I thought Benedict might reimburse me in real-world money since this was all for his benefit, but he wouldn't. He got testy about the whole thing, and said he couldn't see the point of me dressing up. That was a bit rich, since he was already in fancy-dress himself, but I couldn't get him to agree and so we entered the medieval world already upset with each other. I'd been hoping that we might have an interesting meeting between me as a knight, him as the unicorn and some girl who might be there, but it didn't happen. The problems really started when Benedict refused to use the proper language.'

'You mean you had to speak medieval English?' asked Giles, who had spent many wearisome hours learning it for his course, so that he could read medieval poems like 'Gawain and the Green Knight'.

'Not proper medieval English, of course', Jacqui hastened to say. 'A kind of made-up olde-worlde style of speech. These specialist areas in the Alternative World have their own customs and rules, and you really have to abide by them if you're going to be there. People become very possessive about their own world they've created and you have to respect their way of doing things. You can't just crash in. You won't be welcome. Benedict absolutely refused to play the game. You know how blunt he could be, and I'm afraid he was very rude, mocking the other players for their artificial speech which he thought very comic, and said so.'

'Ah! said Giles triumphantly, 'Players. It is a game after all. I thought so.'

'I should have said "role-players"', retorted Jacqui. 'They got angry, and then a whole herd of unicorns turned up to defend their domain. I thought that Benedict recognized one of them, but I can't be sure. It was the way that he or she was speaking that gave the clue he seemed to pick up. I say speaking, but I mean that words you type appear in speech-bubbles attached to the avatars. Anyway, they crowded round Benedict, pushed and jostled him, and lowered their horns to do some real damage.'

Giles remembered his own experience in Montmartre and shivered.

Jacqui went on, 'At that point he pressed the exit button and vanished. I stayed on a bit and tried to calm things down, but I have to say that I was as angry with Benedict as they were. I was also pretty disappointed that the experience hadn't brought me closer to Benedict – in fact quite the opposite. We were never the same with each other after that.'

'Did he ever enter the Alternative World again?' asked Giles.

'I have no idea', replied Jacqui. 'We didn't speak about it. Of course, I went back lots of times. I'd caught sight of Alexia in the medieval area, as a dashing-looking knight calling himself Alex, and on another one of my visits we met again, by the seashore of a desert island where we were both shipwrecked. You might say we rescued each other. Alexia told me later that she had guessed that I was really a woman – intuition you know – and I didn't mind at all when we met in this pub and I discovered she was a woman too.'

Giles resisted saying that the way they'd met again looked to him like a game. Some of his hunches had been confirmed by the story, and Jacqui had been quite open about her bisexuality and attraction to Benedict. He thought he would probably not repeat the story to Hannah, however, given her present state of mind. He bade farewell to Jacqui and promised to meet again before long, though he was unsure about how sincere he was being. One thing he had resolved was at some point to try entering Alternative World as a unicorn for himself.

A week later, when he again had no work in the supermarket, he decided to follow up the advice of Françoise and search for Leonardo da Vinci's 'Maiden with a Unicorn' in the Ashmolean Museum. He had found an image of it on the Museum site online, but wanted to see it in the flesh, or at least represented flesh. He made his way through the impressive neo-classical columns of the portico and found himself in the spacious and lofty atrium which he had visited only a couple of times before. A maze of galleries ran off each side and ahead he could see a wide flight of stairs leading to yet other galleries above. At hazard, he took the immediate gallery to the left of the door and passed through a dramatic throng of white classical statues clustering on each side of the aisle, some gesturing at him with extended arms but no heads, others turning their faces towards him but bereft of arms, still others blankly confronting him as disconnected heads or torsos or even feet. There was no evidence of unicorns here, nor any when he arrived at cases where miniature Egyptian statues of gods grimaced at him. Though many were in the form of animals – cats appeared to be especial favourites – the familiar uni-horned shape was missing. Giles' head was already spinning and he realized he would never find the drawing by guesswork, so he reversed his steps back to the information desk and asked directly where the Leonardo could be found.

The friendly girl at the desk informed him that Renaissance paintings were on the second floor, but having consulted her computer she announced that the Leonardo was not hung publicly on the walls. However, Giles could examine the drawing in the Western Print Room. Usually visitors had to book, but today there were few readers, and she would be glad to take him there through various security barriers. Up and down stairs through the rabbit-warren of the building took them to the print room, where assistants found the drawing for him and placed it in a perspex stand on a table covered by a green baize cloth.

Giles looked at it with awe. The miniature drawing was mounted on a card, with another small print placed beneath it. Leonardo's fingers had once moved across this paper, which was not yellowed at all with age, and the image stood out freshly. There was the girl, with the unicorn not on her lap but kneeling in a docile manner by the side of her bent knee, head tilted towards her. The tamed unicorn was wearing a collar, and the girl was holding its leash, pointing towards him with finger outstretched. Between them was the usual tree, now familiar to Giles, though it was sketched in such a rudimentary way, with a few jagged lines, that the kind of leaf was not discernible. The unicorn's horn, slanting towards the girl, seemed to be entangled in the branches so that he was doubly caught, by collar and tree. The girl, gesturing towards the unicorn, was not looking at him but at the viewer, as if drawing attention to the fabulous beast. But what really aroused Giles' interest was her mouth. It was this that made the effort of finding the drawing so rewarding, even though he could view the image online. While only roughly touched in, there was something more enigmatic about the mouth than any reproduction could capture.

The memory of his school visit to Paris suddenly cropped up in Giles' mind. He had queued up for an hour with his group to get into the Louvre, and he had to admit now that he had found the whole visit tiresome. He just was not old enough, and did not know sufficient about the art, to appreciate the riches on offer. He had walked from one room to another as quickly as possible to get out again into the open air and find the McDonalds they had been promised, but he had paused for a moment in front of Leonardo's 'Mona Lisa'.

It was, he supposed looking back, mainly the fame of the picture that had fascinated him. It felt significant to be standing in front of it in a crowd of people holding up cameras and mobile phones, securing evidence for friends and family back home that they had actually been there and seen it. They were modern pilgrims to a sacred relic, and they hoped that something of its magic would rub off on them. But Giles had been startled by one thing. He thought he was familiar with the image, having seen it many times on advertisements, posters, greetings cards and television. The Mona Lisa's smile had made her a celebrity. Yet this same smile made an impact that it had never made on him before – half-amused, half-serious, hinting at a kind of secret inner life – the shape of the lips speaking of young womanhood, the sheer mystery of the feminine. The secrecy was underlined by a gaze which hovered between a direct look outwards, and a slightly deflected glance over the viewer's shoulder, evading direct exposure. The smile was a kind of invitation, he thought, to share her world.

It was just this feeling that Giles was now having with the maiden's lips, a girl that Leonardo had seen one day. The reproduction online had hardly prepared him for the effect of this mere blob of brown ink, a line for the top lip and a more swelling shape beneath. Like the Mona Lisa, the eyes were more or less directed at the viewer, but just a slight degree askance, enhancing the ambiguity of the set of the mouth. Pointing to the unicorn at her side, the maiden was declaring something, asserting something and asking for something all at the same time. She was expecting the viewer to know what it was, or at least to guess it.

Giles tried to fit the drawing in with what he had learned from looking at the Lady in the Cluny Museum. There it had been a matter of choosing love, and letting love stir all the emotions and senses of the body. He supposed that this drawing was the same kind of thing, but he felt that it was also making another sort of appeal that just at the moment he could not pin down. Perhaps later it would come to him. This image was not one of the postcard series but it might be connected.

Before leaving the print room, he was reminded that his quest was not only about a woman but about a unicorn. His eye moved down to the second small drawing mounted on the card. There Leonardo had sketched another episode from the natural history of the unicorn, portraying the beast crouching down by the bank of a stream, dipping a long, slender horn into a ribbon of water which was tersely but clearly indicated. Giles knew from his conversation with the president of the unicorn society that he was looking at a scene of the unicorn purifying waters that had been polluted, perhaps by the venom of snakes. The unicorn was in a curiously convoluted position, flexibly curved around itself for all the world like a cat, and giving the impression of vulnerability to the cruelty of human hunters who might pass by. The quite tiny sketch managed to convey an act of service at a cost paid by the beast to its own comfort. It seemed appropriate that the assistants in the museum had also provided him with another Leonardo sketch of the same period, a mere trace of a nativity scene, mother with child, both looking fragile and open to being hurt.

Thoughtfully he left the drawings on the table for their guardians to replace, and was glad that they were kept there safely to be seen by the many eyes that cared to search for them.

On the way out he thanked the young woman at the desk of the print room for allowing him to see the drawings, and on an impulse asked whether she remembered a French girl named Françoise who had worked in the Ashmolean.

'Well, of course,' replied the woman, 'she was a great person to have around – so enthusiastic as well as knowledgeable. We were all sorry when she went back to the Sorbonne. Actually, now I come to think of it, that Leonardo drawing of the maiden with unicorn was her favourite piece in the collection. She said she had personal reasons for being so fond of it, but never said what they were. Is she a friend of yours?'

Giles explained that he had only met her briefly, but she had urged him to look at the drawing, and he was glad she had. The girl bade him a friendly farewell, giving him her card and saying that he would be welcome back in her domain at any time. He glanced briefly at the card and saw that her name was Clare Wright.

Stirred and a little tired by the experience, he decided to call in at the 'Bird and Baby' for a restorative pint. Sitting down at a table whose surface was still sticky from previous drinks he was sinking into a reverie when his attention was caught by the name 'Benedict Green' spoken in anger and contempt. Looking around he saw Nick Stoney sitting on a nearby barstool, with a small group around him he was haranguing.

Giles thought he knew him well enough to interrupt, and so called over, 'Nick! What's the matter?'

'That bloody Benedict Green's the matter', spluttered Nick.

'But he's dead', said Giles in a perplexed tone.

'But his influence goes on', said Nick bitterly. 'My fellowship's not being renewed and it's his fault. The college says it's a result of the research assessment procedure and my lack of output. I wasn't included in the Faculty return of those it reckons to be its world-class researchers, its three and four star people, though how they can tell I don't know.'

'Surely that's got nothing to do with Benedict', protested Giles.

'But is it really the reason?' asked Nick sarcastically. My college is looking for funding from the Great and the Good, and they reckon my past reputation might be a liability. That's what I suspect anyway. There are people around who know the story of how I got to Oxford, and why I didn't come the normal route. I don't think I'll ever shake it off, and bloody Benedict Green got me into this. I thought that when he died it would be the end of it. I hoped it would. But apparently not.'

He stopped suddenly, and seemed to think he had said too much.

Nick sounded more paranoid than rational to Giles, and seemed to be in the grip of an obsession, but he had certainly given Giles something to think about. Giles now wondered whether Benedict had made other enemies in his short but tempestuous career who had nothing to do with unicorns and who might be responsible for his death. Perhaps the postcards were just part of his research and there was no one sinister behind them at all. Hannah might be right that it was a wild goose-chase. There might be another explanation for the threatening message on the sixth one. He had the sudden idea that he would take them and show them to Benedict's supervisor, the Revd Mark Goodall. He was suspicious about him anyway – he'd behaved in such a guilty way at the memorial service – and perhaps he might give something away if he had a good reason to look him up. He emailed the chaplain, and explained there was something he wanted to consult him about. Although he got a terse reply it was still an invitation to go round on the next Friday evening.

After a hard day's work at the shelves, he arrived at the chaplain's lodgings in St Paul's College at about 7.00 pm. The door was in the main quadrangle, tucked away in one of those smallish stone arches in the wall with which medieval architects liked to perforate blank surfaces and which were now almost hidden under a blanket of ivy. He was just about to knock when the door flew open and a young man, obviously an undergraduate, staggered out looking upset. The chaplain came after him to the door and said goodbye in a solicitous way, calling out, 'Don't forget next week at the same time!' The undergraduate muttered something inaudible in reply and lurched away unsteadily.

'I'm sorry about that', said the chaplain, and obviously felt he had to add, 'I've taken on young Tom Naylor, replacing Benedict as his tutor. Tom's not very well at the moment, and it's not helped matters that he was probably one of the last people to see Benedict alive. His tutorial was the final one of the day that awful Friday.'

'He still seems very upset', remarked Giles. 'He must have thought a lot of his tutor.'

'It wasn't quite like that,' replied the chaplain unwillingly. 'Actually they'd had an argument about a stupid prank that Tom had got involved in, something to do with taking a car away without permission. I'm not sure of the details. Anyway, he respected Benedict as a teacher and wanted to go on having tutorials with him despite everything. I thought that said a lot for his character.'

Giles stood stock-still at this revelation, as if thunder-struck, his mind going back to the irascible barman in the 'Bird and Baby'. So it was his son who was the student in the last tutorial that day, just before the evening of the tragedy. His thoughts were racing, but he recovered himself and remembered why he'd come. Following up the matter of Tom, if he had the chance, would have to wait.

The chaplain remembered his duty to be hospitable, asked Giles in, sat down opposite him and urbanely offered him a sherry. When Giles had declined what seemed to be a purely formal invitation, the chaplain looked enquiringly at him.

'What can I help you with?' he asked, helpfully enough.

'I've come about these postcards that Hannah and I found among Benedict's things,' Giles explained. We found them a bit puzzling, and I wondered whether you'd seen them before as part of his research.'

The chaplain took his time in looking at them, and seemed interested. 'I can see that they might have been relevant', he said, 'but I've not seen them before. I mean not as a collection, not in this form. I'm familiar with most of the images, of course. They're quite well known. You're sure they were bundled together?'

'Oh yes', said Giles. 'I'm sure about that. Are you certain you really don't know?' he went on daringly, taking what he knew to be an illogical leap, 'because I got the sense that you and Benedict knew quite a bit about each other. He once said something to me about that.'

The chaplain started, and coloured. The look of guilt on his face that Giles had seen at the Memorial Service flitted across his features once again. 'You need to be careful what you're saying,' he replied, attempting a jocular tone but sounding heavy-handed, 'or you might just find yourself in trouble'.

'I don't think I could be in more trouble than I am at the moment, with my suspension and everything', said Giles cheerfully.

'I didn't know about that', said the chaplain, 'and I think it's best in the circumstances if we end the conversation here. I'm not at all sure you should be in Oxford at all. As I've explained, I can't help with what you *said* you came about.'

Stiffly, but – to his credit – still trying to be courteous, the chaplain showed him out. Giles now had a whole flock of suspicions aroused and in full flight, but he decided to do nothing more about enquiries in Oxford until he had made his planned visit to see the original of the third postcard in Rome. He did tell Hannah about Tom, and they agreed this was a trail worth following later on. In fact, Hannah seemed distinctly more enthusiastic about this path of enquiry than the way marked out by the postcards. Giles did not tell her about his visit to the chaplain, some instinct prompting him that she would not be happy about it.

A UNICORN DIES

As he had expected, he found a request from Jacqui, asking to be a Facebook friend, and clicked on 'accept'. He was surprised, but pleased, to find a similar request from Clare Wright, and supposed that she was part of the network around Françoise who had become a 'friend' after the Paris visit. As he accepted, he remembered the afternoon in the Ashmolean.

13
Afternoon in Rome

As the 'Leonardo' express pulled into Termini station in Rome after its journey from the Fiumicino airport, Giles noticed the streaming and exploding smears of graffiti all along the walls, the equipment boxes and the railway carriages flanking the line. Initials in lurid colours burst out of their frames like ballooning pustules in a diseased skin. While this was a usual sight in all cities, it seemed especially disturbing when the railway line was also edged by ancient Roman walls and arches, the mellow red brickwork, now some two millennia old, testimony to Roman architecture and engineering. The graffiti and the ancient buildings coincided and jarred in the eye, even where the monuments themselves had not actually been vandalized. This was, Giles supposed, the way that all great cities now welcomed travellers. They gave evidence of the disaffected young people of their streets, determined to leave their 'tag' of identity on the public stage, awarding themselves by means of a spray can the kind of immortal name claimed by a Julius Caesar and an Augustus Caesar – to name two rulers of Rome that Giles slowly dredged up from his memory as he mused.

Giles reflected that he seemed to be making a habit of staying by railway stations, since he had again booked a low-cost backpackers' hotel close by the Termini. This, however, was different from the lower reaches of Montmartre. Five-star hotels jostled for space in narrow backstreets with cheap lodging houses, fast-food outlets sat cheek-by-jowl with traditional trattorias, shops with international logos were wedged between small *tabacchi* and open-air secondhand book stalls, and expensive limousines fought for parking with buzzing clouds of motor scooters. Drivers leant on their horns continuously in the forlorn hope that this would disperse the traffic blocks in front of them. Giles learnt immediately that unless there was a pedestrian light at a crossing, no vehicles would stop unless at least a foot had already been placed on the road.

Everyone visiting the city seemed to be packed into this sector along with Romans who had lived there for generations. The visitors, it seemed, were reluctant to wander far from the umbilical hub of the Termini, which offered taxis, buses, trams and bicycle rickshaws to all parts of the city. As Giles walked down the street in search of his own accommodation, he noticed that even recent buildings of no great architectural distinction were dignified by brass door handles and knobs, by rows of shutters and by Latin inscriptions which declared this very house to be part of a proud history. While Giles' Latin was poor, even he could pick out resounding words like 'imperium' and 'orbis'. Not that this prevented graffiti cropping up wherever there was a blank stretch of whitewashed wall or a painted steel shutter over an entrance to apartments. The steps leading up to the charming ivy-clad entrance to the church of St Peter in Chains were now bordered by scrawled names and garish hearts.

Giles nevertheless rejoiced in the profusion of life in the blazing afternoon sunshine, and was gratified to find that his cheapest of abodes was close neighbour to the massive and ornate facade of St Maria Maggiore, built on the Esquiline Hill at the point where – so his guidebook told him – snow had fallen miraculously in the middle of summer. Some such refreshment would, he thought, be welcome this sweltering afternoon, but after checking in at the hostel he made his way back to the transport hub of the Termini and took the express bus to Piazza Pia and St Peter's Basilica.

He had been required to book online for entrance to the Borghese Museum and Art Gallery where his Maiden with a Unicorn was housed, and had left the visit for his second day in Rome since he had been uncertain about whether his flight – taken with a budget airline notorious for delays – would arrive too late for an afternoon slot. As it was, the plane had indeed arrived an hour late but the Leonardo Express – aptly named, he thought, remembering the Da Vinci 'Maiden' he had examined in the Ashmolean – had still deposited him in Rome in mid-afternoon. This left him with time to visit a few famous sites, and he was keen to see St Peter's which appeared on television news items whenever the Pope made some pronouncement about climate change, the needs of the poor or sexual scandals in the Church. Reporters were invariably filmed in the square in front of the basilica, and he was curious to see it. He had already promised his friends on Facebook that he would give them his impressions of it. Alighting from his bus in the Piazza at the end of the 'Street of Conciliation' the Basilica bulked so large at the end of the avenue that it seemed nearer than it was, and he was surprised that it took him nearly 10 minutes to walk there.

The proportions of the piazza in front of the Cathedral, flanked by two semi-circles of huge colonnades, were so large that the wooden barriers for crowd control seemed like mere matchwood. He had to queue between them with several hundred other tourists and had time to get the feel of his environment. Figures of saints high up on the pediments of the colonnades stood out sharply against the blue afternoon sky and, circling the square, they formed a kind of aerial congregation for this outdoor holy space. Huge statues of Pope Pius IX, celebrating his munificence in restoring and extending the Basilica now stood over large video screens provided for transmitting the image of the Pope to the throngs in the square when he spoke from the balcony. The nineteenth-century Pope appeared to be drawing attention to the screens like a modern college lecturer, with an attitude more fussily didactic than pious. The theme of modern technology was repeated when Giles reached the entrance to the basilica, which he found guarded by airport-type security scanners. While these excluded suspicious metal objects, human stewards excluded tourists showing too much bare flesh.

He was scanned, approved, and duly admitted, and made his way into the basilica, marvelling at the scale and rich decoration of the interior. From the far end of the basilica, a golden window high over the altar shone like a fiery furnace whose door had been opened to expose the blazing coals inside, and he could just make out the shape of a dove hovering in the middle of the circle of light. His eye travelled up to the top of arches on each side of the nave, decorated with rich gold and white squares and flowers. It was there that he saw what he had never expected to see. In this sacred place there was a large white carving of a woman, lying back with an exposed breast, scarcely covered in diaphanous draperies, and holding the horn of a golden unicorn which was trying to nuzzle her with a look of desperation on its face. One elegant front leg bent over the edge of the arch, it was evidently trying to scramble into her lap, while the woman seemed to be bending her shapely legs away from its huge bulk

'My God'. The expression, perhaps spoken too loudly for the hush around, escaped from Giles' mouth as he stared at this scene.

'I hope he is,' said a mild voice with a strong Italian accent. Giles looked down to where the voice was coming from, and saw a monk in a brown habit, girded with a white, knotted rope and sitting on the marble base of the column which was surmounted by the unicorn arch. Next to him was a capacious basin for holy water in the shape of a shell, held by two large cherubs who seemed to be running to excess fat. Giles had seen these water stoops in previous churches, but this and a similar one on the opposite side of the nave were more like baths – and the memory of Benedict popped up into the surface of his mind. The monk had been trailing his hand in the water, and now looked Giles steadily in the face. Showing old, heavily lined features and a shock of white hair, his robe was untidy and Giles could see signs of a breakfast, or probably a whole month of them, plentifully spread out on its front. But there was something compelling about this figure.

'I'm sorry, Father', said Giles hastily, 'I didn't mean to be blasphemous. I wasn't thinking about what I was saying, I was just so surprised, shocked even.'

'Please don't apologize,' replied the monk pleasantly, 'my master once said something similar when he was shocked, and I'm not sure he knew what he meant by it either.'

'I'm afraid I don't understand', replied Giles.

'I'm sorry too,' responded the monk, 'I'd forgotten that young people today don't know their bible stories. I was talking about Jesus Christ when he was crucified – you must have noticed all the crosses around in this place – and he cried out, "My God, my God. Why have you forsaken me?"

Theologians have been debating ever since what he might have meant, but over the years I've come to think that Jesus only half knew himself. Have you seen the *Pietà* by Michelangelo just opposite, on the other side of the nave? Mary holds the dead Jesus in her arms after he was taken down from the cross. Michelangelo's caught something of the mystery, the desolation and yes – the hopelessness – that you can hear in the earlier cry from the cross.' He paused, and repeated softly, 'My God, my God.'

Giles let a moment go by, driven into a reverie himself, but more centred on Benedict in his bath of death. 'I was shocked to see the woman and unicorn up there,' he said at last. 'They seem so out of place.'

'Well, yes and not really,' replied the monk. 'The figures are part of a whole series of Christian virtues depicted by relief statues on the arches.' He recollected for a moment and then went on: 'There are seven – as I remember them, authority, divine justice, virginity, obedience, humility, patience, human justice and fortitude. They sit underneath an inscription that runs all along the top of the arches, words of Jesus to Peter before the crucifixion, "I have prayed for you, Peter, that your faith may never fail; and you, when you turn again, must strengthen your brothers." Peter was the chief Apostle, you know, and the first Pope. It's said that he's buried here, under the altar.' A look of doubt passed momentarily over his face, and he added quickly, 'but that's neither here nor there. What matters is what he did, and the inscription reminds us of it.'

'So what's the unicorn got to do with all that?' asked Giles in perplexity. I've seen unicorns before – images I mean – in some strange places, but this is the strangest.'

'It's the symbol of the third virtue, virginity,' replied the monk. 'I know that's odd, given the beast's reputation, but it's by association with the old story that only a virgin maiden can catch a unicorn. Women took to having themselves depicted with unicorns to stress their purity – either actual virginity, or faithfulness in marriage. They were often painted like that on the verge of marriage or just afterwards.'

With mounting excitement, Giles began to see a connection with the painting he was due to see the next day. 'But this is in a church, and under that inscription,' he objected.

'Well, it probably signifies faithfulness in a general sense,' explained the monk. 'After all, it's under the words 'that your faith may not fail.'

Giles felt a pang of disappointment. Things seemed to be getting highly religious, and the statue itself burst out of the arch with an animal energy and with what felt like suppressed desire.

'I don't quite get what the woman's doing', he said. He hesitated for a moment, and wondered whether he ought to say what he meant. But the monk seemed an understanding person, and quite unusually open. 'In a tapestry I've seen in Paris, the woman is holding the unicorn's horn as an expression of desire. She's excited by the unicorn and wants to touch him.'

'It's a bit hard to get that feeling out of the image,' conceded the monk. The unicorn stresses the woman's virginity, given the story, but you get the sense things might not remain that way. She's holding a flower in her other hand, the one that not grasping the horn, and she almost seems to be beating him back with it as a kind of talisman. It's a very complicated image, but then life is complicated, you know.'

Giles' mind went back to Benedict, and the series of postcards, and he could not help agreeing that it was. 'Thanks so much, You've really helped,' he said, and went back to gazing up at the gold and white figures high up on the arch.

'I always think of Perpetua and Felicity when I look at that arch,' came the gentle voice again.

Giles was startled. 'Who?' he asked, wondering if they were the monk's sisters, perhaps now dead.

'Perpetua and Felicity', repeated the monk, 'Two women who were martyred for their faith, thrown to wild animals in the arena in the early centuries while Christianity was illegal in the Roman Empire. They became saints, you know.'

'I'd like to hear about them,' said Giles, knowing that he was going to anyway.

'Perpetua was a noble Roman lady, and Felicity was her slave-girl', explained the monk. 'They both became Christians, and of course Perpetua got all the attention since people tried to persuade her to renounce her faith. It seemed a terrible waste. But it was the slave-girl who said the really important thing. Perpetua had refused to marry and really was a virgin, but Felicity gave birth to a child in prison just before her execution. As she cried out in the pangs of childbirth, a jailer mocked her. "If you can't bear that pain," he laughed, "how are you going to bear the agony of being torn apart by a lion?" Her reply has gone down in Christian history. She said "Now I suffer what I suffer, but then another will suffer in me, as I suffer for him." That's faithfulness, I think.'

He looked down, and Giles could see that he was wiping away a tear. Giles was also deeply affected by the story, and thought he would never forget the words of Felicity, spoken in the monk's gentle tones.

'Have you visited the Colosseum?' asked the monk after he had recovered his composure. 'You really ought. The two women were martyred in an arena in Carthage, not here, but similar dreadful things went on in Rome.' He stopped, and Giles could see that he wanted to be scrupulous about historical accuracy. He continued, 'The Colosseum's been consecrated as a holy place, and there's a large cross standing there, but there's actually some doubt now about whether Christians were thrown to the lions there at all. Other victims of human cruelty certainly were, and so it's absolutely right to have the cross there. You can see the underground cells and tunnels where animals and prisoners were held before being pushed out onto the floor of the arena.'

Giles promised to go there, and said goodbye with thanks, before crossing the nave to look at the Michelangelo *Pietà*. Safely behind glass in a side chapel, having been attacked by a man with a hammer forty years before, it was being photographed by dozens of tourists. In defiance of the rules clearly posted up at the entrance to the Basilica, flash was going off from all sides, lighting up the white marble which evoked tired flesh spent of all life, sprawled in Mary's lap, limbs hanging wearily in her arms after torture and death. People were taking 'selfies', wanting to be recorded with the famous statue. Perhaps they imagined it would save a few years in purgatory, thought Giles ironically. Another idea suddenly occurred to him and he hastened back to the pillar where the monk was still sitting.

'I'm sorry to trouble you again,' he said, 'but I've just been wondering. There's an image of Mary with Christ in her lap on one side of the nave, and a woman with a unicorn nearly in her lap on the other. I know that when the unicorn's not being a love-beast it can be a symbol of the passion and death of Christ, since it's killed by hunters in the story. But I can't help thinking there's another kind of connection between Mary and the maiden. I don't know what it is, but I just feel it's there.'

The monk smiled. 'I'm glad you've felt that,' he replied. 'But I'm not going to tell you what I think. You'll have to discover it for yourself, I'm afraid. It'll mean a lot more when you do.'

Giles reflected glumly that he sounded just like his English tutor back in Oxford, but still he bade the monk farewell with renewed thanks. Before leaving he dipped his hand in the water bath and dabbed the water on his forehead, facing the still glowing circle over the altar ahead of him, as he had seen other pilgrims doing. As he did so he thought of Benedict and supposed this would – as on other occasions – stand in for a prayer. As he emerged into the bright light of the square once more he noticed what he had missed on the way in, a fountain on each side of the square, jetting up and emptying themselves into basins, mirror-images of the two cherub-held shells inside. Rome was full of fountains, every piazza and street corner holding a potential memory of Benedict, though Giles had come to realize that it was only in moments of stress, or exhaustion that he would lapse into a waking dream where the water turned red.

Following the advice of the monk, he determined to visit the Colosseum, and took a bus from the Piazza Pia to the Piazza Venezia. From there his guidebook told him he would have to walk. There was in fact a metro station near the Colosseum, but it did not connect with anything inside Central Rome where the metro-moles had curiously failed to dig their way, and where he was dependent on buses. Taxis he could not afford. Following hundreds of other tourists he began to walk in the hot sun alongside the ancient forums, resisting the noisy appeals of modern-day Romans dressed as ancient Roman soldiers to be photographed with him, for a fee of course, and was rewarded after a while by a sight of the Colosseum in the distance. It rose, massive and sinister, with its arches and windows like gaps between teeth in a mouth whose face its designers may have intended to be entertaining but which was in fact frankly ferocious. He could not understand why postcard sellers along the way were offering pictures of the Colosseum bathed in a romantic glow at sunset. Even in its partly ruined state it had been, and still seemed to him, like a gigantic machine of death.

As he entered the gate marked 'those without tickets' he remarked how ingenious and efficient the killing-machine was. Rising three levels above the ground it needed a high order of engineering skill to support ranked tiers of marble seats accommodating tens of thousands of Roman citizens who all wanted an unhindered spectacle of suffering and death inflicted on those below, eager to see the massacre of those deemed criminals or enemies of the state, and ready to turn down their thumbs to demand the execution of a loser in gladiatorial combat.

Queuing for his ticket with hundreds of others, Giles regretted that he had not booked beforehand online as he watched those who had the foresight to do so stride smugly past the waiting throng to be quickly admitted. But it did give him the time to imagine himself part of a similar queue in ancient Rome, surrounded by voyeurs of actual death rather than the present-day voyeurs of the memories of death. Since the ticket desk was at the lowest level it also gave him opportunity to peer into the tunnels of the underground maze of misery for the waiting animals and human beings. Finally furnished with a ticket he made his way, as instructed to level two. He climbed up a concrete staircase, modern though bordered by ancient drainage channels, and complete with the actual Roman herring-bone brick formation on the landings, worn smooth by generations of feet eager to see what death in the afternoon looked like.

Before emerging onto the terrace as ancient games-goers would have done before him, he passed an exhibition which gave him pause for thought. Graffiti, it seemed, was not solely the preserve of modern youth. Here were sections of marble removed from the original seating on which spectators had scratched rough sketches of gladiators, names of their favourite fighters and occasionally their own names too. The quest for immortality was ages-old, but there were no names for the mere victims who had been brought from all corners of the empire to die for the entertainment of the masses, helpless men and women faced by wild animals driven mad for the purposes of human statecraft. They were nameless all.

A UNICORN DIES

Giles reflected on what he could remember of Benedict's thesis, and remembered also the story of Clifford's Tower in York. It appeared that the rulers of Ancient Rome knew well the power of the scapegoat to release the pent-up pressure towards conflict in society, puncturing the danger of revolt against them by the common people, giving them a substitute sacrifice. The shadow of the unicorn, in its role as a scapegoat rather than love-beast, lay over the Colosseum.

With these disturbing thoughts in his mind, Giles stepped out onto the terrace, surrounded by a jostling crowd of tourists. From this vantage point he could look out over the vast arena. A notice nearby informed the visitor that the whole floor area could be flooded for the performance of sea battles, and Giles imagined boats with their sailors grappling with each other, not in a mock battle but in deadly conflict. This floor had long rotted away, and he could see clearly the cells and tunnels underground. There was a retaining wall to stop the modern visitor from falling, but it was interrupted at spaces by stout wrought-iron guard railings which allowed the spectator to see the arena below more clearly. Giles looked down a hundred feet and went weak at the knees. There was a sheer drop into the depths and he could not imagine anyone who fell surviving. The barriers, fortunately, seemed strong enough as the crowd pressed up against them, and security guards were on hand. Giles walked around the terrace and then took stairs down to level one.

Again he looked out onto the arena. This time the terrace was about twenty feet higher than the passageways below. Again there were gaps in the wall with barriers in the spaces at about waist height. These were not as substantial as those in the second tier, but sturdy enough, with metal posts and heavy cables running between them. Most of the gaps protected like this had an outcropping or rough platform of brick in front of them for about 15 feet, probably part of the original floor, before there was a drop into the depths. But at one point, right opposite the cross installed on the far side, there was a broken outcrop of only five feet or so. He moved there to get a better view of the arrangement underground. He heard a guide instructing his charges to look at the grooves in the stone where ropes had run, moving lifts up to the level of the arena floor. This was the grisly mechanism by which animals and humans would find themselves plucked from the fetid darkness of the underground caverns, transported upwards and bursting into the light and fresh air, only to be surrounded by thousands of jeering spectators eager for them to be tortured and die slowly. He leant over the barrier and knew instantly that, with the sun beating down and with a stuffy and noisy crowd around him he was about to lapse into a familiar dream state.

The arena in front of him filled up with water, boats appeared and he heard the swish of oars and the clash of steel. To his horror, the water was slowly turning red from the blood of the combatants, and the colour grew deep vermillion as veins pulsed in his head. He heard the gentle tones of the monk saying, 'Another will be in me and suffer for me.' It was then, in a half-waking condition that he felt the pressure of the crowd behind him, forcing him hard against the barrier, and he sensed that he was being lifted and pushed over the top.

14
Maiden

As Giles fell onto the rough stone surface on the other side of the barrier he snapped out of the dream and had the presence of mind to stop himself rolling over the edge into the underground area beneath. Several people who saw him fall screamed and shouted, calling for the security guards to help. Two rushed forwards, leapt over the barrier and helped him, first to stand up and then to clamber back over the rail. At the same time they were addressing him volubly in Italian, with vigorous hand gestures, and he could tell that they were not pleased with him. Their manner was not soothing.

They took him to a supervisor's office where someone fortunately spoke English. He was asked whether he wanted to go to hospital, and he hastily declined. The less fuss, in his view, the better. It took Giles a while to persuade the official that he had not climbed over the barrier deliberately, but she was obviously puzzled by what had happened. It must, she thought, have been a freak accident with the pressure of the crowd raising and pushing him over. All kinds of odd things happened in a crush. Giles consented, wanting nothing more than to get away, but privately suspected that he had been deliberately lifted and heaved over. He was unlikely to have been killed with the drop as it was, but he would certainly have broken bones and been put out of action for a while. Was it possible that someone had been following him from the hostel, waiting for an opportunity to stage an accident?

Deciding what had happened was complicated by the fact that he had been hovering on the borders between dream and wakefulness. The supervisor kept him longer, taking his personal details and making out a health and safety report. She was rattled, he could tell, and he was still feeling shocked.

At last she let him go, and he strongly suspected that she did not want to see him back in her domain again. The feeling was mutual, and, though shaken, he set off to walk the half mile or so back to his hostel. Sustaining himself first with a burger and coffee from a fast-food shop just outside the station, he turned in for an early night. He emailed Hannah, staying silent about the incident but reassuring her that he was pressing on to visit the Borghese Gallery on the next day. He spent a restless night, dropping into vivid dreams and nightmares. In one he had made it up to the third tier, alone, without a guide. He felt himself pushed over the edge and was plunging to the ground far below, while all around thousands of spectators were cheering and jeering him in equal measure. He fumbled for his forehead and there, as he expected, there grew out a single horn. Expecting the impact with the ground, deep in the dark of the underground passages, in the dream he could not understand why he could not fly. He woke up in a sweat, blaming the lack of air conditioning in this basic accommodation for the way he felt.

His fellow bunk-dwellers were not slow to inform him in the morning that he had been shouting all night, something garbled about 'Now I suffer what I suffer', repeated over and over again. They also told him he had been shouting names – they could just make out 'Hannah' and 'Felicity'. He got the impression that, like the supervisor in the Colosseum, they would be only too glad never to see him again. Picking up a cappuccino and a croissant in a nearby cafe, Giles shouldered his rucksack and made for the buses at the Termini. He got off on the Via Pinciana, close by the entrance gates to the Borghese Museum and Gallery, and made his way down a tree-lined avenue, arriving in a semi-circle of grass surrounded by stone images of eagles that looked like nothing so much as dragons.

Giles had arrived at the next planned stage in his hunt of the unicorn, and was eager to see the painting of the Maiden, but he had the curious sense that he had already, the previous day, made progress in the quest without intending it. He entered the undercroft of the Gallery to collect his pre-ordered ticket, deposited his rucksack in the cloakroom and found himself in the shop. Immediately he saw that reproductions of the Maiden with the Unicorn were everywhere. His guide to Rome did not even mention the painting among the half-dozen 'must sees' at the Gallery, but since the book had been published the Maiden had evidently become the poster-girl of the Borghese. She adorned the front cover of the Gallery's own guidebook, as well as a book called 'Masterpieces of the Borghese'. Although he knew from his internet explorations that there were questions about whether Raphael was solely responsible for the painting, she occupied the front cover of the book dedicated to Raphael's art, the familiar postcard had pride of place in the shop, a poster of her was prominent, and she decorated book marks (unfortunately minus the unicorn to fit the long shape) and children's colouring books. No one could escape her. She looked out at the visitor from every corner.

Giles had a spare half hour before the allotted time of his admission, and he wandered out into the Borghese gardens, noticing as he went that the souvenir stall outside carried medallions with the image of the Maiden along with its trinkets, pictures of Mary, crucifixes and miniature models of famous statues of Rome. She was apparently not just the poster-girl but the presiding saint of the place.

Giles made his way down a pleasant avenue between shady trees and found himself in a piazza. At its centre was one of Rome's multitude of fountains, with a basin carried by four horse-like beasts, from which water spurted and fell into a larger basin below. He stood in front of the fountain, curious to see if the semblances of horses were in fact unicorns, but he saw immediately that they were fabulous sea-horses, their hind quarters dissolving into fishy fins. As he looked at the water jetting up between their front legs and over their snorting nostrils he felt that he was slipping again into a dream. The water was just beginning to turn a delicate shade of pink when he felt himself violently jerked in the back and propelled forward towards the rim of the fountain, half falling over it. At that moment a small vehicle flashed by him, almost grazing his side, and he saw as it vanished down the path that it was one of the buggies used to transport visitors around the park, but driven at a furious pace that certainly exceeded any conceivable speed limits.

'Are you OK, Sir?' enquired an anxious voice, and, recovering his balance, Giles turned and saw a bear of a man behind him. Large of size and resonant of voice, the man repeated 'Are you all right?' adding, 'I'm sorry I had to push you like that, but I'm damned sure that buggy would have hit you otherwise. Must be driven by a madman. Italian drivers, you know.'

Even in his shaken state, Giles knew an American voice when he heard it. Oxford was full of them. His anxiety at nearly being run over was slightly alleviated by the charm of being addressed as 'Sir' by a man twice his age, but he recollected that this was a piece of Southern courtesy, suitable for an apology.

'Please don't apologize', he said quickly. 'I'm really grateful for your quick thinking.' More than a little confused, with his dream state ebbing away, he blurted out, 'Otherwise I'd never have seen the Maiden with the Unicorn.'

He didn't know why he'd said this to a complete stranger, but the big man reacted with surprise. 'Well good night,' he exclaimed, 'I've come to see her as well.'

'What do you mean, "Good night"?' Giles could not help asking, though he realized this sounded rude. 'It's the middle of the morning'.

'Manner of speaking', replied the man cheerfully. 'Where I come from in Georgia it means "Knock me down with a feather",' he explained, changing into a mock-British accent, not very successfully, 'only it's a much older version of the same thing. Elizabethan, I think.' He added, 'I'm Earl King. I enjoy this kind of grammatical conversation seeing as I teach in a liberal arts college at home. I'm in Europe collecting photos for a history of art course and the Borghese's just stuffed with good things, the Raphael among them – if it's all by him. I especially wanted to see her.'

Giles reciprocated this generous self-introduction by explaining that for his part he was Giles Questing, a student at Oxford doing research on images of unicorns. He discreetly said nothing about being suspended or the reason for his research. He had immediately warmed to this large, open-hearted man. They discovered they had the same entrance time, and they retraced their steps to the gallery. Giles felt he had gained a protector in a hazardous situation, reflecting that two near-injuries was too much of a coincidence. Though both could be explained away as – he remembered Hannah's words – 'just the sort of thing that would happen to him' he was even more convinced that someone was determined to stop him decoding the secret message of the postcards.

Earl wanted to wander around the lower part of the gallery, and especially to spend time in the Caravaggio room, taking his photos. Giles was anxious to get to the Maiden which was upstairs, so they agreed to meet there in due course. In a few moments, Giles was standing right in front of her. Given the promotion of her in the shop, there was surprisingly no crowd clustered around the painting and he had plenty of time to stand and stare. The woman looked out into the room, obviously wealthy because of the jewels she was wearing and her fashionable, puffy-sleeved velvet dress, modestly cut. In one hand she held what appeared to be a small and very young unicorn, which looked defenceless and a little pathetic in contrast to the rampant animals he had seen so far. The sight gave the modern viewer a start. The woman looked so true to life, and yet the painter could not have seen her with this companion, though it was possible that viewers of the time would have readily believed that he had. The portrait challenged the boundaries of truth and appearance. Or, as Giles heard a passing tourist put it, 'That's just weird.'

He remembered what the monk had told him about women's assertion of their purity, wanting to be portrayed with a unicorn. The Lady in Paris was probably on the verge of marriage as well, but her message was different. It was 'I choose love, with all its delightful sensations.' What was this woman saying? What was the sender of the postcard, female or male, saying to Benedict through her?

He looked at the Maiden again, trying to be sensitive to the truth that the painter had seen within her, and had expressed so well that she had been made the compelling image of this gallery. Raphael had apparently been influenced by Leonardo's *Mona Lisa*, painted just a few years before. That much was evident from the posture of the woman. However, Raphael's woman was gazing, not directly at the viewer but over the viewer's shoulder, glancing more obviously to one side than Leonardo's Lisa as he remembered her. Giles' mind went back to his earlier thoughts about the *Mona Lisa* and Leonardo's sketch of the maiden and the unicorn in the Ashmolean. With these he had been fascinated by the set of the mouth, the sense that the other two women were about to declare something. Here there was the same sense. The mouth, not exactly smiling, was questioning, challenging, even slightly stubborn.

'She is about to speak', he thought, 'and when she does she will interrupt any complacency, any assumption that she is owned by the rich man who is about to marry her or has just married her.' Her eyes, evading direct contact, preserved her own sense of who she was. Moving to one side of the painting, to his right, he noticed that even when he followed the apparent direction of her eyes she was still keeping her own identity. Suddenly he heard her voice sounding within him, speaking in concert with the women of Leonardo. 'Yes,' he thought, 'what she is calling for is commitment to her, the same loyalty and faithfulness that she is offering through the symbol of the unicorn in her hand. I am giving myself, she seems to say – but will you?'

He was suddenly reminded of Benedict as he saw right next to the painting a large bowl of yellow alabaster, standing on a green marble plinth. Inside it was all flecked with veins of red running across the interior surface. He was sufficiently in control of himself to know that this time he was not going to lapse into a dream state, but he imagined what the sender of the card might have been saying to Benedict through this golden-haired avatar who had sat for Raphael. It was unlikely that he or she was asserting literal virginity, given the message of the Horn of Ulph and the Paris tapestries, but an appeal for faithfulness was much more likely. If the message of the Horn was 'I think there is an attraction here: do you?' and if the Lady in Paris was signalling, 'You excite all my senses; I want to touch you all the time...', this lady was taking things one stage further, making the appeal, 'Will you commit to me, and not just play with me?'

Earl had now arrived in the room and was also looking at the Maiden with admiration and wonder. For a while he just stood there, absorbing the impact she made on him, but after a while the instinct of the teacher to instruct became irresistible. Turning to Giles, he asked, 'You know that the unicorn's only been uncovered in the last century, of course?'

Giles was surprised. The unicorn had been in his thoughts from the beginning, and he could not conceive of the painting without it. 'No, please tell me', he replied, sensing that Earl could not restrain his desire to teach, but not minding being the pupil on this occasion.

'She was painted about 1505, but in the seventeenth century she was turned into a portrait of St Catherine of Alexandria who was martyred by being broken apart on a wheel. She was given all the appropriate religious clothing, and the unicorn in her hand was overpainted by Catherine's symbol, the wheel. It was through restoration in the 1930s that the unicorn was discovered, and she was re-classified as a noble woman of the Renaissance, though it's still not clear who. But here's the thing, the killer-fact you might say. Further restoration in the 1950s revealed that the animal in her hand wasn't originally a unicorn, but a small and cute dog. Much more likely, don't you think? The dog was a symbol of faithfulness, like the unicorn, but there were actually examples around to paint. Someone, for some reason, replaced it with a unicorn of the same size, possibly Raphael himself, or possibly a pupil. There are still mysteries about the painting that nobody's solved yet.'

Giles stood stock-still, absorbing the unexpected information, and re-assessing his conclusions. This new fact did not alter his impression of the message that the maiden, and the postcard in turn, was delivering. And after all, the finished work included the unicorn, whatever processes of art and social standing lay behind it. He moved closer to the surface of the painting and examined the baby unicorn carefully. One of its small front legs was curled around the maiden's thumb, hairs on the leg brushing the fine hairs on her own arm. The maiden's forefinger was caressing its other bent leg. Fingers and legs were intertwined in an attitude of affection. Whoever had added the unicorn had made a good job of it.

Suddenly Giles noticed the much larger painting, hanging on the next wall of the small room, at a right angle but close by the Maiden. It was again by Raphael, a 'Deposition from the Cross', painted at about the same time. The Deposition, he thought, was a kind of elaborated pietà. There was the dead Christ, stretched over Mary's knee in a posture reminiscent of the Michelangelo statue, but there were other biblical characters around, another eight of them, helping Mary carry the dead body of Christ away. In a masterly composition, the body of Christ in the middle linked two circles of disciples and friends, to the left and right of the canvas. But Giles' attention was caught by the Virgin Mary. She had braided yellow hair, just like the Maiden, and her fingers were wrapped around those of the dead Christ as the Maiden's were intertwined with the unicorn's small legs. He looked from Mary to Maiden and back again. The features were curiously similar.

He drew Earl's attention to the two women, and a quiet 'Well, good night!' escaped from his lips as he looked from one to the other. 'Are you trying to tell me it's the same woman?' he demanded.

'Not really,' replied Giles hastily. 'I don't know enough about the history or the art to claim that. I know my limits. I'm just interested in the parallel themes – maiden and unicorn, Mary and Christ. There are two kinds of unicorn hunt, you know – the hunt of love, and the hunting to death. The second can get religious, as a symbol of Christ. Perhaps they get laid over each other in a painter's mind and the associations just happen.' He added, 'But ever since yesterday I'm haunted by the thought that there's some other connection between Mary and the Maiden. Something more significant'. He nearly added 'significant for Benedict' but he remembered in time that Earl knew nothing about that. 'I can't see what it is at the moment, but perhaps it'll become clear later.'

Earl could not help him, despite his superior knowledge of art history, and Giles pushed the puzzle to the back of his mind. 'I'll tell you what, though', Giles said to Earl. 'Have you noticed that there are seven paintings of Mary with the baby Jesus in this very room, some by Raphael?'

'Madonna and Child', corrected Earl, 'That's what they're called, or the *Theotokos* in the east.'

'Whatever', said Giles impatiently. 'Isn't it interesting how the same ideas crop up all the time? Mary with the child Jesus, Mary with the crucified Jesus, Maiden with a unicorn, and here, Maiden with a *baby* unicorn? I'm not sure what it means. I'm just enjoying the connections.'

'Well, you've given me something to tell my class about,' replied Earl. 'But I'll need to take a few more photographs.'

They went off together to look at some of the several other 'Depositions from the Cross' that were scattered about the gallery, to get what Earl called 'background and context'. None of them, Giles noticed, had the fingers of the Virgin and Christ touching. A 'Deposition' by Pieter Paul Rubens, painted in 1602 came closest to the gesture, but not by the Virgin Mary. Christ was draped, not over his mother's knees, but on an antique stone altar, and while the dark-haired Virgin looked up beseechingly to heaven, his hand was being held by another Mary, Mary Magdalene, with yellow hair and one breast exposed. The knee and leg of the dead Christ projected from the canvas towards the viewer in a posture that reminded Giles of the way that the front leg of the golden unicorn thrust out of the arch in St Peter's.

Further food for thought was supplied when, about to descend the stairs, Giles noticed a copy of a lost painting by Leonardo da Vinci, titled 'Leda and the Swan'. Original and copy were from about the same time as the Maiden, and the swan – Zeus in one of his many cunning disguises, Giles remembered – was pointing its beak towards the woman who was cuddling him, in a way suggestive of the yearning muzzle of the unicorn in other paintings and drawings, including Leonard's own sketch in the Ashmolean. Downstairs he passed a classical statue from second-century Asia Minor in which Leda was sitting with the swan fitting comfortably in her lap. The idea flitted across his mind that there was a theme here that pre-dated Christianity, and that it might be relevant for his puzzle, but by now his head was spinning and he had no inclination for further explorations. What mattered, he thought, was that he had decoded the message from the postcard.

Outside he bade farewell to Earl. The big man seemed sorry to see him go, and after taking his photograph on the stone steps of the gallery remarked warmly that their time together had been 'quite good'.

'I thought it was more than "quite" good', responded Giles. 'Myself, I'd have said "very good." And I'm very grateful for your saving me from injury earlier.'

Earl was covered in confusion. 'There I go, I keep forgetting that you Brits don't say "quite" in the way we do. Yes, very good indeed, splendid, awesome in fact. If you're ever in the States, look me up. I'm quite near New York City.' He pressed his card on Giles, and suggested they keep in touch online through Facebook. Giles thought that there might be something in Earl's invitation beyond the typical American desire to be liked that he had often noticed before. He glanced at the card and saw that Earl's college was in the State of New Jersey. Giles realized that he must have moved there from his native Georgia, and a glimmer of an idea about seeing the fourth post-card passed through his mind. He would be interested to discover what Earl told his class about the morning in Rome.

15
Alternative World

'So, she's asking him to marry her. Is that what you think?' demanded Hannah in her usual abrupt beginning to the conversation that she and Giles were having over breakfast around the kitchen table.

'Perhaps', conceded Giles slowly. 'Marriage is certainly in the background of the painting. But I think it's a bit more flexible than that. The postcard-sender is asking for some lasting commitment. It needn't be marriage. And I'm still keeping an open mind about the gender.'

'Not sure about that', retorted Hannah. 'You appear to have fallen in love with this unknown woman from the way you talk about her.'

Giles was strongly tempted to take this opportunity to say whom he was actually falling in love with, but judged this was probably not the moment. He thought again how attractive she looked when she was arguing her point with passion and humour. The way her hair fell over her face was nothing like the carefully braided hair of Raphael's maiden, but the effect was just as powerful.

'I'm trying not to confuse the actual woman who sat for Raphael with the avatar I think she becomes for the sender of the postcards,' he explained, 'but I admit it's hard to keep them separate. The modern person could still be male as well as female. I do think it's a third stage in a relationship that didn't end well.' He hesitated, and stopped himself from adding what he was thinking, which was: 'It couldn't have ended well or you wouldn't have been engaged to Benedict.' It hardly seemed sensitive.

'Don't forget,' warned Hannah, 'that I'm still not convinced there's a story here in the postcards at all. And if there is, that it has anything to do with Benedict's death. And', she added for good measure, 'you seem to be muddling things up with all the religious business about the Virgin Mary. I appreciate that you're taking Benedict's theological outlook seriously, but I can't help thinking that all these pietàs, depositions and nativity scenes are muddying the waters.'

Giles wondered if Hannah had used the word 'waters' deliberately, but he realized he was becoming obsessed by the mental image of Benedict in his bath of death.

'All right, I know that I'm getting taken over by research into unicorns', Giles admitted, 'But I can't help feeling there's a connection. Don't forget that the sixth postcard, with the odd message, is a picture of the Virgin Mary. I wouldn't be surprised if it weren't the key, but I can't yet see how. It seems best to get there step by step.'

Despite being shaken by his two near-injuries, Giles had said nothing to Hannah about them. He was too fond of her to want to annoy her, and he had the sneaking feeling that she might not go on supporting his quest if she thought he was accident-prone. He *had* told her about the monk and Earl, and she had been intrigued and amused by them both.

'Meanwhile', said Hannah, 'there's the rent to be paid, I'm afraid, and I suppose you're determined to make more trips as well. That all costs money, and I'm losing out on the room I rented to Jacqui.'

'I'm glad you've raised the point,' said Giles eagerly, 'because I've had an idea. Stacking shelves isn't bringing in much of an income, and I've got a trip to New York to fund. I want to help you out a bit more too, though I'm really grateful that you're being so reasonable about the rent. I've been thinking about becoming a hospital porter over the summer, and I thought you might know how to go about this.'

'Portering's been outsourced', replied Hannah. 'It used to be run by the Trust, of course, but now it's been handed over to a company in the private sector called "Progress".' She added in a bitter tone, uncharacteristic of her,

'It's all in the name of economy and so-called efficiency. It's a big claim, "Progress". I doubt it myself.'

'You sound upset,' observed Giles. 'Why are you so worried about porters?'

'It's part of a bigger trend at present to weaken the National Health Service, in my humble view', explained Hannah, 'and I suspect my own job's going to go the same way before too long. It's adding to the whole load of anxieties I've told you about already.'

Giles wondered whether to offer the opinion that it might be better for her to have her problem outsourced, but wisely he refrained from saying so, and instead came back to the issue of porters. 'How do I find this Progress company?' he enquired.

'You don't', responded Hannah. 'You go to an employment agency, and see if they're advertising vacancies for porters. They often are. Then you might get sent to an interview with the healthcare company that's looking for staff. The agency mostly used by Progress is called "Superior", and I believe you'll find it in the High Street.'

The very next day, since there was no call to stack shelves, Giles made his way there and found a card recruiting for porters, as Hannah had predicted.

'You've come to right place,' a portly, fussy-mannered man told him. 'I always say that you're all at sea without SEA – the Superior Employment Agency, I mean.'

Giles laughed in an obliging manner and as a reward found himself with an interview with a manager of Progress for a job, he was glad to find, at the John Radcliffe Hospital. It was only a short journey on the bus from near the end of his street, and he was looking forward to travelling there are least some of the time with Hannah. Perhaps he could help with her early-morning worries, he reflected. It wouldn't have been so pleasant to have been assigned to a hospital in Banbury or Swindon.

On this occasion he took the bus up to the stop close by the main entrance. He had never had occasion to go to the hospital in the past, being a generally healthy young man, and he was interested to find that it was a cluster of different styles of buildings sprawled over a hill. Two units covered in grey tiles had the appearance of scientific research centres, nestling next to a building with tall vertical windows and coloured panes of glass that looked like a cathedral attempting to be at ease in a modern age. This in turn abutted two buildings that were even more colourful and resembled nothing so much as piles of giant Lego bricks. He was to learn that these were respectively the Women's Centre, and then – added successively down the hill – the main hospital, the cardiac centre, the children's hospital and the West Wing. The interview was straightforward enough, including what seemed to him to be an absurdly simple intelligence and literacy test. The manager was happy enough for a nine-month placement. The company often recruited undergraduates over the summer, and Giles was promising a longer commitment than usual. He learned that he could start the next Monday morning, and would be put with a more experienced porter to learn the ropes – or, as the manager put it whimsically, the trolleys – for a couple of weeks until he could be trusted on his own.

Having resigned his zero-hours contract with the supermarket with some satisfaction, Giles duly reported to the manager's office on the stipulated day, and was sent to meet an older porter named Gregory. He was fortunate to be placed with Gregory, explained the manager, since he had been with the hospital for decades and was greatly respected by everyone, including the medical establishment. Tall, grey-haired and scholarly-looking, Gregory met him kindly with a steady and keen gaze directed straight into his eyes. Giles warmed to him immediately, and later he was to learn that Gregory was a voracious reader, well-informed in a wide range of subjects, and entirely self-taught without benefit of higher education. He never heard his family name in the whole time he worked in the hospital.

'Like to hear a thought for the day?' enquired Gregory.

A little startled, Giles responded that he certainly would.

'You'll recall that Mother Teresa spent her life caring for the poor and the dying in the slums of Calcutta. Well, she once said, "It seems to us that what we're doing is just one drop in a vast ocean. But remember that the ocean would be less if it missed that drop".'

Giles had the feeling that Gregory had selected that quotation to encourage him on that particular morning. Gregory added, 'I like that better than the more pious things she's recorded as saying. The Pope's just declared her a saint, you know, but I have some sympathy for those who raise questions about her methods of medical care.'

Giles spent the rest of the day shadowing Gregory. He noticed how good Gregory was at calming elderly patients who were to be transferred from a bed to a wheel-chair or a trolley. They were often confused and distressed, asking 'where am I?' and 'what's happening to me?' He would take their questions completely seriously, and would then say something like, 'You've had a lot of experience in life. What tips have you got for younger people like me?' Giles hoped he would, in time, become half as good as Gregory at the job, and said so.

'Thanks, but I'm afraid that portering isn't all that it used to be', responded Gregory. 'We used to be grouped in sections with senior porters coordinating us who were here on the job and could see what was needed for themselves. It was like a sort of family. Now the porter managers sit together in an office and plot our movements over the whole hospital through a computer, following where we are with this personal tracking device we carry around and just sending us instructions by wi-fi.' He pointed to the green line of text on the small screen of the PTD. 'And you'll have noticed that when we've finished the job a nurse or care assistant signs us off by swiping their identity card through the machine. It's quite difficult to interrupt them to get the work approved, and it's like we're being checked up on all the time.' He added, with a sense of fairness, 'I realize it's not much fun for the managers either, trapped in one room all day.'

After a couple of weeks Giles was equipped with his own PTD and followed its instructions to the letter, finding his way over the complicated site whose units were linked by winding corridors and bridges. He still made mistakes, but was getting skilled at pushing chairs, beds and trolleys whose wheels insisted on going in different directions. He had learned the hard way that in taking a patient from Accident and Emergency to the Short Term Medical Ward on the sixth floor he needed to stand with the trolley at the rear of the lift, or he would obstruct the crush of people, some with crutches and all with reproachful looks, trying to get on at the intermediate stops. He noticed that some porters had still not acquired this basic strategy.

One evening after a hard day's work, enlivened only by Gregory's thought for the day ('All the darkness in the world cannot extinguish the light of a single candle', St Francis of Assisi), Giles decided to start an internet adventure. He had intended for some while to follow in Benedict's tracks and explore 'Alternative World' in the form of a unicorn. It was not as straightforward as he had hoped, and he realized that Jacqui had cut out a lot of the detail in aiming to amuse Giles with her story of Benedict in the land of the Middle Ages. After he had registered, he discovered that he had a basic range of avatars to choose from, and none of them were in the least like a unicorn. He could easily, at no cost, modify his avatar with new gender, new body parts, different size and new clothes, but if he were entirely to replace the handsome and muscular young man he had first assumed and take on the form of a fabulous beast, he would need to equip himself with AW dollars and visit the AW store.

There he found dozens of unicorns 'ready to wear' and marked with the pledge of delivery to him in Alternative World 'unpacked and ready for use.' However, many of these avatars were 'petites' unicorns, of the size that Raphael's maiden had carried in her hands, and he realized that in much popular culture unicorns were regarded as denizens of a miniature fairyland. You could also purchase these tiny creatures to follow you around, sprinkling gold dust and scattering rainbows wherever they went. Pink was a favourite colour for these beasts. Larger sizes were available, including 'anthropomorphic avatars' which were half human and half unicorn, of either sex, and distinctly sinister. He remembered the surprising sexual exploits of unicorns he had unwittingly stumbled across on the internet, and wondered fleetingly how the avatars might be employed by their users. But the best way forward was to buy a horse-avatar and then a unicorn conversion kit consisting of mane, hooves and horn in white, black or purple. In a confusion with Pegasus some also came complete with wings. Giles could see that he was going to spend a fair proportion of his week's wages on acquiring a unicorn form, but he decided to persist and chose a conventional white colour. Perhaps there was a clue somewhere in this cyber-world to what had happened to Benedict. If he was willing to pay to fly to Paris, Rome and New

163

York on his quest, he ought – he reflected – to be willing to pay for a cyber-journey.

In his room in Hannah's house he settled down to enter strange regions. He was required to give himself a name, and puzzled over what a suitable unicorn name might be. From the depths of distant memory there rose the name 'Jewel', though he could not think where he had come across it. It took a while to master the art of getting his legs to articulate properly at the click of a mouse, following a sub-menu of directional arrows that appeared on screen, and he was quite proud when he managed to rear and wave his horn. It took him a whole evening to become fully mobile and confident in walking, trotting and galloping around. The next night he transported to the area that was advertised as a 'fairly friendly' place for new inhabitants of the world, called Holiday Island. There he attracted more attention than he had wanted.

At first he had the sensation of being alone in an alien universe, surrounded by empty buildings, but discovered that from another sub-menu he could see what other people or animals were nearby, and could hold conversation either by text ('chat') or by voice ('talk'). If they wished they would take on visibility. He chose a few names at random and decided to use text communication until he was more confident in his cyber-identity. Some of the comments he received were flippant, and he was evidently providing an opportunity for other residents to show off their wit: 'No unicorns on the beach, except on a leash'; 'All unicorn poop must be scooped'. Some, despite the promise of friendly natives, were frankly abusive: 'F off, unicorn. Only humans welcome'; 'Touch me again with that horn and you'll be minced unicorn.' Some were frankly sexual, such as: 'Are you for real? Here's our mobile number – come and horn in on us both,' while he suspected that baffling codes like 'R U a HBB?' were probably sexual. Others were just sentimental, such as 'Unicorn share my dreams' and 'Unicorn, make me a rainbow.'

One conversation was more interesting. An avatar in the form of an attractive young woman enquired, 'Why are you kitted out like that?' and after thinking for a moment he replied, 'I'm expressing outwardly how I feel inside.' He thought that was accurate enough, though somewhat economic with the truth.

'Did you get the name "Jewel" from the Narnia stories?' she went on.

Of course, he thought, that's where he'd come across the name – C.S. Lewis' *Chronicles of Narnia* that he read avidly when he was a child. That's where the unicorn called 'Jewel' appears, fighting on behalf of the good lion named Aslan (who was not, the author underlined, a 'tame' lion). Apparently, in these modern myths the lion and the unicorn were allies rather than opponents. He had failed to notice the religious allegory that critics either applauded or strongly deprecated, but he was grateful that the tales had opened a world of imagination to him that he had been exploring ever since in his literary studies.

'Now you remind me, yes,' he replied.

'So you feel you're in a battle between good and evil, like in the stories?'

'I suppose so, in a way, though the world seems a lot more complicated than that simple dualism.'

'If you insist on travelling through Alternative World as a unicorn you'll find just how complicated it is. Be prepared.'

'Thanks for the advice', he responded. 'Can you give me any other help?'

'In the last of the Narnia stories when Aslan opens a door through a stable into eternity Jewel exclaims that he's come home at last. He's arrived in the land he's been searching for throughout his life, without knowing it's what he wanted all the time. I hope you find the door *you're* looking for.'

It occurred to Giles that this scene must mean a great deal to her, and he resolved to read the book again before too long.

'Another thing', went on his companion, 'You might look up the index of sites to visit under the heading "unicorn", though I advise you to avoid the medieval world until you're more experienced.'

After Jacqui's cautionary tale, Giles had already decided that for himself, and he followed the advice of the friendly avatar and consulted the pop-up menu on the side of the screen. He was fascinated to find a site called 'Unicorn Gallery', which looked harmless enough, and transported there immediately.

A UNICORN DIES

He found himself in front of what seemed to be an art gallery with Greek columns and an ornate door. It was set in a classical landscape of green fields, cypress and olive trees, a winding river and distant mountains. Inside, the walls and an elegantly curved ceiling were entirely covered by paintings and tapestries. The effect was colourful and quite overwhelming. He was amazed and startled to find that all the unicorn images on the postcards he was familiar with were there, together with the Leonardo and others he had never seen before, interspersed by mythical-looking paintings that lacked the unicorn element. He moved slowly round the gallery, bringing up the pictures on the screen in more detail, and becoming increasingly perplexed about how they could all be there, collected so neatly together. It was almost as if someone knew the quest he had been on.

After about ten minutes of examination he became aware from a drop-down map that that there was another avatar in the gallery, identified by the name 'woman_in_red', though he or she obviously intended to remain invisible. He became increasingly uneasy about this behaviour, and his wariness was justified when a group – virtually a crowd – of assorted avatars appeared at the door of the gallery through which he had entered himself. There were humans, fabulous animals and eagles, and they all seemed to be hostile. They started towards him and he instinctively reacted by running – or galloping – towards another door set in the rear of the gallery.

If the situation was already surreal it became even more fantastic when he found himself in a corridor leading off the main gallery. As he ran he caught a glimpse of what looked like a library off to one side, and a little further on a large, antique wooden wall clock. All along the corridor there were doors on both sides. He wondered fleetingly whether they opened into other galleries, but he was too busy manipulating the legs of his avatar to give them much thought. Afterwards he questioned why he had been in such a panic. Like Benedict in the world of the Middle Ages he could have pressed the quit button at any time, and in any case he was not exposed to harm in his own person in what was an online escapade. But in the moment he had become the unicorn, the danger seemed real, and he lived out the scenario someone had prepared for him.

The corridor wound around until it reached a small bridge over what seemed a bottomless chasm beneath, and just before the bridge there hung an impressive large canvas on the wall. He did not have time to examine it, but a woman with a vivid red mouth faced him boldly, her body merging into a background of glittering mosaics of different shapes – squares, triangles, circles, spirals and eyes everywhere. As he ran past he was quite dazzled by the gold and silver shining out from the mosaics and the patterns on her dress. Over the first bridge he came to a second one, and some kind of entrance portal loomed up in front of him, but by now he knew he had lost the race and was about to be brought down by his pursuers, some of whom were already jabbing at him with sharp weapons. He pressed 'quit' and the programme crashed. He had no heart to start it up again.

That night he suffered nightmares in which the vast bath of red water was combined with the winding corridor, linked somehow in his dream-state by the bridges over the void. He woke with a start, sweating and exhausted. Fortunately he was on night duty for the next week, and so was able to sleep in a little longer to recover. Going down late to breakfast he found Rosie having coffee with Hannah in one of their regular meetings. With his online experience fresh in his mind, he could not help giving the two women an edited version of it. He said nothing about his pursuers and his panic-induced flight, but gave them a brief description of his conversations on Holiday Island, the gallery and the corridor. For some reason he left the image of the glittering woman out of his account, and also omitted any reference to the postcards since he'd said nothing to Rosie or Justin about them in their past conversations.

'Sensible woman, that person on Holiday Island who spoke about the Narnia unicorn', was Hannah's comment, 'Sensitive as well. I like the sound of her.'

Rosie too wanted to talk about the interactions on the island, but she reminded Giles that art-history was not her thing.

'I can tell you were impressed by the virtual gallery, but that's not what interests me as a cultural specialist. The avatars on sale in the shop and the comments of the people on the island seem to reinforce the place of the unicorn in popular culture that I told you about. For instance, "HBB" stands for "Hot Bisexual Babe", and some people claiming to be unicorns are happy to be called HBBs. I'd like to reference your experience in an ethnographic paper on myth in the modern world I'm writing, at least in a footnote. Is that all right with you?'

Giles was flattered at the prospect of being enshrined in a footnote, and said so. His talk with Rosie had also given him the idea of discussing suitably-edited accounts of his experience with Justin and Jacqui, who might both have further light to shed from their own expertise.

He made a start by arranging to see Jacqui next morning after he had come off his night shift, meeting at an Italian coffee shop near his lodgings, in the part of Oxford that locals call Jericho. Ordering cappuccino, they were ushered to a table under the shade of an olive tree that was flourishing in the restaurant, with luxuriant dark green foliage reaching from its planting in the floor to a skylight above.

'Is that a real tree, or is it an artificial one?' asked Jacqui as they sat down.

'Real – or perhaps we should say organic', replied Giles. 'Wouldn't you say that an even an olive tree in Alternative World was real in some sense as well? It's surely made of "real" digital pulses of electrons and stored on a "real" computer somewhere. I don't have the proper terms for it, but you're the scientist. Isn't it the *kind* of reality that matters? Why do we speak of a "virtual" world? Don't we just mean it isn't exactly this one?'

'This reminds me of conversations with Benedict that I've really missed', replied Jacqui with a laugh. 'Yes, I'm a scientist, but I think you need to talk to a philosopher or a theologian. We scientists are interested in what works rather than what things are. Thanks for your Facebook blogs from Rome, by the way. Is that why you're talking about olive trees? And what's this new interest in alternative worlds?'

Giles told her, briefly, about his internet adventure, including the gallery in the grove of olive and cypress trees. He missed out the story of the postcards, but did tell her about being hunted, wanting to see how she would react to hearing about a similar escapade to Benedict's. Jacqui remarked that it was probably a good thing that Giles, with so little experience of the

Alternative World, had not tried entering the Middle Ages site without a guide like her. She *was* interested, unlike Rosie, in the gallery, but from the technical rather than the art-history angle.

'Someone went to a lot of trouble to make that', she judged. 'They would have had to raise the money to buy the land, get permission to build, and then have known how to programme it or at least have the skill to use existing templates. It's not the sort of thing you could knock up in a day.'

'Could you have done it?' asked Giles suddenly.

Jacqui seemed taken aback, but quickly recovered. 'Of course, it's well within my own capabilities,' she preened herself, 'but why would I bother? Why would anyone bother? And why go to all the business of adding a corridor to the main hall? I'd say you had a bit of a puzzle here.'

Giles could have added that it was one more puzzle to add to the one he was trying to solve. But even he, with all his suspicions about Benedict's death, could see that it was improbable that someone would construct this elaborate building on the chance that Giles might just wander by there and it would be a good way of warning him off the trail. In fact he had, he believed, been given one more warning, but unless the designer of the gallery knew Giles was going to go online there seemed to be something accidental about the confrontation with him.

Perhaps, thought Giles, Justin might throw more light. He sent him an email and arranged to meet in his rooms at the weekend. Once again he went through the story, this time missing out any reference to the chase as well as to the postcards. Justin smiled at the encounters on Holiday Island, but Giles was fairly sure that he had looked startled and even disturbed when he came to the account of the gallery. He strongly disavowed any acquaintance with Alternative World, but Giles had the feeling that he was keeping something secret. He was reluctant to pass any opinion on the incident, but when Giles pressed him he did come up with one piece of information that Giles thought might be useful in the future.

'I think I can identify the artist of your glittering woman', he said. 'Gustav Klimt created portraits of women like that. Working in the early twentieth century he developed the technique of combining female figures with mosaics and used a lot of gold leaf and gold and silver paint. And he used symbols from the ancient near east like eyes and spirals.'

He went to his bookshelf and pulled down a book on Klimt, showing Giles a 'Portrait of Adele'. 'Is that what you saw, or something like it?' he asked.

Giles was excited. 'Absolutely', he said. 'That's wonderful – it's really cleared up one mystery.'

Oddly, Justin looked anxious at this response. 'I can't see why', he replied discouragingly. 'It's completely the wrong period from the other art you mentioned to me. I'd say it was a bit of a puzzle.'

It's all a puzzle, thought Giles, but I may be on my way to solving it.

16
In class

It had been an uneventful flight. Without incident – as police reports put it, Giles reflected – unless you wished to count being squashed between two male American travellers of a girth that matched their general confidence towards life. Their outlook was on display in the conversation that played to and fro across his hapless body. Not wishing to join the discourse on current events, of a highly conservative political kind, and hoping only to be ignored, Giles had no option but to play the silent meat in the human sandwich. As far as possible he shrunk into his own territory, marked out by the largely ineffectual borders of the arm rests. Some mitigation was offered by the entertainment system, and Giles was grateful for the island of solitude offered by the headphones, even though the sound quality was so poor that he could only surrender to what seemed to be the background noise of the universe.

Further distraction arrived with the meal, spread out across the plastic tray in small pots like colours on an artist's palette, and as he stirred the contents with the plastic cutlery they became even more reminiscent of splurges of viscous oil paint. However, juggling dishes and drinks when the space between the seats was largely filled with heaving flesh searching for ease proved a task of Herculean proportions for his neighbours, and the floor around them gradually began to fill with the detritus of their failed efforts to cope with the location puzzle set them by the airline with the meal. When

A UNICORN DIES

Giles had described to his Facebook friends his plan to experience life at an American college and to visit The Cloisters museum in New York, they had posted conventional messages of envy. He wondered how many would now wish to be in his shoes, or rather, in his seat.

Occasionally, during the eight uncomfortable hours of the flight, Giles dropped into a fitful sleep, waking when his neighbours infringed too abruptly on his space, but he was grateful that in his sleep neither of his dark dreams pursued him – whether falling into a vast basin of water or being chased along an endless corridor hung with paintings. He spent some of his waking hours looking at the two postcards of the tapestries he had come to New York to view, numbers four and six in what he was increasingly confident was a series telling a story. While consuming the bread roll and red wine he had salvaged from his meal tray, he examined the postcards closely, one coming directly from The Cloisters, and the other showing the duplicate of a Cloisters' tapestry which was hanging in Stirling Castle.

Under careful scrutiny, he could readily see that the tapestries came from different hands, or different studios, although they were both marked with the monogram 'AE', with the 'E' reversed. The image of the fourth card, showing the unicorn in captivity in some kind of enclosure, was marked by a pattern of thousands of tiny flowers, which he had come to know from his internet researches as the 'millefleurs' style. The sixth card, showing the unicorn at bay from the hunters, bore no such pattern, but it did show an oak and a holly tree in the upper left hand side, and Giles recalled their appearance in the scene of conflict in the tapestries of the Cluny Museum.

As Benedict had carefully explained to him in the Oxford pub in the last weeks of his life, the image on the fourth postcard belonged to the theme of the 'love hunt', the unicorn as lover captured by his beloved. Benedict had also mentioned the image which had turned up on the sixth postcard, the unicorn about to be killed, and had explained that it belonged to a different kind of hunt, one that allegorized the death of Christ. As he looked at the detail of this card he could just make out that the hunter at the bottom left-hand side had some kind of slogan embroidered on the scabbard that hung beneath his tunic. He recalled what Benedict had told him, that it read 'Hail, Queen of Heaven' in Latin, though he found it impossible to read the letters in the small photograph on the postcard. The hunter was evidently, Benedict had said, the angel Gabriel in disguise, the heavenly hierarch who had greeted Mary with the words, 'Hail, Mary, full of grace' as he gave her the news of the impending conception of Jesus. Presumably the same Gabriel was now marking his imminent death by blowing his horn, a kind of last trumpet. This was the card that carried the ominous message, 'Think you're an archangel? You bastard', but Giles failed to see the link between text and image.

As in his visit to Rome, the connection with Mary also nagged at Giles' mind. There was something significant here he could not quite get hold of. He wondered if the visit to The Cloisters would help him find it. He also wondered why this image was taken from the reproduction in Stirling Castle rather than from the original set in The Cloisters, and why there was a fifth card in-between them. In a drowsy state which anaesthetized him from the behaviour of his neighbours, he felt, rather than witnessed, his descent into Newark airport, pre-warned by the thump of the undercarriage being released and the liturgical bidding of the captain to the flight attendants to take their seats for landing.

Having made his way through passport control and customs, Giles was relieved to find a young man of about his own age holding up a roughly-lettered cardboard sign with his name on it. 'There'll be someone there to meet you', Earl had written, and here he was.

'Hi', the young man greeted him. 'I'm Sam, Sam Warner, and you're rooming with me for the week at Horne Grant College'. He added the information 'We're in the Alpha Muse dorm', or at least that was how Giles heard what he said.

Giles made a mental note that he would have to ask for this curious phrase to be explained in due course, but for the moment he simply felt a pang of disappointment that he would have to share a room with a stranger. This had not occurred to him when Earl had issued his invitation, as no undergraduate at Oxford would have tolerated living with someone else in the same room. Having a mate dossing on the floor for a night or two, or sharing the bed with a boyfriend or girlfriend for the few nights the college permitted at any one time was, of course, a totally different matter.

A UNICORN DIES

Sam had a car in the parking lot, and Giles was surprised to hear that this was not unusual for undergraduate students in the USA. Sam assured him that half the students, about a thousand of them, had their own cars and that this was almost a necessity since Horne Grant College was isolated in a rural area a few miles outside the quaintly named township of Bethlehem. The line of the old nursery rhyme, 'how far is it to Bethlehem?' ran through Giles' mind, and the answer turned out to be about fifty miles west from Newark airport.

As they made their way down route 78 Giles observed dozens of farms alongside the road with rows of fruit-trees, greenhouses and polytunnels, bearing witness to the agricultural specialities of New Jersey in fruit and vegetables. Sam kept to a steady 60 miles an hour, and stayed in the same lane the whole way to Bethlehem. When Giles expressed surprise that Sam was failing to take the opportunity of a clear road for a bit of overtaking and racing, as his peers would have done in the UK if they had the kind of powerful, three-litre car that Sam had, his companion was genuinely shocked. He wanted to keep his licence, he protested; freeways were designed to allow several lanes of traffic to proceed at a uniform speed from one place to another. It was all rather like parallel conveyor-belts, thought Giles, and he could now see why giant computer companies were developing driverless cars.

In their fifty-minute journey, Sam explained that he was an undergraduate student in his third year of a four-year course, named the 'Junior' year. When Giles asked him what subject he was reading, he got another lesson in cultural difference to set alongside road behaviour. He was 'majoring' – and Giles guessed this meant specializing – in Art History and Sociology, but he was required to take courses in most of the other disciplines of the Humanities, and in at least two science subjects. This was, apparently, typical of a 'liberal arts college' of which Horne Grant was an example. Sam did not seem to know of any other form of education, and was amazed to hear that Giles was studying nothing except English Literature for a whole three years.

'Don't you find that tedious?' he asked. 'I admit that it can be a bit frustrating trying to hold everything together in our system, but at least you get an overview of a lot of subjects, and you can try some things out before choosing a major. When I started on my degree I had no idea of doing Art History, but classes with Dr King really fascinated me and at the end of the first year I signed up to this as part of a joint major.'

'No, it's not boring just to study English', Giles replied, 'and there's a huge amount to cover, from Old English to the present day. But I do wish I knew more about art, and about theology as well.' He added, without thinking what he was saying, 'I might be a bit less puzzled about unicorns than I am at present.'

At the word 'unicorn' Sam started violently, and his foot slipped on the accelerator so that for a moment it looked as though any passing police car might confiscate his licence after all. But he quickly recovered and returned to his sedate pace. It appeared that he was going to say something about unicorns, but he checked himself and instead explained the name of the college.

'Patrick Horne Grant was a local lawyer, born in Bloomsbury, which is part of the Bethlehem District. He made good, first practising law in Bethlehem and then entering politics. He became a Democrat Representative in the House of Congress for one of the New Jersey Districts. But here's the point. He had to go to another city, Hackettstown, for his education and so when he made some money and got a reputation he vowed to give Bethlehem its own college. He needed the help of the Presbyterian Church to do this, and so the college has a Presbyterian tradition and we all have to go to chapel at least once a semester. It's not so bad when Dr King shows us some art in the service.'

'So I suppose you come from Bethlehem', commented Giles.

'Oh no', replied Sam. 'I'm from down South like Dr King, in my case from Kentucky. Now we get people from all over.' He added, 'They need the best grades from High School because we're in the second rank of liberal arts schools nationally. Our football team's in the NCAA Second Division as well.'

Giles did not entirely understand the last statement, but he got the general sense that Sam was as proud to be at Horne Grant as his own friends were to be at Oxford. He was inclined to be dismissive about this, until he caught sight of what Sam called 'the Campus'. Having passed through the small township of Bethlehem, with one main street almost hidden under a dense spider's web of overhead telephone wires, they entered stone gate posts bearing imperial-looking lions and he found about 50 acres of rolling parkland dotted about with stately buildings, many of which boasted towers. Tall, white Corinthian columns fronted buildings of mature red brick. There were marble steps everywhere leading down to neatly-trimmed lawns. He could see a sports arena that looked Olympic size, and a football field that would have been coveted by an English first-division team – though he realized that this was a sacred space devoted to American football and not to what Americans call 'soccer'. In several places there were huge parking areas containing the thousand student cars to which Sam had referred, and as they drove towards Sam's residence a van passed them marked 'campus police'. From the tower of a vast Gothic chapel there sounded out a hymn played on a peal of bells.

Later Sam told him that Horne Grant was not unusual. There were over 90 similar colleges in New Jersey, and Giles began to realize that education was on a different scale in the USA. It also, he learnt, cost students more than twice the fee in UK universities, and it had to be paid up-front. Somewhat subdued in spirit as he visualized his own ancient college in Oxford that could have been put in one corner of a Horne Grant parking lot, he followed Sam into his hall of residence – or 'dorm' as he called it – which was marked on the outside by three huge Greek letters, glinting in the winter sunlight. Giles determined to ask Sam about this when he had a chance.

Giles settled into the room he was sharing with Sam for the week, and then followed him to the Student Union for an evening meal in the refectory. Again, everything was on a grander scale than he was used to. There were a whole series of different serveries, devoted to Italian, Mexican and native New Jersey food, long bars of salad and counters piled high with fruit, biscuits, and cake. Serried rows of taps offered a variety of fizzy drinks, coffee, tea, chocolate and milk. If driving down the freeway had helped Giles to understand why driverless cars were a sound investment for the future, the cornucopia of food on display began to explain his situation of entrapment between twin obesities on the plane.

The next day Sam took Giles to Earl King's class on Art History, and Giles met his erstwhile saviour and museum-companion once again. The class was meeting twice a week, for a total of three hours out of the 15 that students were expected to spend in class instruction. In the first class, Earl explained, he would like Giles to describe something of his life in the University of Oxford. It would, said Earl, 'broaden their cultural awareness.' In the second class the next day he wanted Giles to give some account of his research into unicorns in art, including his visit to the Borghese Gallery where they had met.

Giles did his best to communicate the life of an undergraduate at Oxford, but it was difficult to cross the cultural divide. The twenty students in the class were frankly incredulous that Giles sometimes only had one hour of formal tuition a week at which he was obliged to attend, and that more discussion than teaching went on in this hour anyway, with 20 minutes of it taken up by his reading an essay out loud to his tutor. Disbelief was only deepened when Giles related that lectures were usually an optional matter for humanities students, and if students did not feel sufficiently entertained by the lecturer they might leave in the middle. He felt he was wading through a fog of incomprehension when he further reported that undergraduates wrote at least one 3,000 word paper every week, that persistent failure to complete this task might result in a student's being expelled, and yet this serious work contributed nothing in terms of marks to a final grade in their degree.

'The idea is', explained Giles desperately, 'that writing the essays teaches you how to think and develops the critical skills that are tested later in examinations. The point of Oxford is to give you plenty of time to read for yourself in libraries and come to your own conclusions.' He went on to speak about the resources for scholarship that Oxford offered to its students.

'I suppose that the university supplies all its undergrads with laptops linked up to smartboards', commented one young woman.

'Well, not actually yet,' replied Giles uneasily. 'But here's an example of what I mean. I know a visiting student from an American university who went for a tutorial with the great-great nephew of the poet William Wordsworth who was a Fellow in English in one of the colleges. The tutor noticed that the student had failed to bring a copy of the 'Lyrical Ballads' with him, and so reached a copy down from his shelves, which happened to be a first edition signed by the poet, and let him use that for the course of the tutorial. This action, and his inspiring interpretation of the poetry was a life-changing experience for the student, who promptly changed from a science major to an arts major, and went on to take a doctorate in the humanities.'

A murmur ran around the class, some of whom were deeply impressed, but others of whom had not actually heard of either the Lyrical Ballads or Wordsworth. Giles pressed on, and described how he had been allowed to handle for himself the Leonardo da Vinci drawing of 'The Maiden with a Unicorn'. For some reason this made a stronger impact on the group. They wanted to know what it felt like to be so close to a da Vinci, and whether he was afraid that he was going to damage it. Giles suspected that he was basking in some reflected glory from the reputation of the much more famous 'Mona Lisa' – perhaps any da Vinci would have impressed – but it seemed a positive note on which to end his contribution. Earl took over, and summed up differences between the educational systems of their own college and that of Oxford, and Giles judged that he made a good job of assessing their respective strengths and weaknesses.

On the next day, Earl began with a 'pop quiz'. The students had been required to read a chapter from Odell Shepherd's book on *The Lore of the Unicorn* between classes, and a list of questions requiring one-sentence answers was handed out. Five minutes were spent on completing this assignment, and then the results were collected with a warning from Earl that their responses would make some difference to their end-of-semester grades. Giles had to admit that this was a successful means of ensuring that some reading was done, though he thought that beginning a tutorial in this way would probably lead to student revolt in Oxford. Earl then sprang a surprise on Giles.

'Giles told us yesterday about the da Vinci drawing of a maiden with a unicorn. When I met Giles in Rome, I had just visited a painting with a similar theme that I don't believe he got to see. Actually, it's difficult to get into the Farnese Palace where it's a fresco on the wall, because this splendid building's now the French Embassy and entrance is limited. The woman holding the unicorn's neck in the painting there is probably Giulia Farnese, who married the wealthy Orsino Orsini in Rome in May 1489. All the accounts of the time report her to be a most beautiful woman, as her picture shows, with dark hair, black eyes and an ardent spirit. Orsini is said to have been ugly with a squint, so perhaps it's not surprising that Giulia became the mistress of another man – who just happened to be the Pope, Alexander VI. In the rumours of the time she was sometimes called sarcastically "the bride of Christ"'.

Some nervous laughter came from the group, although the joke evidently escaped many of those present, and some seemed to regard it as blasphemous,

'I suppose the painting was made for her marriage,' commented one of the young men in the class, 'like other unicorn paintings and tapestries that you've told us about. It must be affirming her purity and faithfulness.'

'Here's the odd thing,' replied Earl mysteriously. 'It was painted about 1602 by Domenichino, after the palace had been re-built and extended to reflect the new wealth and power of the Farnese family, largely based on the influence of Giula's brother who became Pope Paul III. And *he* had been launched on his career in the Church by Giulia, who persuaded her lover, Pope Alexander, to make him a Cardinal. The coupling of the lady and the unicorn was created long after her death, to fit on the wall of a new gallery, which was mostly decorated by a series called 'the loves of the Gods', painted by Annibale Carracce. This particular painting is highly ambiguous. It shows all the confusions of love. Love can be a messy business, you know.'

Again there was a scattering of nervous laughter in the class. Some did seem to know. But the students were undeniably fascinated. At this point Earl switched on the video projector and the Gallery of the Farnese Palace leapt to vivid life in front of them. The domed ceiling, and the side and end walls were covered in mythological scenes in glowing colours. Earl identified the exploits of divine lovers like Jupiter and Juno, Perseus and Andromeda, Orpheus and Eurydice, and made the point that placed among them were Giulia and the unicorn. Giles felt a sudden shock run through him. All this was familiar to him from his adventure in Alternative World, repeated in many nightmares. He recognized the scene, or something very

179

close to it, as the hall of paintings and tapestries which he had entered in the form of his unicorn avatar and from which he had fled with nameless enemies in pursuit. In the on-line gallery there had hung all the other examples of the unicorn images he had come to know through his quest, but otherwise the appearance of the room was very similar. The only explanation could be that the person who had designed the on-line gallery knew the Farnese Gallery well and had used it as a model.

Giles' head began to spin, his vision swam, and he felt the symptoms of a fit beginning, but he fought the attack and kept conscious. Earl, apparently oblivious to the effect his visual aid was having on Giles, switched to a close-up of the Giulia painting. Giles recognized this immediately as one of the images in the cyber-gallery he had not identified at the time, and now, despite his simmering panic, he observed with interest the way that the unicorn had hooked both its front legs around the maiden's legs, and the way that she was placing both hands around the unicorn's neck to caress it, one high up on the neck and the other lower down. Images from the Ashmolean, Cluny, and the Vatican only showed a one-handed approach, and the Raphael painting from the Borghese Gallery had the baby unicorn sitting in the woman's hands which were clasped like the Mona Lisa's. Giulia's stance was an outright committal. It was the most intimate interaction of the two that Giles had yet seen, and he had recovered enough poise to be able to say this when Earl asked him for his reaction in front of the class.

Earl then switched to the Raphael image from the Borghese. Recovering still further, Giles was able to respond to Earl's invitation to relate his impressions of their visit together. He said nothing about his 'mother and child' theories but spoke about the way that the direction of the woman's eyes, eluding the viewer, seemed to preserve her own sense of dignity about herself and issue a challenge to the viewer. He could see women in the class nodding their approval.

'What about Giulia's eyes in the picture from the Farnese?' asked one of the women in the group. Earl switched back and forward between the slides, and a lively discussion followed.

'Giulia's not looking up at the viewers, or even past us,' commented one of the students. 'She seems lost in a world of her own thoughts, far away.'

The general consensus was that Raphael's woman was boldly confronting the world, while Giulia, with eyes more downcast, seemed to be absorbed in a private contemplation of herself and – perhaps – of her love. Earl seemed pleased with the way that Giles had helped to engage the class, and then added his own comments about the Raphael, largely technical. First he spoke about the over-paintings and the puzzle of the replacement of the dog by the unicorn, but then returned to the question of the eyes.

'The painting reminds us of the more famous painting of the 'Mona Lisa' by Leonardo da Vinci', he told them – though Giles already knew this. Earl had an image of the painting from the Louvre ready on his computer, and it was greeted by a sigh of recognition from the class.

'Raphael saw the painting and made a sketch of it before he painted his own woman', he informed them, and then went on to add a detail that was new to Giles. 'It's possible that he didn't see Leonardo's *Mona Lisa* as we now know her,' he announced. 'A French scientist has used a hi-tech camera on the picture to produce images showing that there was an earlier version underneath, in which Lisa isn't yet smiling, like Raphael's woman. And here's the clincher – she's looking obviously to one side, again just like the Raphael. But what about the Lisa we all know and love?'

The class considered the painting they had thought they knew well. Finally one brave voice spoke out. 'It's difficult to say, but I think she's looking more directly at us, though she's still not – like – exactly in your face.' The class laughed.

Earl smiled his approval. 'Leonardo may have worked on the painting over the years, turning the actual woman Lisa Gherardini, the wife of a silk merchant in Florence, into a mythical being in whom we can find Every Woman. Perhaps she doesn't need to protect who she is with her gaze in the same way as Raphael's woman does – or the actual Lisa did.'

Again he was underlining the element of mystery, and Giles could see that this was the method by which he kept their attention. He wanted them to feel that they were being let into a secret world that others were excluded from, and that there was a game to be played, a conundrum to be solved. For all his bluff heartiness, there was something secretive about Earl himself, felt Giles. He had learnt nothing about Earl's personal life, and did not even know whether he lived on campus or some distance away. He had said nothing about a wife or family, and Giles sensed that he wanted to keep a separation between his home, wherever it was, and his professional life. If anyone was looking askance at them, he was.

The class ended, and Giles reflected that he would hear no more about unicorns until he got to The Cloisters at the end of the week. He could not have been more wrong.

17
Alpha Mu Omega

Lunch in the cafeteria was just ending, and Sam and Giles were sitting together at a window overlooking one of the verdant green lawns outside the student centre building. Suddenly Giles heard a raucous noise outside, and looking up he saw a group of about twenty students bursting out from a house opposite. The house was a neat, stone-built building in a nineteenth-century style, a little Disneyesque in its coy windows and chimneys but attractive enough, and Giles noticed for the first time that it carried proudly on the outside the same three Greek letters that were placed on the wall of the dorm in which he was staying. His attention was now, however, drawn to the students who were wearing a kind of fancy-dress, obviously meant to be vaguely medieval, and one or two – he noticed with a shock – were wearing unicorn heads. The students were raising their arms, jumping about, engaged in small improvised dances, banging a drum and uttering a ragged chant. Giles heard a phrase repeated over and over again in a foreign language, but he could not make out what it was. The row sounded cheerful enough, and the general mood was one of celebration, though Giles caught just an undertone of potential menace. Things, he sensed, could go wrong with this joyous throng or with the people who got caught up with them.

'What the hell's going on here?' demanded Giles. He was still shaken by his experience in class, and was in no mood for further surprises.

'It's the new alpha muse', replied Sam – or at least that was the way Giles heard the words, as he had in the car on the way to the college. 'They're new Greeks, celebrating being made members of the fraternity after the rushes last night.'

He might as well have been speaking the Greek he was referring to, and Giles asked him, impatiently, to tell him more in plain English.

'Don't you have Greek societies at your university?' Sam asked with surprise. Most colleges and universities in the U.S. have student societies on campus called "fraternities" – for men – and "sororities" for women. You get elected to them by the existing Greeks after introductory sessions called "rushes" where you can bid to become a member. Celebrations for successful initiates, or "pledges", happen the day after.'

'I still don't understand the "Greek" bit', complained Giles, 'and what's this about a muse?'

'They're called Greek societies because they've got names usually made up of three Greek letters. I don't know how they began, but they're very old, and used to be really secret societies. Now they're much more open, but they've still got their own rituals. You're looking at the society which has the unicorn as its symbol – so the three Greek letters are Alpha, Mu and Omega. Alpha and Omega come from the Bible, you know. It's a title given to Jesus Christ in the Book of Revelation, meaning 'the beginning and the end'. In between there's an 'm' for 'monoceros', the Greek word for a unicorn. The unicorn, I think, is a symbol for Christ and this fits in with the fact that we're a sort of Presbyterian school. Perhaps being founded by someone whose middle name was "Horne" has something to do with it as well. For short, we're called the "Alpha Mu"s or "AMO"s.'

Things were getting clearer for Giles, but he picked up immediately on the word 'we'. 'What do you mean, 'we'?' he asked. Are you a member?

'Of course,' replied Sam. 'Didn't you know that you're staying in the Alpha Mu dorm?'

Giles was staggered. 'But I'm not a member', he protested. 'I had no idea about all this.'

'That's OK,' said Sam kindly, 'it's just convenient to have you taking up a spare bed. Most Greek societies are national organizations, and have

enough houses on campus for all their members to live together in them.
Here we've got fraternals like that as well, but Alpha Mu Omega is a "local"
society. It doesn't exist anywhere else except at Horne Grant. So it can't
afford housing for all its members, and the college provides a dorm assigned
to the Alpha Mus. It belongs to the college, and the Dean of Students can ask
to use dorm space when he needs it. We voted to allow you in because you
sounded interesting – we've all heard of Oxford and some of us would like to
go there to study some time.'

Giles had a lot of food for thought, and he continued to reflect as the
hubbub outside began to die down. Was it just a coincidence that Earl was
running an art-history class on unicorns in a place where one of the Greek
societies had a unicorn symbol? Or was it part of his academic ploy to
interest students by taking up something they were already familiar with?
Why hadn't he told Giles about the Alpha Mu dorm arrangement? Something
else occurred to him.

'What are they shouting?' he asked. 'Is it some kind of slogan?' 'It's
Greek, I suppose,' he added with a sudden insight.

'Yes, it's '*boulesetai soi monokeros douleusai*', replied Sam speedily,
obviously used to repeating it. 'It's a verse from somewhere in the Bible. I
think it's from the Book of Job, but I'm not sure. It means "Can you bind the
unicorn?"'

Giles recalled that just this verse had been read at Benedict's memorial
service, and reflected that the President of the Unicorn Society in Oxford
would have been able to give him exact chapter and verse. He also thought
that the phrase contained a touch of mystery, as well as a lot of aggression
when re-used by a group of students who didn't want to be tied down to rules
and regulations.

'Tell you what,' said Sam, 'We've got a party in the frat house tonight
for the initiates. Why don't you come as my guest? You can see more about
us close up, as it were.'

Giles hesitated, and then said he'd be glad to come.

That night the party was in full swing when they arrived at the house. Music
blared out from every corner of what Sam explained was the club-room, and

no notice seemed to be taken of the campus prohibition on alcohol, or the state prohibition on drinking under 21. Coke, Dr Pepper and orange juice were on open display for any college authorities who happened to stop by, but Giles saw cans of more potent stuff being circulated in a clandestine way. The fraternity was for men only, but women were present, and Giles suspected that the party wouldn't have worked without the suppressed excitement of relationships being made, progressed and broken all around him. Stacks of pizza, burgers and doughnuts were on offer, and students whom Giles had seen enjoying trays piled high with food in the cafeteria were still tucking in with a hearty appetite, as if they had not seen food for days. His experience in the plane came back to his mind again and he had a mental vision of these young people in twenty years' time when they weren't any longer burning the calories on the track or the football field. Despite his inner warnings about reaping the same fate, he helped himself to a burger, and also accepted an open can of lager surreptitiously pressed into his hand by an unknown benefactor.

'You're the Oxford student, aren't you?' shouted one of the women in his ear over the pulsing beat of the rock music. 'We've heard about what you said in the art-history class.' She added with a smile, 'Would you like to look into my eyes?'

Giles was flattered by her attention, but hastily diverted the conversation as he remembered Hannah. 'Are you a member of a fraternity too?' he enquired. 'What's in it for you?' Recalling the proper language to use, he added, 'How many of the students at Horne Grant are Greeks? How many different societies are there?'

'What a lot of questions', she responded with a laugh. 'In the first place it's sororities for women, not fraternities. I'm a member of the AMO sorority here for women. About a third of the students enjoy Greek life, and there are chapters here for another four societies. What's in it for us? Well, I felt a bit lonely and isolated when I came here. I was missing home and 2,000 students were a lot to get to know. AMO gives me a sense of belonging. I know 50 people really well. It gives me a home-base. I guess that Oxford must be much bigger than Horne Grant. How do you manage there?'

'Every college has a Junior Common Room, and all students belong to it,' he replied. She did not seem to be inclined to follow up these alien concepts, and so he added, 'What do students feel who don't get accepted?'

'You'd have to ask them', she replied, 'though there aren't any here. Tonight everyone's a member or initiate of AMO. But I know some people don't want the extra hassle of membership of a fraternity or sorority, and some know that their GPA just isn't high enough.'

Once again Giles felt he was in a strange world. 'GPA?' he queried.

'Grade point average', she explained. 'You need at least a 3.0 to get in, and the AMOs are really exclusive – we want a 3.5 or you haven't got a chance.'

The numbers, and what they signified, were as Greek to Giles as the letters had been, and in a spirit of earnest research he wanted to ask further questions but the party was getting increasingly noisy and he could hardly hear himself speak. The woman moved away and Giles had a few more fragmentary conversations. He ate and drank more and was beginning to feel he had had enough of the evening when a young man banged loudly on the table and called for silence. He was dressed flamboyantly, in a yellow waistcoat and a bow tie that Giles could just see was covered in tiny unicorns. He had obviously drunk quite a lot out of the circulating cans but was still able to speak fairly clearly. His neighbour nudged him and whispered 'It's the student president of the Alpha Mus.'

'Among us tonight', he articulated slowly and deliberately, 'we have a visitor from across the Atlantic, from the famous Oxford University – that's Oxford, England, not Oxford Mississippi, or Oxford Ohio, or Oxford Massachusetts. He waved a hand dismissively, as if to banish all these other lesser Oxfords to the outer margins of the world. 'Your AMO committee has met, and we want to give him a special sort of initiation to remember us by. Perhaps he might start a chapter of Alpha Mu Omega in Oxford, you never know. Step forward please, Giles.'

Giles was overcome by embarrassment and wished he had returned to the dorm earlier. He felt himself being jostled forward by those around him, and as the crowd parted he found himself facing a chair on which sat an attractive young woman with braided tresses of blond hair, a low-cut bodice and wearing a long skirt. Altogether she had an approximately medieval appearance.

'Meet your maiden', commanded the president in formal tones. More conversationally he added, 'I can't guarantee all the traditional virtues of the maiden, but I think you'll like Abigail.' Returning to his more reverent, if slurred manner, he enunciated: 'Kneel down, Giles, and do the sacred unicorn action.'

Giles hesitated and looked puzzled. He could not think what was meant.

'Put your head in her lap', explained the president. 'Isn't that what all good unicorns do?'

Strong arms pressed Giles down onto his knees directly facing the girl and forced his head into her lap. She spread her legs to make room for him, and as she put her arms round his neck all the images of the maiden and the unicorn he had seen or imagined flooded into his mind. Her embrace was warm, her scent was enticing, her belly soft, her thighs entwined around him and he could feel their supple muscles against his own body. The weight of rounded breasts rested gently on his head. It was not unpleasant, and he felt a curious mixture of impulses. Sexual desire stirred within him, and at the same time a longing for safety and refuge as distant memories returned of burying his head in the lap of his mother. He had the sense that he was searching for entry somewhere he belonged but from where he was, for the moment, excluded. He surrendered himself to the experience as the chant arose around him, '*boulesetai soi monokeros douleusai.*'

But then the hands of the onlookers pressed him further into the girl's lap and he found it more difficult to breathe. He was beginning to suffocate and to choke as the chant grew ever louder. Panic mounted inside him, and images of the hunters who would surely be hidden in the bushes around the maiden came to his mind. He feared what might happen next and felt himself lapsing towards unconsciousness and into a velvet darkness. '*Boulesetai soi monokeros douleusai*' rose the chant again, and as if in answer to the question in the Greek words the pressure on him lessened and he felt himself being released.

'Who will bind the unicorn? You are unbound', intoned the president. 'Arise as a new unicorn.'

Giles scarcely knew how to respond. He did not know whether he had been attacked as an unwelcome outsider or been given a great privilege. He wasn't sure whether the ritual had been done in a spirit of friendship or sarcasm, whether he had been honoured or mocked. Perhaps it was all these at once. Friendship, like love, was – as Earl had said – a messy business. He mumbled something and stumbled off to the edges of the party. A few people congratulated him, but again he couldn't tell what motives lay behind the words. Sam rejoined him and seemed as embarrassed as he was about the whole thing.

'You might have warned me about what was going to happen', complained Giles, feeling that he had been let down by his new friend.

'I didn't know what the President had in mind', protested Sam, 'I'm not part of the house committee. They just asked me to invite you to come. If it's of any consolation, I can tell you that I had the same test myself when I was initiated.'

In a subdued mood the two returned to the room they shared, and Giles dropped into a fitful sleep. He had to admit that he had been sexually aroused by his contact with the young woman in the ritual, but his near-suffocation also triggered recollections of bad experiences in the past, not least the death of Benedict.

When he awoke in the morning he became aware immediately that something was wrong with him. He had a raging headache and felt hot, there was a nagging pain in his stomach, and he felt sick. His muscles were aching and he felt weak. He did not feel like getting out of bed, but shortly had to rouse himself and stagger to the bathroom where he vomited violently and was exhausted further by an attack of diarrhoea. Two more visits in the same direction in the next hour ensured that his stomach was empty of the food he had consumed the night before, and yet his stomach muscles did not seem to get the message and insisted on trying to empty an already voided vessel. Alarmed, Sam summoned the campus medical team, and a doctor diagnosed mild food poisoning. The doctor asked what he had eaten and ventured the guess that Giles had been unfortunate with a burger, left out too long in the atmosphere of a super-heated room in the afternoon before the party and then undercooked. The cafeteria food seemed above suspicion, as there seemed to be no evidence of mass poisoning, or indeed even one other victim.

Giles remained in bed that day and most of the next, nursing a gnawing pain in his stomach and occasional cramps, sustained only by water and supplements the doctor had given him. It was now the Thursday of his week in the USA, and he was due to take the return flight late Friday afternoon. It seemed that his planned visit to The Cloisters on the Friday morning would have to be cancelled. Earl had told him that he had an appointment in Manhattan on Friday morning, and the plan had been for him to take Giles to Grand Central Railway Station nearby his venue, from where Giles would take a subway train to Fort Tryon Park and The Cloisters, giving him enough time to look at the tapestries, have lunch in the café there and then take public transport back to Newark airport. Sam now suggested that, if he felt he could travel, he would take him directly to Newark airport the next afternoon.

Giles was bitterly disappointed. He could not but conclude that once again he was being prevented from looking at the originals of Benedict's postcards. Had someone slipped something toxic into his drink or food, with the expectation that he would be too ill to make his visit to The Cloisters? Had it got anything to do with the sudden appearance of the gallery of paintings in Earl's video show? Giles was also worried that he seemed to have lost the fourth postcard showing the image of 'The unicorn at bay' from the Cloisters series, and he wondered whether anyone had taken it from his shared room. Fellow-students were in and out to see Sam all the time, and it was clear that no work got done in his room which was effectively consigned to being a social area.

On Thursday evening, however, Giles began to feel better and even managed to eat the bananas and dry toast recommended by the medical team. Sam sent a message to Earl and a conversation ensued over the mobile phone. Earl tried to persuade him to abandon the trip, urging him strongly to play safe and not endanger his health with the extra effort needed to traipse about over New York and take the long walk uphill to The Cloisters. He'd like to take him directly to the museum, he explained, but he could not cancel his meeting with a publisher. Giles had insisted, and Earl finally had to give way. Feeling more optimistic about his situation, Giles took an hour that evening to post photos of the impressive campus on his Facebook 'wall', and to blog about some of the more amusing differences between student life there and in Oxford, but he took care to say nothing about the unicorn ritual.

The next morning Giles bade a warm farewell to Sam, whom he had come to regard as a friend during their eventful week, promising to keep in touch by email. The journey to Manhattan in Earl's car was a largely silent one. Earl was unusually quiet, and Giles slept most of the way in a state of exhausted recovery from the ravages inflicted on his internal organs over the last couple of days. The silence was broken for a while when Earl gave Giles careful directions. From Grand Central he was to take the number 7 line to Times Square station. Earl had consulted the subway map, he said, and it seemed that for the next leg of the journey he should change onto the number 1 line going uptown and to get off after a 30 minute journey at Dyckman Street. Leaving the station he should turn left down Broadway and after a 5-minute walk take a path entering Fort Tryon Park. It all seemed easy enough to remember, especially the number 1.

After suitable farewells and thanks, Giles got out of the car outside Grand Central Station and hefted his rucksack onto his back. He wondered whether he should have felt more regretful that he was unlikely to see Earl again.

18

The Cloisters

rand Central Terminal was grand. There was no doubt about that, thought Giles. Huge columns framed three tall arched windows, surmounted by a massive cornice which in turn was topped by a sculpture of figures surrounding an ornate clock. The effect, it seemed to Giles, who had some practice now of looking at paintings, was to draw the eye both vertically and horizontally at the same time. The result was to yield a sense of the unlimited, even the sublime. It was an unexpected marvel, nestling in its classical grandeur among the towering skyscrapers of Manhattan, the older stone contrasting dramatically with the glass and steel of modern life.

If the outside was impressive the Main Concourse inside was astonishing. Giles found himself inside a vast hall, which he estimated to be roughly 300 by more than 100 feet. Marble covered the floors and walls, and stately balconies with winding stairs bordered it on three sides. Lofty windows on east and west with lunettes high in the ceiling overhead let in light which gave the marble a translucent appearance, while arches led off on all sides over which the inscriptions pointed to 44 platforms and more than 100 tracks. But what struck his eye most was the blue-green dome of the ceiling, covered with mythological figures which Giles realized after a second or two marked out the heavenly constellations, through which points of light shone like the major stars. While the hall was filled with several thousand travellers, its size gave it a kind of awed hush which one would expect to find in a church or art gallery. And it was a gallery that Giles was reminded of immediately.

Weakened by his days in bed and the repeated evacuations of his body, Giles recognized that the lapse into unconsciousness he had resisted on several occasions during the week was about to overtake him. The Main Concourse swam around him and was transfigured first into a larger version of the Farnese Gallery shown him by Earl, and then into the cyber-hall of images he had experienced through his avatar. He realized he was sinking to the ground and, just as his eye had been drawn vertically and horizontally by the facade of the station, he seemed to experience both familiar nightmares concurrently – simultaneously falling into an immense pool of water and chased along an endless corridor – or perhaps one followed the other with the absence of time that often marks dreams.

When he regained consciousness he found himself the centre of a concerned group of people, one offering him a glass of water and another asking if he wanted to go to hospital. Grateful for the water, he rejected firmly all mentions of medical help and lurched unsteadily to his feet. The people around appeared relieved that no more was required of them at a time when getting to work was the urgent matter at hand, and after sitting for a while on the marble steps of one of the balconies Giles made his way through one of the arches underground to the subway.

Here the mood of his surroundings changed totally. While above all was airy with an extravagance of space, built on the principles of lavish generosity, below ground all was confined and cramped. Narrow corridors, whose walls were faced with what looked like the cheapest lavatory tiles, converged on each other in a rabbit warren for commuters. Bare steel columns were topped by iron girders, through which it seemed that hundreds of travellers were slowly crawling. Narrow circular stairways wound up and down linking the corridors, issuing onto platforms which were scarcely wider than the yellow danger zone provided on the platforms of the London Underground. Following the signs to line 7 Giles turned a corner at the bottom of the stairs and followed a path no more than three feet wide between the stairway and the railway tracks. He was surrounded by a hundred jostling commuters, and feared that he was being pushed remorselessly towards the edge of the platform.

While there was no evidence of an attack, afterwards he wondered whether some of the pressure might have been deliberate, and even questioned whether he had been followed into the main concourse by someone determined to stop him, who had witnessed his moment of weakness and decided to exploit it. The possibility even flickered into his mind that it was Earl, but he suppressed the thought as paranoid. As it was, a voice had shouted 'watch out!' and helpful hands had guided him back against the wall, so that he had arrived safely at the platform for line 7 and taken the subway train to Times Square as directed.

There he changed platforms for line 1, walking through the same kind of iron landscape as at Grand Central. It felt like being inside a machine, supplying in his own person with many others the moving parts of some manufactured engine. He had never felt so much like a product of industry. In the train compartment the theme continued as everything felt hard – polished fibreglass seats, plastic floor, stainless steel walls. At Dyckman Street station he got off according to instructions, and found himself in a similar confined environment. Of a 'Broadway' there was no sign. The street was full of traffic, but narrow and made even narrower by road works. Buildings around were crumbling, the shops which lined the street were shabby, people hurried along with eyes fixed to the ground and there were piles of rubbish everywhere. Nothing seemed less like a neighbourhood which housed a large park and a museum of medieval art. Giles began to panic, a frame of mind not helped by his residual weakness. Would he have sufficient time to get to the museum and then back to Newark airport? He checked the name of the station several times. It was indeed Dyckman Street, but where was this Broadway?

He began to walk along the road, with the hope that the name would change further along, as often happened. But the further he walked the more despair he felt. Seeing a road-crossing attendant, wearing a yellow hi-vis jacket, he asked whether she knew where The Cloisters were. She had never heard of them, was the reply. But then he looked up, and saw in the distance, on a kind of hill, a building that looked a little medieval in aspect. He thought he could see a tower. He drew attention to it, but she had no idea of what it was, and seemed never to have noticed it before. Nevertheless, he crossed the road and began to walk along a side street in the direction of this sign in the sky. Meeting another crossing attendant – at least, he reflected, this part of the city was safety-conscious – he enquired again. Once more, the attendant had never heard of The Cloisters, and professed complete ignorance of the building that Giles showed him. But he did know where Broadway was, and pointed up the side street two blocks ahead. Encouraged, and growing in hope, Giles forged on.

Broadway turned out to be like its name, and very different in atmosphere from the huddle of streets several blocks down. At the junction at the end of the street was another station, different from the first, but also named 'Dyckman Street'. He resolved to solve the puzzle later, and quickly turned onto a path leading into a large park, the track winding round and up a large hill bordered by stone walls with vistas over grass and stately trees, mostly bare at this time of year. The golden leaves of Autumn were fallen everywhere, carpeting the path with a soft, yielding surface very unlike the hardness of the subway. A line from Milton's *Paradise Lost* entered his mind: 'Thick as autumnal leaves that strow the brooks in Vallombrosa...' The view also included a vista of the surrounding area of the city, and he could just make out the two road crossings whose guardians had never looked up to wonder about the treasure-trove that was placed above their heads.

As he made his way up the path to his destination at the top of the hill, all his emotions changed. Images of mother and child were constantly in his imagination, and now a more organic picture superimposed itself over his sense of having been trapped in a machine on his journey. It seemed that after inhabiting the spacious womb of the Main Concourse he had been pushed into and through the constricted birth canal of the subway and of the narrow streets below the hill. Recovery and strength grew upon him as he climbed towards the pale light of the Autumn day. He had been in the valley of the shadow for the last couple of days and reached the lowest pitch four levels down in the subway on track 7. From there he had risen, and the phrase 'resurrection on the third day' sprang to his mind. He felt renewed, born again. It crossed his mind that leaving the subway at Dyckman Street as he had been instructed had resulted in one more obstacle to getting to the unicorn tapestries, but he pushed the thought to the back of his mind and determined to enjoy the walk and the visit.

In this exalted mood he climbed the stairs into the museum, left his back-pack in the cloakroom and paid a voluntary entrance fee at the entrance counter. He made his way into one of the cloisters that gave the building its name, transported (so said the information card on the wall) from a twelfth-century monastery in the Pyrenees. A fountain played at its centre, surrounded by plants, and Giles could well have lingered to enjoy the tranquillity, but he walked forward into a Gothic hall which led towards the 'Hall of the Unicorn'. In the first hall he discovered clustered together no less than three statues of Mary with the Christ-child, which information cards told him were from thirteenth and fourteenth century France. The same cards informed him that in these artefacts Mary took the form respectively of the 'throne of wisdom' – her lap providing a seat for the child Jesus as the divine wisdom – a courtly lady and the 'Queen of Heaven.' With mounting excitement he passed by them towards the room of the tapestries, entering through a doorway of volcanic stone surmounted by a shield featuring two unicorns.

Standing in the middle of the hall, he had the sense of being immersed into a sea of shapes and colours, with most of the tapestries full of movement like restless waves. He saw immediately the origin of the fourth of Benedict's postcards. It hung to the right of a large window which looked out onto the cloister. He was familiar with the image of 'The Unicorn in Captivity' from the postcard he had studied dozens of times before he had lost it. The unicorn lay in a fenced enclosure, with a dense mass of flowering plants sprinkled over the ground inside and outside the circular garden. But now, seeing it in actuality, several new impressions came to him. One came directly from his experience of initiation among the Alphas Mus, though he had not been particularly grateful for it at the time. This round enclosure, he thought, was itself a kind of lap. There was no need for a tapestry showing the unicorn literally laying its head in the maiden's lap, even if there had once been such a portrayal in this series which was now lost. The unicorn rested in the most intimate garden of his lover's body, outside and inside.

A second impression was the sheer vitality of the scene. Everything was alive to an ultimate degree – the small flowers, the tree to which the unicorn was chained, and a larger flowering plant right in front of the fencing. Though the unicorn carried a wound on its chest – presumably a wound of love – this had done it no harm; to the contrary, the unicorn was alert and sprightly, with bright eye, lifted head and bouncing tail. The collar by which he was chained to the tree stood out in vivid blue, drawing attention to itself. This utter liveliness contrasted with the mood of the tapestry on the left hand side of the window, showing the beginning of the hunt of love which was ending in the chained beast. This tapestry too was covered in hundreds of small flowers, and showed five hunters with five dogs setting out on their expedition, with a sixth figure acting as a scout among the trees. Compared with its paired tapestry, however, there was something about this picture that was pedestrian – not only in the literal sense that the hunters were walking and not yet running, but also in a certain static quality. It was pleasant enough, but it only threw into relief the vivacity of the unicorn, though in captivity. The observer got the impression that to be captured by love, to be committed irrevocably to the beloved, was the most delightful life imaginable.

Giles thought he could now understand the message of the fourth postcard. The sender was saying: 'you are caught in my love for ever and this is life for us both'. If the third postcard had been calling for commitment, this one was celebrating a commitment that had been freely given, since no unicorn could be caught unless it consented to enter the lap of the beloved. The story had moved on to a stage of mutual promise and pledge of faithfulness. Giles was deeply stirred by the narrative he had discovered, and it moved him in turn to make his own resolve – that he would declare his love to Hannah when he returned to Oxford.

Giles had now resolved the enigma of the fourth card, at least to his satisfaction, and strictly speaking he knew he should wait for his visit to Stirling Castle to unravel the mystery of the sixth one. But there on the walls was its original, and he gave some attention and thought to it. It appeared to be the third tapestry in a set of four, which he had already decided was a different series from the two on each side of the window. The first group showed the first kind of hunt, or the 'hunt of love', featuring the capture of the unicorn through the lure of a maiden. The next four tapestries, beginning on the right hand wall and continuing around the remaining two, made up a second kind of hunt, the 'religious' hunt, or the allegory of the passion and death of Christ. Since writing his essay on the unicorn for his tutor in Oxford, an event that now seemed ages ago, he had been aware of this second kind of hunt, and Benedict had spoken about it in his conversation with Giles and Emily in the pub. But this was the first time he had seen it portrayed. He could now see how the image on his sixth postcard, called 'the Unicorn at Bay' came after the first two tapestries hanging on the walls, named on their information cards 'The Unicorn is Found' and 'The Unicorn Leaps out of the Stream', and how it was followed by the final tapestry called 'The Unicorn is Killed.'

In the first episode of this second series, the huntsmen were gathered behind a marble fountain, and the water in the basin was spilling out through the mouth of a lion mask into a stream running below it and across the foreground of the tapestry. The unicorn was kneeling in front of the fountain and dipping its horn into the stream. Giles immediately recognized the theme. Just as the President of the Oxford Unicorn Society had recounted the myth, the unicorn was purifying the water of any poison with the antidote of its horn. Grateful animals who were to drink the water clustered around him – a couple of lions, a panther, a genet, a hyena and a stag. Giles supposed that if the unicorn represented Christ, then he must be cleansing the world of sin through his death which was shortly to be portrayed in the remainder of the series.

Giles looked at the huntsmen standing back from the basin, oddly not pursuing the unicorn of whom they had caught sight for the first time, and the sight triggered a memory in his mind. He had, not long ago, been invited to the baptism of the young child of a cousin, and the huntsmen here looked just like the congregation there. They were standing around the basin which was like a font, and witnessing a sacred action. If this was indeed the first episode in a hunt which was an allegory of the passion of Christ, this must represent the baptism of Christ through which he began his ministry of purifying human life. Giles spent some time working through the detail of the tapestry, and decided to come back to it when he had viewed the others.

The second episode depicted the unicorn jumping out of a stream, and Giles supposed that it had entered it with the aim of depriving the hounds of its scent, just as a stag would do when hunted by hounds. In fact, this second series had no reference to a maiden. The hunting and killing of the unicorn, representing Christ, was apparently being modelled, Giles realized, on the way that a stag hunt usually proceeded. Three of the scent hounds had entered the river in pursuit of the beast, and four hunters with their two greyhounds had positioned themselves on the far bank to attack the unicorn as it emerged from the river. Another five hunters and four dogs remained on the hither bank, and altogether four spears in a circular formation were directly pointing at the unicorn which occupied more or less a central position in the picture. Despite its hazardous situation, and the blood streaming down its rump from a dog bite, Giles had the impression that the unicorn was the master of the scene. Its horn, standing proudly upright, seemed more than a match for the threatening spears. The beast seemed full of strength and vitality, giving the confident impression that it could break free and outrun its hunters at any time it wished. The light glinting off the leaves of the surrounding oak trees and holly bushes accentuated this sense of energy.

The same impression was given by the third episode, which was Giles' sixth postcard, 'The Unicorn at Bay'. Although the attack on the unicorn was accelerating, all the hunters surrounding it and the hounds jumping up in a frenzy around the beast, the unicorn at the centre was still moving with balletic grace, rear legs kicked up in the air, front legs firmly planted on the ground and horn pointing down to gore one unfortunate dog. The hunters were poised to deliver the death blow with their spears, but Giles got the odd sense that if it wished, the unicorn could still escape and save its life. Giles noted the presence of the angel Gabriel disguised as one of the hunters, blowing his horn, whom he had first noticed on examining the postcard. Close up to the tapestry he could now read the slogan on the scabbard of his sword. Benedict was right: it was 'Ave Regina C.', or 'Hail Queen of C.', and he had just enough Latin to know that the 'C' was short for 'Caeli', or heaven. But he resolved to give more attention to this scene when he finally got to its copy in Stirling, and he passed onto the final episode of the series in front of him.

This tapestry, named 'The Unicorn is Killed and brought to the Castle' showed a complicated scene made up of two episodes. Giles saw that the top left section of the tapestry represented the death of the unicorn at the hands of the hunters. On a hillside the beast was faced by two hunters thrusting spears into its neck and chest, down which blood was streaming, while hounds were jumping up and biting it. Another hunter was slinking in from the rear to deliver the death blow with his sword. A hunter with a yellow cap was blowing a horn, and it seemed that the blood of the unicorn was dripping down into the mouth of the horn like a chalice.

In the foreground of the tapestry the final episode was being played out. The dead unicorn, slung across the back of a horse, was being brought back to a castle, with dogs and hunters walking alongside. Round the neck of the unicorn was a wreath or crown of oak twigs that seemed to have sprouted thorns, identifying the unicorn as Christ. One of the hunters was grasping its horn with one hand, while gesturing with the other to the richly-dressed man and woman who were coming out of the castle to the right, evidently its lord and lady. The pair were, Giles noticed, not looking at all happy despite having presumably arranged the hunt. They were wearing what seemed to be expressions of deep sorrow.

Giles stood in the middle of the room and let his gaze pass over the four episodes, moving backwards and forwards. At that point what seemed like a revelation struck him. A conviction suddenly gained hold on his mind that was nothing to do with the message of the fourth postcard with its joyous assertion of commitment. The story played out before him was of someone who had willingly given himself up to death. The unicorn, representing Christ, had died violently but not simply as a hapless victim. The key was in the first tapestry of the series, an image of purifying the water which, when it became an allegory for baptism, was easily understood as cleansing sins *through* water. Was it possible that Benedict had thought he was somehow making atonement for sins through dying in water? Benedict had said he was familiar with the tapestries. Had he intended to replicate the stone basin of the fountain in the bath where he had slit his wrists? Who could tell what curious connections were being made in his original and fertile mind in a state of anxiety and depression, exacerbated by the LSD he had taken? In a state of drug-induced hallucination, had he taken on the identity of the unicorn?

Hannah had certainly spoken about a mysterious sense of guilt that Benedict carried with him all the time. Perhaps, in addition to his own sins, he dared to think – with the help of a mind-transforming drug – that he was sharing in the sufferings of the Christ who took away the sins of the world. Basin and bath merged together in Giles' vision as the room swam around him for a moment.

Giles was having to revise all his assumptions. He had always intended to keep an open mind, but had – he realized – become fixated on the belief that Benedict had been murdered. He began to think that Detective Inspector Longley was right all along with his judgement of suicide 'while the balance of mind was disturbed'. Hannah had found it difficult to believe that Benedict had taken his own life, but she was curiously opposed to accepting that the postcards contained clues to a murder. She seemed to have been right about that. All the incidents that had happened which seemed designed to stop him from visiting the originals of the postcards could just be coincidences. Everything could be explained as an accident, even his most recent experiences, down to getting off at what appeared to be the wrong station. He recognized that he was – as Hannah put it – accident prone. A sense of relief swept over him, and he felt he had been released from a nightmare. Benedict had taken his own life. He could forget about his own unicorn hunt and go home to Hannah.

There were, however, some loose ends that were still worth clearing up to satisfy his own curiosity. How did Benedict get from the state of mind disclosed in the fourth postcard – a captive of love – to the despair that was revealed by his suicide? How was the gap to be bridged between the two stories Giles could see depicted on the walls in front of him? Then there were still two postcards to be followed up, and there was the odd business of how Mary and the whole mother-child motif fitted into the unicorn narrative. He was, in fact, perplexed by the apparent absence of Mary from the second set of tapestries, especially as she was much in his mind from passing the three statues in the outer hall. She was perhaps present by implication because Gabriel was there, and his greeting to her – 'Hail, Queen of Heaven' – was included in the third tapestry of the series. This was the scene reproduced on his sixth postcard ('The Unicorn at Bay'), though – curiously – from the copy at Stirling Castle. He noticed that the Gabriel-hunter in that episode was the only figure wearing a gold-coloured cap, a kind of substitute halo, and then saw that there was one figure in each of the four tapestries wearing a gold or yellow cap. Perhaps Gabriel was there, a hidden presence, in each of the scenes.

It was then that Giles glanced up to the lintel of the unicorn doorway and saw two fragments of tapestry hanging high above the door. They seemed to be two parts of one torn tapestry which belonged to neither of the two series he had been looking at. The left hand piece showed a hunter hiding among the trees and bushes outside a fenced enclosure that looked like the one in the 'Unicorn in Captivity' tapestry, although this one lacked the 'millefleurs' design. The hunter had two dogs with him, and was blowing his horn. The second fragment showed the enclosure again, but the scene was now inside it. A tall woman in a red dress was looking slyly at the hunter outside, and was apparently betraying the unicorn to him. The beast was couching down, its gaze transfixed by someone who was missing from the fragment, but whose hand could just be glimpsed holding its neck. Two more dogs were inside the fence, one biting the unicorn's back and causing two streams of blood to flow down. This was the familiar 'unicorn with the maiden' theme, and so did not, it seemed, belong to the allegorical hunt. But who was the woman in red? Was she the elusive Mary? That hardly fitted in with her presentation as a deceiver and betrayer.

Giles gave up the attempt to work it out, and made his way out of the hall. Everywhere he looked as he quickly passed other exhibits seemed to confirm his conclusion about Benedict. Over the doorway of the outer Gothic hall was placed a fourteenth-century fresco from Tuscany in which Christ displayed his wounds, freely received. The figure was rising out of a stone receptacle that looked equally like a tomb and a font. Next to the gift shop stood a reconstructed chapel from Spain, and at its doorway was an eighth-century stone sarcophagus that the information label said had been converted from a container for the dead into a font, adapted ingeniously by adding a hole in the corner for the water to run out. Giving Giles further pause for thought, this object was decorated with a medallion showing Mary and the Christ-child. Giles recalled his many nightmare visions of basins of bloody water, and they all now seemed to point to Benedict's surrender of his own life.

In the shop he purchased another copy of the 'Unicorn in Captivity' image to replace the one he had lost, and also bought copies of all the other unicorn tapestries in the hall.

'Wouldn't you like to buy one of the guidebooks to the unicorn tapestries?' enquired the young woman serving at the counter. 'It includes an explanation of all the symbolism.'

'Thanks,' replied Giles, 'but it's really too bulky and heavy to go in my rucksack.' He added with the confidence of youth, 'Anyway, I think I've figured out most of the meaning myself. I've seen a lot of unicorn pictures already.'

'Well, can I help you with anything you don't think you've worked out?' the young woman persisted generously.

Giles wanted to respond to her offer, and something did occur to him. 'You know the scene where the dead unicorn is carried, slung across the back of a horse, to the palace of a nobleman and his wife. Why do they look sad when they've arranged the hunt in the first place?'

'Good question', replied the woman. 'They're probably meant to be Adam and Eve. They're responsible for the hunt because it was their disobedience in the Garden of Eden that brought the sin into the world which Christ has expiated through his death. They look sad because salvation has needed the sacrifice of the Son of God.'

Giles thanked his informant, though he realized afterwards that he really should have asked about the woman in red, and was at a loss to know why he had not. He was certainly anxious to get to the airport on time, and he was aware that he had spent longer looking at the tapestries than he had intended.

He quickly made his way down the leaf-strewn path to Broadway, his head full of thoughts about his discoveries in the Unicorn Hall and his new conviction about the fate of Benedict. He could hardly wait to get back to Oxford to confess to Hannah how right she had been, and to declare his love for her. He turned left down Broadway instead of returning to the narrow streets from which he had come earlier, and soon arrived at the second station he had seen named 'Dyckman Street.' Here he now understood his previous mistake. This was the Dyckman Street Station on Line A, where the other had been on Line 1. It seemed that Earl had misread the subway map and told him the wrong line. As he travelled back towards Times Square the train took on a different, less depressing aspect than before. The hard seats were the same, but now he saw opposite him a young woman carrying a violin and accompanied by her young child. They were obviously delighting in each other's company, and he wondered whether the child would soon be listening to the mother's music-making. As he got off the subway train at Times Square he heard a different kind of music, an infectious beat coming from a young black man drumming up a storm of sound from a set of plastic buckets, singing along and throwing in some snatches of rap between the syncopation. Like others, Giles could not help but smile and enjoy being serenaded as he waited for the Express Airport Bus to Newark. It seemed a small return for such a gift to throw in a couple of dollars to his proffered plastic cup.

Giles' elevated mood continued as the bus bounced and rattled its way over uneven roads towards the airport freeway. Fifteen minutes along the freeway, however, some of his former sense of weakness from his illness returned, and with it a more sombre outlook. On each side stretched an industrial wasteland. Heaps of gravel bordered the road, deserted factory buildings erupted between them, vast parking lots and container parks filled the flat landscape, pylons and rusting bridges dotted the desolate scene and in the gathering darkness Giles could just discern ponds and pools of stagnant water everywhere. As he boarded the plane an hour later he reflected gloomily that it was not only in tapestries that toxic water needed to be purified.

19
Another death

'Do I gather you think she's pretty satisfied with how things are going?' enquired Hannah. They were sitting, as usual, at the kitchen table on the evening of Giles' return to Oxford.

'She or he', responded Giles. 'You'll remember that we're not being dogmatic about the sex of the sender of the postcards. But yes, I think the maiden, or the person using her as a mask, believes that Benedict has given the commitment that she – or he – desires.' As soon as he said this, he realized that this was not news that would be received altogether well by Hannah as Benedict's fiancée, even some time after these events.

'So we've got to stage four of the story', Hannah summed up. The first message is 'I think there may be some attraction here', the second is 'You inflame all my senses', the third, 'When are you going to make a commitment?' and the fourth 'We're going to be happy ever afterwards.'

'Well, yes, more or less,' replied Giles, amused as ever at her briskness, but feeling that this brief account did not quite do justice to the complexity and depth of emotion he had been experiencing as he viewed the artworks that had yielded up the narrative.

'And what about the list of suspects for murder, at least as you see them?' enquired Hannah. 'I suppose that on the male side you suspect the secretive chaplain, the angry former school-mate and the unstable undergraduate. Then, according to you, there's the unknown sender of the postcards. But if the supposed maiden is happy about the way the relationship is developing, it's a bit of a stretch to see her as the murderer.'

Giles could have replied that something must have gone tragically wrong to interrupt the running smooth of the true course of love, or Hannah would not have been Benedict's fiancée, but he had something more important to say. Now that some of the immediate impact that the tapestries had had on him had drained away, he no longer had the absolute conviction about Benedict's suicide that had come to him in the moment of revelation in the museum, but he still sincerely felt that this was the most probable explanation of what had happened. He swallowed hard, his throat went dry, and he croaked rather than spoke.

'Actually, I think I may have been wrong all along about the postcards. I'm not completely sure about it, but I'm now inclined to believe that they don't point to a murderer. In fact, I'm beginning to think that Benedict wasn't murdered at all, but was so unhappy about something that he took his own life.'

Hannah appeared thunderstruck. 'I suppose I'm glad you're not obsessed with the cards any longer, since I didn't think this was doing either you or Benedict's memory any good. I don't know what to think about Benedict's death itself. I'm still a bit doubtful about suicide, but perhaps there's no other answer. Are you sure about this? The unicorn hunt has meant such a lot to you – are you really going to give it up?'

'Well, no,' replied Giles, 'I didn't mean that. There are puzzles about the unicorn symbolism that I want to work through, and I do want to explore the meaning of the other two cards. There's a story there, I'm certain, but I'm going to be much more cautious about the idea of murder from now on.'

'I think that's all I can expect at the moment,' replied Hannah generously. 'What brought you to this change of mind? Was it something that happened at the college or at the museum? Do tell me about it.'

Giles gave her a brief account of his eventful week, and his thoughts about the second series of tapestries in the museum. He had, of course, already related his conclusions about 'The Unicorn in Captivity'. Hannah showed particular interest in the AMO ritual. 'Tell me again how the initiation went, in more detail', she asked.

Greatly daring, Giles asked, 'Will you let me show you?'

Hannah hesitated, looked him straight in the eyes, smiled and then replied, 'Yes, all right.'

Trembling a little, Giles got down on his knees in front of her and placed his head in her lap. She put her arms around him. Unlike the young woman in the Alpha Mu house, Hannah was wearing a short dress, and as Giles demonstrated how his head had been pushed deeply into Abigail's lap, there were almost inevitable results. Whether it was because Hannah had been moved by his giving way about the death of Benedict, or whether she really did reciprocate his intense feelings about her, Giles was not sure, and just at that moment did not greatly care. This was the situation he had imagined about all the way on the plane from Newark, and a deep spring of joy welled up within him, akin to the sense of blissful life he had felt emanating from the tapestry of the unicorn in captivity, lying chained among the thousand flowers. He was at last entering the garden of earthly delights, the fenced enclosure which was opened to a unicorn who submitted to be wounded by love. The scents and the moisture of the garden enveloped his senses as, with exquisite kindness, Hannah bent over him and fulfilled the promise of the many images by grasping the horn of the unicorn. She took him by the hand and led him upstairs.

The next morning Giles woke up, somewhat jet-lagged, but almost entirely recovered from his bout of illness, to find himself in Hannah's room rather than his own. Clothed in her usual honesty, though – charmingly – in little else, she said, 'I'm not sure there's any future in this, but I'm really fond of you and I'm glad we've had this time close together. I think it's better not to repeat it, at least until we're more certain about each other. It's also a bit soon for me after the loss of Benedict. I don't feel I'm ready for a new relationship yet. Don't you agree?'

All Giles' resolves about telling Hannah that he loved her dissipated in face of this bracing, practical realism, and he lost the courage he had gained in face of the tapestry of the chained unicorn. He told himself that he would be more convincing about his feelings for her, and would be more worthy of her, if only he could show her the solution to the riddles that remained about the postcards. So, with some disappointment, he consented to her proposal and returned to his own room. It would be difficult to live so close to her in this state of separation, which he felt to be an expulsion from the garden no less than had been experienced by the Adam and Eve of the final tapestry in the series on the fatal hunt of the unicorn, but he determined to be faithful to his lady and to win her at last through persistent devotion.

A first step in what he felt to be his 'new life' (he had a vague memory of Dante's *vita nuova*) would be to go and have a frank conversation with the chaplain, Dr Goodall. Now that he was released from harbouring the hostile suspicion he had felt earlier they might have a more productive exchange. On his next half-day off from the hospital, he made his way to the chaplain's college on the off-chance that he would be in and free from teaching. He had thought it more politic not to give him warning by email. Entering St Paul's College by the lodge he found the chaplain's archway in the main quadrangle, knocked and waited. The chaplain opened the door, welcoming smile at the ready, but the smile disappeared and he seemed about to close the door forcefully when he saw it was Giles.

'I'd be grateful if you could spare a few minutes,' interjected Giles quickly, 'You could really help me. I'm sorry if I was at all rude last time we met.'

The chaplain hesitated, and then seemed to recall his pastoral duty. 'You'd better come in,' he said reluctantly, 'but I hope you realize that nobody was more sad than I when poor Benedict took his life. Please don't imply anything else, or I'll regret letting you in.'

'I appreciate that,' replied Giles, 'but I just wanted to clear up some things that have been worrying me.'

They sat, facing each other in the chaplain's easy chairs provided for conversation, the chaplain having learnt early on that nothing inhibited pastoral counselling more than the counsellor sitting behind a desk.

'Please don't think I'm being offensive,' Giles began, 'but I have to mention that when he was talking to me about unicorns, Benedict once let slip that you had been a bit fond of the love hunt. Would you be so kind as to explain that? I'm sure it was just a harmless comment.'

The chaplain sighed deeply. 'I knew this would come back to haunt me', he said wearily. You've really got no right to know private matters, but since Benedict mentioned it, and since I can see that you're not going to give me any peace until you know, I can tell you what it's about. A couple of years ago I had a brief affair with a young post-doctoral Fellow here in college. I assure you it was consensual, and the young woman never complained about it to the college authorities, but I judge it was unprofessional as the chaplain. I think Benedict mentioned it because he knew the girl and he thought it was of no consequence, but I'm not proud of my behaviour and I probably took it more seriously than he did.'

Giles also, he had to admit, thought it of no great importance, especially in the light of his own sexual behaviour, but he could see that it mattered a lot to Mark Goodall. For all that, it seemed odd that this past history had caused the chaplain to react in such a guilty way on previous occasions.

'It's really generous of you to explain that,' responded Giles, 'and I assure you that I'll keep it in complete confidence. But it doesn't seem to account for the way you seem to feel guilty when I've mentioned Benedict.'

For a moment it seemed as if Dr Goodall was going to lose the air of patience he was strenuously cultivating, and would explode in a distinctly unclerical kind of way, but finally he sighed again. 'I really don't know why I'm telling you this,' he began, 'but it's probably best for both of us to clear the air. I was, of course, thoroughly familiar with Benedict's thesis since I was his supervisor, and after Benedict died I incorporated a couple of ideas from his work in some academic articles I was writing – actually about the connection of Girard's theories with the unicorn myth, but that's by the way. You won't know this, but when you're supervising a thesis it's quite difficult to sort out which are your original ideas and which are a student's. Sometimes you suggest an idea to a student that he takes up and develops, and then he supposes he thought of it in the first place and gets quite possessive about it. Sometimes it's the other way round. Anyway, on reflection I thought I hadn't been altogether fair to Benedict and I felt guilty, even though he wasn't around to be hurt by it.'

On the face of it, this seemed a handsome confession, although Giles couldn't help feeling there was something slightly self-justifying about it.

There was just a hint in the way the chaplain had put things that he was tweaking the truth, frank though he had seemed. It also struck Giles immediately that he had offered the best motive that he had heard so far for anyone killing Benedict, supposing that plagiarism had happened before Benedict's death, not afterwards. If Benedict had read his own original ideas in an academic journal under Mark Goodall's name, the chaplain's professional reputation would have been at risk and perhaps destroyed. But, in his new benign mood of disavowing a murder hunt, and still in the afterglow of his night with Hannah, he was inclined to let the chaplain off the hook of anything more nefarious than mild academic theft. More pleased with each other than when the chaplain had opened the door, the one offered and the other accepted the conventional glass of sherry.

A few days later Giles was at work in the hospital, where he was now trusted to do a porter's job on his own, when he received a message on his personal tracking device instructing him to collect medication from the pharmacy and deliver it to the Women's Hospital. Leaving the counter of the pharmacy on the entrance level, he realized that he did not actually know the way to his destination. With a quick burst of affection he thought of Hannah, and how she could have helped him at this point. On his return to Oxford she had told him that her job as accommodation officer had finally been out-sourced to 'Progress', how she had been made redundant and encouraged to apply for another job in the Hospital Trust. She was now Signage Officer for the hospital, responsible for all the signs steering patients and staff around a hospital that in the last few years had sprouted its new wings untidily all over the hilly slope on which it was built. For a moment he even thought of trying to find her office, since the pharmacist had disappeared on some errand, but to his relief he saw Gregory in the corridor, and greeted him.

'Hi, Gregory. Have you got a thought for the day for me?' he began.

Gregory looked him in the eye in his usual steady, serious way, and responded, 'Well, Dostoyevsky's Ivan Karamazov asked the only question about suffering that really matters."

Giles really wanted to know how to get to the Women's Hospital, but he had become curious about Ivan, as Gregory had intended. 'What was the question?' he asked.

'Is the whole universe worth the tears of one tortured child?' replied Gregory. 'Is there anything else I can help you with?'

Giles explained his immediate need, and Gregory thought for a moment, 'You can go outside, round the side of the hospital and in through the separate entrance to the Women's Hospital,' explained Gregory, 'or you can stay inside and take a longer route. Go to the next floor up and then make for the academic block and the library. Follow the signs on through the corridor, and then walk across two small bridges when you'll see the entrance. It's a really winding way, but I've occasionally taken it with a frail patient when it was too cold outside.'

Giles thanked him and decided to take the internal route. Even if less direct it would be worth getting to know more of the hospital, he thought. It was in the corridor just beyond the library that he made a disturbing discovery. His surroundings seemed strangely familiar, though he had never been to that part of the hospital before, and exactly why this might be suddenly came to him when he found himself facing a large portrait just before the first small bridge that crossed the gap between the levels of the hill-built hospital. There hung the dramatic figure of a woman from his 'Alternative World' experience that the President of the Unicorn Society had identified as a Klimt. Here he saw immediately that this version was an amateur, though charming, imitation of the artist's style. A roughly sketched woman was wrapped with flowing robes of shining gold and silver pieces of paper, and overlaid with glittering, multi-coloured fragments of glass, beads, stones and plastic. A label informed him that the montage had been presented by pupils from a nearby primary school, and it crossed his mind that this work of young children was a fitting icon for a corridor which wound its way past the neo-natal and special-care baby units.

Giles realized with a sense of shock that the corridor had a striking resemblance to the passageway which had led away from the virtual art gallery in his on-line adventure, and down which he had fled in panic in the guise of a unicorn. On one corner there was a medical library, and a little further on the Hospital Trust office with an antique clock visible through the glass partition. The doors on each side of his path he now saw were offices, marked by the names of various directors, managers and supervisors. Nothing, however, was as striking as the pseudo-Klimt which had first alerted him to the similarities between the hospital and cyber corridor. His head began to swim and he swayed and staggered a little as he continued unsteadily towards the Women's Hospital. Fighting off a lapse into unconsciousness he arrived at the reception desk and managed to hand over his package. The receptionist looked concerned and enquired whether he was all right, and he just managed to croak that he was, before she summoned a nurse who swiped her card over his tracker and signed off the job.

Immediately a new message appeared, and through blurred eyes he saw that the line of green characters was summoning him to take a patient from Accident and Emergency to the X-Ray Department. Not wanting to face the ominous passage again, he made his way back to the entrance of the required department by the outside path. Feeling revived by the cool breeze, he hardly knew what to make of his unexpected discovery. Could anyone other than him have been familiar both with the Farnese Gallery and a corridor at an Oxford hospital? Why would anyone have thought of creating a scenario in which they both figured? Could this possibly have anything to do with Benedict's fate?

A couple of weeks later Giles made preparations to travel to Colmar by air and train shortly after Christmas to look at the original of the fifth postcard, in which the Virgin Mary appeared for the first time in the series. As he thought about the message written on the sixth card he had a hunch that one particular archangel, Gabriel, would re-appear as unexpectedly as the heavenly messenger had once appeared to Mary. If he had still been convinced that Benedict had been murdered, then he would certainly have been anticipating a key development in detection. However, he still hoped for light to be shed on the story told by the cards as well as on the new mysteries that the quest had opened up.

In fact Giles' new, if tentative, conviction that Benedict had taken his own life had begun to waver with the extremely odd event of the hospital corridor and he became even more unsure when, one morning in the hospital, he glanced at a copy of the *Oxford Mail* that had been left on a seat in the Accident and Emergency Department. His eye was caught by the small headline towards the bottom of the front page, 'Graduate Student Killed in Bizarre Accident'. He read on:

> 'A 27 year-old graduate student at New College, Oxford, Justin Webber, was killed at Oxford Railway Station yesterday afternoon. He fell in the gap between two carriages as the train was gathering speed to leave the station. Details are uncertain, as nobody seems to have seen the accident happen although there was a crowd of travellers on the platform. It is possible that Mr Webber was trying to open a door to get on and was unaware that the doors are locked automatically seconds before departure. If he was holding and pulling at the door handle he might have lost his footing, slipped and been dragged under as the train accelerated. Great Western Railways which operates the train has commented that the safety of passengers is a priority, and that all travellers should be aware of safety procedures and not try to board moving trains. This was, the company says, a one-in-a-thousand accident. It will hold an internal enquiry to try and establish exactly what happened. GWR and the police are anxious to hear from any passengers who saw the incident and have not come forward. The Warden of New College has issued a statement regretting the tragic loss of this fine young student who, he says, was full of promise as a scholar of the future. He had already been teaching undergraduates and they had appreciated his lively approach to history.'

Giles was shocked at this news, and had a vivid image of his own near-accident at Grand Central Terminal. That night, over the kitchen table, he discussed the event with Hannah.

'This will be a terrible blow for your friend Rosie, I suppose, since she seemed close to Justin through the Unicorn Society', began Giles.

'I'm seeing her for coffee later this week,' replied Hannah, 'so I'll find out then how she's affected.'

Giles was not sure about how to approach the next thing he wanted to say, but he plunged straight in anyway. 'Justin always seemed to me a possible candidate for the person sending the postcards. He knew all the unicorn art that Benedict was referring to, and also seemed familiar with the images on the cards. We agreed that the sender didn't have to be female – it could have been a man taking on the identity of the 'maiden' – if it was possible that Benedict had bisexual relations.' He sensed Hannah prickling up at this point, but she did not object. Giles also reflected that Justin had all the expertise to create the cyber-gallery he had stumbled into on Alternative World, but he did not mention this as he had told Hannah nothing about his adventures there. 'I'm not sure whether his death makes any difference to my quest. I'm a bit confused and I hope you might be able to help me sort my feelings out.'

Hannah seemed pleased to be appealed to like this. 'Well, his death doesn't make any difference to the story you're trying to uncover', she pointed out. 'If he *was* the sender – mind you, I'm not saying he was – then that's just a past fact. If you were looking for a murderer, and he was the killer as well as the sender, then it would obviously affect the situation, because you couldn't bring him to justice any longer – but then, I think you've given that idea up.'

Giles thanked her for the clarity of her thinking, though he could see other possibilities that he did not want to speak about for fear of damaging the fragile harmony that seemed to exist between them. For some reason he could not articulate well, the accident to Justin had made him just a little more uncertain about his reading of the tapestries in The Cloisters. Suppose Justin knew something that had to be suppressed and his death on a crowded platform wasn't an accident at all? Suppose, then, Justin wasn't behind the postcards, and there was a murderer still around? Or suppose Justin was responsible for the cards but not for the murder?

On balance, Giles was still convinced by his own reconstruction of Benedict's death as an expiatory, if deluded, act of self-sacrifice. But he was keeping just a little more of an open mind as he set out for Colmar in the days following New Year. When he announced to his friends on Facebook that he would be visiting Colmar 'to look at art' – no mention of unicorns – he received postings along the lines of 'Where did you say?' He aimed to enlighten them in due course.

20
Colmar

In a hotel room in the heart of the old town of Colmar, Giles felt safer than he had done on his previous unicorn hunting trips when he had stayed in back-packer hostels. He no longer had to look around him and wonder whom he was sharing his sleeping space with, or guard the precious cargo of the postcards. It was only a budget hotel, but he could afford it with his wages from portering at the hospital.

He reminded himself that there was actually little to fear, since he had decided Benedict's death was probably suicide, but there was an ominous black hole at the centre of the word 'probably', and despite his avowals to Hannah he felt increasingly sucked into it. Taking the shuttle bus from Basle airport to the St Louis railway station he had looked nervously around him at his no doubt harmless fellow-travellers, and catching the regional express to Colmar he had taken care to keep some distance from the designated danger zone outlined in white at the edge of the platform.

On the hour's railway journey he had spent the time looking carefully at the fifth postcard. Features of it puzzled him, though the central tableau seemed clear enough. The Virgin Mary, identified by her golden halo, sat in a walled garden, not unlike the enclosure in which the captured unicorn had been lying contentedly in The Cloisters' tapestries. This was the first unicorn picture he had seen in which Mary had appeared, though she had frequently come to his mind while he was chasing up the other images. In the traditional manner of catching unicorns, the beast was half-lying in her lap, and in a trusting way he was allowing Mary to hold his front hooves in her left hand. The eye visible to the viewer was cast down and shut, as if he were about to fall asleep. His horn too was dipped low, and Mary was holding it with her right hand, her fingers gently stroking it. The maiden was looking at the beast tenderly, welcoming it to her with a slight smile of humorous recognition. 'Here you are, then – you've come at last', she seemed to be thinking.

The postcard carried the attribution, 'Martin Schongauer and his entourage, 1420', and the printed legend, 'Mystic Hunt'. Giles had no idea what this title meant, and had concluded so far that it was another instance of using the unicorn imagery to assert the purity and faithfulness of the maiden concerned. The posture was reminiscent of the unicorn in the lap of Giulia Farnese, although this was obviously a more religious scenario, and the virginity of Mary was, he knew, an important dogma for Christianity. Filling the scene were other symbols that seemed to him to be vaguely religious. A large altar was placed incongruously in the garden, covered by a white lacy cloth and behind it stood thirteen tall, wooden staves. A golden bucket stood near Mary, filled with objects he could not identify, and sprawled by her feet was a white lamb that looked curiously like a hearth-rug or a child's stuffed toy. Scrolls with Latin letters he could not decipher were attached to these objects (one seemed to be floating from the lamb's front left hoof) and next to the unicorn there sprouted a single, slender stem of a plant which was crowned by a profusion of white lily flowers. Matching the castle-like crenellations of the wall, the garden also appeared to boast a tower beside which Mary was seated. Although puzzled by this seemingly odd assortment of symbols, Giles could not mistake the dominating figure floating in the air above Mary's head, transported by a kind of green, flying bush out of which broke tongues of fire and flashes of lightning. This was evidently God the Father, presiding over the whole affair, whatever it was. Why had the sender of the postcards chosen this picture, and what stage in the person's history with Benedict did it represent?

Giles hoped that the meaning of the picture would become clearer to him when he saw it in actuality in the Museum Unterlinden, which he knew from his investigations on the internet to be housed in a former Dominican convent dating from the thirteenth century. He had arrived in Colmar late on a Tuesday afternoon, and intended to visit the museum on the next day. Meanwhile he used his time in tramping round the historic town in the gathering dusk. He was impressed by the busy intersections of narrow, cobbled streets, lined by colourful half-timbered houses endowed plentifully with shutters, balconies, and turrets. In many places canals ran beneath the surface of the road, exposed for a few dozen yards in deep, railed culverts and then disappearing underground again. In this first week of January Christmas lights were strung across the road, but they had now been turned off, awaiting removal. Glittering coloured balls, here and there catching the light of streetlamps, still hung in the branches of the trees bared by winter, but the scene had the desolate quality of something ended but lingering on, outstaying its welcome. The party was over, but nobody had yet cleared away the festive decorations and returned the scene to normality. In a chastened mood Giles slept fitfully in his own small enclosure of a room overlooking an old courtyard now used as a car-park, waiting for a morning when perhaps the message of the fifth card would be revealed.

The former Dominican convent loomed over the picturesque square around it, its gloomy bulk contrasting with the clutter of gaily painted houses on every side. Standing in its cloisters next day, in front of the picture whose image he had poured over so many times, Giles saw immediately one detail he had missed in the slightly-blurred reproduction. Mary was – shockingly – guiding the lowered horn of the unicorn into her body, somewhere between her breasts and her stomach, since a slight discoloration on her dark dress showed that she had been pierced by the sharp, twisted weapon. But that was not the only surprise the picture had in store for Giles. He now saw it was part of a multiple-panel piece, and in the painting to the left was the archangel Gabriel in his role as a hunter, familiar to Giles from his presence among the other hunters in The Cloisters' tapestries. Running in full flight, his wings flapping to propel him on, his richly-decorated cloak streaming out behind him, blowing his horn and with a sharp spear held over his shoulder, Gabriel was holding four fierce dogs who were straining forward on a leash. Latin labels were attached to each of them, and more Latin floated on curling scrolls out of the end of his horn, appearing to fill the air with clamorous

218

sound. The low walls surrounding him showed that the angelic messenger was inside the same garden where Mary sat; he was passing by an elegant, gushing fountain set in the middle of the garden with a padlock holding down its top cover, and behind him there stood a tall wooden door in the wall, shut fast with an ornate iron hinge.

There had been no sign of the pursuing archangel in the postcard Giles had found, and he now realized he had previously missed the obvious. His card was not just a maiden with a unicorn. Mary was not just another pure and faithful woman. The painted panel portrayed the event in the Gospels called the 'annunciation'. Gabriel's message was the same as on his sixth postcard, a greeting to Mary and an announcement that, although she was a virgin, she would give birth to the Christ. But this time he was not just giving news. He was, it seemed, actually chasing the unicorn onto Mary's lap. He and his dogs were driving it to seek refuge with her. The momentum was concentrated onto the tip of the unicorn's horn, impaling Mary, virtually impregnating her. The unicorn was being hunted into Mary's own body. Giles suddenly, in a shattering moment of revelation, saw the meaning of the symbolism. Christ as the unicorn was entering not only Mary's lap but her womb. Indeed, the lap *was* the womb, or the way into it. A wonderful child was to be born from Gabriel's hunt.

'Please notice', said a familiar, husky voice behind him, 'that the enclosed garden depicts the womb. Any woman's vagina can be represented by the circular, walled garden. In Mary's case it is shut in behind the locked door you can see in the left hand picture and so it symbolizes a virgin womb, a vagina with an unbroken hymen which has not yet been opened by any male entry. The early theologians called it *hortus conclusus*. The symbolism is taken from the Hebrew book called the Song of Songs where the lover declares, "my bride is a garden locked, a sealed fountain", and then "if she is a wall, we will build upon her a battlement of silver; if she is a door, we will board her up with cedar." You can see in the two paintings the wall, the battlements, the door and the fountain. The painters have left nothing out in this poetic picture of the womb.'

Giles swung round in amazement to see Françoise standing there, tall and slim in a red coat which exactly matched the usual vivid red of her mouth.

He realized immediately that she was not actually addressing him, but a group of Americans who were shifting nervously at what they evidently felt was altogether too much anatomical information. Their whole body language said plainly that they were not expecting this kind of brutal fact on a morning intended for a gentle blend of culture and piety.

Giles was amused once more at Françoise's frank and efficient manner, a trait he had admired when he first met her in the Cluny Museum. At the same moment she also recognized him, and they exchanged warm smiles.

'It's great to see you', said Giles, delighted. 'I'm astonished to find you here. I can see you're busy at the moment, but when you're free, can we repeat that cup of coffee? I'd love to catch up.' Then he added 'and discuss these paintings, of course!'

'There's a *winstub*, a winebar, just opposite the museum,' replied Françoise. 'How about meeting there in about half an hour? I'm not so surprised to see you. Don't you remember that I became your friend on Facebook? I've been waiting for you to turn up as you posted you'd be here this week.'

Giles willingly agreed to the winebar, and when Françoise turned away to take her group to less embarrassing works of art, he consulted the information labels fixed to the wall next to the paintings. They were part, he read, of a 24-panel altarpiece in oil paints on pine boards made for the Dominicans by Martin Schongauer, or at least by Schongauer in collaboration with other artists in his studio, depicting the infancy and passion of Christ. The collection of labels in the room gave disappointingly little explanation of the works of art contained in it, and nothing to help Giles with the Latin. He got the impression, perhaps unfairly, that the writers were more anxious to tell visitors that Schongauer was a son of Colmar than to inform them about Gabriel and the son of Mary.

Nevertheless Giles realized now, in a flash of illumination, that he was quite wrong to think there were only two kinds of unicorn hunt – the secular theme of the love-hunt and the religious theme of the hunting and killing of Christ. The unicorn did not just represent *either* a lover or Christ. There was a third sort of hunt, where Christ *was* the lover. Any human lover entered the enclosed garden of a woman, and Christ entered the sealed garden of Mary, chased there by Gabriel. This, apparently, was called 'the mystic hunt'.

Other puzzling pieces now fell into place in his mind. There was the parallel between the images of maiden-with-unicorn and Mary-with-Christ-child which had been teasing him ever since his trip to Rome. Others in the past had obviously noticed it too and had exploited it for devotional purposes. There was the strong hint dropped by the Franciscan monk in the Vatican, and possibly another hint left to future generations by Raphael himself. He now realized what the third hunt was that his tutor had wanted him to find for himself a year ago, and which it seems that Benedict had intended to tell him about, but had not had the time.

As he wandered round the museum, idling away the half hour before his appointed meeting with Françoise, he noticed other, more conventional, examples of Gabriel's alarming visit to Mary. In these, including one by Schongauer himself, it was the Holy Spirit in the form of a dove that was being sent by God the Father and announced by Gabriel. In the 'mystic hunt' the descent of the dove was replaced by the hunt of the unicorn. He wondered whether it had literally been replaced in the altarpiece, since the two annunciation panels were of a different colouring and style from the other twenty-two, and alone carried Latin tags. Had someone wanted a more allegorical scene than had been provided there before, perhaps someone, like him, fascinated by unicorns?

He also asked himself what the sender of the postcard could have meant by choosing this image, and how it might fit into the relationship between this person and Benedict. Discounting unlikely claims to a virginal conception, the clue must lie in the promise of a child. If the last episode, from The Cloisters postcard, indicated that a pledge of faithfulness had been received from Benedict and that the sender thought the relationship was secure, this could only be a joyful announcement that the sender was pregnant. 'You have entered me,' she was saying, 'and I am expecting a child.' It was now plain that the sender could only be a 'she'. All thoughts that the maiden might be an avatar for a male had evaporated with the declaration that she would be giving birth. What a poignant way, thought Giles, for her to give Benedict the news. And yet, in all the time he had known Benedict, he had no idea that he was a father. The thought quickly followed: did Hannah know it?

It was with sombre feelings, mixed with excitement at solving a mystery, that he met up with Françoise inside the winebar opposite, watching through the window as she first neatly deposited the stub of a *Gauloise* in a nearby litter bin. He began by expressing his surprise in finding her in Colmar.

'It's really not so surprising', responded Françoise. 'I'm an art-historian and I've recently got a new post in the Department of Art History and Musicology in the University of Basle. Didn't you see it on my Facebook posting? Well, Colmar's near Basle, and I'm still earning some extra cash by conducting art-appreciation tours.'

'I'm not sure that the last group *did* appreciate the 'mystic hunt of the unicorn' very much, said Giles with a grin.

'Well, they're a group of American evangelical Protestants,' replied Françoise, with what Giles suspected to be a slightly surprising touch of Catholic disdain, 'and they know their Bibles very well. They've read the Song of Songs and remember the lover's invitation to his lover to meet her in the garden, and I expect they spiritualize the two characters as Christ and the church, but they've missed the erotic sense of the garden completely.'

'*I* appreciated your explanation of the garden', Giles hastened to assure her. 'The meaning of this particular unicorn hunt had only just occurred to me.'

'Haven't you come across it before?' asked Françoise. 'If I'd realized that I would have told you about it in Paris, but the Cluny Museum tapestries were really nothing to do with it. The "mystic hunt" was quite a popular theme in the Middle Ages. I could name you another dozen examples in paintings and tapestries – I think you say "from the top of my head" – but an interesting one is from the Mary-cycle in the Unser Frauen Church in Memmingen, where the child Jesus is portrayed riding the unicorn into Mary's womb. That's a rather heavy-handed explanation of the allegory, and actually destroys its effect altogether. It's a bit of a mess, really.'

'Off the top ...' corrected Giles, absently.

Françoise tossed back her head, so that her black hair streamed down her back, and she gave one of her quick smiles. 'If you're so good at English, I assume you've read the medieval English poem by William of Shoreham in praise of the Virgin Mary?'

With a surge of excitement Giles suddenly remembered that this was the very poem mentioned by his English tutor in his unicorn tutorial with Emily the previous Spring, a poem that he had totally failed to follow up as he had been advised.

'No, I ought to have read it but I haven't', he confessed.

Françoise startled him by pushing back the table, getting to her feet and drawing herself up to her full, elegant height. 'Here's a verse I translated myself from the medieval text,' she announced with a glint in her black eyes, 'using my rather poor English'. She declaimed, startling other patrons of the winebar around:

> 'In you has God become a child;
> In you his anger has become all mild;
> The unicorn, which was once so wild
> By a chaste maiden has been brought to rest;
> Tamed by a woman others call blest,
> Calmed by milk from your breast.'

Their neighbours were beginning to look nervous, behaving somewhat like the group of visiting Americans, confronted by the phenomenon that was Françoise, and Giles hastily urged her to sit down again.

'I wish I'd followed the advice of my tutor and read that earlier,' he confessed. 'It would have answered a lot of questions, though it's strong stuff – especially that bit about the unicorn sucking Mary's milk. Can you also help me with the Latin tags in the paintings? I suspect I might be missing something, though I get the general picture.'

'I thought you were at Oxford', replied Françoise playfully, subsiding into her chair. 'Don't all Oxford students have to know Latin?'

'Not for the last forty years, I think, replied Giles, adding in self-justification, 'I've got a smattering of the language, but the painted letters are difficult to read.'

'Well, everything's very well labelled in case you don't get the allusions from the Bible', replied Françoise. 'The door's labelled "closed door" –

porta clausa – and the fountain's labelled 'sealed fountain' – *fons signata*. The message coming from Gabriel's horn is his greeting 'Hail, full of grace, the Lord is with you', and underneath it the painter's put a prophecy from Isaiah, "a virgin shall conceive".' The four dogs are named *misericordia*, *justitia, pax* and *veritas* – that's mercy, justice, peace and truth.'

'They look very fierce dogs to have such pleasant names', observed Giles.

'Well, it's an allegory', explained Françoise. 'They have to be fierce to drive the unicorn into seeking safety in Mary's lap. Actually, in devotional literature of the time the four names are also given to four women called "the daughters of God", who debate together about the best means for humankind to be redeemed. The names come from Psalm 85, "Mercy and truth are met together, justice and peace join hands". But here women would obviously not fit in. It *has* to be dogs.'

She paused and then added, in an unexpectedly bitter tone, 'Anyway the miraculous birth does cause her terrible pain as a mother in the end. The death of Christ is foreshadowed in his birth. The penetrating of Mary by the unicorn's horn recalls the prediction to Mary by Simeon in the Gospel story as he blesses mother and child: "A sword will pierce your own heart also".'

Giles was silent for a moment, but pressed on. 'All's very clear on the left, but what about the right hand panel? I'm puzzled by the odd-looking squashed lamb and by the bucket.'

'The typology there is a bit more obscure,' replied Françoise, 'but familiar enough to those who knew their Bibles. That's not a lamb but a fleece, which is why it looks flat. It's labelled "Gideon's fleece" – *vellus gedeonus*. Do you know the story of Gideon in the Old Testament? He put out a fleece all night to get some guidance from God, and got his answer when it was sodden with dew in the morning. It was a sort of divination or fortune-telling. An early Christian hymn about Mary says that the Word of God came into Mary's womb like the dew into Gideon's fleece.'

'I'd never have guessed that,' exclaimed Giles. 'That's what I call obscure. And the bucket?'

'That's from the Book of Hebrews in the New Testament', replied Françoise with a superb swiftness. 'The author's listing items that were

224

believed to be in the Holy Place and the Holy of Holies in the Hebrew temple and among them there are the golden urn full of manna, the holy table, and Aaron's rod that miraculously grew buds. You'll see behind the altar or table wooden staves standing for all the tribes of Israel, and the tallest one is budding – it's obviously the one for the tribe of Aaron, and so it's Aaron's rod. The point being made by the artist is that the enclosed garden of Mary's body is also a holy sanctuary, nothing less than the Most Holy Place on earth. What you call the bucket's the urn, and it's labelled "golden urn" – *urna aurea* – in case you need any help with it. On another level of allegory, Mary herself *is* the golden urn full of manna and the rod that buds with flower.'

'I'm hugely impressed,' responded Giles. 'Your American class didn't know what it was missing. But I don't think any of that's added anything to the basic message of the painting,' or, he added in his mind, the message of the unknown woman to Benedict.

'I think you're right', admitted Françoise, 'but we art-historians are absolute pedants for detail. I can't help completing the lesson by pointing out the lily which underlines Mary's purity, and the patch of three-leaved clovers in the grass that allegorize the Trinity.'

'That last bit I *have* come across before,' exclaimed Giles. 'I once heard it in a very boring sermon in college chapel where the preacher was trying to explain the complicated doctrine of the Trinity.'

'Some religious images just go on surviving from century to century,' said Françoise, 'but I'm not sure that's true of the unicorn.'

'It's still everywhere today,' said Giles, 'but with a very different meaning.' He did not elaborate.

They paused in their conversation while they ordered a light lunch. Françoise recommended *croque monsieur* as a traditional French snack since Giles was in France, but he was disappointed to find when it arrived that it was little more than his college chef called 'Welsh rarebit' and he had always called 'cheese on toast'.

'I have to say that I'm amazed by the symbolism in the paintings,' he commented after they had eaten for a while.

'You think *that's* amazing', said Françoise in a surprisingly heated manner. 'I'll tell you what I find amazing. Just let me tell you. It's the fact that, in the eyes of the church, it was all right for Mary to have extraordinary relations with a unicorn while other women were condemned as witches, and were absurdly accused of copulating with demons in the shape of animals. It's male arrogance about women, and it all comes from the image of God the Father who's arranging everything for Mary – whether she wants it or not – from his burning bush that Schongauer puts up the sky. You know, in the Old Testament story God spoke to Moses from the bush that wasn't burnt up, but ever since it's been women who've been bossed around by men. Just look at the famous Cranach.'

Giles was taken aback by the vehemence of her speech, revealing something fierce about her he had not noticed before, and yet he remembered her saying something similar in Paris.

'Do you mean Cranach the painter?' he enquired. 'I've heard of him.'

'Yes, Lucas Cranach the Elder,' she replied, 'famous artist and close friend of the Protestant Reformers. One version of his painting called *Melancholy* is on postcards and souvenirs all over the gift shop at the Museum here. Look at the top left. Two naked witches, one riding on an ugly-looking pig, are poking a worthy knight with sharp sticks. It's fitting that this painting's ended up in Colmar. This region of Alsace had dozens of witch trials in the sixteenth and seventeenth centuries. In 1572 twenty-five witches were burnt in one day in Colmar alone. We don't exactly know where, but after the process in court they were probably taken to the river to see if they floated – if they did, their guilt was confirmed and they were burnt, if they sank they were innocent but drowned. Victims either way. Now I come to think of it they were like unicorns, hunted to death – or perhaps "scapegoats" is the better term.'

This speech sounded astonishingly like what Benedict had said to Giles, and so he asked Françoise the question he'd first asked her in Paris.

'Are you quite sure you didn't meet a theology research student called Benedict Green while you were in Oxford? He was writing a thesis about unicorns and scapegoats.'

Françoise, for once, seemed impatient with Giles' questioning. 'I've told you before, no, I didn't know him. But he sounds as if he might have been on the right track. If you really want to please me, would you go to the river in

Colmar and think for a moment about men's violence to women? Promise me you will. You see the canals running under the streets? There are two open canals on two sides of the museum here – in fact, we're sitting by the side of one. Just follow them down until they run into the River Lauch. It's in the area of the town called 'Little Venice', and you'll see lots of street signs to it. Most of the houses are more recent than the witch-trial period, but the river was there then. I feel the experience will have a good effect on you for the future, and you won't become one of the oppressors.'

She was so earnest, and Giles anyway liked her so much, that he readily gave his promise. He would have time to make this walk on the way to the railway station from where he was to begin the journey back to the airport that evening.

Before they parted, he had one other thing to tell her. 'I want you to know that I did what you advised me in Paris. I went to look at Leonardo's little sketch of the maiden and the unicorn in the Ashmolean Museum. One of the assistants there remembered you well and said it was a favourite of yours. I've been intrigued by the smile he gives his women.'

Françoise seemed pleased. 'Oh yes, the smile', she agreed. 'Do you know that Leonardo practised drawing the shape of the human mouth? I've been to the Royal Library in Windsor Palace and seen a manuscript of his which just has a smile on it, with no face attached. It's like the smile on the face of the Cheshire Cat in your Lewis Carroll's *Alice in Wonderland*. When the cat disappeared you know, only the smile was left.'

They said *au revoir*, Françoise urging him once more to visit the river in Little Venice, and Giles promising again to do so. It seemed to mean a lot to her. When she had left, he decided first to visit the official town Information Centre, which was in a building directly opposite to the entrance door of the museum, across one of the canal bridges. Perhaps, he thought, they would know exactly where the witch trials had taken place. Françoise's directions had been vague, to say the least. But he received an unexpected reply when he asked the young woman at the desk his question.

'Oh no,' she exclaimed, in excellent English. 'There were no witch trials or burnings in Colmar. You must be thinking of two other nearby villages, Bergheim and Rouffach.'

227

She seemed a little offended that this slur could be cast on such a friendly and hospitable town as Colmar. Clearly, she did not want any reference to the execution of witches to be part of the story of the town for which she was an advocate with tourists.

'Are you quite sure?' persisted Giles nevertheless. 'I was told there were witch-trials by a friend of mine who's a historian in the University of Basle.'

'In that case I'll check with a colleague who knows more about history than me,' she replied helpfully, lifting the phone and having an animated conversation in which he could catch the word *sorcières* repeated.

'No,' she said, 'I thought not. There's even a witch festival in one of the neighbouring towns, but not in Colmar.'

He thanked her for taking such trouble, but, since he was inclined to trust Françoise over even the most official tourist information, he resolved to make the detour on the way to the railway station anyway, and set off.

21
Another hospital

Giles followed the canal system and signs to *Petite Venise*, as instructed, and made his way down the street named Grand Rue. Cobbles and overhanging ancient houses did not prevent traffic from making its disruptive way up and down, claiming the right of access in order to scatter heedless pedestrians to either side. As in the area around Unterlinden, Christmas decorations hung forlornly from lampstands and houses, from church windows, towers and balustrades. Especially pathetic were the remnants of what had been carefully constructed heaps of fir twigs, painted cones, coloured baubles and short silvered branches which had been placed on small wooden platforms all the way down the railings of the canal, and which had evidently been pillaged for their contents by passers-by stocking up for the next yuletide – unless they had been robbed by wintering jackdaws looking for glittering objects. It was time to dispose of the remains of the body of Christmas past.

At the bottom of Grand Rue, as the road turned off the main thoroughfare towards the lanes of Little Venice, he found a small square in which there still stood several dozen wooden huts, constructed like little fairy-tale houses, which had evidently served as stalls for the winter market and were now shut fast. Like the street decorations, they called for clearance. In the shadows of the late afternoon it was a desolate scene, and Giles wished he had been there a couple of weeks before when lanterns would have been lit, a scent of mulled wine filling the air, the huts open for business and an infectious anticipation gripping the crowds who were buying presents and awaiting the coming day. As it was, he seemed to be the only person out in the open air, though some shop windows around were still lit.

He pressed on through the deserted square to the first bridge over La Lauch where several canal streams poured into the river and painted houses bordered the water. A notice informed him that fishermen had once plied their trade along this stretch of the river, and he made his way down a narrow, cobbled street alongside the banks, between timber-frame houses plastered in different coloured stuccos and past several bridges that offered undeniably charming vistas despite the fading light. He could quite appreciate why it was called 'Little Venice'. As he walked along he turned over in his mind what had been for him the astounding discovery of the third hunt of the unicorn, the 'mystic hunt'. He imagined the pleasure of the unknown woman in sending Benedict the news that – in the ancient words emerging from the horn of Gabriel – she would 'conceive and bear a child'. Benedict was the unicorn who had penetrated into the centre of her secret, enclosed garden and the result was new life in the world. In the quaint metaphors of early Christianity, she was the golden pot filled with manna and the fleece into which the dew had come. Her battlements had been breached and her fountain was unsealed.

But like the passing of Christmas in Colmar, the joy of nativity had somehow faded – he did not yet know how or why – and Benedict's own life had ended – again he did not yet know how or why. Giles was not sure in what direction these reflections were going, but somehow they were getting mixed up in his mind with Françoise's passionate campaign against the abuse of women. Giles stopped and wandered to the middle of one bridge, looking down into the water. Now was the time to think seriously of the scapegoating of women, and he made what felt like a religious vow that he would never be one of the oppressors. As he gazed down into the darkening stream, he felt the onset of a familiar fall into a watery vortex, and he began to see the surface of the river redden with the blood of martyrs, just as the great bath in the chaplain's lodgings had once turned red from Benedict's open veins. Yet he resisted the drop into unconsciousness, fighting off the fit of blackness until he felt able to walk on further, though unsteady on his feet.

He judged that in the gathering dusk it would be better not to try to find his way through narrow lanes to the station, but to retrace his steps slightly to the Grand Rue and then take a route across wider and better-lit streets to his destination. Another panic began to grip him, however, as pacing along the cobbled paths reminded him of his flight down the corridor of his online adventure, and it was with a sense of relief that he found himself back in the quiet square with the market huts. In a moment, he assured himself, he would be treading a broader way. He stopped for a couple of seconds to look at the statue of some local worthy, hand uplifted, outlined sharply against the dying light of the sky and still wrapped in Christmas tinsel.

It was at that very moment that a figure stepped out from the shadow of a hut into his path and he felt a sudden blow at the very point where the unicorn's horn had pierced the body of Mary. He had the briefest of impressions that his assailant was a woman. There followed the sharpest pain he had ever felt in his life, and when he automatically put his hand under his coat where he had felt the blow it came away wet and sticky. He just managed to shout 'help' weakly before he fell and before the oblivion that had threatened him shortly before, and that he had staved off on the bridge, finally overcame him. He had fallen into the black hole of improbability.

Later he learned that his shout, tremulous though it was, had been heard in a nearby shop, someone had come to investigate after only a few minutes and had – horrified – called an ambulance. He returned to consciousness in the emergency department of the hospital, with a stabbing pain in his chest and struggling for breath. A medical assessment had established that the knife point had penetrated the wall of his chest, nicking a rib, but had stopped a couple of millimetres short of his heart. As he lay on a trolley, anxious about what was to come, the phrase that Françoise had repeated to him kept going round in his mind: 'A sword shall pierce your own heart also.' He was told that his left lung had collapsed because of a build-up of blood and air between the chest wall and the lining of the lung, and that a drain would have to be inserted immediately. When this was done under local anaesthetic he felt an immediate relief, as well as immense gratitude that he was not going to die after all.

He received the final pouch of blood from a transfusion to cope with his blood-loss, and when this was replaced by a saline drip on the intravenous line a tangle of cables was attached to monitor his heart and blood pressure. He would need, he discovered, to spend two weeks or so in hospital while his wounds – both from the stabbing and from the drainage procedure – healed. Then he could return home, though a careful watch would have to be kept that he wasn't developing any infection. He would be given an X-Ray in his own hospital after a couple of weeks to check that all was in order. For the most part he had been remarkably lucky, as his doctors told him. While the injury was life-threatening, when dealt with promptly, he learned, it became much less serious.

The next couple of days while fluid continued draining from his chest cavity into a jar beneath him, he lay luxuriously in bed in the Louis Pasteur Civil Hospital in Colmar, enjoying the care of the medical staff, and looking out through his window. He could catch glimpses of bare branches in the trees which softened the appearance of the utilitarian concrete hospital blocks, interspersed with winter evergreen. His eye could not escape the most dominating feature of the scene, a tall chimney constantly belching smoke, and he idly wondered whether this came from the heating system or from burning hospital waste. It did not seem worth asking. He could hear the trains bumping over the gaps in the rails as they arrived at or left the railway station, and his nights were broken now and then by the distant hooting of engines. The ambulance had taken him precisely in the direction he had been intending to walk that early evening, then over a bridge spanning the tracks and just half a mile further on. He counted the days until he could get back on the train himself and make his planned journey back to the Basle-Freiburg airport.

He was interviewed by an English-speaking officer of the local police who visited him at his bedside. The clumsy nature of the attack and relative lack of damage to his internal organs by the stabbing showed, the police thought, that this was not the work of a professional criminal. The fact that his mobile phone and wallet were missing from his pocket had led the police to think this was an opportunistic attack by some vagrant, and they regretted that there was little they could do except warn him not to wander around less-frequented parts of the town after dark. They stressed that this was an unusual occurrence, and that tourists generally had little to worry about in the friendly and safe environment of Colmar. He gathered that he had become a somewhat unwelcome addition to the local crime statistics.

For his own part, he spent the unexpected – and unwanted – gift of the extra hours given him for solitary thinking in turning recent events over and over in his mind. Did this attack mean that he was being targeted after all by some person who wanted to prevent him getting at the truth of Benedict's death? Did this mean, in turn, that Benedict had been murdered? Or was it just another instance – though a much more dramatic one than before – of his propensity for getting into trouble? He thought he knew what Hannah would say.

Then there was the startling disclosure of the 'mystic hunt' to think about. For the first time he mentally reviewed the various women whom he knew had been acquainted with Benedict, or whom he had come across in following the trail of the postcards. Some suspicions began to grow in his mind, but nobody in his view stood out as fitting the Mary of the annunciation, and so perhaps there was an unknown woman lurking somewhere in the shadows of Benedict's life whom he had not yet met. The situation was somewhat simplified by the revelation of the fifth card that the sender of the postcards must have been a woman, but even if Benedict had been murdered, the sender and the murderer were not necessarily the same person. Even if he himself had been attacked because he was getting too near the truth, his attacker could have been a man or a woman. He could not completely trust his intuition that the one who struck the blow was female. Then there was Hannah. This brush with death – for so it was – had prompted him to resolve that he would make a bolder declaration of his love for her than he had attempted so far.

He had the opportunity to develop his thoughts and intentions further when Hannah came to visit him, just four days after his admission to hospital. The ward staff had lent him a mobile phone, and he had first contacted his parents, giving them a sanitized version of the incident,

233

assuring them that he was recovering fast, and urging them not to trouble about coming to see him so far from home. He had phoned Hannah's mobile too, to explain why he had failed to return to her house on the scheduled day. He had, it must be said, not put as much effort into persuading her not to make the journey as he had with his parents, and was very glad when she turned up just as he had been allowed to get out of bed and sit in a chair beside it. After greeting her warmly, he expressed his surprise that she had been able to get to Colmar so quickly.

'Well, I was owed a few days holiday, and I was lucky to get a last-minute air-ticket,' explained Hannah, 'but how are you? I've been so worried.'

'Feeling sore,' admitted Giles, 'and I have to be careful when I move not to disturb the stitches and the staples. But it could have been a lot worse.'

He briefly gave her an account of the attack, and then went on to outline his discoveries in the Unterlinden Museum.

'Let's sum the story up, then,' said Hannah after a while in her usual brisk way – 'at least as *you* read it. Stage one: "I think I'm attracted to you." Stage two: "I was right, you arouse all the senses of my body". Stage three: "But will you be faithful to me?" Stage four: "Good, now I know you're committed." Stage five: "Marvellous news – I'm pregnant." Is that it?'

Giles smiled. 'You haven't plumbed the emotional depths or explored all the nuances of what seems an intense relationship, but I think that's more or less the coded meaning of the cards up to number five. From the message written on the last one something goes badly wrong after that, but I suppose we know that anyway because Benedict was engaged to you when he died.' He had only just said this when he suddenly realized the effect that the uncovered story, and especially the fifth episode, must be having on Hannah.

'You must understand,' said Hannah slowly, 'that it's hard for me to come to terms with what you're saying about this last card. Somebody conceived a child with Benedict. Possibly she gave birth to the child. If you're right, Benedict concealed a huge truth from me, though I admit he dropped enough hints about feeling guilty for something in the past. It's devastating. I just don't know what to think. I'm not sure I'll ever accept it. It's a terrible conclusion to build on a farrago of medieval images – pots of manna, dew on a fleece, budding rods, fountains and locked gardens. Even you must admit that it sounds fantastic. Are you sure this woman Françoise hasn't just been encouraging your imaginative streak? Don't get me wrong – I'm as fascinated as you are by the iconography, and that's why I've been happy for you to explore the postcards, but for me it's part of religious history. You seem to think it's about life here and now.'

Giles could have replied that the multiplying of unicorns all over the media showed just how strong a grip the image had on people's minds today, and how they used it in different ways to express how they felt about themselves and relations with others. But for the moment he said nothing.

'And another thing,' Hannah added, 'how long ago is all this supposed to have happened? I knew Benedict for about two years altogether, with a year before we agreed to get engaged.'

Giles reflected. 'It must have been not long before he met you, I would guess. He was working on the thesis for five years, and it must have taken the first year to develop the kind of interest in unicorns that would make sense of the code in the postcards. I guess the relationship with this woman must have begun three to four years ago.'

Hannah brooded for a while, and they sat together in silence for couple of minutes. 'Let's suppose you've decoded the postcards accurately', Hannah finally broke in. 'The plot's certainly ingenious, I grant you that. To me it makes it more likely that Benedict killed himself. He must have been eaten up with guilt and remorse, about the way he was treating me as well his previous lover, and besides, none of our speculations about possible killers seem to have worked out. I hope you're not going to cite the attack on you as evidence otherwise?'

Giles decided to use discretion and say nothing about his increasing doubts about his previous concession to Hannah. Instead he mumbled something non-specific, and went on with a rush into what he had resolved to say, before his courage failed him.

'Lying here, Hannah, I've been thinking about the image and message on the fourth card, and I want to offer you the same kind of commitment. I love you, and I want to make our relationship more permanent, if you'll have me. I know it's still soon after the death of Benedict, but do you think we could live together as well as just being in the same house? I'll be going back to college next term for my last year, and during that time that we could plan for our long-time future together.'

Hannah did not seem altogether surprised by this declaration, but she looked at Giles with a curious blend of pleasure and sadness. 'That's truly sweet of you Giles, and I'm really fond of you, but I'm not sure just at the moment. I've been meaning to give you some news that complicates things a bit. Mark Goodall has asked me to help him with putting Benedict's thesis in order for publication. He's going to complete it, giving Benedict all due credit, and to add some of his own research as well. I'll be able to look after Benedict's interests and reputation, as well as giving Mark the kind of assistance he needs with computers. You know that I use them all the time in my work, and I've developed quite a bit of expertise in constructing databases that Mark finds invaluable.'

Giles was immediately suspicious of her familiar use of the name 'Mark', and asked anxiously, 'But why should that stand in the way of our plans together? I don't mind you working on the thesis, in fact I think it's a splendid idea. Benedict had something really original to say, and it's important that other people don't exploit it for their own benefit.' He had only just managed to say 'other people' instead of 'Dr Goodall'.

Hannah flushed slightly. 'I know that Mark's had strong feelings for me for some time, and I'm fond of him – as I am of you. But because of Benedict I've known him for much longer than the short time I've known you. I'm a bit confused about how I feel, and I don't want to do anything final too quickly.'

Giles had to be content with her promise not to take anything personal further with Mark for the moment, but he felt undeniably anxious, and wished he were back in Oxford. They parted with a friendly kiss.

A couple of weeks later, shortly before being discharged from the Louis Pasteur, Giles had a call on his borrowed mobile from Françoise. She'd read about the attack on him in the local newspaper, she explained with a note of concern in her voice, and had contacted the hospital. She'd like to meet and see how he was. He suggested that they meet the next morning in the hospital café, close by the main gate. It would do him good to start moving around in preparation for travelling home. At the appointed time he took the lift to the ground floor, and walked stiffly the short distance across the road to the café, ignoring the slight ache in his chest. It felt good to be in the open air again, and he looked with appreciation at the only splash of colour he could see among the greens and browns of winter; a japonica bush, still bedecked with a few yellow fruit from earlier months was now flowering red, lighting up the area around the café's rubbish bins. Giles negotiated his way around the bicycles parked at the café door and went inside to find Françoise waiting for him.

They greeted each other warmly, and Françoise burst out, 'I feel so guilty for sending you in the direction of Little Venice that day! I presume that you were doing what I asked you, as the newspaper piece said that you were found stabbed in the little square of Rue Saint-Jean. I wanted to tell you this before you went back to Oxford.'

Giles assured her that he was recovering well, and that he did not blame her in the least. 'It could have happened anywhere,' he reassured her, 'and I do understand your concern about the oppression of women. Is there anything else I should do?'

'Were you going back to the Unterlinden Museum,' she enquired?

'I *was* thinking of making another visit', replied Giles. 'It seems a waste of being here so long not to make the most of the opportunity.'

'If you do, be sure to visit the Issenheim Altar-piece, painted by Matthias Grünewald in the sixteenth century', urged Françoise. 'It was painted for the chapel of a hospital run by the Order founded in memory of St Anthony in Issenheim, near by Colmar. Sufferers from a disfiguring plague called St Anthony's fire would be brought to the chapel and at Advent and Lent they could gaze at a figure of a Christ who was also terribly disfigured, with a pallid and tortured flesh like theirs. Other pilgrims would venerate the image of St Anthony on the altar-piece and either pray for protection against illness or thank him for recovery.'

'Is that why you think I should visit it?' enquired Giles. 'To express gratitude for my own recovery?' The suggestion seemed more pious than he would have expected from Françoise.

'Well, I suppose there's a kind of appropriateness there, but that isn't what I meant', replied Françoise with a laugh. 'Most people go to see it for the massive central panel showing the crucified Christ, but I advise you to look carefully at the side panel on the theme of the annunciation by Gabriel to Mary.'

'Why? Is there a unicorn there, like the Schongauer?' asked Giles.

'No, not a breath, nor a hide, nor a hoof', answered Françoise. 'But look at it long and carefully and I believe you'll see why I'm so passionate for the cause of women. The image might even justify the danger you ran in going down to the river to remember the women who were scapegoats of men's fear – men afraid of what they can't control.'

She would not say any more, but she spoke with her usual intensity and humour, and Giles was impressed. They parted with further *au revoirs*, and Giles wondered whether and when they would meet again.

Later that week, when the stitches from his drainage wound had been removed, and ahead of his discharge, the hospital authorities allowed him off the premises to visit the Museum, and he took a bus to the town centre which left directly outside the hospital. In the cloister he made a brief, farewell visit to the room with the Schongauer unicorn panels and then continued round the ambulatory to the chapel. The altarpiece occupied most of the massive space, the panels disassembled and spread out so they could be easily meditated upon in one viewing, when originally only a selection would be visible at any one time for the different feasts of the year. He quickly found the annunciation, and wondered what message it would give him from Françoise.

Mary, he thought, sits in a room that is more like a Gothic chapel than her bed-chamber. The Holy Ghost in the form of a white dove hovers in a halo of light streaming in from high windows. Gabriel has arrived and still seems in movement, his golden hair blowing behind him. He is pointing with his finger in a stern and warning manner at Mary, the energy of his arm emphasized by the flowing red mantle that lies over it. He does not appear to be speaking comforting words but issuing instructions like a stern teacher to be carried out to the letter, an admonition echoed by the prophet Isaiah high up on the left hand side who is pointing insistently at his written prophecy. Mary has been reading a book with the words of the same prophecy, and the pages show the words 'a virgin will conceive and bear a child'. The book lies open on a chest and it looks as though it has been dropped from her hands at the shock of the encounter.

Giles remembered other annunciations he had seen in this and other art galleries and thought: she's not looking at the archangel with the look of humble submission and joyful anticipation that I've usually seen written on her face, but instead she's turning away with a critical look, almost of distaste. As he gazed intently at the painting, it seemed to him that here was a woman trapped between the demands of two men, voices from the past and the present. Gabriel appeared as an enemy, even though he was not equipped with a sharp spear and four dogs but carried only a lily over his shoulder. The annunciation was a threat. A sword would surely pierce her heart. These heavenly authorities wanted to use Mary for purposes long foretold, and yet she was turning aside into her own space, her own world. There was no unicorn in the painting unless it was Mary herself, victim and scapegoat.

Giles was well aware that he was interpreting the painting through Françoise's eyes, with the help of the hints she had given him. It was a feminist reading, that was undeniable. Yet Giles felt that Françoise was also telling him something more, about her own life, her own painful experiences that he did not yet entirely grasp. There was something she wanted him to understand about her. Perhaps one day he would. In any case, seeing the Grünewald painting had given him more material for the blog he wanted to post on his Facebook page, justifying his choice of this small town for an art-viewing trip, which had earlier on been met with such bafflement by his friends.

22
Oxford again

For a few days after returning to Hannah's house, Giles felt disinclined to move around much while the wound in his chest continued to heal. He had agreed with the agency not to return to work for another couple of weeks, and he spent his time catching up with reading in preparation for his return to college and tutorials in the next term. Twentieth-century literature was on the agenda, and he preoccupied himself reading T. S. Eliot and W. B. Yeats. Unexpected surprises lay in wait for him, such as finding a play by Yeats in which a young princess of extreme religious sentimentality devotes herself to serving a unicorn, evidently meant to symbolize Christ. He found himself disliking the heroine intensely, prone as she was to submitting obediently to the unicorn's advances, desiring to be trampled underfoot and generally embracing a life of self-denial and martyrdom for its sake. He was relieved when the common people in the story turned against her, feeling she had received her just dues for being a feeble specimen of humanity, and realizing that Yeats meant the audience to share this reaction. He could not help comparing the milksop Diotema with the feisty assertiveness of Françoise and the sharp critical insights of Hannah.

It was Hannah he found at the breakfast table one late Saturday morning, having her regular coffee with Rosie Jones. The other woman hailed him with concern.

'What's this I hear about your being mugged? Hannah's been telling me all about your adventure. Remind me, what were you doing in Colmar anyway? Hannah told me you were going to be there, but she was a bit hazy about why exactly. She said something about research.'

Giles assured her that he was well on the way to recovery, but was cautious about telling her the whole truth about his visit. 'I'm using this year out of my course to travel a bit and to look up the background for my studies in literature.' That was just about true, he reflected, or near enough to pass as true. 'Have you heard of the famous Issenheim Altar-piece, painted by Matthias Grünewald?' he went on. 'It's kept in the museum at Colmar, I was very glad to see it, though it cost me a couple of weeks in the local hospital.'

She took in this information. 'Well, you know that my interest isn't in the history of art but the culture of the present day. That's the real cutting-edge, in my view. I don't go poking about in musty museums. But you might be interested in a lecture we're putting on next week as a kind of memorial to my good friend and colleague Justin who died in that tragic accident the other month, and we're also going to mention Benedict as well. We've lost two really good members in one year, and by "we" I mean the Unicorn Society. We give a public lecture once a term, and this one's got quite a bit of history in it – but then that's what Justin and Benedict enjoyed, so it seems right. I know from our talk together that you're interested in unicorns, and I thought you might like to come.'

Giles mused over the fact that he had, for some reason, not been counted worthy to be a member of the inner circle of this society, but replied enthusiastically that he would come to the lecture, and took the details. Among its attractions was the possibility of going there with Hannah. He imagined she would be there, since the event was partly in honour of Benedict, and he broached the subject with her after Rosie had gone.

'I'll be there,' Hannah assured him, 'it's the least I can do to keep the memory of Benedict alive. But I have to say it's going to be difficult with the pressure of work I've got at the moment. I thought looking after signage in the hospital was going to be less stressful than accommodation, but it seems I was wrong.'

Giles remembered his pledge to be more interested in her daily work, and encouraged her to share her frustrations with him.

'It's not the staff,' she exclaimed, 'but the patients, who have problems with finding places when they arrive at the hospital. They think that the department they want is going to be posted up at the entrance, but there are so many that this would only be a confusing list. Like road signs, we give the departments immediately ahead, and then we expect patients to follow the arrow to "all other departments". They'll find the signs they want nearer the place they're going to if they just follow the main arrow. But they want their destination flagged up right at the beginning. It's like arriving at Dover and expecting to find a sign to Oxford. Then they send us letters of complaint, lamenting our incompetence and lack of consideration, and those end up with me. I try to answer them all, and explain our method, but they often write back with follow-up suggestions. The situation's a nightmare because the hospital's expanded all over the hill, and what was marked as the ground floor in one section when it was built is actually the second floor in a newer one, and so when patients enter the West Wing they find that it's not the ground floor but level minus two. I've been having particular problems over a whole year now in deciding how to sign the internal route to the Women's Unit, and I've spent a lot of time there.'

Giles had only been half-attending despite his resolution, admiring the sound of her voice and the intensity of her passion rather than following all the content. But his interest was awakened by the mention of the corridor which had appeared – or a fantastic version of it – so unexpectedly in 'Alternative World' and which featured frequently in his dreams. Regretfully he did not feel he could let her know why it intrigued him, since he knew her views on the subject of the postcards, but he asked her to say more. She seemed gratified by this interest.

'It's no great deal,' she replied, 'just a fussy detail, but the question is at what point we put up a sign to the Women's Unit in this winding corridor, which is really filled up by the Trust offices and the academic section. Visitors who've been using the shops in the main hospital to get gifts for their friends and loved ones, and then don't want to go outside again in the cold, are particularly vociferous about this. In the end I decided to start

242

outside the main restaurant on the third floor, because I thought that visitors and patients from the Women's Unit might want to go there and find their way back, but I had to walk around several times to get the hang of what it felt like to be looking for the route. Then that's only the beginning of the job. I've got to knock up a design for the sign on the computer before I sub-contract the manufacture, and that means conforming to a whole set of regulations laid down by the NHS.'

Giles expressed his astonishment at this world of daily work which had suddenly been opened out to him. 'What do you mean, regulations? Surely signs are just signs.'

'Oh no', replied Hannah. 'There are rules for the size, the typeface and even the colour. We have to keep within a certain range of specified tones, though we've managed to squeeze in a sort of Oxford blue to make the point that we're a university hospital. I had to go on a special computer course to learn to use a visual design package before I was allowed to take the job on. I suppose it might be useful for other things in the future. The greater expertise with the computer I've gained is certainly helping with the work that I'm doing with Mark on Benedict's thesis.'

Giles was fascinated by the coincidence that he and Hannah had both had the same corridor in their minds for a while, but did not pursue the issue. Nor did he make any further comment on the vexatious matter of Hannah's collaboration with Mark, though it was causing him a good deal of anguish. Better to let it lie in silence, he thought. He simply arranged to go with her to the unicorn lecture, which carried the mysterious title 'The Unicorn and the Platypus', and which was being held in an Italianate Anglo-Catholic Church deep in the Jericho district.

Meanwhile he determined to use some of his time not earmarked for reading in following up a loose end in the story of Benedict that had been troubling him. He sent an email to the student, Tom Naylor, who had brawled with Benedict in the pub and had curiously ended up being the last student he taught on the afternoon of his death. Giles was quite surprised that Tom had agreed to meet him, but on further thought realized that if he'd killed Benedict he would be anxious to steer him off the track, and if he hadn't he might be glad to get the whole affair out into the open. They arranged to meet in the Jude the Obscure pub in Jericho, named after Thomas Hardy's working-class character Jude who had failed to get into the élite halls of Oxford despite going to all the trouble to learn Greek and Latin. It seemed a suitable venue since Giles himself was suffering exclusion from charmed academia for a while, and Tom seemed to be on the verge of being thrown out altogether.

'I didn't bear him a grudge', burst out Tom after they had got drinks and sat in an uneasy silence for a minute or two. 'I know it looks bad, and I was a fool. I felt angry at the time that Benedict didn't appear to mind messing up my life. He could be a bloody prig, you know, as well as a bloody good tutor. But after we had the fight I didn't hold it against him.'

Tom was shifting around on his seat, his eyes looking nervously over Giles' shoulder and searching here and there in the room, as if worried who might be listening to his confession. 'I was smoking a lot of cannabis at the time, the strong stuff, skunk, as well as popping a few amphetamines. I did get into a crowd who used to amuse themselves by borrowing people's cars to race around in at night. When the college made me go to a psychiatrist later, he told me that I probably had a "cannabis psychosis". Not many people know about that, but I met other students like me in the hospital.'

He hesitated, as if he had said too much, and then said defensively, 'So I wasn't completely responsible for the business with the car. I thought Benedict might see that, but I'm not sure he ever did.'

Giles was not sure he did either, but passed no judgement, asking only, 'What happened the afternoon Benedict died?'

'Nothing really, as far as I was concerned', declared Tom hastily and robustly. 'We had the tutorial, which wasn't a great success because I'd failed to write an essay. It was supposed to be about science and creation. I did stay up all night but I couldn't get started somehow. To be fair, he filled me in with what I should have done – bloody good stuff, actually, I took a lot of notes – we walked out of college together and then parted. It was the last I saw of him.'

Tom had begun truculently, but ended close to tears. That was how Giles related the interview to Hannah later, commenting 'I'm inclined to believe him – I think he's a nicer person than his father – but I also think he was quite capable of doing something violent, given the state he was in at the time. We mustn't forget that Benedict could have ruined his university career by reporting him, and he seems to have been uncertain about what Benedict was likely to do. I haven't tried to work out how he could have got back into the chaplain's lodgings again. Perhaps they went out for a drink and came back together.'

'How does it fit in your theory about the postcards?' enquired Hannah softly, adding 'just supposing there's something in it. Aren't you making things more complicated all the time?'

'I believe that I've decoded the message of the first five cards,' asserted Giles firmly, 'and this means that the sender must have been a woman. But of course we've agreed that the sender may have nothing to do with the way Benedict died, though she might have pushed him into the state of mind where he took his life. Or someone like Tom might have killed him for completely different reasons. Having met Tom he seems a less likely killer, but we can't rule him out.'

Giles did not add that he was not ruling Mark Goodall out either, though every time he thought about the puzzle he swung wildly between agreeing with Hannah that – sadly – Benedict had ended his own life, and his own hunch that Benedict was the victim of somebody else's vengeance, someone who was targeting him as well. Each ache in his chest underlined the second supposition. Meanwhile there was more to learn about unicorns, he thought, and looked forward to accompanying Hannah to the evening lecture in St Barnabas Church, Jericho.

The church was a breath of Italy, with its square tower in the form of a Campanile and its mixed brick and stucco finish. It should have been standing in a sun-soaked piazza, hugging the side of a hill in Umbria, but instead was almost hidden behind a huddle of building hoardings, fencing off a piece of land which bordered the dark waters of the Oxford canal and which had once boasted an ancient boatyard. Now there was only an air of dereliction, although various notices pinned to the ugly barriers promised development and re-creation in an eschaton known only to the builders and planners and continually postponed. Giles had never been inside the church and was startled to find himself facing a shining apse of golden mosaic

245

stones bearing not a grisly cross but the triumphant figure of the resurrected and exalted Christ. Down one side of the nave, between the lofty windows, marched a succession of saints on their way to glory in the apse, while the other side was completely blank, as if the money had run out sometime in the nineteenth century.

It was a memorable setting for a memorial occasion, and Giles took his seat alongside Hannah with a sense of expectation. Looking around before the proceedings began, he was startled to see – apart from Mark Goodall whom he had expected to be present – two other faces he knew. One was Clare whom he'd met at the desk of the print room in the Ashmolean, and the other was Nick Stoney. He determined to speak to them both afterwards over the glass of wine promised, and settled down to listen. Rosie began, as the secretary of the Unicorn Society, speaking about Justin and paying tribute to his many qualities as a scholar and as a friend. She spoke well, with affection and humour, and it seemed to those present and listening that it was fitting that he had not as yet been replaced as President, and that there had been a decent gap in which to celebrate his life. Rosie then went on to mention Benedict, looking into the audience at Hannah while she was speaking, explaining that the Society had lost not one but two good members during the year, both with a brilliant scholarly career ahead of them. Finally she introduced the speaker, a distinguished Professor of the History of Art who was also – remarkably – a scientist.

He took an intriguing subject. What counted as evidence when a fabulous-sounding animal was asserted to exist? The duck-billed platypus, he explained, seemed on first reports as unlikely a combination of features from different animals as the unicorn was. What kinds of proof could be adduced for the one which were missing for the other? And what does this tell us about the way that scientific investigation works? The argument itself was provocative and interesting, but this was not what gripped Giles. The speaker illustrated his talk with visuals about the platypus and the unicorn, and Giles found to his astonishment that the sequence of slides about the unicorn almost exactly matched the postcards and the other portrayals he had come across on his journey of discovery. He was still thinking about whether this coincidence was bound to happen as soon as one spoke about the 'natural history' of the unicorn, or whether there was some mysterious connection at work here that he did not know about, when the lecture came to an end. In something of a daze Giles hardly listened to the few questions and answers that followed the enthusiastic and well-merited applause.

As people got to their feet and there was a general surge towards the table set up at the back with wine and canapés, Giles abandoned Hannah and managed to insinuate himself into the crowd and alongside Clare from the Ashmolean. He greeted her a little shyly.

'Hello there! Do you remember me from my visit to the print room last year? I was looking at the Leonardo drawing of the unicorn, and then you signed up as one of my friends on Facebook – but I expect you have dozens of friends and don't keep track of them all.'

She smiled at him. 'As a matter of fact, I do remember you well, for two reasons. You fell asleep on my watch, and you knew Françoise. I've read about your journeys now and then on your blog.'

Her first recollection did not seem to be entirely to Giles' credit, but he pressed on. 'I was a bit surprised to see you here. Did you know either Justin or Benedict?'

'Well, of course,' replied the young woman, 'I knew them both well through the Unicorn Society. I've been a member of it for a long while. Like all societies, members aren't necessarily friends, but they happened to be both friends, and I admired both of their work in different ways. Benedict and I particularly go back a few years together.'

'It seems quite difficult to become a member,' remarked Giles with feeling.

'I wouldn't worry about that,' said Clare quickly. 'It doesn't mean a lot. Most people just come to the termly lectures like this one. What did you make of it, by the way?'

'Fascinating', said Giles. 'The argument was interesting, of course, but I was most taken by the sequence of visuals about the unicorn. I noticed that the Leonardo was there among others.'

'I have to confess that was my doing', said Clare. 'Our speaker is an expert on Leonardo and I often see him in the print room. I expect he would have chosen that particular image anyway, but I did suggest it to him when he was last in the museum. He was kind enough to ask me for some advice about which pictures and tapestries to use. I think he asked other members of the Society as well, but I helped.'

'You certainly did', agreed Giles warmly. 'The result was marvellous. One more thing, if you don't mind. Was Françoise a member of the Unicorn Society while she was in Oxford?'

'I'm sorry', said Clare, and a slight note of frostiness seemed to have entered into what had been a friendly manner. 'We make it a habit not to give out that kind of information. You'd have to ask her about that directly. Please understand, I'm not saying yes or no.'

Giles felt snubbed, in a conversation that had been pleasant up till then. An unnecessary note of secrecy, even the cultic, seemed to have been introduced. It was with some relief that he saw Clare was drifting off to get a glass of wine and talk to others, and he turned round to find himself facing the glare of Nick.

Giles did his best to be conciliatory. 'Hello, Nick. I'm a bit surprised to see you here. I thought you'd moved away to a new university.'

'Didn't work out,' growled Nick, 'and we all know whose bloody fault that was. Once you've done the dirt on someone it sticks. I'm back in Oxford teaching A-level students at one of the crammers – young people who want to get into Oxford, God help them.'

'If you still feel like that about Benedict, I do wonder why you're here', observed Giles.

'It's not just about God-awful Benedict,' Nick almost shouted, 'it's about Justin, who was a good type, and the subject of the lecture interested me.' Sarcastically he added, 'I suppose that members are allowed to come to meetings of their own society.'

Giles started. He had had no idea that Nick was a member of the Unicorn Society, but then he recollected what Clare had rightly pointed out, that members were not necessarily friends. Nick had moved away to re-fill a glass that Giles guessed had been topped up several times already, and he looked around for Hannah, feeling guilty at having neglected her and suddenly missing her company. It would be good to walk home together, but he failed to see her though he scoured the room. Then it struck him that Mark was missing as well. He had only himself to blame, he reflected sorely. He pushed his way courteously through the throng and then, near the door, came upon someone else he knew whom he had missed in his earlier scan of the room. There stood Jacqui with a woman who was, presumably, Alexia. Resorting to a well-tried phrase he offered a 'Hello! It's a surprise to see you here.'

'Not at all,' replied Jacqui, in a lively manner, 'I could say the same about you. I'm interested in unicorns, as you well know, and the speaker tonight is a distinguished scientist talking about scientific method. It's a topic of absorbing interest to all scientists, and I judged his exposition of what counts as evidence to be superb. Fancy taking the illustration of the unicorn to explore method – only someone who's both a scientist and an art historian could have possibly imagined it.'

Giles hastened to agree, and wondered whether his interest in the visuals had distracted him from the verbals. 'Actually I didn't know you were quite so interested in unicorns', he added. 'I thought that your adventure with Benedict in Alternative World was the beginning and end of the interest. I got that impression from our various talks together about the subject'– and here he recalled silently their conversation in the Italian restaurant on the unicorn gallery, when Jacqui had given no clue of her familiarity with the iconography.

'Well, no', replied Jacqui. 'I'm sorry if I misled you – not that it really matters, surely. After our badly-conducted expedition to the medieval world I read quite a lot about the lore of the unicorn, and looked at a lot of pictures online. And you picqued my interest with the pictures of unicorns you put on your blog from your journeys.'

Giles was now puzzled. He was having to re-think Jacqui's relationship with Benedict. 'Tell me, just when did the medieval adventure happen? I assumed it was quite recent, not long before Benedict's death.'

Jacqui paused and seemed to consider what to disclose. 'No, about four years' ago when we were both just beginning our research. That's gone on longer than I anticipated – a common complaint – but I've nearly finished now.' She added, with a significant look at Alexia, 'it was way before Alexia and I met online,' and she repeated with emphasis, 'way, way before'.

A UNICORN DIES

Giles took his leave and walked home deep in thought. At this one meeting of the Unicorn Society he had met up with quite a number of the actors in Benedict's story. He had been compelled to adjust his thinking on a number of scores. It had been an extraordinary evening, and not just because of the excellent lecture.

A week later he made his way to the John Radcliffe Hospital for a check up in outpatients, and to have the X-ray that would show whether his chest cavity was now clear of damage. All went well, and on the way out he ran into Gregory. He greeted him warmly, and explained that he hoped to be back on duty soon.

'That's good news,' enthused Gregory, 'and would you like a thought for the day?' Giles agreed he would. Gregory pronounced solemnly, 'Robert Louis Stevenson said, "It's better to travel hopefully than to arrive",' and then added with a laugh, 'though I suppose that's better advice for life in general than for the work of a porter.'

Giles laughed as well, but the saying had triggered off a desire to visit the scene of his dreams, in which he could never actually arrive at his destination at the end of the passage. He made his way to the corridor between the main hospital and the Women's Unit. It was a curious experience to be walking down it again, after all that had happened in Colmar. As the Klimt woman came into sight round the bend of the passageway, his experience of the attack flooded back into his mind. Despite the good news of the X-ray his chest still ached from time to time, and – whether in fact or imagination – he suddenly felt the sharp pain of the knife penetrating him. The familiar darkness was beginning to engulf him, to suck him down into the black hole. He collapsed onto a chair placed conveniently at the side of the corridor and set his mind to resist the dark forces. He would not, he determined, succumb and lapse into unconsciousness. He could not say why, but it seemed essential to keep awake, to avoid danger, to escape the terror that was lurking beyond the borders of the light.

Just at that moment he looked up to see the wonderful sight of Hannah, standing pensively in the corridor and looking at the signs to the Women's Unit. His heart leapt up within him, and he knew with the certainty of his faith that salvation lay in her, as it had once lain for nine months in the womb of Mary. He had never loved her more, and with this thought he wrenched himself out of the void and was able to stand up and greet her in quite a normal voice.

23
Stirling Castle

'Why bother about it, then?', enquired Hannah in her usual, straightforward way.

They were sitting around the kitchen table, and Giles had raised the subject of the sixth postcard. He had been expressing his doubts about whether there was any point in chasing up to Scotland to look at a tapestry that was only, by all accounts, an exact duplicate of the one he had seen already in The Cloisters. The card was there, lying in front of them on the table, and Giles had examined it dozens of times already. The unicorn was at bay from the hunters, in balletic pose, scoring a direct hit from its sharp horn on the upturned stomach of one of the attacking dogs while streaming with blood from a bite-wound on its back. It looked as if it could still escape, but Giles knew the fateful end of the story as told in the next and last tapestry in the series. And there was Gabriel, in the guise of one of the hunters carrying the message of the annunciation on his scabbard at what seemed an incongruous moment. 'Ave Regina' it announced in elaborate script. On the back of the card was the message he had read many times: 'Think you're an archangel? You bastard.' Something had evidently gone badly wrong to turn the joyous tones of the Magnificat, celebrating a coming birth, into this sour accusation. The dates on the postcards showed a gap of about six months between the fifth and the sixth – a world enough and time for disaster to have struck the relationship.

'I can see what the message *might* mean', said Giles slowly. 'If we connect the figure of Gabriel in this tapestry with the Gabriel of the "mystic hunt", then the woman sending the card is saying something like, "You think you're like the high and mighty archangel, making me pregnant, but you're not. You're the unicorn in this picture, and something nasty's going to happen to you." That's what I've been thinking, but I'm not happy about it. Things don't quite fit.'

'I'm a bit surprised to hear you say that', said Hannah, with a note of laughter in her voice, mocking him in a charming way. 'You seem very good at making the pieces fit. What can possibly have worried you?'

'Well,' replied Giles defensively, 'that sequence of tapestries in The Cloisters isn't about the "mystic hunt" at all. There's the love hunt, and there's the hunt of the death of Christ, but no trace of the hunt that I saw at Colmar, the one with Gabriel and Mary. I'm having to read that into this last image. I'm supposing that's what the woman sending it must have done, but I'd like to know why she went back to the set of tapestries from The Cloisters for a second go. There's a missing link there, and it leaves me feeling a bit uncomfortable.'

'I'm glad to see you've still got some sense of proportion', responded Hannah. 'You're making some big guesses and leaps of thought in concocting this tale behind the postcards.' After waiting a moment for this to sink in she added, 'I'll tell you another reason why it doesn't fit. It takes a woman to see this. You've been very keen on the symbol of Mary, but it seems all out of character for a woman identifying herself with Mary to write a message like that, let alone follow it up by slitting Benedict's wrists with a paperknife. The message you're finding in the sixth postcard depends on being spoken by the one whose been made pregnant, and that's "Mary". But it doesn't sound like Mary – the tone's all wrong, "bastard" and all that. I'm just not convinced that the two images connect as neatly with each other as you're supposing, and if they don't then perhaps you've got the whole story wrong from the beginning.'

Giles was instantly struck by the brilliance of her observation. He had always thought that Hannah had a quick mind, but this perception was making him re-consider everything, at least momentarily – and Hannah really was delightful when she became intense about something. He had lived so long in the story he had constructed from the postcards and his visits to their originals that he had come simply to assume that it was true. Now he saw readily that the whole structure might be a mere rickety pile. How could someone speaking through one card with the loving voice of Mary then send the hateful message through the other? Without admitting how well aimed Hannah's missile had been, he fell back on his own doubts.

'I'm not saying the woman followed up her threat and actually killed Benedict. She could just have been venting her anger at him, for whatever reason. But I don't see how looking at the tapestry in Stirling Castle is going to tell us anything we don't know already. There seems to be no possibility of discovering who the mystery woman is,' adding to please Hannah, 'if she exists.'

For all that, Giles was irritated by this loose end in his own unicorn hunt, and had a feeling he failed to shake off that he might always regret not actually seeing the tapestry whose image was on the sixth card, even though this tapestry was only a duplicate. Besides this, he had the oddest conviction, which he knew was illogical, that seeing it might somehow help to resolve his position with Hannah. Over the next few days following their conversation, he came to recover some modicum of confidence in the story of the woman and Benedict, despite the problems, and hoped that – against all the evidence – Hannah might be impressed by further discoveries. With the hopeless optimism of love he was inclined to put a positive spin on her remark that he was good at putting the pieces together.

Guiltily he confessed to her that he had decided to take the train up to Stirling. Her reaction was better than he had expected.

'Well if you insist on it, I'd better come as well to keep an eye on you. You're not completely recovered yet from the adventure in Colmar, and you seem to get perpetually into trouble.'

Giles broke the habit of many years and deliberately omitted to post his coming trip on Facebook. He had realized, from the beginning of his journeyings, that his Facebook friends would know more or less where he was, but he had been reluctant to think any of them responsible for the attacks against him. Now he decided to play things as safely as possible.

Hannah made the arrangements for train tickets to Stirling and one night's accommodation with a bed-and-breakfast place near the castle, and at mid-morning not much later they set off from Oxford station on what Giles intended to be the last of his own unicorn hunts. He had been looking forward to eight hours close by Hannah's side, but it seemed that she had either been unsuccessful in booking two seats together, or else had her own reasons for wanting an isolated journey that Giles hesitated to enquire into. As a consequence, for the first hour of the journey he was forced to listen to the continuous drumming sounds and tinny tones of a singer from the earphones of the woman next door to him, who took the liberty of interpreting 'Quiet Coach' to mean permission for personal stereo at full volume. This background noise was punctuated at various points by amplified announcements from train staff who were evidently exempt from any restrictions on their creativity at all, so that as well as announcements of stations Giles was treated to the news that they were running slowly because the 'train in front has terminated' and that 'the shop situation is now open.'

Amused rather than irritated by these experiments with the English language, he was further entertained by reading Lewis Carroll's account of the meeting of Alice with the unicorn in *Through the Looking Glass*, which he had packed in his rucksack with other books. In Carroll's story the lion and the unicorn were constantly scrapping with each other in a friendly manner, living out the nursery rhyme that Alice recalled in her mind:

'The Lion and the Unicorn were fighting for the crown:
The Lion beat the Unicorn all round the town.
Some gave them white bread, some gave them brown;
Some gave them plum-cake and drummed them out of
town.'

Giles made a mental note to chase down the origins of the rhyme, and meanwhile was intrigued by the remark of Carroll's unicorn as he 'sauntered by with his hands in his pockets' that Alice was herself a 'fabulous monster'. Giles spent some time pondering on the bargain proposed by the unicorn to Alice that 'If you'll believe in me, I'll believe in you,' and before he knew it the train was passing through the Lake District on the way to Carlisle.

Grassy slopes showing outcropping of rock bordered the track, opening out to the vague shape of mountains at the horizon. Winding streams, showing erratic patterns of stones breaking the surface were accompanied by stone bothies and occasionally by farm buildings with corrugated iron roofs. Giles fell into a daydream in which he envisaged living in this pleasant area alone with Hannah, and this soon modulated into hopes of what might possibly lie ahead in the night to come. From time to time he took out the sixth postcard from his pocket and entertained himself by fitting the hunting scene into the passing landscape outside the window, overlaying the streams he could see with the brook at the bottom of the tapestry. As often before he wondered idly what viewing the duplicate of the Cloisters tapestry could possibly tell him more than the original he had already seen in New York, and he questioned again why the sender had chosen a postcard showing the Scottish copy of it. The printed caption on the reverse of the card informed him that the image had been woven, together with copies of the rest of The Cloisters set, by the West Dean Tapestry Studio for Stirling Castle in celebration of Scotland's heritage. He was aware that the unicorn was a symbol connected with the history of Scotland, but he was still puzzled by what seemed a highly elaborate way of decorating a castle.

After Carlisle, as they meandered through the Scottish lowlands the sheep continued to be omnipresent, fattening themselves on every grassy knoll and watched over by a late-afternoon, pale moon, but the backdrop of mountains had vanished and only re-appeared as they neared Edinburgh. Haymarket Station, where they changed trains and had a takeaway meal on a platform seat, was a bubble of shining glass and aluminium hovering over tracks which disappeared into a tunnel blackened by past aeons of smoke and surmounted by equally discoloured tenement buildings. A largely suburban journey to Stirling was broken by occasional green fields, the shadow of distant hills and a solitary oil flare from the Firth of Forth.

From the railway station Giles and Hannah followed the map to their bed-and-breakfast house along a path winding around the castle mount which bore the utilitarian name 'Back Walk'. It did what it promised, since high above them, through sparse trees and vegetation loomed the massive shape of the rear walls of the castle, hewn from grey granite. Giles looked at Hannah, striding steadily ahead of him through the gathering dusk, the bottom edge of her hair curling gently inwards at the collar, unveiling a patch of bare neck now and then as she moved, her shoulders sitting neatly under a red padded jacket, her back falling straight to a short skirt fringing legs clad in black leggings, bent at the knee at a point he wanted desperately to touch. He looked, and longed to be closer to her with feeling that was compounded of respect, love and lust in equal measures. Spring was in the air.

Arriving at their lodgings, Giles' spirits rose as he discovered that Hannah had booked one room for them both, but sank again when he discovered that this arrangement had been driven more by reasons of economy than sex. The room contained a double and a single bed and Hannah, emerging in silk pyjamas from the en-suite bathroom to occupy the single bed, seemed to indicate that she intended to continue the same policy of 'near but separate' as she had shown on the train. It appeared that a frustrating time for Giles, sleeping in the double, could be eased only by his anticipation of viewing the set of tapestries on the next day and by whatever else to which he cared to resort. The modern sexual nuances of the unicorn which surged through his mind in the darkness hardly helped the situation. But in the middle of the night he was awoken by a delightful disturbance in the duvet covering him, and he discovered to his surprise and joy that all his fevered imaginings of the journey would be fulfilled after all.

In her matter-of-fact way at the substantial Scottish breakfast the next morning, Hannah mentioned that she had left the option open of joining him for the night, and had in the end been influenced by the romanticism of the trip and her affection for him. He should not expect, she continued, that the situation had essentially changed, but she was grateful for his response. For his part, he admired her handling of the night's events, and he was content enough that his hopes for a more long-lasting relationship with Hannah were still alive, even if his clerical rival still lurked in the shadows. He did not dare to ask her whether she had also been stirred, in his case, by the romantic situation of revising Benedict's thesis.

Buoyed up by the sensations of the night past, he returned with Hannah along the Back Walk to the historic centre of the town. As they walked under the grim mass of the castle they noticed wooden figures carved out of the ends of tree stumps on the slopes above them, but could not make out what they represented. They agreed that, on the way back, they would take the higher path they could see around the castle mount in order to view the carvings more closely, even though this would be a longer way back to the station.

Emerging from the Back Walk into Broad Street, Giles became aware that he was entering the land of the unicorn. In the middle of the street, flanked by granite houses, there stood what appeared to be a market cross, but it was crowned by the ancient stone emblem of a unicorn holding a crest. A notice nearby informed him that this was a 'Mercat Cross', and that these crosses were often surmounted by unicorns, since they were used for royal proclamations and the unicorn supported the royal arms. In this case the unicorn had affectionately been dubbed 'Puggy' by the inhabitants for centuries. The notice concluded by quoting the nursery rhyme, *The Lion and the Unicorn were fighting for the crown...* Giles wondered briefly whether a unicorn on a cross would provoke confusion between the king and Christ, but then realized that this was probably the idea anyway.

At the end of the street the road rose towards the Castle gates, and there came into view the Great Hall within the curtail of the castle, painted in a striking golden-yellow, on whose roof ridge two unicorns and two lions stood out against the sky. Paying their entrance fee, Giles and Hannah were given tickets bearing the head of a unicorn. Entering the gift shop nearby to buy a guidebook, they found shelves full of fluffy pink unicorns for children, unicorn brooches and key-rings, and postcards of the unicorn tapestries among which Giles spied the one he had been carrying with him. They discovered that the tapestries were housed in the Queen's Inner Hall in the Royal Buildings, and as they walked through a succession of rooms to get there the unicorn emblem continued to proliferate around them.

In the King's Outer and Inner Halls huge painted banners depicted a pair of unicorns supporting the royal crest of the red lion of Scotland, and unicorn bosses were scattered over the ceiling of the King's bedchamber. Prominent in the Queen's bedchamber was a crest supported by a unicorn and an eagle, uniting the arms – so a notice informed them – of James V and his Queen, Mary of Guise. The same device of the unicorn and the eagle hung on a rich red banner in the Queen's Inner Hall, and everywhere there were unicorns, their horns crossed on wall friezes and supporting crests on iron fire grates. After hunting for solitary and hidden examples of unicorns in different cities of the world, Giles was overwhelmed by an environment where it seemed that unicorns gathered in herds and showed themselves openly. Stirling Castle, a principal home of the Kings of Scotland since James IV might as well be renamed 'Unicorn Castle'. He began to get some inkling of why the modern refurbishers of the castle wanted to reproduce a set of unicorn tapestries from elsewhere.

And there they hung, in the Queen's Inner Hall, covering the four walls. Entering the room, the tapestry of 'The Unicorn in Captivity', the image of the fourth of Benedict's postcards, caught Giles' eye immediately, hanging over the fireplace. Immediately to its right, on the next right-angled wall, he spied the tapestry depicted on his sixth postcard, 'The Unicorn at Bay'. To its right on the same wall there hung the tapestry depicting the killing of the unicorn and the carrying of it to the castle. The modern weavers had accentuated the Christ-allegory by making explicit the dripping of the unicorn's blood into the horn of a hunter, making the flared rim of the horn red and giving it the appearance of a chalice. On the wall opposite to these Giles noticed the first and second tapestries from the sequence depicting the hunt to the death, and on their left on the right-angle wall the 'Start of the Hunt'.

The six images were quite familiar to him. He had spent time studying them at the Cloisters, and he had two of them on the set of postcards inherited from Benedict. The colours of the wool stood out with a freshness, especially the blue of the sky. In 'The Unicorn at Bay', lighting from the bottom edge brought out vividly the movement into flight of the water-fowl, and the bounding up of the dogs to snap at the unicorn, but nothing really new came to mind on seeing the image in actuality. He was pointing out the details in the tapestry to Hannah, and explaining the five others briefly, when she interrupted him.

'But what about that one?' she asked, pointing to a narrower tapestry hanging between two windows. 'That's really striking.'

A UNICORN DIES

Startled by her question, he swung round to see something totally unexpected. There was a seventh tapestry opposite the fireplace, brightly lit by a spotlight. It seemed at the same time oddly familiar and yet entirely strange. A young woman was seated with her hand around a unicorn's neck, its front legs lying in her lap. After a moment he recognized the pair as being just like the Lady and the unicorn in the tapestry portraying 'sight' in the series hanging in the Cluny Museum. The posture was the same, though reversed right to left, and the woman was holding the unicorn's neck instead of a mirror. He did not recall anything like this being among the Cloisters' tapestries at all. Then he suddenly remembered the two mysterious fragments he had seen hanging over the doorway in the Unicorn Hall, which he could make no sense of at the time. They had had been joined together by the modern weavers and a seated woman had been added. The first piece had shown a hunter in the bushes with his four dogs. The second piece had shown a lady in red standing with the unicorn at her feet, wounded in the back from the bites of two of the dogs. But now the pieces had been reunited and a second woman had been added, and Giles suddenly saw that the scene was an annunciation, just like the painting at Colmar. The hunter concealed in the bushes was Gabriel who was chasing the unicorn into the lap of Mary, now present as the seated woman.

When he had looked long and hard at the tapestries in The Cloisters, Giles had felt that Mary was missing in the sets, but she was there after all, present and yet absent, ripped out of the fragmented tapestry. He could not help exclaiming out loud, 'So who's the woman in red?'

'Why, Eve of course', replied a familiar American voice. He turned sharply to see who was speaking, and Professor Earl King was standing behind him, with a curious smile on his face.

'What on earth are you doing here, and what do you mean, Eve?'

'Answering your questions in order: collecting material for my art class, and the first woman.'

Getting over his surprise at seeing Earl, Giles replied shortly, 'Well, of course I know who Eve was. But what's she doing here? And where did Mary come from – I suppose it is Mary?'

'Full marks, well done,' replied Earl in his best lecturing manner. 'It's Mary of course. The designer of the tapestries wanted to complete the tapestry which exists in two fragments in the Cloisters collection. It was damaged in the period after the French Revolution when it was looted from a chateau and used by the peasants for keeping their vegetables frost-free in the winter. When you saw it in the Cloisters, didn't you notice a couple of fingers just visible round the neck of the unicorn? It's a clue that someone was holding him who went missing when the tapestry got torn up. Given all the other images from the Middle Ages, it was obviously a virgin spreading her lap for the unicorn, and remarkably the Lady from Cluny slotted right in. Since Gabriel appears in the third tapestry from the hunt to death sequence, it's odds on that he's the hunter in the bushes.'

'But why Eve?' persisted Giles.

'She's the other side of Mary. The first woman sins in the garden by taking the forbidden fruit. There's the apple tree to tell you that, next to the usual holly and oak trees. It's an apple tree that Mary's sitting under – there's a nice touch – put the virgin under a tree, and it's the tree of fatal disobedience. Mary is the new Eve, obeying God by consenting to becoming the mother of the Saviour.'

Giles thought of Emily's protest against the slandering of Eve in a tutorial that now seemed long ago, as well as his tutor's protest against the slandering of apple trees, but he said only, 'Eve looks very sly.'

'She's betraying the unicorn to the hunter, and his dogs are wounding the unicorn.'

'But the hunter's Gabriel. Isn't he on God's side?' asked Giles in some perplexity. 'I don't quite get the plot.'

'Well, the picture's working on all kinds of levels' replied Earl. 'It's a hunting scene, so of course the quarry gets hurt. Then it's certainly the purpose of God for the Saviour to be born from the womb of Mary, but he's also born to die, and Gabriel knows this. It's the sin of Eve that makes it necessary, so she's a betrayer, but her sin is also part of the divine story of redemption. Some early Christians used to say "O happy fault!". Making her into a betrayer of the unicorn at least keeps Mary innocent. In fact, Eve makes an appearance in several medieval "unicorn annunciations".'

'It's hard to take it all in', confessed Giles. 'But I'm just astounded by the way this new tapestry brings together the images I've seen in a number of places. It's a kind of climax to my quest for the unicorn.'

In fact, he could hardly suppress his excitement. The woman in red was – he believed – the final clue to the decoding of the postcards, but he said nothing about this to Earl. He was saving it to share with Hannah, and only with her.

Meanwhile Hannah, standing beside Giles and listening to their conversation, had been bursting to say something to Earl. Finally she broke in, 'I've met you before, in Oxford. I remember you – you're actually hard to forget. You came into the hospital where I work. I even remember the spot I met you – upstairs in the corridor to the women's hospital.'

'I asked you for directions to outpatients,' Earl agreed. 'I'd been stung by a bee and I was having a bad reaction. My throat was closing up and I needed anti-histamine quickly. I'd got myself lost in your maze of a hospital and I was on the wrong floor.'

Giles was astounded at the news. 'Wait a minute', he exclaimed, 'All the time we talked about Oxford you never told me you'd been there.'

'I never denied it,' said Earl. 'I was there collecting material – do you know the da Vinci maiden with a unicorn in the Ashmolean? I was anxious to see it, and I did. The curators were very helpful, especially one young woman whose name I forget.'

Giles' suspicions about Earl had been doubled by this admission, confirming the conclusion he had reached on his American trip that Earl was a man full of secrets who told you only what he wanted you to know. However, he decided that it would do no harm to make the most of Earl's indisputable expertise on the subject and continued, 'Now you're here, perhaps you can explain why there are images of the unicorn everywhere. This seems like unicorn castle.'

Earl dropped back into his teaching mode. 'James the First of Scotland seems to have picked up the motif during his imprisonment in England, where it was becoming fashionable on coats of arms. He needed animals to support his armorial shield which bore the red lion of Scotland, and so he purloined the unicorn, using two of them as supporters. The household manifests for James the Fifth show he had two sets of unicorn tapestries, though none are left today, and he had two ceremonial barges that he named 'The Lion' and 'The Unicorn'. Then James the Sixth used it to unite the two national thrones when he became James the First of England on the death of Elizabeth – a golden lion for England, a unicorn for Scotland, though Scotland already had its own red lion. Do you know the nursery rhyme which first appeared in 1603?'

To Giles' embarrassment he began to sing *The Lion and the Unicorn were fighting for the crown* in a rich baritone voice, and was immediately shushed by the attendants who looked ready to throw out this alarming American.

'My own theory', continued Earl unabashed, 'is that "the Lion beat the Unicorn" means that the English lion supplants one of the Scottish unicorns on the royal arms, but I have to admit it's all a bit obscure. Perhaps it's just the English getting their revenge because they're upset having a Scottish king foisted on them when they were used to beating them in battle over the years.'

'So it's political, not religious,' Giles summed up.

'Probably both', corrected Earl. 'Have you seen the Mercat cross? I take it this is a claim that Christ is backing Scotland.'

'Is that why there's a kind of altar under the seventh tapestry?' enquired Giles. He pointed to a tall wooden chest topped off by a white cloth and two candles. It was actually covering up about a foot of tapestry at the bottom of the picture – he could just see a rabbit hidden behind the canopy of the cupboard if he squinted, and he felt some compassion for the weaver who had lovingly created the woollen animal only for it never to see the light of day.

'That's probably just an accident of arranging furniture in the room', explained Earl. 'It's not an altar – though I agree it looks like one – but a buffet. In a wealthy household their silver and gold plates would be arranged on top, to show visitors how rich the family was. There aren't any plates here, and there's probably too much of a risk of their going missing with people like me around.' At this remark, the attendants looked even more nervous than before, and made a distinct move towards Earl.

'The arrangement reminds me of something I saw in the previous room', remarked Giles hastily, and took Earl to have a look at it, thinking it safer to remove him from the scene in the Inner Hall. There too was a cupboard with a white cloth on top, this time surmounted by a triptych showing the Madonna and Child in the central panel. The designers of the room had evidently wanted it to represent a typical object of veneration by the Catholic Mary of Guise.

'Do you remember we talked about the parallels between the maiden and the unicorn and the virgin and child in the Borghese museum in Rome?' Giles asked Earl. The connection puzzled me then, but I figured it out when I saw a picture of "the mystic hunt" in Colmar. We've got the same linking here with the seventh tapestry.'

'I'll use your ideas for one of my lessons,' responded Earl, and Giles chose to take the remark seriously.

Returning to the Inner Hall, where the attendants seemed to have relaxed in the meanwhile, Giles studied the face of the Virgin in the newly completed tapestry. There was something about the set of the mouth that gave the same impression as the Raphael portrait in the Borghese. It was not the same shape at all – unlike the mouth of Raphael's maiden, it drooped at one corner – but it had exactly the same determination about challenging the world and taking on all comers. He pointed this out to Earl, who had – as usual – something further to add.

'The face as it looks now is quite different from the early drawings for the tapestry that have been published', Earl remarked. 'Some people think it now bears a remarkable resemblance to the modern artist Tracy Emin, and the project manager in fact had a close collaboration with Emin and was influenced by her intimate self-portraits'.

Giles and Hannah said farewell to Earl, uneasily. There was something about his failure to mention being in Oxford that nagged at Giles, though he still thought he had solved the puzzle of the postcards and he could not wait to tell Hannah about it when they were on their own.

The seventh tapestry

24
The upper path

Hannah and Giles left the Queen's Inner Hall through an Outer Hall which boasted yet another large insignia of the unicorn and the eagle, walked past yet another gift shop bearing a unicorn design on its glass doors, and made their exit from the castle as an excited and noisy group of schoolchildren came in chattering about finding unicorns. Giles hoped they would find more than the fluffy pink kind. He and Hannah had decided to return to the station by a longer route, along the upper path of the Back Walk, looping back onto the lower path and so through the streets to catch their train in the early afternoon. On the way they planned to look at the wood carvings placed on the slope of the castle mount.

Heading for the upper path, they skirted the dark medieval bulk of the Church of the Holy Rood where James VI had been crowned King of Scotland. Church and gloomy graveyard passed, Giles had his opportunity to tell Hannah about his discovery in the Queen's Hall and get her reaction.

'As I thought', began Giles, 'the message of the last postcard is a threat. Benedict may think he's the archangel, but he's the unicorn and is about to be killed.'

'You'd already decided that,' objected Hannah, 'and my point still stands. It doesn't sound like a woman who thinks of herself as being Mary. And why send a postcard with the modern copy of the tapestry instead of an image of the original? I've enjoyed coming here, but I don't think I'm any wiser.'

'But don't you see?' broke in Giles. '"The Unicorn at Bay" is hanging opposite the new, restored tapestry of Mary and the unicorn. The woman who sent the postcards from the Cloisters series saw the two images together. It shows that it's not just a wild leap to read "The Unicorn at Bay" as an episode following the annunciation story, and to link the Gabriels who appear in both. The same woman who conceived a child like Mary is now telling Benedict that he's the unicorn heading for death.'

'I can see that,' replied Hannah slowly and reluctantly. 'But could a woman who identified with Mary send the "bastard" message?'

'That's just what seeing the tapestries together solved for me. It struck me like a blinding light. The vicious message isn't coming from Mary. It's coming from the other woman in the new tapestry – Eve, the woman in red, as red as the blood trickling down the back of the unicorn. Or rather, it's coming from the "Eve" side of the unknown woman's personality. With her Mary part she rejoiced earlier on in the coming child. With her Eve part she's blaming Benedict for something that's now gone wrong. The woman in red betrays the unicorn and she's threatening Benedict with death as well.'

Giles felt quite exhausted. He had put all he had into explaining the mystery and had spoken passionately. If he could not persuade Hannah, his only love, he thought, he had no chance at all of convincing sceptics like D.I. Longley – if the time ever came to tell him the whole story.

Hannah was frowning. 'I thought you'd given up the idea that one person had sent all the cards and was responsible for Benedict's death.'

Wearily, Giles responded, 'I admit that you made me doubt it, but now this seventh tapestry has made all the difference. It's the same woman who has sent all the cards after all, and when you decode the message it's probably the same woman who killed him. I know it's not proof that she carried out her threat, but it's at least likely. Of course, I still don't know who she is and perhaps I never will.'

Hannah was silent. Giles wasn't sure how she was taking his announcement, but he hoped that his passion on the subject – as well as his passion last night – might have had some effect. It appeared, however, that she had decided to change the subject. 'We're near to where we saw the tree carvings', she said. 'Let's go and look at them.'

Giles preferred this suggestion to an argument, and not much further along the path they came to some steps winding downwards to the left. Giles climbed down a narrow platform looking down to the lower path about seventy feet below, and across to fields and hills in the distance. There was no rail provided, and the slope covered by vegetation was a steep one, though it fell short of being a sheer drop. About fifteen feet down from the lookout point he could now clearly see three life-size wood carvings, made from the tree stumps on which they still stood. One figure sat with some kind of tool in his hand, while another figure was kneeling backwards with his head cut off and fallen in a grisly manner at his feet. Between them stood an ominous figure in a long cloak, with his face hidden in a cowl and an upraised axe. A notice at the spot, headed 'Baird & Hardie' explained all, and Giles read it carefully.

'John Baird and Andrew Hardie were hung and beheaded at the Stirling Tolbooth by surgical student, Thomas Moore, in 1820. Moore had been draughted in as the local hangman refused to carry out the executions.

John Baird and Andrew Hardie are now counted among the pioneers of Scottish democracy. They were weavers who led a call for reform during the Radical War of 1820, also known as the Scottish Insurrection.

The Radical War called for fairer working conditions and a more responsive government to the high employment rate and high food prices which had up until that point been largely ignored. For this they were charged with treason.

Original relics including Moore's cloak and axe are on display in the Smith Museum and Art Gallery.'

Giles stood there, appalled. He had noticed the Tolbooth or courtroom situated opposite the Mercat Cross in Broad Street, and he was now learning that this was where their trials had taken place. The act of brutal execution had happened under the gaze of the stone unicorn, supposedly representing royal justice. There flashed back into his mind the substance of the doctoral thesis on which Benedict had been working, reflecting on the many scapegoats that society had persecuted, and their resemblance to the fate of the mythical unicorn. He recalled the Jews dying in Clifford's Tower in York, the Christians thrown to wild animals in Roman arenas and the witches burned in Colmar. That year in Stirling the lion and the unicorn had certainly been struggling in a radical war, and the unicorn was embodied in these weavers and not in the uncaring crown. *The Lion beat the Unicorn all around the town...* Perhaps, he imagined, these victims had been weavers of tapestries, even weaving the gorgeous hangings of the unicorn for the castle from which the soldiers had been despatched to defeat the revolutionaries. With these thoughts there came the memory of Benedict himself, and his bloody death, and he felt the inevitable onset of dizziness and the opening of a black hole beneath him.

As he fought back the sensation and struggled for consciousness he saw Hannah coming down the steps towards him, and it seemed that she was having difficulty in putting one foot in front of another. She was crouched over, clinging onto the face of the vertical rock into which the steps had been cut, and appeared half-paralyzed.

'Hannah, what's the matter?' he managed to call out. 'It's not very steep here – it's quite easy to get down.'

'I get vertigo,' she panted, 'I can't help it', and with this she fell against him heavily. They swayed together on the lip of the lookout platform and as he finally blacked out he fell over the edge, bouncing against one of the carvings as he careered down the slope into the void that threatened to swallow him up.

He recovered consciousness on the path at the bottom. He found he was aching all over, and blood was oozing from cuts on his face and hands. His ribs felt badly bruised, and he suspected that he had twisted an ankle and wrenched a knee, but almost miraculously he seemed to have rolled down the slope without breaking any bones. Even the knife wound to his chest had not re-opened. Looking up, he saw that he might have hit any one of the trees or large rocks that stood sparsely on the slope beneath the carvings, and that his fate would have been very different if he had, but luckily he had missed them entirely and the soft vegetation had cushioned his body. In a couple of minutes Hannah reached him. She had apparently been released from her frozen state of vertigo and had made her way up the steps and round the upper path to where it descended and joined the lower one. She bent over him, tears in her eyes and full of apologies for any part she might have played in knocking him over the edge. He reassured her that no great damage been done, but it was obvious that he could not now walk to the station. They cleaned up his cuts as best as they could with handkerchiefs, and hobbling along, he made it to the main road at the further end of the Back Walk. Hannah phoned for a taxi on her mobile as he sat down heavily at the side of the road.

They just managed to catch the last train to Edinburgh that connected with the Oxford train, and on the long leg back home Giles lay back in his seat, eyes closed. The nursery rhyme, *The Lion and the Unicorn*, kept running inanely through his mind with its insistent rhythm, like the beat of the drum-set from the earphones of his neighbour on the outward journey. In waking dreams, he struggled to get out of a deep bath from which water-fowl were oddly flying up – woodcock, ducks and snipe – and there the figure of the woman in red appeared, bending over him with a sly look on her face. She was Eve ... she was the betrayer ... she was ... suddenly he believed he knew who she was. He sat bolt upright, and the worst thought in the world fixed itself in his mind. She was Hannah.

But surely she couldn't be. His Hannah. He glanced across the aisle of the carriage where she was sitting opposite him, again in separated seats. He loved everything about her – the profile of her face, her serious look as she attended to what she was reading, the delicate curtain of hair falling around her cheeks and chin, her mouth set with determination, and above all the liveliness of her mind. Surely she could not be the lion to his unicorn, the Eve as well as the Mary in whose role he had – he now realized – implicitly cast her.

Silently he reviewed the possible suspects for the sender of the postcards and the killer of Benedict – if in fact he had been murdered. It was just conceivable that the two suspects were not the same person, though he was inclined to think that they were after the revelation of 'the Woman in Red.' His head began to spin as he considered the permutations. There were the men – Nick, Tom, Justin and Mark. As time had gone by it had become clear that they could not have sent the cards, and yet they remained in the frame, even Justin, for a possible murder. Earl was now raising similar nagging questions in his mind, especially after the revelation that he had been in Oxford. As Giles had decoded the cards, the figure of a woman had begun to take the central role in the love-hate drama he was uncovering, and he now wondered for the first time whether Jacqui or Françoise, or even Clare or Rosie might fit the part. It seemed inconceivable that any of them would have acted so ruthlessly to try and stop him finding the truth. The cast of suspects was a large one, but at first he resisted making Hannah any part of it. However, in an agony of mind, with his world turned upside down, he gradually faced the most terrible possibility of all. As the train carried him past Carlisle and towards Wolverhampton he ticked off all the damning points in his mind.

All his friends knew where he was going on his various travels from his Facebook postings, but it was only Hannah who had known the actual addresses where he was staying. It wasn't absolutely necessary (he comforted himself) for an attacker to have known these details, but it would have made things easier. She could at least have been behind the attacks on him, and now she had offered of her own accord to come with him to Stirling where he had had another accident in which she was certainly closely implicated. He shivered as he thought of her bending over him on the path in her red jacket, like the woman in red standing over the wounded unicorn. Further, she was familiar with the corridor to the Women's Centre in the course of her work, and had sufficient expertise in computer design programmes to produce the online version of it. She had been discouraging about the conclusions he was reaching in reading the messages on the postcards, and had poured cold water on the idea that he was the target of attacks. He knew nothing about her history with Benedict before her engagement, and it was quite feasible that their early partnership had included the conception of a child. At the time when he knew them both it was obvious that their relationship was under a strain. It was difficult to imagine that it had reached the depths of the accusation "bastard!" but if the woman in red had a divided personality, perhaps the Eve part of her was capable of this kind of hatred. Really, Giles reflected, he knew so little about Hannah.

A few things stood against her being the woman in red, thought Giles with a surge of hopefulness. First, she seemed genuinely upset, even broken up, by the death of Benedict. But then a divided personality could explain this too. She might lament with Mary but plot with Eve. She had been ready to begin a new relationship with Mark Goodall and even with himself – though even as he thought this he realized how unfair to her he was being. He knew Shakespeare's play *Othello* well enough to recognize that this was the very argument of the villain Iago ('She did deceive her father, marrying you...').

Giles also hadn't entirely ruled out that the woman who had loved Benedict, carried his child and then sent him a threatening message was not after all his killer. He was now convinced of the story of love and hate that the decoded cards had yielded up, and it was (as he had told Hannah) more likely than not that the woman was the murderer. But there was still just the possibility that someone else had killed Benedict or that he had even taken his own life. It was a remote chance, but it opened up a crack of light if Hannah were the woman in question behind the cards.

If ... but that was the point, and the most powerful factor of all stood against it. This was simply his love for her, and his innate feeling that she could not have deceived him. He believed in her and – as the unicorn had said to Alice – he wanted her to believe in him with all his heart. But was this enough in face of all the evidence? As the train rattled on between Birmingham and Oxford, playing the tune *The Lion and the Unicorn* as it went over the gaps in the rails, he could not make up his mind. His world had been torn apart as violently as the seventh tapestry had been torn, and he could only hope for the same kind of restoration by a skilful weaver.

25 The river

Back in Oxford Giles continued to live in a broken universe after his devastating experience at Stirling Castle. Just two days had been enough to turn his own heart against him. His time there with Hannah had begun with the joy of a Springtime comedy and had ended in the worst tragedy he could imagine.

He did not know what to do about his doubts in her and re-reading *Othello* had only made things much worse. He could not bring himself to ask her directly whether she was the woman in red and the sender of the postcards, in case this blighted his relationship with her for ever. At times he felt unsafe in the house and locked his bedroom door at night, and at other times he felt thoroughly ashamed of his suspicions. At times he wished he had never begun the unicorn hunt, and at others he remembered with gratitude the moments he had spent with Hannah around the kitchen table. At times he was intensely jealous of the work she was still doing with Mark Goodall on preparing Benedict's thesis for publication, and at others he was inclined to say 'let her go!' He was living in a state of suspended animation, and he had no idea how to resolve the conflict or still the storm beating away in his mind.

Meanwhile he was fit enough to return to work at the hospital following the healing of his knife-wound, and after a few days he was also none the worse for his precipitation down the castle slope at Stirling. A few weeks remained before he was due to return to his college to continue his degree in Trinity Term. Leaving the surgical ward outpatient clinic one afternoon, he was glad to run into his former colleague Gregory pushing an empty wheel-chair, obviously on the way to pick up a patient.

They were both pleased to see each other, and Giles asked straightaway, 'Do you have a thought for the day for me?'

Gregory looked him in the eyes in his usual serious way, seemed to sum him up, and then offered 'The heart has its reasons for which the reason knows nothing', adding after a pause, 'That's from the philosopher Blaise Pascal, though I expect you knew that.'

'I didn't, actually,' responded Giles, 'but your quote's more apt for what's happened to me than you can possibly have known. I've been injured in the course of a sort of quest of the heart. It's a very long story, but I've been hunting unicorns, or at least paintings and tapestries of unicorns. Some day I'll tell you all about it.'

'It's a funny thing,' responded Gregory, 'but I had a patient a few years ago now who was mentioning unicorns. I've always remembered it, as it seemed odd at the time.'

'I'd really like to hear about that', said Giles curiously. 'I'm due for a coffee break now. Are you free any time soon?'

Gregory was, right after his pending errand, and so in twenty minutes time they were sitting together in the League of Friends coffee shop enjoying a couple of cappuccinos at an amazingly low price.

'It happened like this', recounted Gregory. 'I was summoned one day in winter to pick up a patient in a wheel-chair from near the reception desk on the entrance level, and instructed to take her to the Women's Centre. It seemed she'd come for an appointment, but was in a terrible state. She should have gone directly to the Women's Centre entrance, but had somehow ended up in the main hospital. She was very distraught, and appeared to have had a sort of collapse. The receptionist was rightly worried about her and had rung the porters' management room for help. Other women have turned up emotionally upset, usually when they're facing a termination of a pregnancy, but I don't recall anyone being quite as bad as that. She was wearing a thin, red dress with no coat and she was shivering.'

Giles remembered his own journey with the ordered medication from pharmacy to the Women's Centre, and made an informed guess. 'I suppose, because of the cold outside, you took her the winding way inside, up in the lift and round the corridor over the bridges?'

'Exactly', said Gregory. 'It seemed the kindest thing to do. She was too disturbed to walk, and all the way she kept muttering about unicorns. I remember she said something like, "I should never have let the unicorn near me," and "I always knew the unicorn was an unkind beast".'

Giles was gripped by a sudden excitement. 'Tell me again', he said. 'You're sure you did take her through the corridor where all the offices are, past the academic block and the library?'

'Absolutely', Gregory assured him. 'I remember because the local primary school had just donated that large picture which looks like a Klimt woman, and it was hanging there. As we went past it she laughed in a hysterical way and asked, "Is that supposed to be me?" She had calmed down by the time we got to the reception desk. Perhaps the ride in the chair helped.'

'I think you've just solved the most important mystery in the world for me', said Giles in what was now a wave of excitement. At last the end of the quest was coming into view, and his doubts could be resolved. He was ready to face the truth and to act courageously on it, whatever it might be. Only one question remained to be asked, and he asked it.

'What did she look like?'

Gregory told him.

Later that day Giles was sitting with a woman at a kitchen table. She had made them cups of coffee, and he sat letting it warm his hands, taking an occasional sip. 'I can't believe it was you all the time', he said. 'You really hid it so well.'

She laughed bitterly. 'I didn't know much about the art-history of the unicorn, but Benedict talked to me a lot about it, and when the idea of the postcards came to me I had the help of Justin – you know, the President of the Unicorn Society.'

'Is that why you had to kill Justin?' Giles asked gently. 'I suppose you did and that his death wasn't an accident.'

'Oh yes, I killed him all right', she admitted. 'He was beginning to become suspicious, especially when you asked him about the Cluny tapestry. Then he was stupid to tell you about the Klimt, but he thought that since it wasn't to do with the postcards it wouldn't matter. It was a crowded platform and it wasn't difficult to push him off the edge. Everyone always ignores the yellow line and he wasn't an exception.'

Giles shivered, despite the heating and the coffee. 'But how could you bring yourself to kill Benedict?' he asked. 'I suppose it was you, and that you didn't just drive him to suicide?'

A steely look he had never seen before came into her eyes. 'Yes, I killed him. He was an insufferable hypocrite', she said with heavy emphasis, close to shouting. 'His thesis was all about the oppressed and the marginalized and how we should give them priority – God's preference for the poor, he even called it – and all the time he didn't seem to care how much he'd hurt me. Perhaps women weren't in his list of the persecuted. I'll never forget that terrible journey along the corridor and past the children's painting in the John Radcliffe hospital on the way to have my baby aborted – terminated they call it. It seemed an extra insult to be wheeled past the 'Care of the New-born' unit. No nativity for me. No new-born child. Remembering that and the copy of the Klimt woman gave me a new slant on the Gabriel-Mary story. Gabriel wasn't a joyous messenger at all but a cruel hunter like all males.'

'But why didn't you have the baby?' asked Giles gently.

'Don't you realize how difficult it is to start a career with a young child when you've got no support?' she retorted angrily. 'You're no better than Benedict. I'd left the pregnancy for 17 weeks because I was hoping he'd come round and accept the baby, but he was too taken up with his own career to want a child, and kept urging me to end the pregnancy. Finally I needed a surgical procedure. It wasn't difficult to get the consent of two doctors on "social and mental grounds" given the state I was in. I won't trouble you with the sordid details of vacuuming out the womb, but I bled for days afterwards and developed an infection. Later they told me at the hospital that I'd been the unlucky one in a thousand and I was unlikely to be able to have other children.'

Giles was shocked by her account, and reflected once again that Benedict had been a very mixed personality. He understood now why he had been left with a sense of guilt that had obviously still been haunting him when he was killed. 'Why did you create the "Unicorn Gallery" in Alternative World?' he asked.

'Well, I didn't do it to trap you – don't compliment yourself on that!' she replied. 'I suppose it was a kind of catharsis. Putting the unicorn story together after I'd killed Benedict, commemorating all the women that men and a male God had abused and then including the Klimt woman in the corridor helped me come to terms with my own tragedy. I kept telling you that I wasn't interested in the paintings and the tapestries to put you off the scent, but in fact I became obsessed by them. I use the computer a lot each day, and I went on designing the site while I was supposed to be doing my proper work. Justin had given me a picture of the Farnese Gallery and I got a programmer friend to help me with the technical stuff. Now I've finished it I spend a lot of time just sitting in the gallery, and I couldn't believe it when a unicorn – or someone with a unicorn avatar – came along. I felt he was trampling all over my sacred space and I immediately contacted a group of my friends who were online in Alternative World to help me expel the intruder. I didn't know it was you until you told me what had happened that morning over coffee.'

'So when did you start the scheme of the postcards?' enquired Giles, trying to get the story straight in his mind.

'They began while Benedict and I were still in the first stages of our relationship. I wanted him to know how I felt about him and I don't find it easy to say these things directly. Justin helped me choose them since he knew far more about the art than I did, and I bought them online. It was a kind of game, like sending unsigned Valentine's cards. You must have worked out by now what they mean. They seem an innocent part of the relationship to me now – I can't believe how happy I was when I sent him the Colmar card telling him I was pregnant. By then Justin had told me about the sacred hunt of the unicorn and I was ridiculously pleased about the way I could give Benedict the news. I thought he'd welcome it, but I couldn't have been more wrong. After the abortion I wanted him to realize his cruelty and to feel threatened, so I sent the last postcard, again with the aid of Justin's expert knowledge.'

'I was a bit perplexed by that at first,' interrupted Giles. 'I couldn't see why you'd sent a postcard of the copy from the Stirling tapestries rather than the original at The Cloisters. It was only when I went to the castle that I got an idea why.'

'Justin told me about the completion of the seventh tapestry. I happened to be up at Stirling University giving a paper in the School of Social Sciences, so I decided to visit the castle for myself. It was then that I saw that the two women in the restored tapestry were really one – Mary and Eve. I felt there was something of me in both of them, and I wanted the threat to come from the same place where they showed themselves together. Benedict might have thought he was the high and mighty Gabriel presiding, unscathed, in a lordly way over my conception. I wanted him to know that he was the unicorn, and that one day he would suffer as much as I had when I'd gone to the hospital wearing a red dress, just like Eve. Later on I decided the day had come to follow the plot of the unicorn hunt and kill Benedict. It seemed the only way to come to terms with my pain and be able to start again. Anyway, by then he'd become the unicorn in my mind and he just had to die. It's what happens to unicorns, you know.'

Giles had the strong urge to correct her about the unicorn hunt – it was only in one kind of hunt, he wanted to say, that the unicorn was killed. But he could see that she was not open to reason, and perhaps by now was not entirely sane. He kept silent as her voice rose into a kind of rapture.

'I am Eve as well as Mary', she chanted. 'I'm both the betrayer and the virgin mother. Benedict was both Gabriel and the unicorn. I am the woman in red. My name, after all, is Rosie. It was all destined from my birth.'

Giles thought that the best thing to do was to humour her and go along with her mood, which was curiously one of confession. He wondered whether she realized the consequences of what she was revealing so readily.

'I got really worried when you found the unicorn tabs. That was much worse than discovering the postcards', went on Rosie. 'I thought you might have shown them to them to the police inspector. If the police had analysed them they would have found them soaked in a solution of LSD. The members of our Unicorn Society were all in on the secret, sucking the tabs to get a high – some of them even saw unicorns. Benedict had been using them for months to get rid of writer's block with his thesis, and when I went back with him to the chaplain's rooms that night for us to take tabs together I slipped him PCP in a glass of wine. The combination was disastrous for him. I'd arranged to meet him in a pub earlier on and he thought I'd forgiven him, poor sod. Once the concoction began to take effect he was willing enough to take up my suggestion to have a bit of fun together in the bath. I knew all about his arrangement with the chaplain, and we'd taken advantage of his generosity together in the past. Benedict just managed to run the bath and got into it first while I started to undress. When he slipped into unconsciousness I leant over and slit his wrists. I hardly needed to get wet at all. The woman in red made the water red, and the unicorn was well and truly caught in a woman's lap. When it was all over I turned off the heating. I had some vague memory that it would confuse the police about the time he'd died, and I'd made sure that I was seen at a restaurant earlier in the evening.'

'Weren't you afraid the police would find traces of you in the lodgings?' asked Giles. 'You don't seem to have taken any precautions.'

'The police are fools', Rosie snorted. 'I made sure I visited the chaplain earlier in the day to invite him to give our termly talk at the Unicorn Society. I picked up his lethal little paper-knife to admire it and I used his bathroom. I took my wineglass and the used tabs away with me. If the police had looked they'd have found my fingerprints and DNA everywhere, and I'd have had a damn good explanation, but they gave up early in the case anyway and accepted it was suicide.'

'So you were the person who tried to stop me solving the clues on the cards', cried Giles. 'I thought the accidents I had were more than coincidences, though I couldn't convince Hannah. She was so reluctant to accept my theories that I even suspected her.'

'Hannah – there's another fool', retorted Rosie contemptuously. 'She had no idea about my previous history with Benedict – typically, he hadn't told her – so she took my sympathy at face value. He'd taken up with her a couple of months after I'd turned against him and sent him the last card. I suppose it might have been him moving on that finally pushed me into planning to kill him. He actually got engaged to her – engaged! He wouldn't know what commitment meant. Perhaps I had the idea that women needed to be saved from him, even a poor sap like Hannah.'

'How did you know where I was going?' asked Giles curiously. 'You weren't one of my friends on Facebook, so you didn't see my postings after my first couple of trips. And you concealed yourself well at each of the places. I never recognized you there.'

'Hannah told me the places where you were planning to go over those tedious cups of coffee, and she didn't mind answering my friendly enquiries about where you were arranging to stay. I guessed for myself from the postcards what you were aiming to look at. And of course I didn't follow you around myself. I've got links with unicorn societies all over the world, in museums, galleries, colleges, arts groups. Didn't you listen to anything I told you about the cultural significance of the unicorn? Members were glad enough to join forces against someone I said was an enemy of unicorns, and so I could get them to try and stop you working out the puzzle even though they didn't know why. But none of them wanted to go as far as murder, even that bumptious American Professor I met and recruited to the Society in Oxford. He was useful enough to me in trying to stop you getting to The Cloisters when you turned up at his college, though I never knew whose side he was on. So when Hannah told me you were planning to visit Colmar, I finally had to go there myself and follow you from the museum.'

'You do realize,' said Giles, 'that I'm going to have to repeat this whole confession to Detective Inspector Longley?'

'I don't think you will', replied Rosie. 'I didn't bother to follow you to Stirling because I thought you'd probably guessed the truth and I'd planned to deal with you this time back in Oxford. Your coffee contains a dose of LSD and PCP, and you'll discover you're about to become the unicorn. I hope you're going to die the unicorn's death, but I've got to the point when I don't much care any longer. I doubt whether your credibility level will be high with the police anyway.' Under her breath she added, 'With any luck it'll be the case of another undergraduate high on drugs drowned in a flooded river.'

Giles' head was beginning to swim and the room was revolving slowly around him. He heard Rosie say to him slowly and deliberately, 'You are the unicorn. You must go to purify the waters. Go to the river.' She repeated this twice and then demanded, 'What must you do? Tell me!'

He was seeing a burst of coloured lights and suddenly everything began to make sense. The universe was wonderful and beautiful. The table, the books on the shelves, the papers lying on chairs were etched in the sharpest outline. Every detail stood out and there were halos of light around them. He knew with a sudden certainty that the universe was a perfect circle, that every rock and stone, every star and planet, every animal, insect and person had their place in the whole and he was at one with them. But there was contamination there. Poison had been allowed to enter the stream of life. If Rosie was the woman in red he was the unicorn, and she was right – it was his task to purify the waters with his horn, whatever it cost him. He knew just where to go, where he had first thought about the way to catch a unicorn nearly a year before. The place in the Parks was called the 'Rainbow Bridge,' and so everything fitted together – unicorns and rainbows. He laughed at the thought, and was happy that he could be of service.

'I must purify the water. I must go the river', he dutifully repeated to Rosie.

With her ironic laughter ringing in his ears he staggered off across Magdalen bridge, down Longwall Street and into the side gateway of the University Parks. As he went on his unsteady way the image of Hannah came into his mind, and he felt once again the strong pulse of his love for her. He felt contaminated by ever having suspected her and knew instinctively that he could not cleanse the universe unless he spoke out his love. He took out his mobile phone and sent her a garbled text message: 'I Lov u. Frgiv me. Im going to end of Rnbow.'

As he started along the path by the bank of the Cherwell, in his state of heightened awareness he thought he could see every blade of grass in the early evening light, and at the green, curled tips the early evening dew glinted like jewels. Spring flowers were sprinkled everywhere over the grass in bright constellations and he knew that he was the unicorn at peace in the myriad-petalled enclosure. The sensation was delightful, but was immediately replaced by a frightening feeling that all was not well. Before he could catch his breath, the path had become the winding corridor in the hospital and, as in the matching corridor in Alternative World, the hunt was on. Indefinable enemies, menacing figures in the gathering gloom, were pursuing him and now there was no 'escape' key to press. A lion reared up in his path in front of him and he desperately beat it away, avoiding its bared claws and feeling its hot breath on his face and the rough fur of its mane. He had reached the bridge, but now it looked like one of the bridges in the hospital, not the familiar rainbow shape he was expecting. The rainbow, sign of hope for a drowned world, was gone and all that remained were the dark waters that lay on each side, waiting for his sacrificial ministry.

He plunged in, winded for a moment by the shock of the cold water, and immersed his head once beneath its surface, coming up gasping. At the edges the water was fairly calm and he could keep his footing, but out in the middle there was a strong current moving, swollen by the rainwater which had collected from the fields around. He must get there, he thought desperately with a kind of mad logic, there where the stream was flowing if he was the unicorn who had dipped his horn into the flowing waters of the fountain. But now something else was happening. The water all around which had been muddy black was turning red. He seemed to be floating in the large bath that had troubled his dreams. He felt himself being dragged along by the current and falling into the black void that he had experienced so often before. Images flashed through his mind – Leonardo's girl, Raphael's maiden, the Cluny Lady, the woman in red, Mary in her walled garden, the Klimt woman in glittering dress, and the quiet face of Hannah. He was Benedict. He was the unicorn. He prepared to immerse his head again, feeling the weight of the long horn that projected from his forehead.

What Rosie had not reckoned with when she dosed Giles with LSD was that he had a long history of fighting off unconsciousness. He had developed mental practices of delaying the downward slip into darkness that came to him periodically, and these now stood him in good stead as the mind-altering drug took hold of him. He remained conscious enough to hear a car horn in the distance, a long, persistent blast of an impatient driver that Giles heard as if it were the trumpet of Gabriel the hunter.

The archangel, he realized, was chasing the unicorn into the womb of Mary, accompanied by his hounds of redeeming mercy and peace. The hunt that really mattered had already happened, and had caused a shift in the revolving cosmos. He did not have to cleanse the waters on his own, since this service had already been offered in many times and in many places and the artists and poets had faithfully born witness to it. The fate of the whole universe did not depend on him after all. He could resign his avatar and just be Giles, Hannah's Giles, and all would be well and all manner of things would be well. He would be at home in the country he had been seeking.

With a huge effort he struggled out of the strong current into the quieter eddies at the edge of the river and heaved himself up onto the bank. Then darkness came and swallowed him up.

After a while, streaks of wan light appeared at the edge of the black cloud he was inhabiting. He was still lying on the damp grass and night was coming on but he felt calmer and wrapped around with a warm sense of well-being. He heard a voice speaking, and it was the voice of Hannah.

'I've come to catch a unicorn', she said.

42255983R00159

Printed in Poland
by Amazon Fulfillment
Poland Sp. z o.o., Wrocław